THE
PRIME
TREES

JEREMY THOMAS FULLER

BOOKS BY JEREMY THOMAS FULLER

THE METALWOOD SAGA

SEASON ONE

The Metal Wood

The Stone Flame

The Death Edge

The Fatal Cure

The Prime Trees

SEASON TWO

The Absent Memory

The Crystal Curse

The Silent Binds

The Twin Fury

The Splinter Soul

STANDALONE

Attention Deficit

THE PRIME TREES

THE METALWOOD SAGA
BOOK 5

JEREMY THOMAS FULLER

STARMIST ENTERTAINMENT

STARMIST ENTERTAINMENT

166 Geary Str STE 1500 #1259
San Francisco, CA 94108
United States

jeremythomasfuller.com
instagram.com/jeremythomasfuller
facebook.com/jeremythomasfuller
bsky.app/profile/jeremythomasfuller.com

Cover designed by Maria Spada
Author photo by Zack Griset
Set in Stix Two

PART
ONE

PART
ONE

ONE

TREY SAT in his chair in the Town Hall, stunned. The room was silent for a long moment. "That was...quite the story," he said finally. He felt numb at first, but something was growing inside him, suffusing his body.

The Sundering. The Ascension. The things the elves had done. It was almost too much. It was almost far too much to bear.

He stood.

"I would never have believed it," he said, "but I've seen you. I've seen how you work. How you think." He felt his hands start shaking. He walked up to Silanar, finally understanding the feeling that was shooting through his veins.

It was anger.

"You killed them," Trey said. He was standing right in front of Silanar's chair, glaring down at the man. "*You* killed them. Seven billion living human beings. It wasn't a virus at all. It was *elves*."

Silanar just sat there, looking at him with those elven eyes, expressionless.

Trey leaned down until he was inches away from the man's face. *"How dare you,"* he said, his voice almost a whisper.

Then he spun and left the room.

"WELL, THAT WENT WELL," Bellas said. Arra could hear the sarcasm dripping in his tone. She glanced over at Fenian, trying to gauge his reaction. They'd both heard parts of the story before, but never in this much detail. And never from the Cothellon's side.

It was...sobering.

Fenian seemed nonplussed. This business of killing most of the humans didn't seem to bother him much. Well, it bothered Arra. It bothered her a lot. She wondered, not for the first time, just what kind of a man her father was.

"He'll be back," Silanar said, referring to Trey. "I hope. In the meantime, we have a meeting to continue."

"Hold the fuck on," Orym said suddenly.

"That language isn't necessary," Silanar said. "What do you want?"

"You've heard it all now," Orym said, "every detail. You know what the Fennas Elenathon device will do. And I've already told you that they plan to activate it soon. Very soon."

"It's been what—296 years?—since their first failure," Silanar said. "How do you know they'll activate it now?"

"Because I still *work* for them, you idiot," Orym said, his voice dripping with contempt. "How can you not understand, after all this? I've been undercover the whole time. I arranged all of this. Trey, your new Prime Mage, is down here because of me. And this entire planet is going to be destroyed if we don't do something. Right. Fucking. Now."

"And just what do you propose we do?" Daylor said.

"We need to destroy the cities once and for all," Orym said.

"How? They're invisible, and even if they weren't, they're also shielded by those forcefields you described. They can't be destroyed."

"They can be," Orym said. "There's something very few people know about the forcefields."

"And I suppose you're going to tell us."

"Picture an egg," Orym said, ignoring Daylor. "Picture it standing on end. Got it? Now cut the egg neatly in half." He made a sideways chopping motion with his hand. "Now you have two shells: one on the bottom, and one on the top."

"Very descriptive," Silanar remarked. Orym glared at him.

"The city shields used to be the whole egg—a full circle around the entire city. But over time, forcefinder Talent atrophied in the population. People just aren't as genetically predisposed to it as they are to the other Talents. As a result, we don't have enough darkmages to maintain the full Shield. So only the bottom half is active."

Arra saw her father thinking that over. "But why even keep the Shield up at all?" he asked.

"To keep people like you from getting in."

"Are all the cities like this?"

"Yes," Orym said.

"So all we have to do is get our people three thousand feet in the air—high enough to clear the forcefield—then, what, throw explosives at the city? Shoot it? And we have to do this six times, in locations all over the planet?"

"Seven times," Orym said. "New Tokyo has been rebuilt."

"It's just not feasible," Silanar said.

"That's why I brought you the Prime Mage."

"He's really only half a Prime Mage, and a very weak one at that. How is that supposed to help?"

Arra was looking at the window, watching Trey. He'd left the village, stomping out into the forest with a murderous expression on his face.

"He's not going to be able to do anything if he's not here," she said.

Everyone looked at her.

ARRA FOUND Trey in a clearing deep in the forest, nearly a mile away from Sylrantheas. He was sitting on a fallen tree, glowering at the ground. Arra made sure to make noise as she approached so he wouldn't be frightened. He looked up as she neared, his expression dark. She didn't say anything, just walked up and sat beside him on the log.

They were both silent for several minutes. Then Trey drew in a ragged breath. "What kind of person commits genocide?" he asked, still staring at the ground.

She looked at him, at the hunch in his back, at his hair where it met the nape of his neck. She put a hand on his forearm, the touch awkward.

"I'm not going to defend him," she said quietly. "How could I? I think it's unspeakable what he—what they—did."

Trey looked at her then, and she could see tears glistening in his eyes. "What could have become of us?" he asked, his voice quavering. "What could we have accomplished in all this time? We might have *saved* this planet, not killed it." He looked out at the forest.

Arra squeezed his arm. "I know."

She felt something, then, as she touched him. As if in a

long-lost life, she had once known him. She withdrew her touch, suddenly confused.

He looked at her again, his blue eyes finding hers. "Everything I've ever known was a lie," he said, "and the truth—the truth is *far* worse."

He reached for her then, needing physical contact, needing comfort. She wrapped one arm around him and held him as he cried.

"SO YOU'RE AN ELF?" Rylan asked. The boys in the tent were staring at him, watching his reaction.

"You got it," Dill—Dillon—said.

"How old are you?"

"We don't really keep track in the Under. I guess I'm something like 430, give or a take a few decades."

"Holy shit," Rylan said.

"Well said."

"And you've been down here the whole time? Who else knows?"

Dill looked around the room. "Just these guys, mostly," he said. "Oh, and him."

Someone new stepped into the tent. He was older than most of the boys in the Under—much older. He had shaggy gray hair and walked with a slight hunch, making him seem short. He was wearing a dirty, floppy black jacket made of cloth, and baggy black pants. The strange man walked up to the table and sat, dropping a heavy bag onto it with a loud clanking noise.

"Rylan," Dill said, "meet Smoke. Smoke, Rylan."

The man named Smoke turned to look at him, but he

didn't stand. His eyes were gray, glinting like steel. He didn't say anything.

"Smoke here makes mergeguns," Dill said.

"Mergeguns?" Rylan asked.

"Yup. Same as what Shot uses, and the guards that chased you."

"Stupid name."

Dill laughed. "It is pretty stupid, now that you mention it."

Rylan eyed the man named Smoke. He seemed like he was hiding something. But then again, it seemed like *everyone* was hiding something around here. He looked over at Elanil. She hadn't reacted much during Dill's story. Maybe she'd heard it before.

Her expression was one of pity.

"I found Con," he said, changing the subject.

Dill quirked an eyebrow. "Oh?"

"She's in an old jail in Planner Central. They aren't feeding her. She looks like she's about to die."

"We don't rescue people from Planner Central anymore," Dill said. "It's too dangerous."

"I thought you wanted to take over the city."

"Sure," Dill said, "but I don't see how saving her will help do that."

"Con can help," Rylan said. "We have to rescue her."

Dill looked at him for a moment as if weighing his options. "If we get her out," he said, "will you help us?"

"I was already going to help you," Rylan said.

"Not much of a negotiator, are you?"

Rylan shrugged.

Dill turned to Elanil. "What about you?"

Elanil looked surprised at being addressed. "I want to go home," she said. That haunted expression was back in her eyes.

"I don't see any way of getting you back there," Dill said. "Unless Dad knows a way. Grime, is the radio working yet?"

Grime shook his head. "Not yet, boss. It works for short-range stuff, but something's wrong with the antenna. We haven't been able to raise Orym on it."

"Get it fixed," Dill said.

"Sure thing, boss."

"In the meantime, there's something I want you to see."

"Not until we get Con," Rylan said. He wasn't going to budge on the subject, not this time. He needed to save her, and time was rapidly running out.

Dill sighed. "Fine. Shot, go find Small. You and him and me will go with Rylan to get Con. Elanil, you coming?"

Elanil looked around the room nervously. She was probably afraid of what would happen if she were left alone with the boys. "I guess," she said.

Dill went over to the big chest and rummaged around. "Here," he said, turning back to Rylan and handing him a handful of dark wood.

"Maple?" Rylan asked.

Dill nodded. "Dark maple," he said. "Heard you were out."

"Thanks."

"I don't suppose you have any prime elm on hand?" Elanil asked.

"Nope," Dill said. "You didn't bring any with you?"

Elanil looked crestfallen. "I used it all getting here."

Dill stroked his chin. "Grime, will the radio reach Greyson?"

"Sure will, boss."

"Get him on the line. See if he can get us some prime elm. Real prime elm, not the dark stuff. I know the Planners still have some. Tell him to use the dead drop just outside Planner Central. And Grime?"

"Yes, boss?"

"Tell him to hurry."

Dill turned to Rylan, sticking out his hand. "We'll get your friend out," he said, "and then we'll fix this city. Deal?"

"Deal," Rylan said, shaking Dill's hand.

He hoped they wouldn't be too late to save Con.

TWO

"COME BACK TO THE VILLAGE," Arra said, her arm still around Trey. It felt strange, holding him like this. He was a human, after all, and still a relative stranger to her. But she could see that he was hurting, and she was the only one there. She needed to be his shoulder to cry on.

Truth be told, she didn't mind.

"Why should I go back?" he asked. "I just want to get away. From the elves, from the magic, from everything."

"From me?" Arra asked.

She didn't know why she had said that.

Trey sat up, looking at her, his face close to hers. She found herself licking her lips.

"Not from you," he whispered. "Never from you."

They stayed like that for a long moment, neither one making a move. She felt her face growing hot. What was happening to her?

"Don't let me interrupt," a voice said suddenly. Arra jumped, pulling away from Trey. She looked toward the voice and saw Fenian standing there, leaning on his crutches.

He seemed upset.

Trey shifted down the log, making space between him and her. And Fenian walked up to them, swinging on his crutches, obvious anger apparent on his face.

"Nothing happened," Arra said.

"That didn't look like nothing." Fenian's voice was low. "If you want *him* over me, just say so."

Arra stood. She tried to put her arms around Fenian's neck, but he moved back, away from her. "No," he said, "I know that look. You're in love with him."

"What?"

That was out of the blue, even for him. Arra wasn't in *love* with Trey. She'd just tried to comfort him—the man *was* hurting, after all. Yes, there was some kind of connection between the two of them...some kind of shared history...but that didn't translate to *love*.

At all.

"Fenian," she said, "I want *you*. Only you. I love *you*."

Fenian just stood there, glaring at her.

"It's my fault," Trey said, standing. "I'm sorry. I'm sorry about everything."

Then he left, heading in the direction of Sylrantheas.

Arra let out a breath. "He doesn't mean anything to me," she said. She stepped forward, trying to get close to him again, and this time he let her. "Please don't be angry," she said. "I was just trying to comfort him. He was really shaken up by the story."

Fenian glared at her for a moment longer, then he sighed, his expression softening. "I guess I can't blame him," he said, putting one arm around her. "I'd be mad as hell if I'd just met the man who'd killed most of my species. I'd probably try to kill him."

Arra looked up at Fenian, alarm growing in her mind. "Do you think he'll try to kill Father?"

Fenian snorted. "Trey? Kill Silanar? There's a better chance of the Earth crashing into the moon."

That was an odd choice of phrase.

"Forgive me?" Arra asked, looking deeply into his eyes.

"How can I resist that look?" he said, leaning down and kissing her. She returned the kiss, squeezing him tightly.

But her moment with Trey still stuck in her mind. She could still feel what it had been like to hold him. She could feel her face flushing. She'd come very close to kissing him.

She would have to be more careful around Trey in the future.

WHEN ARRA and Fenian got back to the Council room an hour later, everyone was arguing. Orym was pacing around the room, clearly angry about something. They stepped into the room quietly, closing the door and sitting down to watch the proceedings.

Trey was nowhere to be seen. She hoped he'd made it back to Sylrantheas, and hadn't run away again. She'd have to be careful around him, sure, but that didn't mean she wanted him to leave. He was part of this now, like it or not.

"I'll say it one last time," Bellas was saying, "it's impractical. Can't be done. Even if we had a way to get up to the cities, we don't have any way to quickly communicate with the other elven villages. We can't coordinate an attack of this scale. Not anymore."

Ever since the Sundering, the elves had let technology crumble around them, wanting to go back to simpler times. The Cothellon split had been too fresh a wound, too hard a lesson. Now all the elves wanted was to remain at peace, with the land and with themselves. They wanted the Earth to heal.

And even if they hadn't wanted to eschew science, all the scientists were up there in those floating cities. Lost to them forever.

So there were no radios, no satellites. No planes or cars or elevators. There wasn't even electricity, most of the time. It just wasn't necessary.

"We have to try," Eloen said. "Surely Orym can assist us, or we can find someone else. We can get an old plane or helicopter running. Or we could even use hot air balloons."

"But then what?" Kharis asked. "We don't have explosives, or guns. The Guardians aren't trained for infiltration. We can't do any real damage to the cities. And besides, Orym has told us about the Cothellon. They have police, security, even a small military. We can't go up against that. Not with bows and arrows."

"We have magic," Nuvian said. "Magic that the Cothellon don't have access to anymore. Unless they have stockpiles of primewood, still?"

Orym stopped pacing and shook his head. "They only have a little," he said. "They gave up Woodway magic centuries ago. They wanted to be rid of the old ways, as they called it." He looked out the window, his voice taking on a bitter tone. "I agreed with them, once."

"We're very nearly out of primewood," Silanar said, "thanks to the Remnant. And from what you've told us, Orym, darkprime magic is in many ways more powerful than our own."

Orym sat down. "It is powerful, yes," he said, "but also dangerous. There's a side effect. It's like a drug—it feels incredible at first, but if you use too much..." He let the sentence hang unfinished.

"I wonder if we can use that to our advantage," Silanar said.

Nobody had a reply to that.

"I still think this whole thing is folly," Bellas said. "We have no assurances that this...device...of theirs is going to be ready anytime soon. If Orym is right, and this gate machine is capable of destroying the planet, then I agree: we need to move against them. But let's not be hasty. We need to plan and discuss. We need to hold a High Council meeting."

"We haven't held a High Council meeting in nearly three hundred years," Orist said. "What makes you think anyone will even come?"

"They'll come when they hear this," Bellas said.

"If they believe it. Which I find unlikely."

"We don't have time for this!" Orym shouted. "I am telling you, Fennas Elenathon is ready *now!* They will be putting it into action within weeks, if not days. The time to act is now, or it may be too late!"

"Then why not come to us sooner?" Silanar asked. "I find it hard to believe you've been planning all this time, and the best you could do was warn us mere *weeks* before it was going to happen."

Orym stared daggers at Silanar. "Surely by now you know that if I could have done this sooner, I would have." They looked at each other for a long moment.

"What about sabotage?" Bellas said. "Put a bomb in each of the cities. Like Dunedar did."

"Won't work," Orym said. "After what happened during the Uprising, all the darkmage legions are heavily guarded and fortified. We'd need an army to get in. And that's putting aside the problem of getting back to the cities at all."

"Wait," Silanar said, "you don't have a way back?"

Orym shook his head sadly. "This was a one-time deal. Make or break. I can't return to New San Francisco, or any of the other cities. None of us can. There's no way up anymore. At least no way that we can use."

The room was silent for a minute.

"Let's put it to a vote," Silanar said, breaking the silence. "Those in favor of immediate action?"

Eloen and Orist raised their hands.

"Those against?"

The other six members of the Council raised their hands.

"The motion is settled," Silanar said. "We will arrange for a World Council meeting to discuss this further."

"No!" Orym shouted, pounding his fist on the arm of his chair. He looked furious.

Silanar stood, coming over to Orym and laying a hand on his shoulder. "I'm sorry, old friend."

Orym looked up at him with fear in his eyes. "You still don't understand," he said. "The entire *planet* is about to die."

"I killed over seven billion people," Silanar said, his voice cold. "I understand better than you think."

He turned and left, the other Council members filing out of the room after him.

Orym stayed in his seat, looking devastated. Arra didn't know what she should do. She couldn't influence the Council. She couldn't attack the cities herself. She couldn't stop the devastation that was about to come. But somehow she knew, in her heart, that Orym was speaking the truth.

The world was about to die.

Fenian put a hand on her leg. "Let's go," he said.

Arra stood with him numbly, still watching Orym in his chair.

There was nothing she could do.

THREE

"REPORT," Quynn said into the mouthpiece. He hated using this old radio technology.

"They tested him," the voice on the other end said. The tinny sound made Quynn wince, so he turned it down a little.

"And?" Quynn asked. The man he was talking to was intolerably slow. Quynn willed himself to be patient.

"They found something...unusual."

"Yes? Spit it out, man."

"They're calling him a Prime Mage."

Quynn felt his blood run cold. Could it be? Had his suspicions been correct all along? He spoke into the communicator slowly and clearly.

"Which Talent did he Align with?" Quynn asked.

"All of them," the voice said.

"You're sure?"

"I'm sure. Although he can only use half the magic."

"What does that mean?"

"I don't know. I'm not a mage." The man sounded flustered. "He can only do three of the magics, not all of them."

What? Quynn had never heard of anything like that

before. He paused for a moment, tapping two fingers together as he thought. "Thank you for your report," he said. "Let me know if you hear anything else."

"Wait," the voice said, "there's something else."

"Yes?"

"He's using an artifact—some kind of book. It enhances his power, makes him stronger. Without it he can't do much of anything."

So *that's* where the Book went. If he could pair the Book with the Staff...the possibilities were endless.

"Get your hands on that Book," Quynn ordered.

"Sir? You want me to have it stolen?"

"Yes. Is that a problem?"

"No, sir."

"Good. Contact me if you learn anything else."

Quynn clicked the communicator off and leaned back in his chair. Lights flickered and flashed along the rows of desks. The screens ahead were dark, the control room empty.

Quynn allowed himself a moment of glee. This was it. After all his work, all his planning, his project had finally succeeded. When everyone had said it was impossible, he'd done it. He'd found one. Or at least half of one. He wondered if that could be fixed. Regardless, it was time to bring the boy back into the fold. The elves on the ground had outlived their usefulness.

He tapped his communicator and waited for the call to connect.

"Yes?" Grathgor's voice said.

"I found one," Quynn said. He tried to keep his voice from revealing his excitement. "I just have one more thing to attend to, and we'll have a Prime Mage in our midst again."

"You really found one?" Grathgor asked. He sounded skeptical.

"My oldest project made it through in the end," Quynn said. It was more than he'd dared to hope for. "He just needed some...inspiration."

"That is excellent," Grathgor said. There was a pause. "You're sitting in my chair, aren't you."

Quynn smiled in the dark. "Sorry, old friend. You know how I like to come here to think."

"It is of no concern. Will you inform Lorelei?"

"I will. She will be very pleased." She would be less pleased if she knew his next move, but he saw no need to tell her.

"Indeed. Such interesting timing," Grathgor said. "Our first test was a success, so we are on schedule for starting the Conjunction. You'll have until we do to wrap up your business."

It was all finally happening. "Very well," Quynn said into the communicator.

"And Quynn?"

"Yes?"

"When all this is done, I owe you a drink."

Quynn chuckled, the laugh sounding strange in his own ears. "You have a deal," he said, and clicked off.

Quynn ran his hand over the polished surface of the deep black desk. Purple and blue lights played along the metal like dancing fireflies in the night. He smiled a wide smile, then stood and strode out of the room.

He had one more task left to accomplish.

FOUR

TREY FOUND Callan at the blacksmith workshop, pounding a piece of hot metal, an angry look on his face. When Orist saw Trey, he stepped in and took over from Callan, motioning that he was free to go.

"What's up?" Callan asked, turning to Trey.

"I'm leaving," Trey said. "I came to say goodbye."

Callan looked at him with concern, stepping out of the workshop. "I don't understand," he said. "Where are you going?"

"Away," Trey said. "I just have to get away. From the elves, from Arra. Out from under the city."

"Can we at least talk about this?" Callan asked, taking off his apron and laying it on a table.

"I'm going, Callan."

His friend looked at him for a long moment, then shrugged. "I'm not going to stand in your way," he said, "but let me at least buy you one last beer before you go."

"The elves don't even use money," Trey said.

"I know," Callan said. "Weird, right? It was just a figure of speech."

Trey didn't want to stay in Sylrantheas even a moment longer. He couldn't look at the elves anymore without his stomach twisting, without wanting to punch someone—or worse. After what they'd done...he just couldn't think about it. The thoughts blurred in his head, terrifyingly close.

But on the other hand, he could really use a drink.

"Fine," he said. "One last beer."

It was still fairly early in the afternoon, so they were the only ones in the tavern. Meriel smiled at them as they entered, stacking glasses behind the bar. Trey couldn't bring himself to smile back, though. To him, her smile had been the grin of a cadaver. He saw destruction everywhere he looked.

His stomach lurched again.

"Where will you go?" Callan asked once they'd gotten settled in a booth. The wood stank of death.

"Away," Trey said. "I might wander the forest for a while, teach myself to hunt. Or, hell—maybe the Remnant will take me in."

"That sounds like a terrible idea," Callan said. Meriel dropped off their beers, smiling at Trey again. Trey felt repulsed.

"How can you be so calm about all this?" Trey asked.

"About what? The Sundering? That wild story?" Callan snorted. "Even if I believed half of it, it was three hundred years ago. What's done is done."

He was being awfully cavalier about the whole thing. Trey looked into his mug, unable to bring himself to take a drink. "I guess I'm just not like you," he said. "I can't ignore the past."

He lifted the mug to his lips. The beer tasted like tears.

"You seemed to be getting pretty cozy with Arra," Callan said.

Trey slammed his mug down on the table, beer sloshing over his hand. "I'm a married man, dammit. And even if I weren't, Arra is taken."

"Okay, okay, buddy," Callan said. "Jesus. I didn't mean anything by it."

"Sorry."

"You really think you can do it? Survive in the forest on your own?"

Trey felt the walls closing in, his mind running in circles. "I don't know," he said. "I just have to get away."

"I never thought I'd be swinging a blacksmith hammer, either. I guess neither one of us are who we thought we'd be."

They were silent for a few minutes. A group of elves came into the tavern, talking excitedly to each other. They saw Trey and Callan sitting in the booth and stopped, looking at them askance. Then they went to a table at the other end of the room and sat, resuming their conversation in quieter tones, pointedly ignoring the humans.

"Looks like the feeling's mutual," Callan observed.

Trey tried another sip of beer. It tasted more like beer this time, at least. He took a longer draught.

"The Waychoice Ceremony is tomorrow, you know," Callan said.

Trey looked up from his mug. "Waychoice?" He knew he'd heard that term somewhere, but he couldn't remember where.

"It's like their school graduation or something," Callan said. "Can you believe they don't graduate from school until age *fifty*? You should come. Arra's going to be graduating."

"Why is it called a Waychoice Ceremony?" Trey asked.

"Something about their Ways," Callan said. "They have to pick one when they graduate, and that becomes their job, basically. It's how they keep their economy working without actual money."

How *did* their economy work, anyway? He knew from his reading that humans had tried similar things in the past, but it had never worked. Maybe there was some fundamental difference between elves and humans. Maybe they just *thought* differently.

Maybe someday, if he ever returned, he'd ask them.

But as for now, he couldn't stomach the thought of staying in the city even an hour longer. He started thinking about what he needed to pack, and how he would get it without arousing suspicion. He wasn't sure the elves would even let him leave.

"You should stay for the ceremony," Callan said again.

"Why do you want me to stay so badly?" Trey asked.

Callan shrugged. "It's your life," he said. "I just thought you'd like to see Arra's big moment."

Trey studied his friend. Callan was looking fit and healthy, more so than he ever had in the city in the sky. Blacksmithing agreed with him, apparently. But Trey could also see lines of worry there on his face. Adjusting to life among the elves hadn't been easy for either of them. Callan was doing a better job of adapting than Trey was, but his friend still needed a familiar face. Perhaps Trey should stay just one more day.

"Fine," he said, "I'll stay. But just until the ceremony is over."

"Good," Callan said, grinning, but the smile rang false.

"Do you think I'll ever see my wife again?" Trey asked.

"In all the years we've been alive," Callan said, "has anyone ever come back from Civil Service?"

Trey sighed. "I guess I figured that if the virus is a lie, maybe Civil Service is a lie, too. Maybe there's a way I can see Lora again."

Callan reached a hand across the table, placing it on Trey's forearm. "I know how you feel," he said quietly. "A day doesn't go by where I don't think of my sister. Wherever she is—and wherever Lora is—they're okay. They're doing good things. I know it."

"Even after all we just heard? The cities are just some *machine* built by the elves."

"It must be like this," Callan said, motioning to the beer and the booth they were sitting in. "In a closed society like the sky cities, some resources must be shared, including labor. I mean, New San Francisco does have a money-based economy, but it can't all work like that. Maybe Civil Service is how they keep things running. For the greater good."

That didn't make sense at all, and the words didn't sound like something Callan would even think of. Trey quirked an eyebrow at him. "How can you say that?" he asked. "They take our loved ones from us—*permanently*—and we never see them again. How could that possibly be for the greater good?"

"I don't know," Callan said, looking away. "I'm not smart enough to understand things like that."

Trey frowned. Things weren't adding up. First Callan was trying to get Trey to stay in the village longer—which made sense—but now he was defending Civil Service? What about Deirdre? Callan had lost his own sister. He'd been furious.

Trey sighed, letting the subject drop. He was too mentally exhausted to care any more. He just needed to leave.

He sipped his beer, missing his wife.

"YOU'RE GOING TO DO GREAT," Fenian said. "I wish I was Choosing tomorrow."

"You will be soon enough," Arra said.

Fenian wasn't old enough to Choose. Not yet. He was two years younger than Arra, so he had to wait. He seemed in a hurry to graduate, to become an adult.

Arra couldn't blame him.

This year, three elves were Choosing: Arra, Imra, and Allain. It was rare to have three at once, since so few children were born every year. It would make for an interesting Waychoice Ceremony.

Melenora bustled in, coming through the front door with an armload of cloth. "Arra, dear," she said, "I have a surprise for you." She looked meaningfully at Fenian, who seemed to take the hint.

"I'll see you tomorrow," he said, giving Arra a kiss on the cheek.

She squeezed his hand. "Wish me luck," she said.

"You bring your own luck," Fenian said, winking. Then he left, and it was just her and her mother.

"Well?" Arra asked, looking at her mother questioningly. "What's this surprise?"

"It's something I had made for you," Melenora said. "As a Waychoice gift. I hope you like it."

She stepped forward, handing Arra the cloth bundle. It looked like clothing of some kind. Was it a dress for Waychoice? Her mother was always trying to get her into dresses. It wasn't that Arra hated dresses, exactly, they just weren't very functional. She preferred something more practical, especially when she was hunting.

As Arra unfolded the clothing, she gasped. It was a beautiful, matching pair of pants and a shirt, cut slim and made out of supple, dark brown leather. She felt the material—it was soft, almost luxuriously so. She could tell the outfit would be silent as she moved, not squeaky like most leather. The craftsmanship was impeccable. She'd never owned anything half this nice before.

"It's waterproof, too," Melenora said.

Arra beamed. "This is beautiful, Mother! Can I try it on now?"

"Of course," Melenora said, smiling.

Arra bounded to her room and shed her clothes, throwing them on the bed and slipping into the new outfit. It fit perfectly: close-fitting, but not tight enough to restrict her movement. She crouched experimentally, seeing how the fabric responded. It moved with her, stretching to accommodate the pose. Fantastic.

She straightened, looking at herself in the mirror. The shirt was snug around her chest, with a deep v-neck that she laced closed with the included leather laces. The shirt was long enough to drape over the pants or to be tucked into them. The pants were also laced up with strips of leather. Both pieces were simple, not ostentatious—no fringes or unnecessary ornamentation. A tiny emblem was embroidered on the pants on her left hip: a bow and arrow.

She turned back and forth, admiring the outfit. Would it be too much? She'd likely be made fun of, wearing this with the other Hunters. But maybe she didn't care. Maybe she *wanted* something to make her stand out. Something of her own.

A knock came at her door and Melenora entered. "You look beautiful," she said. "Do you like it?"

"Oh, Mother," Arra said, "I love it!" She embraced her mother with a quick hug.

"I want you to wear it tomorrow," Melenora said.

Students were allowed to wear whatever they wanted, as long as it was respectable and appropriate. Often, students wore outfits that reflected their Choice. Wearing this outfit would mark her as a Hunter, but was that the Choice she wanted to make? There were so many other things she wanted to do, so much else she enjoyed. Archery was near the top, sure, but it wasn't her only interest.

She felt the weight of the Choice crashing down on her again.

Her father appeared at the door. "Everyone decent?" he asked.

Arra brightened. "Look, Father!" she said, twirling. It wasn't a dress, but she still felt inexplicably feminine in the outfit. Like the clothes knew her, somehow. Improved her.

"It suits you," Silanar said. Were his eyes watering? "My little girl, all grown up." He stepped into the room, handing Arra a long package wrapped with brown paper. "I have a gift for you as well."

Two Waychoice gifts? It was her lucky day. Arra grabbed the package and tore into it, feeling like a kid again. She should be nervous, should be thinking about her Choice tomorrow, but this was nice. This was a welcome distraction.

The package contained a beautiful quiver. It was made from reinforced leather, the color matching her outfit perfectly. She put it on, adjusting the strap so the quiver sat comfortably on her back. She looked like a true archer.

"It's amazing," she said.

"There's one more thing," Silanar said, handing her a leather pouch. It was the traditional primewood pouch, meant to be worn around the waist or attached to a belt.

"Father," she said, "you know I don't need this."

"It's tradition," he said, "even if you aren't a mage. It was given to me for my Waychoice, and I want you to have it now."

Arra felt emotions warring within her. The primewood pouch was a stark reminder that she was not a mage, and for that she hated it. But it was still a touching gift, a personal item that Silanar would not have dared to part with unless he meant it as a great kindness. She should accept it, regardless of how it made her feel.

"Thank you," she said, trying not to let tears come. It was okay—magic wasn't everything. She could do a lot with her bow and arrows alone—more than most mages. It would be enough.

She hugged her father and mother. "Thank you both," she said. "It's all so beautiful."

"Whatever you Choose tomorrow," Silanar said, "you'll always be our daughter. Our Arra." There *were* tears in his eyes. It was unlike her father to be so emotional.

She hugged him again. Most of the time he wasn't very lovable, but tonight was an exception. She wished she'd had more moments like this growing up. But as of tomorrow, she'd be grown, her childhood in the past. It was time to shed childhood fantasies, time to determine her future. Time to Choose.

At least she'd look damn good doing it.

ALLAIN WALKED through the village streets, idly carving at the wood block in his hand. Tonight he was making a hummingbird. They were hard to get right—the beak was especially problematic. He whistled lightly as he walked, enjoying the brisk night air. He was in a good mood—the Waychoice was tomorrow. He would finally be considered an adult.

It was about time.

He stopped whistling when he heard a voice coming from just off the road, in a little grove of trees. It was pretty late—

usually Allain was the only one out at this time of night. He moved off the road, skirting around the trees so he wouldn't be seen by whoever was inside. The voice continued as he silently approached. He didn't recognize it.

"I convinced him to stay one more day," the person said. Allain heard someone respond, but the other voice was too quiet and garbled to make out. He crept closer.

"I don't have it yet," the first voice said. "What are you going to do?"

The other voice said something, but Allain still couldn't hear the words. "Trey will be here," the first voice said. "You're not going to kill *everyone*, are you?"

Allain grew alarmed as the other voice spoke. What was happening here? Who was going to be killed?

"Okay. Sorry," the first voice said. "Yes, I'll get it." Then there was a hiss and a click, and the conversation stopped.

Allain held his position, crouching behind a pair of bushes. He wanted to see if he could get a glimpse of whoever it was that had been speaking. He heard footsteps, and someone emerged from the grove, looking both ways before departing.

It was too dark to see anything—he had only seen a silhouette. Still, the man had been big, and tall. Something about his shape seemed familiar, but Allain couldn't quite place it. Who had it been? What was Trey involved with?

And who was about to kill everyone?

FIVE

ARRA INSPECTED herself in the mirror. The Waychoice Ceremony was in less than an hour. These were her final moments of being a child.

She turned from side to side, looking at her reflection. She looked like a character in a fantasy novel, although her quiver was empty, somewhat spoiling the effect. It wouldn't do to go to her Waychoice armed, though.

The brown clothing looked good on her, accentuating her body in all the right places, while still remaining comfortable. She thought about what Fenian would do when he saw her, and she blushed. He'd waste no time getting her out of these clothes tonight.

She was looking forward to it.

She hadn't been planning on wearing the primewood pouch her father had given her, but at the last moment she strapped it on. It completed the picture, making her look like a bladedancer mage. It was a lie, but it was a pretty lie. She had been surprised to find primewood chips in the pouch— not just poplar or yew, but all six of the deciduous woods.

With primewood so limited, Silanar shouldn't have wasted any of it on her. He'd probably wanted her to feel like she belonged, but it was too much. She resolved to give it back to him after the ceremony.

Her aunt and mother entered the room, nodding appreciatively at her appearance.

"Look at this hottie," Nuala said, grinning devilishly.

"Shush, Nuala," Melenora said. "Don't give her any ideas."

"Oh, I'm sure she's already had plenty of ideas," Nuala said, poking Arra in the side. Arra squealed, laughing. Her aunt always used to tickle her like this when she was younger. "Now, Arra," Nuala said, "the Planters will be so happy to have you, when you Choose Cultivation."

"Nuala!" Melenora said, acting shocked. "You aren't supposed to tell her what to Choose. And besides," she looked at Arra, "my daughter will be Choosing Artisan."

Arra wrinkled her nose at her mother.

"No?" Melenora said, looking her up and down. "Well you're good enough at it. But no, I suppose you'll be Choosing Hunter, won't you? You're certainly dressed the part." She smiled, not intending her words to hurt.

"You'll find out when everyone else does," Arra said.

"Can't you give us even a tiny hint?" Nuala asked. "Normally it's so obvious. But with you"—she leaned in closer, whispering conspiratorially—"there's a pool on what you'll Choose. I put in twenty pieces of birch you'll pick Cultivation."

Arra put a hand to her mouth, shocked. They were placing bets with *primewood*? That was wrong on so many levels.

"I shouldn't have told you that, I see," Nuala said, frowning. "Well, don't let it bother you. Just some fun."

Melenora swatted her sister on the arm. "Don't frighten the poor child," she said, "she has enough on her mind already." She reached out to gather Arra in a big hug. "Just Choose what you think is best," she said.

TREY HAD DECIDED to leave right after the ceremony. He shouldn't have stayed this long—he was itching, jumping at shadows. He couldn't help but see the elves as evil ghosts of their former selves. When he'd first landed amongst them, he'd been entranced by their beauty, by their magic.

But after Silanar's story, everything had changed.

He had debated what to take with him. In the end, he'd settled on a simple pack with some clothes, food, and a few supplies—flint and tender, rope, a small lantern. The elves didn't have anything truly useful like flashlights, so that would have to do. He also took a pouch of prime birch, ash, and elm—the deciduous woods he could actually use. He knew it was stealing and wrong, especially with the elves having lost half their primewood, but it was better to be safe than sorry.

He'd almost taken the Book of Amplification with him, knowing that it was the only way he'd actually be able to do any useful magic. But, ultimately, he couldn't bring himself to do it. It was a precious artifact, and he had no right taking it. So he had left the book in its usual place, inside the chest at the foot of his bed.

He had brought the pack with him. Once the ceremony was over, he'd slip away.

He wasn't going to say goodbye.

The ceremony was about to start. It was being held in one of the gardens in Tarwa Matso, the city Cultivation center.

Apparently this was one of the places they held important events—weddings, Council election speeches, things like that. The garden consisted of a field of grass, bordered by trees and beautiful plants of every type. Flowers bloomed everywhere Trey looked, birds and insects flitting about. A large gazebo was at one end of the field, decorated with garlands and wreaths. It made an effective, if quaint, stage. Rows of wooden chairs had been set in the grass beyond the gazebo. Trey sat by himself in the back row, watching elves arriving for the ceremony.

Nobody paid him much heed as they came in and sat down. Trey figured he was something of an enigma at this point—a Prime Mage who couldn't do any respectable magic without the Book to help him. A human who'd fallen out of the big machine city in the sky. A human who wasn't supposed to be a mage.

What use *was* he, down here?

Elves kept filing in, well-behaved and orderly, as usual. Where was Callan? Trey hadn't seen him today. He hadn't seen Orym, either, come to think of it. Why was everyone disappearing all the time? Elanil and Rylan still hadn't come back from wherever they had gone. Well, soon enough Trey would be doing some disappearing of his own.

He longed to be away from this place.

A hush came over the crowd as Aolis Talos appeared, coming out to stand in front of the crowd. This was the High Magister of the School, Trey remembered. He'd been the one who'd brought out the Tree of Alignment. Today he looked haggard, as if he hadn't slept, but he still managed a regal bearing. He looked the part of High Magister: tall and stately, bald head black and shining in the sun.

"Greetings," Aolis said, his voice easily loud enough to be heard. Was it being amplified somehow? Maybe it was that strengthshaping magic he'd heard about. One of the three types he couldn't do. "We are gathered here today," Aolis continued, "to witness the Waychoice of three young ones, and their passage into adulthood."

The Waychoice. Trey could have sworn he'd read this exact kind of thing in several of his books. He hoped this ceremony wouldn't involve anything silly like pricking fingers or something.

Aolis was droning on and on, something about how the Ways were life, how Choosing was the gateway to life. Something like that. It was a bunch of nonsense, really, so Trey tuned it out. But when the three graduates walked out on stage, Trey perked up.

Arra was the very picture of a fantasy novel. Trey did a double-take, not believing his eyes. He'd known she was beautiful, but in *that* outfit—damn. She looked like a warrior princess about to save the kingdom. A bow-and-arrows, sword-and-sorcery woman with impossible curves. Trey almost started laughing right then and there. It was ridiculous. This whole thing was ridiculous: the Waychoice, the magic, the outfits. Yes, elves were real, and they were everything humanity had hoped they would be.

He found himself growing angry, then. Sure, on the outside these elves looked like fantasy gods and goddesses, action heroes come to life. But inside? Inside they were cruel, manipulative murderers, on a scale unprecedented by any human.

The elves were pretty, athletic, and skilled. Wholesome and altruistic, in harmony with each other and the planet. Magical and logical and *completely batshit crazy.*

Trey took a deep breath, trying to stop the feelings that kept coming to him. When he looked at Arra, he wanted her, sure. He couldn't deny her beauty. But he hated her, too, hated what she represented. Hated the person she would become. He knew he wasn't being fair to her, but there it was. Elves were elves.

They were all evil as far as he was concerned.

Still, he might as well enjoy the show. He settled into his seat, keeping his eyes on Arra the entire time.

SIX

"WITH YOUR CHOICE," Aolis Talos was saying, "you become a part of this town, of its people. You Choose to dedicate your life to Sylrantheas, to form and function as a member of elven society."

Arra focused on keeping still, motionless on the gazebo platform. She didn't like being the center of attention—not like this, standing in front of everyone. She preferred to be out in the woods, underneath a tree. Or in the gardens, or the hospital. Anywhere but here. She caught sight of Trey sitting in the back of the audience. He didn't look happy to be there, either—his face was gloomy. Maybe she should talk to him after this was over, try to reassure him that not *all* elves were like her father. She studied his face, trying to imagine what must be going through his mind.

Then she caught Fenian's eye. He was sitting in the front row, had seen her looking at Trey. A faint expression crossed his face, unreadable. Arra wanted to sigh, but she couldn't. Not in front of all these people.

Finally, Aolis' speech was done. He turned to Allain, the first in the group. "My son," he said, using the word figuratively, as Allain was becoming a son of the elves, "the Choice has been laid before you. Step forward, and speak true. Choose your Way."

Allain stepped forward stiffly. "I Choose Construction," he said, "that I may serve the Eldrim in this Way."

Arra wasn't surprised by his Choice, but she knew it had cost him. Allain had desperately wanted to be a Hunter, to Choose the Way of Bombardment, but he just wasn't good enough. And so he would follow in his father's footsteps, taking up Construction.

She hoped he would be happy.

Imra was up next. "My daughter," Aolis said, gesturing to her, "the Choice has been laid before you. Step forward, and speak true. Choose your Way."

Imra took a step forward, her movement graceful, almost sinuous. She cut a magnificent pose in her Waychoice outfit, breeches and a shirt not too dissimilar to Arra's. They were both archers, and they looked the part, but Arra thought Imra pulled it off better than she did. Imra looked back at Arra for a second, smiling at her almost shyly. Then she returned her gaze to the crowd.

"I Choose Bombardment," she said, "that I may serve the Eldrim in this Way."

Good. Imra would make a fantastic Hunter; Sylrantheas was better for having her. Arra felt a swell of pride for her friend, and a sudden longing came over her. She could feel her childhood already slipping away. Imra looked back at her again, beaming. She was so happy. Arra smiled back, knowing that her own smile wasn't half as genuine.

Then it was her turn.

"My daughter," Aolis started, but the rest of it was a blur. Arra felt blood rising to her head, her face flushing. This was it. This was the moment she had been waiting for her entire life. The moment she Chose her destiny.

And she still wasn't ready.

She blinked, suddenly realizing that Aolis had stopped talking. The entire crowd was looking at her, watching her. She was the daughter of the Council Leader, the daughter of two Mentors. The best archer in the village.

The expectations were high.

Bombardment, then. That was what was expected of her. It was her most visible talent, the thing she seemed to excel at the most. But something about it just didn't feel right. It didn't resonate.

The other Ways flashed through her mind in quick succession. Restoration, Cultivation. Movement, Engravement. Sculpture, Recitation, Inspiration. Musician, Artisan. Even Conflagration passed by her mind's eye, on its way to being sorted and counted. Each Way held a place in her heart. She felt an affinity towards them all. There was no possible way she could Choose.

She knew what she needed to do.

She stepped forward. "Sons and daughters of Sylrantheas," she said, projecting her voice. This wasn't part of the expected speech. Already, elves in the audience were looking at each other with confusion. "My wish is to serve you all, the best way I know how." She paused, lending greater gravity to the moment.

"I Choose everything," she said, "that I may serve the people in these Ways."

The audience was silent. Nobody had ever done this before, as far as Arra knew. But how could she be expected to Choose when there was no clear Choice? She could have been a Hunter—a very successful one, in fact—but a part of her would always have been missing. She would have been incomplete.

She couldn't have lived a life in just one Way. But would the elves accept that Choice? Or was the mold set too tightly to break?

Aolis cleared his throat. "Our children have Chosen," he said, continuing the ceremony as if nothing unusual had happened. He looked at Arra as he finished the ceremony. "Now they are children no longer. May the Twins guide them and protect them, and welcome them into their hearts."

"Twins guide and protect them," the audience chanted, making the signs of the Twins. Most of them still looked bewildered, as if they couldn't understand why Aolis had allowed Arra's unorthodox Choice.

Having finished the ceremony, Aolis turned to Arra. "Speak to me tonight," he said, his expression stern. Arra felt her stomach drop. That wasn't good. But before she could think on it further, Fenian was there, grabbing her and kissing her fiercely.

"That was amazing," he said breathlessly. "I never thought you'd actually do it!"

Do what? Choose everything? She herself hadn't known until the moment had arrived. Had Fenian actually figured out what she was going to do before she had?

"I think I'm in trouble," she said.

"Nonsense," Fenian said, "you'll be fine. I'll stand up for you. This will be the start of a new age!" He kissed her again, his eyes bright. His ardor was unexpected. She'd have to get to the bottom of this, as soon as she talked to Aolis.

As she returned the kiss, she caught Trey looking at her out of the corner of her eye. He was watching Fenian, his expression filled with malice. She closed her eyes, focusing on the kiss. Something had clearly broken in Trey, ever since he'd heard the story of the Sundering. But that was something she'd worry about later.

"Hey!" somebody shouted suddenly. "Hey! Everyone! Stop what you're doing!"

Arra looked up to see Orym sprinting into the garden, crashing through flowers and trees. Something was hanging from his shoulder, trailing down to his pocket. It looked like a wire of some kind.

"We have to evacuate the village right now!" Orym shouted. People had just started to stand, getting out of their seats and milling about. They stopped when they heard Orym shouting, looking at him with confusion in their eyes.

"What is the meaning of this?" Silanar said, standing from his seat in the front row. Arra instinctively grabbed Fenian's hand, grateful that he was standing beside her on the gazebo's stage.

"They're coming!" Orym shouted. "They're coming right now! We have to—"

Suddenly there was a loud roar, and the sound of something zipping by in the air—once, twice, three times. A woman screamed, and Fenian grunted next to her, suddenly stumbling. She looked at him to see a hole torn in his pants. Blood pooled there, seeping from the wound in his leg.

Fenian had been shot.

SEVEN

ARRA SCREAMED, but the sound was drowned out by more roaring. She had no frame of reference for what the sound was. Could it be some kind of engine? She paid it no more attention—Fenian needed help.

But before she could do anything, a massive vehicle materialized in mid-air. It was a car, but it was flying. There was only one place where it could have come from. One place where flying cars were real.

New San Francisco.

The car was moving rapidly as it faded into view, soaring over the group of elves gathered for the Waychoice. As it flew, it pelted the crowd with something—bullets? Elves went down with screams and cries, blood spraying and chunks of wood flying through the air.

Yes. Definitely bullets.

Arra was frozen. The scene was hard to parse. Why was the flying car here? Why was it shooting them?

Why now?

The sounds of dying elves reached her ears underneath the roar of the machine. Guardians were flooding the scene, marching out with swords and arrows brandished, but more cars were appearing in the air. The flying machines just mowed them down, flinging bullets and blood everywhere. Arra felt bile rising to her throat. Already everything was in chaos, and only moments had passed.

Fenian was sagging against the side of the gazebo, having trouble standing. He'd been shot in his wounded leg, adding insult to injury. He gritted his teeth, pressing a hand to the wound. "We have to get everyone out of here," he said, his voice strained with pain. "Is your bow nearby?"

"You're hurt," Arra said. "You need medical attention."

"I can manage," he said. "The bullet just grazed me. It hurts like hell, but I can still use these damn crutches. Get your bow." His tone was commanding. Even after being shot, Fenian was still a Hunter through and through.

Arra nodded briskly. She didn't want to leave Fenian, but she had a job to do. She had Chosen every Way. Now it was time to put that Choice into action.

Luckily, her bow was just behind the gazebo. She'd brought it to complete the outfit, but hadn't wanted to bring it onstage. She ran over to the longbow, picking it up. Arrows. She needed arrows.

She scanned the area, hoping somebody had brought some. She saw yet more cars materializing, zooming over the frantic crowd. Two guns mounted to the side of them blazed, spouting bullets that ripped through the helpless elves below. As she watched, Aolis took two bullets to the chest and went down in a spray of blood. The sounds of screaming elves and roaring engines overwhelmed her.

Suddenly Kharis was in front of her, thrusting a bundle of arrows at her. "Here," he shouted over the noise, "take these and get behind something!"

Arra grabbed the arrows and shoved them into the quiver

she was already wearing. She ducked down behind one of the gazebo's wooden pillars with Kharis. "Will these even work?" she asked, taking an arrow out and nocking it to her longbow. The bow was absurdly large for this kind of position—she'd have to stand up to even shoot the thing. She wished she had a smaller recurve with her.

"Not against the fallcars," Kharis said. "Look there."

Men were coming out of the forest. Not humans—elves, maybe a dozen of them, dressed in identical pale blue uniforms. They had small silver helmets on, although the helmets weren't very protective—they left the faces and ears open, clearly advertising that these were elves. They were each holding a small silver gun that seemed to shimmer darkly.

The Cothellon had arrived.

How had they gotten in? The wall should have—oh. The wall had been destroyed by the Remnant. Now anyone was free to march all over Sylrantheas. And besides—if the Cothellon had flying machines, no wall could stop them.

The Eldrim were sitting ducks.

Allain appeared suddenly, running past the gazebo. "He's coming for Trey!" he shouted as he passed. Before she could ask him what he meant, he was gone.

Orym plopped down next to where they were hiding behind the gazebo. "Those are mergeguns!" he shouted, out of breath. "They can shoot through anything. You guys are our best bet—take out those troops if you can! I'll try to get as many people out of here as possible. Where's Lhoris?" Without waiting for a reply, he bounded off, ducking to stay low.

Another fallcar flew in from the forest. Or was it one of the first two? Everything was happening so fast. The fallcar razed the crowd again, felling more elves. So many were dead and dying. It was a massacre. Why was this happening?

No time for that now—Arra felt her Hunter instincts taking over. She'd trained for this. Not *this*, exactly, but it didn't matter. She could do this.

She drew the bow back, sighting carefully along the arrow. The Cothellon soldiers in sky blue were advancing on the crowd. Elves were screaming and running, trying in vain to get out of the enclosed garden as quickly as possible. Arra stilled her breathing, focusing on the soldiers. Then she loosed the arrow, watching as it sailed between two Cothellon and flew into the forest.

It missed everything.

Twins! Arra drew another arrow, trying to calm herself. The screams continued, piercing her heart like knives. She couldn't do this. Her people were dying.

She blinked, trying to clear her thoughts. She held her breath and nocked the arrow, drawing it back. The Cothellon were still on the other side of the garden, still moving, but this was a shot she could take.

One of the soldiers slapped a woman hard with his gloved hand, and the elf went down. Arra closed her mind, walling it off from what she was seeing. She couldn't let it affect her. She had to focus.

She loosed the arrow.

It sliced through the air, flying straight and true. It slammed into the soldier's eye, the one who had slapped the poor elven woman. He went down, dead instantly, the arrow sticking out of his eye as he fell.

Arra felt a chill run through her. She'd killed before, yes, but that had always been animals, and sometimes Remnant.

She'd never killed an *elf* before.

She turned, checking her surroundings. Fenian was on

the other side of the gazebo, balanced on one leg behind another wooden pillar. He was clearly in a lot of pain, but that didn't seem to be stopping him. He nocked an arrow, sighted, and loosed, all in one fluid motion. Another Cothellon soldier fell, an arrow piercing his heart.

Next to her, Kharis also loosed an arrow. It flew true, killing a third soldier. The fallcars had stopped coming, but Arra thought she could hear sounds from further away—shots and explosions in the village. She smelled smoke. Twins—the village was being destroyed.

She started to draw another arrow, but the Cothellon had been alerted to the archers' presence at this point. They turned as a group, spreading out. Some of them ducked behind chairs, while a few others advanced on the gazebo. Three of them were heading for where Fenian was hiding. He was fiddling with his primewood pouch, though, and didn't see them.

"Fenian!" Arra screamed, starting to stand.

Kharis pulled her down roughly. "We have to move," he hissed.

Arra started to turn, following her Mentor's orders, but the glimmer of a gun caught her attention.

The world went into slow motion.

The crowd of screaming elves quietened, their movements becoming blurry. Smoke crept in around the edges of her vision, the acrid smell permeating her senses. The gun she'd seen was there, shining strangely, somehow dark and bright all at the same time. The Cothellon soldier holding it was staring at Fenian's location. Arra tried to cry out again, but she couldn't move. She felt like she was swimming through mud.

She saw the soldier lift the gun, pointing it at the wooden post sheltering Fenian. She saw him clench his hand, his finger moving slowly, impossibly slowly, pulling back the trigger of the gun. Arra stretched out to stop him, to do anything to prevent what was about to happen, but she couldn't. She wasn't fast enough. Everything was moving so slowly.

But Fenian was safe. Right? He was behind a big pillar of wood. A simple bullet couldn't get to him. He'd be okay.

The Cothellon just kept moving his finger back, and the bullet began to fly. And Arra realized she was wrong—this wasn't an ordinary bullet. Orym had said so. He had said it could shoot through anything.

Which meant it could shoot through wood.

No.

She saw the bullet move through the air, streaking toward the gazebo's structure, the air rippling behind it, shimmering dust flying out from its path. She watched as the bullet ripped through the wooden pillar like it was paper, splitting the wood into fragments and continuing onward. She saw the wood shards flying, watched them spinning in the sunlight from above. She saw dust, and wood, and metal.

And blood.

She couldn't move as the bullet ripped through Fenian's chest, shattering his skin. She couldn't budge as his face twisted with shock, as his eyes flared. She couldn't prevent the awful spread of blood blooming from his chest.

His shirt was shredded, his eyes already glassy.

He slid down the wooden pillar, a bright streak of blood streaming in his wake.

He fell to the ground, and all his breathing stopped, and time finally—suddenly—returned to normal.

Arra screamed.

EIGHT

RYLAN AND ELANIL trekked through the Under, leading the way to Planner Central to rescue Con. She hadn't been doing well the last time Rylan had seen her—but that was only a few hours ago.

Con would still be alive.

He hoped.

"Do you think we'll have enough mergeguns?" Dill asked. He and Shot and Small were coming with them to get Con.

Shot grunted. "How many will we have?"

"A dozen, maybe. Fifteen if we're lucky. It takes Smoke a while to put them together, and we aren't exactly swimming in dark oak, here."

"Aren't mages the limiting factor?" Small asked. He was always smart like that.

Dill nodded. "Smoke and Shot make two that we have. I'm hoping Dad gets us more. But even if he doesn't, those guns don't last too long. Six shots each, maybe. Having more of them will help, even if we don't have that many mages."

"That's what the police were using, isn't it?" Rylan asked, turning to Dill as they walked. They were using an abandoned subway tunnel, plenty wide enough for them all. It made for a nice change after the Under's normally cramped passages.

"During the meeting?" Dill asked. "Those were merge-guns, alright. They can shoot through anything, as long as a mergemelder is using them. Pretty damn dangerous."

"Anything?" Rylan asked. "Anything at all?"

Dill stroked his bare chin. "Pretty sure. I've seen them go through metal, wood, and water. Haven't tried it with a force-field, but I bet it can shoot through that, too."

"Got no way to make a forcefield, anyway," Small said. He was having to walk faster to keep up, but he didn't seem to mind. "Last forcefinder we knew of is dead."

Phoenix. Rylan tried not to think about his mother.

"So you figure the only way to beat them is to have merge-guns of your own?" he asked.

"That's the idea."

They reached a place where the subway tunnel split, going off to the left and right at angles. Rylan stopped. He didn't remember this part of the Under. Which way should they go?

"Don't ask me," Dill said, seeing his confusion. "You're leading this little expedition."

"Left," Small said.

Rylan looked down both tunnels. They seemed the same to him. Without a map—and nobody made maps of the stuff down here—there was no way to know unless you tried them both. He shrugged. "Left it is," he said, setting off.

The rest of the group followed him, their voices echoing through the tunnel as they went.

TREY DUCKED when the first flying car arrived, primitive instincts taking over. The roar of engines was an unexpected change from the normally quiet forest. Were the Remnant back? Had they acquired new technology?

Bullets started flying, and elves around him started dropping. Blood was suddenly everywhere, and Trey's head began to hurt. He dropped to the ground, trying to stay out of the line of fire.

What the hell was going on?

He crawled over to an elf near him who was bleeding profusely from a bullet wound in her stomach. As Trey drew near, he recognized the woman: it was Eloen, the Restoration Mentor.

"H-help me," she said as she saw him approach. Her eyes were glassy, her breathing shallow.

"Aren't you a Healer?" Trey asked. He fumbled in his primewood pouch, pulling out a piece of birch. "Here. I'm not strong enough."

Eloen pushed the wood away with a shaking hand. "Can't...heal myself," she said. "Too dangerous."

What? But Trey had healed himself before. Maybe only Prime Mages could do that. It seemed strange.

"I'll try," he said.

"You healed Elanil," Eloen said, her breath raspy. "You can heal me."

But Trey wasn't sure. Something was roiling in his head. All the chaos and the danger around him was interrupting him, pausing his thoughts. There was too much going on. He didn't think he could do *anything* right now.

Another line of bullets pummeled the grass just a foot away, making Trey flinch. This was crazy. Who was attacking them?

"Trey," Eloen said, and he could see her fading.

He had to try.

Clutching the primewood piece, he laid a hand on Eloen's arm. Trying to ignore the screams and shots around him, he Willed the bullet wound to heal.

Nothing happened.

He closed his eyes and tried again, harder, focusing intensely on the magic. He visualized a connection from the wood, through his body, to Eloen's arm.

The magic took hold.

But it felt flimsy. Another flying vehicle roared overhead, interrupting Trey's thoughts again. The magic failed as quickly as it had come, and the primewood turned to dust.

Eloen was still dying.

"I can't," he said. "I'm not strong enough. I can't focus. I just...can't."

Eloen looked at him through pain-filled eyes. "Please," she uttered, and then she lapsed into unconsciousness.

Trey was disgusted with himself. He was supposed to be a Prime Mage, an all-powerful magician, something that hadn't happened in five thousand years. But really, when it came down to it, what *was* he? A nothing. A nobody. A failure.

He couldn't heal a thing.

He stood, taking stock of his surroundings. Everywhere elves were running, shouting and crying and trying to escape the deadly flying cars. A group of soldiers clad in sky blue uniforms appeared at the back of the garden, near him. They had strange-looking guns and metallic helmets. They looked like something out of a science fiction book.

Definitely not Remnant.

Trey gave Eloen one last look. She would die. Might already have. Was it Trey's fault? Was it his fault he hadn't healed her? Perhaps.

He was weak.

He made his way down the row of chairs, staying as low as possible. He couldn't be of use to anyone here, not with his weak magic. He should just run. He should leave the city like he'd planned.

He should escape while he had the chance.

An arrow sliced through the air over his head and he looked to see where it had come from. Arra was crouched down behind one of the gazebo's wooden supports, pulling back her longbow, auburn hair flying wildly behind her. She looked scared and determined, all at the same time. As he watched, she drew back her bow and loosed another arrow.

She, at least, was useful. She had the ability to kill, even without magic. She was the action hero Trey would never be.

Not without that Book.

In that moment, Trey decided *not* to leave. Not yet, at least. He was caught up with the elves now, part of whatever was happening here. Eloen would probably die, but there were others he could save. He should at least *try*. If Arra could do it, so could he.

But he needed that Book.

So he stood and started running, sprinting as fast as he could away from the soldiers, out of the garden, heading in the direction of Arra's house. Bullets flew by him as he ran, but none hit him. He moved with a speed he didn't know he had, adrenaline coursing through his blood.

He would get the Book of Amplification, and then those soldiers would see some *real* magic.

ARRA DROPPED HER BOW, struggling to get over to where Fenian was lying. But before she could get to him, something careened into her, taking her down. She heard a shot whiz by over her head.

"Watch it, girl!" It was Lhoris. He slapped her on the arm and grinned. "Close one," he said, then ducked as another bullet flew at him. It hit the gazebo, shattered wood flying everywhere. Dust and smoke filled the air, and Arra looked up. The soldiers were getting closer. She saw her father over by Fenian, dragging him away from the gazebo. It looked like he was still breathing after all.

"Snap out of it," Lhoris said. "Help us out, here!"

He was right. Arra picked up her bow, taking care to stay hidden behind the raised stage of the gazebo. Where had Imra gone? She had been onstage with her during the ceremony.

Then Imra was there, green eyes flashing, a spattering of blood on her right cheek. She planted her longbow next to Arra without a word, nocking an arrow and loosing it toward the soldiers. One of them went down, and dust fell from Imra's hand.

Arra had frozen for too long. It was time to act. She grabbed an arrow, fitting it to her bowstring with shaking hands. The screams of the elves were relentless, assaulting her ears painfully. The sound made her heart twist. Her people were dying.

She loosed the arrow and it flew off-angle, missing her target. "Twins!" she screamed.

She couldn't do this. She couldn't concentrate. Three more soldiers neared their location behind the gazebo, guns out. Kharis managed to shoot another arrow, but it glanced off a helmet, clattering away uselessly. Arra could hear him cursing nearby. She felt panic rising inside her.

Then Imra's hand was on hers, holding it where she was holding the longbow. Her friend's hand was cool, dry. Calm.

"Let me help," she said. She lifted her hand away, revealing a piece of prime poplar. Arra looked at her questioningly, then realization dawned. She nodded, nocking another arrow to her bow.

Imra put her hand on Arra's shoulder, then, so it wouldn't interfere with the shot. The touch from her friend was reassuring. Yes. She could do this.

She loosed the arrow.

She could almost sense the magic as it happened. Quick as a blink, Imra directed the arrow to its target. One of the soldiers went down, but there were two more twenty feet away. They knelt, steadying their guns.

Aiming right for Arra.

NINE

TREY MANAGED to reach Arra's house, staying low and trying to avoid being seen by the flying cars. Explosions rocked the village in the distance, and Trey could see fires erupting everywhere. There was no way to fight this, not without the Book.

This was so much worse than the Remnant attack had been. This was *true* devastation, on a level he'd never seen before. The elves attacking them had flying cars. Flying cars with *guns*.

He didn't think anyone would survive this.

But he had to try.

Just before he entered the house, he thought he saw a strange elf dressed all in black, standing across the street, looking at him. The man looked familiar, but Trey didn't know why. He didn't think he'd seen him before during his time in Sylrantheas. The man just stood there, doing nothing. Odd.

But Trey didn't have time for this. He ran into the house, heading into the guest room he'd been staying in. Flinging open the chest at the foot of the bed, he dug around for where he knew the Book of Amplification would be.

Except it wasn't there.

Trey dug further, going through blankets and articles of clothing. Maybe the Book had just fallen to the bottom, becoming lost amongst the trunk's other contents.

He couldn't find it.

He sat back on his heels, thinking hard. He clearly remembered putting the book there, just before going to the Waychoice Ceremony. He'd almost taken it with him, but had decided not to. It should definitely be there, unless somebody had taken it.

Maybe Silanar had thought better of allowing Trey to keep the Book. Maybe he'd taken it back. That must be it. It made sense.

The room shook, a loud explosion sounding from a few blocks away. He could hear screaming, the sounds of bullets and running feet. It was too much violence—it was too sudden, too extreme. Trey's head began to hurt, and thoughts of his father sprang into his mind.

Trey had a feeling the man would have greatly enjoyed this.

He stood up, making his way out of the house, leaving his bag in the room. If he couldn't find the Book, he couldn't use magic effectively. Part of him wanted to just slink away, to take his bag and leave the elves behind forever. But part of him felt responsible for this, somehow. As if the events that had been set in motion the day he'd first met Orym had led to this. None of it was his fault, but it was all pointed at him. He knew it.

He was the Prime Mage.

He knew what he had to do.

He exited the house, noting that the strange elf in black

was gone. Trey heard screams from all over Sylrantheas, could see fires erupting from various buildings. He looked left, in the direction he knew the Primestore building was. No smoke over there, thankfully. He hoped the last of the primewood would survive the day.

He turned right, heading back the way he had come, back to the garden where the ceremony had taken place. There had been hundreds of elves there. That was where he was needed. He would help where he could.

Allain appeared from somewhere suddenly, carving a wooden figurine in his hand. It looked like a stag, maybe—a half-formed stag, head and antlers emerging from a solid block of wood. Allain twisted and flicked his small carving knife expertly, rendering shapes in the wood.

Another explosion sounded nearby, pieces of wood and dirt falling from the roof of a nearby house. The damage to the city was growing by the minute. The elves either needed to fight back or get out, but Allain was standing there.

Now was not the time for wood carving.

"Allain," Trey said, and the boy looked up, eyes glinting coldly. He smirked at Trey as he approached, still carving.

"This is your fault," he said.

"What?" Trey didn't understand.

"They're here for you."

"*Who's* here? What's going on?"

"The Cothellon, asshole. Why the hell else would they be here? You're the Prime Mage. You're the new guy. It's obvious."

Allain was getting close now, still flicking shards of wood with his knife. What was the plan, here? Was he going to attack Trey with the carving knife? He took a cautious step back.

"How would they even know I was here?" Trey asked, trying to keep Allain talking. He continued stepping backward down the street, keeping his distance. A flying car zipped by overhead, but this time it wasn't shooting anything.

"They know *everything*," Allain said. "They know all about your little secret."

"What are you even talking about?" Trey was growing exasperated.

"You and Arra," Allain said. The wooden stag continued to take shape, looking as if it would bound out from the block of wood at any moment. "We all see you together. We know."

"Know what?" Trey asked. "Jesus Christ, Allain, just say what you're going to say. The town is going to shit around us —can't you see that?"

"You're going to steal her from me," Allain said. "You're going to run away. You're going to destroy this entire village, all our primewood, and take my girl."

"She's not your girl, Allain. And she's not mine, either. She's with Fenian."

"I see the way she looks at you," Allain said. The pair of them continued their strange lock-step, moving slowly down the street, the flick-flick of the carving knife a curious counterpoint to the screams and shots and explosions in the distance. Trey ducked instinctively as yet another flying car zoomed over his head. He needed this to end. Now.

He stopped moving backward and took a step toward Allain.

Suddenly Allain's carving knife turned into a sword, glimmering in the sunlight. It was long and curved, like the scimitars Trey had read about in history books. Allain lunged forward, pressing the metal almost up to Trey's neck, not quite touching him.

"I'm going to kill you," he breathed, still holding on to the carving in his other hand. "You're going to die, and then this attack will stop."

TEN

IMRA SQUEEZED Arra's shoulder and dropped her bow, pulling a chip of poplar from her pouch. Arra could see the soldiers' fingers tightening on their triggers.

Their guns were pointed right at her. She was about to die.

She blanked her mind, pulling two arrows from her quiver and nocking them to her bow in one fluid motion. Imra squeezed her shoulder again, signaling her readiness, and Arra loosed the shot.

The two arrows flew, side-by-side at first, then diverging perfectly, angling off to the left and right. Arra could feel the pulse of Imra's hand on her shoulder as she used her bladedancing magic to direct the arrows to their target.

Both soldiers went down, dead instantly.

Imra let out a yip, flashing a grin at Arra, and Arra released the breath she'd been holding. That had been far too close.

The entire gazebo exploded.

"SHHH!" Shot crouched down suddenly, shushing them. Rylan stopped, the others nearly colliding with him as they came up from behind.

"What is it?" Rylan whispered.

"Guards up ahead," Shot said.

"What? We must have gone the wrong way."

"Maybe not," Dill whispered from behind him. "Guards have been known to patrol under Planner Central. Let's deal with them."

Rylan was pretty sure he knew what "deal with them" meant, and he wasn't sure he liked it.

He looked at Elanil, at her pretty face all smudged. Her hair was messed up, too, and she looked scared. He sidled up to her, still crouching on the cold cement floor of the tunnel.

"You okay?" he asked quietly.

She nodded. "I prefer trees," she whispered, "but I don't mind a little adventure." She looked at him, her tan eyes reflecting the boys' flashlight beams as they played them around the tunnel. "As long as it doesn't get me killed."

"I think Con and you will like each other," Rylan said.

"Guys, kill your lights," Dill ordered. They obeyed, shutting them off one by one. "On me," he said, creeping past Rylan to take the lead.

As Rylan's eyes adjusted to the darkness, he noticed an eerie green light emanating from the ceiling. Where had he seen green light in the Under before? A memory tickled at him, but he couldn't place it.

Suddenly a loud clattering sound echoed through the tunnel. Someone had dropped their flashlight.

"Shit," Small said.

"They've seen us!" Shot cried in a hoarse whisper. "Run!"

"LET ME GO, ALLAIN," Trey said. The mysterious sword was still at his throat, although he couldn't feel it touching his skin. Maybe Allain wasn't as committed to this course of action as he sounded.

"Fuck you," Allain said.

So much for that.

The house next to them exploded suddenly, the force of the blast propelling Trey and Allain sideways and slamming them into a nearby wall. Shrapnel and smoke flew threw the air, slapping into Trey's face and arms. Allain was on the ground, carving knife back in his hand. His sword was nowhere to be seen.

Allain stood up, brushing dirt and wood fragments off his clothing. He was still holding the carving of the stag, although one of the antlers was missing.

He advanced on Trey again.

Trey got up. He hadn't been hurt, thankfully. He glanced at the house across the street now reduced to a pile of burning rubble. Trey hoped nobody had been inside.

He looked back at Allain, but the boy wasn't there anymore. Instead, a full-sized black grizzly bear was standing where Allain had been. Trey had seen one in a video, once. It was a lot bigger in person, and a whole lot scarier.

The bear roared at Trey and set off towards him, sharp teeth bared.

"COME ON," Dill ordered, pulling out one of the mergeguns and standing up. He took off down the tunnel.

Rylan could see the guards now, just up ahead around the bend, little circles of light around them where some kind of electric lanterns were hanging on the wall. One had a radio, and the other had a gun.

He jogged forward, following Dill.

Before Rylan could figure out what the plan was, Shot raised his gun and pulled the trigger, and the first guard went down in a spray of blood. The other guard stepped out of sight.

Dill didn't slow. He continued jogging down the tunnel, heading to where the man had disappeared. He hadn't been armed; he'd be easy to take out. At least Rylan hoped that was the case.

They rounded the corner and found themselves face to face with not one, but *three* guards.

And all of them had guns.

ARRA FLEW BACK, the explosion propelling her out of the garden and slamming her into a tree. She shook her head, dazed, trying to figure out what had happened.

The gazebo had exploded.

Everything hurt. Arra looked down, trying to assess the damage. Her whole body was sliced with cuts and lacerations, wooden splinters and dirt covering her body. None of her wounds seemed life-threatening, but they *hurt*.

Imra, though, had it a lot worse. She was slumped over on the ground, blood coming out of her nose.

She wasn't moving.

Arra got up on her knees, crawling painfully over to Imra. She wasn't breathing.

Shit.

"Imra!" Arra said, shaking her shoulders. "Wake up!"

More gunshots rang out from the garden. The gazebo was

a flaming ruin, reduced to nothing but broken wood. The remaining soldiers had split up, mowing down whatever elves they could find before continuing out into the village.

They were alone.

"Come on, Imra, wake up," Arra said, sobbing. First Fenian now Imra. She couldn't lose them both, not like this. She needed to *do* something.

She'd Chosen all the Ways. All of them, Healing included. So she took a deep breath, ignoring the pain in her own body, focusing her mind to the problem. She needed to use her medical training. She needed to save Imra.

She could do this.

She laid Imra down on her back and knelt down next to her, immediately beginning chest compressions. She remembered Eloen's words to the class as she had taught them CPR—Eloen had always believed that Mundane medical training was more important than magic. Arra had always resented it—she'd wanted to be a mage. But now, when it mattered most, she realized her Mentor had been right.

She could do this.

She continued compressions, counting to thirty, willing Imra to come back to her. And just like that, in less than a minute, it worked. Imra sputtered and started breathing again, her eyes opening wide. Arra hadn't even had to administer mouth-to-mouth.

Imra was back.

Magic not required.

"What happened?" she whispered.

Arra hugged her tightly. "Oh, Imra," she sobbed into her ear. "I'm so glad you're okay. I almost lost you."

Imra hugged her back weakly. "Did the gazebo explode?"

Arra nodded, still holding Imra close. Then she realized

she was missing something. Her bow. Where had it gone? She'd lost hold of it during the explosion.

Then she saw it, sitting on the ground near the gazebo.

It was on fire.

EVERYONE REACTED AT ONCE.

Shot leveled his gun, squeezing the trigger. Dill balled his fists, blue energy shooting out from them. Rylan stuck his hand in his pocket and grabbed a piece of dark maple, shoving the guards' guns down to the floor with his mind, hard.

The guard on the left went down, shot through the head, blood flying everywhere. The guard in the middle fell to the floor, twitching as blue lightning played over his body. And the guard on the right, having suddenly lost his gun, looked confused. Until Small kicked him in the balls, then in the face.

It was over in a moment.

"Nice job," Dill said, bending over and retrieving the guns. "More guns for us. Although I fear we made far too much noise. Everyone in the vicinity will be looking for us now."

"Where *are* we, anyway?" Shot asked.

Everyone looked at Rylan.

Then the sound of a girl's scream echoed from further down the tunnel.

TREY HAD NEVER SEEN a bear in the flesh before. It was *far* bigger than he had expected. Bigger and scarier.

And coming toward him.

His mind didn't have time to figure out how the bear had arrived, or why it was chasing him. Primal reflexes took over, and he ran.

A flying car buzzed overhead as he sprinted down the street, the bear running after him. It didn't seem very fast, luckily—it was only able to keep pace with Trey. Suddenly an arrow shot through the air next to him on the right, missing him by inches. He hadn't felt the wind of it as it passed, oddly. He glanced behind him in time to see a pair of mean-looking birds flying at his face. He ducked frantically, turning and running faster.

What the hell was going on?

More arrows flew by him as he ran, his breath coming hard as he sped through the village. Buildings erupted in flame as he passed, and he could hear elves screaming and crying a few streets away. The street he was on was eerily silent, apart from the bear.

He heard it roar again, could feel it thumping on the ground as it moved. He didn't dare look behind him.

He took a side street, ducking to the left, hoping to lose the bear somehow. But Sylrantheas wasn't the kind of city he was used to—it didn't have alleyways or fire escapes. Or underground tunnels. Everything curved, wending its way through the redwood trees. He wasn't sure where he was going.

The bear was still following him. He saw it from the corner of his eye, slipping on the dirt ground, struggling to change its momentum.

As he watched, the bear suddenly disappeared, turning to dust that blew away in the breeze. In the bear's place, a pack of snakes slithered, moving impossibly fast. Trey turned and ran away from the snakes, moving slower this time.

He finally knew what was happening.

ARRA'S BOW was in ruins. She had owned that bow for twenty years, and now it had been destroyed.

Just...gone.

She sat next to it, watching it burn. There was no point trying to save it now—it was ruined. Fenian had been shot, might already be dead. Imra had nearly died. Dozens, maybe hundreds of elves had just been shot and killed. Even the gazebo had been ruined.

But somehow out of all that, the thing that hit her hardest was the loss of her bow.

She couldn't do this anymore.

She looked around the garden, stricken with grief. Everywhere she looked, elves lay on the ground—bleeding, or crying, or burning, or dead. Arra felt frozen, useless. This was all too big, too impossible to fix.

So she sat and cried, watching her bow burn.

Imra came over to sit beside her. "Arra," she said, "we have to go. They're still attacking us. I can hear them. We need to see if we can help anyone."

"We should just run," Arra whispered.

"We have to help," Imra said. "We have to try."

"I can't. It's too much. I tried to Choose, and it didn't help. Nothing worked. Nothing survived."

Imra reached out to take her hand. "I'm here," she said. "I will always be here. And you can replace that bow—you *know* you wanted to switch to a recurve anyway."

Imra was right. Arra had wanted that.

"I feel stuck," she said.

Imra watched her for a moment, fire reflecting in her bright green eyes. "We all feel stuck, sometimes," she said. "We all feel lost. But sometimes all you need is someone to show you the way. Someone strong; someone willing to break the rules. Someone who cares more about doing what's right than doing what's expected."

Arra looked at her, tears swimming in her vision.

"Someone like you," Imra said. "Now *get up*. Do what you came here to do. You Chose *everything*, Arra, remember? Now your job is us. Your job is me. Your job is this entire village, and if you sit here and cry about your bow, nothing good will ever happen."

Arra saw her friend in a new light, then. Imra had never spoken to her like this before. When had she become so strong? She saw something in those big green eyes—loyalty, perhaps. Respect.

Love.

And so Arra stood, pulling Imra up with her, clasping her friend tightly around the waist and kissing her hair. "Thank you," she said, fire and smoke whirling all around her. "You sure know how to make a girl feel good."

Imra laughed, pulling her away from the gazebo. "Come on. Let's go get you a new bow."

Arra took one last look at the burning garden before she left. Her Choosing, her adulthood, her life was all in flames. But she would do what she had to do—not to save her pride, but to save her people. She would continue on, fulfilling the destiny that she herself had decided on.

She ran away with Imra, focused on the future.

Her bow was a distant memory.

ELEVEN

TREY FOUND himself in front of a familiar building. On the way, he'd been pursued by snakes, bats, a tiger, and a cute little jackrabbit. It was like a zoo from ancient Earth had come to life on the streets of Sylrantheas.

Very funny, Allain.

Mistweaving wasn't one of Trey's Talents, or he'd probably have recognized it sooner. As it stood, he was impressed. He'd had no idea what to expect from mistweaving magic, but he hadn't thought such detailed illusions would be possible. Could Allain actually *kill* him with a fake sword?

He didn't particularly want to find out.

But why did he know this building? It was tall, and very square. Probably the ugliest building he'd seen in the whole village, come to think of it. And half of it appeared to have been burnt down.

Oh. This was the Primestore, where the elves kept all their primewood. Trey had put out a big fire here, back when he'd had the Book of Amplification. The rest of the building was still intact. He'd managed to save a good bit of it.

As he approached, he saw two Guardians stationed in

front of the building, near a small door. Like all Guardians, they were armed with bows and swords. And like all Guardians, they looked ready to kill on a moment's notice.

An explosion rocked the village nearby. Trey could hear bullets firing, the whirring of an engine. The whole day had gone to shit really quickly. Was Allain right? Was it really Trey's fault? How could that be? He had no idea who was attacking them or why.

The guards brandished their bows as they saw Trey approach. He swallowed, suddenly nervous. He wasn't going to hurt anything—why were they acting like that?

He turned and saw Allain nearing, holding what was left of his little stag. The boy had turned back into his usual self, an illusion no longer. He must have grown tired of the menagerie.

"Hey," Trey said, trying a different tactic. "That was some pretty cool magic."

Allain smirked at him. "Jealous?"

Trey could see that the block of wood in Allain's hand had dwindled considerably: only the torso of the stag remained. Allain had his carving knife out, flicking bits of wood off the block. This was one of the Ways, Trey realized, one of the skilled Investments that powered the magic. This was Sculpture. And Allain was *very* good at it.

"I *am* jealous," Trey admitted. Frankly, this mistweaving stuff seemed pretty useful, *and* flashy as hell. "But seriously," he continued, "this isn't my fault." He gestured around him, to the village. Pillars of smoke were rising everywhere, darkening the sky. Screams still echoed around the city, although the street they were on was strangely empty.

"I know you didn't do it on purpose," Allain said, "but that doesn't change the fact that it's your fault."

Trey wasn't sure how to respond to that.

"I'm going to kill you," Allain said. He was getting closer. Were the Guardians just going to stand there and let this happen?

Fighting suddenly erupted on the street they were on, startling Trey. A group of Cothellon soldiers backed in from somewhere else, fighting hand-to-hand with a group of elves. Trey saw Kharis in the group, fighting with a pair of knives. His opponent had a sword and some kind of fist weapon. Not all of them carried guns, apparently. Everyone seemed evenly matched, all skilled fighters.

Orist appeared, wading into the fight wielding a big black-smith hammer as a weapon. He swung it heavily, trying to smash it into the Cothellon troops, but the elves were too agile. They avoided his swings easily.

Orist was the blacksmith, the one who'd been teaching Callan. Wasn't he Allain's father? Perhaps Allain would think better of his plan now that Orist was here. But no, it didn't appear to have any effect on the boy. He just kept carving, smirking at Trey.

Trey looked at the Guardians. "Guys?" he asked. "Aren't you going to help?"

The men just looked at him as if he were the devil. Then one of them turned to the other. "We *should* help," he said.

"We were ordered to remain here," the other one said.

The fight continued, the sounds of elves grunting and weapons clashing clearly audible as they neared the building. Trey wondered what he should do. He had no weapon, and he still had Allain to deal with.

Kharis cried out suddenly, and Trey saw a nasty gash appear on his arm. Blood began streaming out immediately and Kharis retreated, holding his arm. The Cothellon fighting him pressed in, hoping for the kill.

"Dammit," the second Guardian said, "come on." They drew their swords and ran into the fray.

This left Trey and Allain alone in front of the building.

"Ready to die?" Allain asked, stepping forward.

"Is this really the right time?" Trey asked, shifting sideways toward the nearby door. "I mean, your friends are over there getting hurt. Your *father's* over there."

"They can take care of themselves," Allain said. "They don't need me. They never have."

What kind of a life had Allain led that made him this bitter, this unstable? Trey stepped closer to the door.

"What the hell is *that*?" he asked, pointing at nothing. Allain took the bait, looking behind him to see what Trey had been pointing at. Trey took advantage of the distraction to pull open the door and duck into the Primestore building.

This side of the building was dark, the only light coming from the door he had just come through. Trey didn't bother closing the door—Allain knew where he'd gone. Instead, he darted further into the building, hoping to hide somewhere. Further in, the roof was missing—it had collapsed during the fire. Trey avoided that part of the building, preferring to stay in the dark.

Everywhere he looked, shelves of neatly-stacked wood reached to the ceiling several stories above. There was more wood in here than he'd expected. How much magic did these elves need to do, anyway?

He ran down one aisle, barely able to see where he was going. Another aisle appeared to his left, running perpendicular to him, and he turned into it. Behind him, he could hear Allain entering the building.

"I know you're in here," Allain said. The sounds of fighting outside were quieter now.

Trey ran down the aisles, turning randomly, trying to stay

as quiet as possible as he made his way to what he hoped was the back wall of the building. Maybe if he could elude Allain for long enough, something would distract him.

The sound of clashing metal drew his attention. The fighting had moved into the Primestore building itself. Good —that was the distraction Trey needed. He heard men cursing as they tried to gain the upper hand. He couldn't see them, but it sounded like they were still near the entrance. Where was Allain? It was too dark to see anything.

Suddenly he felt a prick on the back of his neck.

"Gotcha," Allain said from behind him.

Trey didn't have time to react before a whirring sound grew in his ears. Was that—

The wall to his left exploded, hurtling fragments of wood at him. Trey ducked to the side, trying to shelter his face from the blast. He felt a wave of searing heat roll over him, and his back was pummeled by wood, shredding the clothing he was wearing. He felt it tearing into him, slicing the skin.

The heat continued, and Trey looked behind him to see the building on fire, a great hole torn in the back wall. A flying car was still there, silver guns trained directly on him.

"Move!" Trey shouted, pushing Allain bodily back, away from the hole in the wall. They fell together, hitting the ground with a grunt.

The car started shooting.

The sound was deafening. Bullets hit the stacks of prime-wood rapidly, tearing into them with insane force. Every-where the bullets hit, shards of wood exploded into the air. One shelf started tipping, angling sideways as bullets pounded into it. As Trey watched, the whole shelf fell back, toppling over to hit the shelf behind it. This started the next shelf tipping, and the next, like a line of massive wooden dominoes.

Trey held his hands over his head as the shelves fell, the sound incredibly loud in the enclosed space. The air filled with dust and smoke, and fire whipped into the room from somewhere, crackling and popping as it burned. The wood finished falling, pieces of it still clattering here and there as it settled to the floor. The flying car flew away, apparently satisfied with its job.

Trey was already having trouble breathing. The fire had started close to him, and it was spreading rapidly throughout the building. The dry primewood caught it up instantly, flaring to life as the flicker of flames grew and grew. Smoke poured everywhere. Trey found himself coughing.

"Fire!" Trey heard from outside. It sounded like Silanar. He hoped they could put the fire out before too much damage was done. They didn't have a Prime Mage this time. Trey didn't have the Book.

He coughed again and rolled over.

Allain was hovering over him, holding the knife to his throat.

"Goddammit!" Trey said. "When will you give this up?"

"Never," Allain said. Something in the boy's eyes flinched, though. Allain didn't seem like a killer. Maybe he wouldn't go through with it.

Trey could hear cries all around him, the clash of steel. What the hell was going on? Allain lifted the knife from him, distracted by something, his eyes suddenly wide. Trey turned.

Just in time to witness another big section of roof cave in, collapsing downward in a shower of wood and sparks. The roof landed at an angle, one side of it leaning on one of the remaining upright shelves. The wood, Trey could see, was burning.

And there was someone trapped beneath it.

RYLAN HEARD the girl screaming again. He followed the rest of the crew as they bounded down the tunnel. What was going on up ahead? The scream had sounded familiar, somehow. He glanced at Elanil. She was running along with them, keeping pace, her expression intense. Then they reached the end of the tunnel, and Rylan and Elanil both gasped in unison.

There was a forest down below them.

The mouth of their tunnel emerged about three stories up, overlooking a massive room. The room was lined with trees as far as he could see. It was a forest of trees, many of them gleaming in that sinister manner he'd seen before. Their wood was dark, and the leaves were also dark, sort of a greenish-gray.

He still didn't know what forests like this were *for*.

"Darkprime Trees," Dill whispered, as if anticipating the question. "This is where we get the darkprime wood we use for our magic."

Okay. But where had the scream come from? Rylan scanned the chamber, hoping to locate the source of the sound. Perhaps they could save the girl doing the screaming. Something about her still sounded familiar.

Movement caught his attention, far below on the floor, almost directly underneath them. Two men in purple uniforms were walking briskly across the chamber, carrying something—someone—between them. It was a girl, Rylan saw. A little girl.

The men arrived at their destination a moment later, depositing the girl next to one of the trees. This tree looked normal, though—the wood wasn't dark, just a normal brown color, and the leaves looked normal. The tree was smaller than the others in the room, and it didn't have that strange shine to it.

The girl slumped to the ground where they had dropped her, motionless. It looked like she was in bad shape; her hair was unkempt, her clothing torn and dirty. And she was skinny to the point of malnutrition.

The guards grabbed her roughly, sitting her down with her back against the small tree's trunk. Rylan squinted, trying to get a look at her face. He felt like he should know her, somehow.

Then he figured it out.

He gave a great cry, unable to control himself. The shout echoed loudly in the chamber, and the two men below looked up at them. Dill clapped his hand over Rylan's mouth, pulling him back from the edge. Everyone else retreated, too. The men below didn't make any sound, didn't give any evidence that they'd seen the group in the tunnel. Rylan didn't care. He had to get down there. He'd seen who it was sitting against the tree, looking almost dead.

It was Con.

TWELVE

"HELP!" someone cried from underneath the fiery roof planks.

It was Kharis.

He sounded pained. Trey could hear him grunting, trying to free himself, but the wood didn't move.

Then Orist was there, setting his hammer down and trying to lift the wood. He coughed from the smoke, his muscles bulging with effort.

But it wasn't enough—the wood didn't budge.

Trey looked back to Allain. The boy still had his knife out, still pointed at Trey.

"We need to help them," Trey said. "You need to stop this."

Allain looked at him, indecision in his eyes. He clearly wanted to help his father, but something was holding him back. He looked again at Orist, still struggling to lift the burning wood. Then he looked at Trey, moving the knife even closer.

"No," he said, his words barely audible over the fire.

Trey shifted awkwardly under the carving knife, trying to

get another look at Orist. The man had planted his feet, trying to get a better grip on the wood. A burning ember jumped from the wood to Orist's leg, setting it ablaze, but Orist ignored it.

Then another motion caught Trey's eye. Behind Orist, another shelf of wood was looming, unstable. As he watched, it began tipping.

It was about to fall on Orist.

Allain didn't see it. He was looking only at Trey. "Allain —" Trey started, but it was too late.

Orist yelled out loudly as he lifted the huge piece of roof. Trey saw veins in his neck and arms popping out as he managed it. Kharis scrambled out, scuttling away.

But the shelf behind Orist was still falling.

It picked up speed, hurtling to the ground faster than Trey would have thought possible. He watched, frozen, as it slammed into Orist, driving him to the ground with a sickening crunch.

Orist was gone.

"No!" Allain screamed, finally leaving Trey. He scrambled over to where his father had been, but there was nothing to see. It was all a jumble of wood and fire and smoke.

Kharis had survived. Trey saw him limping away, still holding his wounded arm. Orist had saved him. But Orist had paid the ultimate price.

So much death. So much disaster.

Trey coughed again uncontrollably. He had to escape. He had to get out. He had to move.

He had to put out this damn fire.

"Allain!" he shouted, coughing and almost retching from the smoke. Allain was crying, unable to even get close to where his father had been buried. The fire was just too strong.

Trey scrambled to his feet, trying not to breathe. He ran

over to Allain, pulling the boy roughly away. Allain had tears streaking down his face, and his muscles were limp. He allowed Trey to pull him out of the building. He had put the knife away.

"I should have helped," Allain said, but the words were too much for him. He fell to the ground on hands and knees, vomiting over and over again.

Trey assessed the situation. Smoke was pouring from the building, but the fire hadn't taken the entire thing yet. There was still a chance to save some of the primewood, if they could put the fire out quickly. Without the Book, without a Prime Mage, how would they do it?

Hadn't he heard Silanar's voice a minute ago?

He left Allain where he was. The boy probably *really* wanted to kill him now, blaming his father's death on Trey. But for now, Allain was useless, out of it. He would be no danger now.

Trey rounded the building, drawing deep breaths of fresh air, feeling it cool his lungs. He found a group of elves standing at the front of the building. Silanar was there, and Kythaela—the elf who had pronounced his magical abilities earlier. Other elves he recognized, but couldn't name. They were doing something, all holding hands in a circle.

Trey ran up to them. "Can I help?"

"Not now," Silanar snapped.

Frustrated, Trey turned to look at the building. Fire was blazing from it, smoke streaming to the sky. He could smell the scent of wood burning, and it made him sick to his stomach. Something about the fire reminded him of his father, of Simon. It reminded him of the torture the man had put him through. Of the animals he had killed. Of the way he'd treated his mother.

Fire, like his father, was evil.

But fire, like his father, could be *killed*.

The primewood pouch was still around his waist. Trey felt an icy calm wash over him as he opened it, pulling out two pieces of prime ash. He didn't have to search for it—he knew exactly which pieces were which. It was an instinct. Part of him.

He grasped the ash in his hand and Willed a storm to appear.

Nothing happened, of course. Trey needed that damn Book of Amplification. He blew out a breath, disgusted with himself. Why even try? It was useless. *He* was useless. He turned back to the group of elves. They had their eyes closed and were chanting something, hand in hand.

Trey suddenly realized what they were doing. He stepped up to them, breaking in, pushing between two of the elves. They looked at him, anger flashing in their eyes, but Trey just grabbed their hands, wordlessly reforming the circle with him in it. The prime ash was still in his left hand, and the elf to his right had wood in his hand, too. The elves looked at each other for a moment, communicating wordlessly. Then, as a group, they bowed their heads.

Trey Willed a storm to appear. All around him, he could feel the elves doing the same thing. They wanted the storm. They wished for it, calling it, pulling it out of the sky.

And the storm obeyed.

The sky darkened, clouds appearing out of thin air. The wind picked up, swirling over and around the circle of mages. The wind fed the fire, and it picked up too, roaring even louder.

Then the rain came, pelting down on them as if the heavens themselves had opened. Thick drops of icy water fell from the sky, instantly soaking everyone in the circle. Trey cracked his eyes, looking at the Primestore building. The rain was falling there, too. Everywhere it hit, it drove the fire back. The sound of sizzling water mixed with the sound of the fire, and a new smell permeated the air as everything became quickly saturated with water.

There was no lightning in this storm. No lightning, no thunder. Just rain—lots and lots of rain. A perfect firefighting storm.

Trey clenched the hands of the mages next to him. He knew he wasn't contributing much—his power was far too weak without the Book. But it felt good to be able to help, even a little. He realized then that there was something else there, something else floating around his mind. It wasn't just the magic, and it wasn't just the storm. Trey felt other minds, other beings, near him, touching him. Other souls. He realized with a start that he was feeling the mental touch of the mages to his left and right. The magic was merging them together, making Trey part of the group in a way he had never imagined.

Part of him wanted to recoil from this new sensation. But another part of him reveled in it, never wanted it to stop. There was a kind of joy in the merging of souls, a joy he had never experienced before. It was intimate, passionate. Euphoric.

It was a circle, he instinctively knew. A circle of souls. It was power merged, magic combined. This was *strong*. This was communing with the gods. The storm bent and blustered to his Will—to the *group's* Will—and Trey knew that the elves didn't actually *need* Prime Mages.

They had each other.

He felt strength flowing in from Silanar and the other strengthshapers in the group. He felt the call of nature from the stormwardens. And above all that, above the swirling miasma of magic, he felt peace. Stillness.

Harmony.

The moment lasted for a long time, until Trey felt the wood finally give out. The magic, as beautiful as it had been, was gone. The merging of minds ended, and with it the storm.

Trey opened his eyes fully. Everything was soaked. His clothes, his hair, his shoes. The ground had turned to mud. Everywhere rain dripped, the sound a strange comfort after the hell he'd just been through. But it had worked. They had done it.

The fire was gone.

The Primestore building was a smoking ruin, but it was only partly ruined. A large portion of the roof had fallen in, and more than half the building was clearly destroyed. But it wasn't a total loss. Some of it had survived.

"Father!" Allain cried from behind the building. Silanar gave Trey a questioning look.

"It's Orist," Trey said. "He's dead."

The group around him gasped, their expressions shocked. But before anyone could respond, two more flying cars appeared, zooming toward them in the air. Their guns were pointed at the group.

"Run!" Silanar shouted.

They ran.

THIRTEEN

"CONTROL YOURSELF," Dill whispered harshly in Rylan's ear. Rylan nodded against the hand that was still holding his mouth tightly shut. Dill released him, glaring at him for a moment. Then he turned and made his way back to the edge of the tunnel.

Rylan followed, looking below. The men were going about their business. Perhaps they hadn't seen anything. It was dark in the tunnel, after all. Maybe they'd just go back to whatever it was they were doing. Or maybe they'd summoned guards, and it was just a matter of time before they were caught.

What were they doing down there? Con almost looked like she was sleeping, slumped over against the tree, breathing shallowly. Rylan ached to go down there, to rescue her from these evil men. He thought back to his first experience in a forest such as this. He remembered what the men had done to the woman there.

They had cut her throat.

Rylan looked at Dill, questions in his eyes. Dill caught his look and shook his head firmly. "Wait," he mouthed. Rylan sighed inwardly. Dill was right—there would be more guards down there, somewhere. He looked up at the ceiling, where the familiar catwalk system was. He didn't see any guards, but that didn't mean they weren't there. It was hard to see very far in the dim light.

He now recognized the catwalk system for what it was. It was a sprinkler system, for watering the trees. The catwalks gave access to the sprinkler heads and piping, for maintenance purposes. They also worked well for observing things from above.

There was a loud sound, and a pair of large double doors opened in one wall. As Rylan watched, a procession of people came through the doors. One at a time, people were being led into the room. They were all handcuffed, their expressions scared. It was a huge variety of people, men and women of all ages. Some were children and teenagers. The younger ones looked like underkids, probably captured on the streets or taken directly from their Crew. Rylan shuddered to think of it.

The parade of people kept filing in. Each manacled person was placed in front of a tree. The trees looked like saplings, mostly, barely large enough to even be called a tree. Each of them were normal looking, not shining like the others, positioned randomly throughout the room. The people were making enough noise down there that Rylan felt like he could talk.

"What is this?" Rylan asked. "What are they doing?"

"Darkprime Ceremony," Dill said, his expression twisting into a grimace. "We shouldn't be here."

"We're here for Con," Rylan said. "We have to get her out!"

"Do you see all the people down there?" Dill gestured to the forest. It was filling up rapidly. Each purple-uniformed man was paired with one handcuffed person, each pair standing underneath a tree. Rylan could see guns and swords and knives glittering on most of the uniformed men.

Rylan didn't know what to do. Dill was right—they couldn't just go down there and face all those men. As if to emphasize his point, more armed guards appeared in the catwalk system in front of them, filing out as if preparing for the ceremony. Rylan and the others shrank back further, trying to keep to the shadows.

Rylan made a fist. This couldn't be it! He couldn't just stand here helplessly and watch whatever was going to happen.

What *was* going to happen, anyway? They weren't going to kill all these people at once, were they? He opened his mouth to ask the question, but Small sidled over to him.

"There's another name for this ceremony, you know," he whispered.

"What?" Rylan asked.

"Civil Service."

Oh.

So *this* was Civil Service. Death by blade, in front of a tree. It made no sense, but now was not the time to puzzle it out.

He needed to save Con.

But they were too late—the window of opportunity had passed. As he looked down at the forest filled with people, he couldn't see any way for them to free her now. They would need an army to get her out.

Rylan wondered if Trey and Callan knew what Civil Service really was. He wondered if anyone knew. He'd heard them talking about the ones they'd lost—Trey's wife, Callan's sister. Were they dead now too, or rotting in a cell? It was probably too late for them as well.

Civil Service wasn't just a lie.

It was a horror.

"What are they doing with all of those people?" Elanil asked softly.

"I think," Rylan said, barely able to see her in the darkness, "that they're going to kill them all."

The room below suddenly fell silent. Rylan crept forward to watch what was happening, his fingers clutching the darkprime wood in his pocket. Could he stop this with magic, somehow? Maybe lift Con up to the catwalks and grab her?

"Don't," Dill said, looking at him. "They're all armed. They'd have us in a second." Rylan shrank back from Dill's stare. The guy was getting awfully good at anticipating what Rylan was thinking. He grimaced, looking back at the forest. Was there really nothing they could do?

The room was still silent. Rylan tried to count how many prisoners were there. Probably at least forty, maybe more.

"Are there normally this many people?" Rylan asked.

Dill shook his head. "Usually no more than a few at a time. They only need it when they lose a Tree. Darkprime Trees don't regenerate when you cut them, you see. Not like real Prime Trees."

It was starting to make a strange kind of sense to Rylan. "The city," he said. "This is how it floats, from magic in the wood. It's how the Shield works, how we get our food."

"Yup," Dill said. "I told you that before."

"And if Darkprime Trees don't regenerate, they have to keep making new ones."

Dill nodded soberly. "You got it. And this is how they do it —through the murder of human beings. This is the dirty secret behind the entire Cothellon Uprising." His voice got even quieter. "This is what my father created."

"Attention!" somebody shouted from down below. The uniformed men snapped to attention, standing straight in front of their victims, legs together.

"You might not want to watch this," Dill said.

Rylan gritted his teeth. If he couldn't help Con, he would at least watch her die. He would remember her.

He would avenge her.

"Draw!" the voice shouted.

Everyone drew a knife. They glittered in the chamber's light, standing out in sharp contrast to the wood and leaves. They held their knives in front of them, blade facing up.

"Position!" the shout continued.

The uniformed men turned the knife sideways, so the blade was facing to their left. The manacled humans looked very afraid.

They finally understood what was about to happen.

Elanil reached out to take his hand, and he could see tears forming in her eyes. But Rylan steeled himself, looking back at Con. She looked so sad, so pathetic, sitting there underneath her tree. Rylan couldn't bear to see her like this. She'd been so happy, so brave. Such a force of life down here in the ugly Under.

She'd been his only true friend.

"Strike!" came the shout.

As one, knives flashed, slicing cleanly from left to right. As one, the blades were sheathed, the men continuing to stand at attention. As one, a line of red appeared on every human's neck.

Nobody moved. Nobody cried out.

The chamber was completely silent.

Rylan felt tears come to his eyes as he watched Con die, slumping to the ground as blood flowed from her neck. Elanil squeezed his hand tightly as he saw her blood, her life force, stream from her body and pool at the roots of the tree. His vision swam with tears as he watched her skin grow white, her hair mingling with the blood and dirt and leaves.

She was dead.

He drew in a ragged breath.

Then the trees *changed*.

They grew larger, fading in and out as if lit from within. The wood grew darker, almost black, acquiring a strange shine that seemed to wiggle away from view. The branches of the trees twisted and changed, bending into grotesque shapes, becoming ugly versions of their former selves.

All the uniformed men bent down together in front of their trees, then, as if bowing to a god. Some of them lay prostrate on the ground, hands clasped together. Was this some kind of religion for them? Rylan thought back to his first experience with the ceremony. It had been the same, the killers worshipping at the feet of the tree.

It disgusted him.

"Guys," Dill said softly, "we should go before someone finds us."

But Rylan couldn't go.

He couldn't leave. He could only stare at the poor, lifeless body down below, at the girl who was his friend. He had failed her. She had helped him, sheltered him when he needed it, fed him when she could. She had worked with him, played with him, made life bearable in the dark and dirty Under hell.

She had been his only friend.

And he had failed her.

What was his life worth now? What were *any* of their lives worth? How could these *people*, these *elves*, these terrible murderers of children—how could they exist? How could any of this happen?

It was Orym. It was the Cothellon. They had made this happen, them and their terrible mission. They'd enslaved humans, *killed* humans, and for what? To warp the planet somewhere else? It was stupid. It was horrible. It was wrong.

And Rylan had done nothing to stop them.

But that would change. Starting now.

Dill was looking at him, concern written on his face. "You okay?"

Rylan took a deep, shuddering breath. "No," he said, his voice quiet in the dark. "I am not okay."

"I'm sorry," Small said.

"We should have gone after her sooner," Shot said.

And Elanil looked at him, *really* looked at him, and he read empathy in her eyes. "She was beautiful," she whispered. A tear tracked down her cheek.

He'd lost her. He'd lost his friend. He'd lost Con.

But he'd gained these others, this fierce Crew, this strong elven girl. They were with him. They could help.

"This," Rylan said, gesturing to the terrible forest down below. "This will stop. It *must* stop."

"Yes," Dill said. "That's the plan."

FOURTEEN

EVERYONE SPLIT IN DIFFERENT DIRECTIONS, bullets blazing from the two flying cars. Trey didn't look to see if anyone had been hit. He ran toward Arra's house, intent on getting the bag he'd packed, the sounds of shots and screams diminishing as he ran. Here and there buildings were on fire, burning unattended. He passed bodies, elves dead on the ground from bullet wounds or explosions, blood and mangled limbs everywhere. He thought he was going to be sick.

He kept running.

He made it to the house without encountering any resistance. He grabbed the bag and looked for the Book one last time. It wasn't there.

So he left.

Perhaps he should have left before the Waychoice, when he had intended. Perhaps Allain had been right. Maybe none of this would have happened if he hadn't stayed. His mind reeled, unable to come to terms with the things he had witnessed. Flying cars. Soldiers. Guns.

And more fire than he had ever cared to see.

More than anything, he hoped that Arra had made it out

alive. He hoped that she was safe somehow, free to shoot her bow and live her life. He didn't want to imagine her dead, her body pierced by bullets or worse. He didn't want to think of her beautiful hair and fierce eyes staring sightless, looking up at him from a chasm of death.

But now that he'd thought of it, the visions were there, seared into the retina of his mind. He felt them there, jumbling into memories, fleeing from the sound of his soul.

It was time for him to go. Time to get the hell out of this devastated city, to seek a new life on his own. He would try to leave this place behind, along with the memories it held. Maybe he would find another settlement, some human survivors.

Maybe he'd be able to forget any of this had ever happened.

He pictured his wife, cooking dinner in the kitchen, wearing that red shirt she loved so much. He remembered their last night together, how it had felt to lay with her and watch the moon. He remembered the city, the streets, the tunnels, the books.

He remembered the look on Lora's face when she'd been taken for Civil Service. He remembered the agony, his aching desire to help her, to free her from the clutches of the Department. He remembered Rylan, the little boy who'd helped him escape his cell. He remembered his first taste of magic— healing Callan, that memory bittersweet.

He remembered Arra. How she had given him an apricot on that first morning. How they had both grabbed the Tree of Alignment at the same time. He remembered her holding him after he'd heard Silanar's terrible tale. He remembered how she had looked on stage at the Waychoice, how she had defied her people and Chosen all the Ways.

But most of all, he remembered the sounds of dead and dying. The scent of smoke, the feel of fire.

He remembered pain.

And he put it all behind him.

ARRA AND IMRA limped into the forest, hand in hand. Arra didn't want to let go of her friend, not so soon after almost losing her. They joined the trail of refugees leaving the village. The attack was still ongoing, still unexplained. Many elves had died, and many more buildings had been destroyed. Arra had seen a fire at the Primestore building, but she hadn't been able to help.

She and Imra had done what they could, helping with the wounded, assisting others in their escape. Then they had snuck over to the archery compound to pick up a new bow for Arra, some arrows, and more primewood. She was now holding a shorter recurve bow, more conducive to shooting from constrained positions. She already missed her longbow, but it was time to leave it in the past.

She winced as she walked, cuts and burns hurting with every step. Healing magic needed to be saved for the truly injured—her injuries could be seen to later. Imra seemed to be fine, having recovered remarkably quickly from her near-death experience.

Ahead of her, Fenian was being carried in a stretcher. He'd been shot twice, but he was still alive, if barely. He'd lost a lot of blood. Soulsoother mages had been able to stabilize him, but he was still in critical condition. She wanted to be up there with him, helping to carry his stretcher, ensuring he survived the trip. But her place was with the Hunters.

No, that wasn't right. She had Chosen *every* Way—she

could be with whomever she wanted. But the Hunters still felt right. Maybe it had been the loss of her bow that had cemented that decision. She could be everything, but she would be a Hunter first. So she stayed at the rear with Imra, guarding the elves as they left the village. Kharis and Lhoris were running point at the front.

Maybe she just didn't want to see Fenian the way he was.

Arra looked back as she entered the forest, leaving the village behind. Sylrantheas burned, smoke trails leaving furrows in the sky. All around her, elves cried or moaned in pain, limping along, doing anything they could to get away. Many were being carried in stretchers like Fenian.

For a wonder, no Cothellon appeared to be following them. The soldiers had seemed intent on destroying the city itself, not chasing its inhabitants down. To what end, nobody knew. It was senseless destruction on a scale she'd never thought to see. She wished there was some explanation, some reason for it all. She felt bitterness return to her soul as she mourned her city. The Eldrim would return, she hoped. Return and rebuild. But for now, the important thing was survival.

She squeezed Imra's hand as they made their way deeper into the forest. She had no idea where they were heading. There was nowhere left to go.

Sylrantheas had been destroyed.

Suddenly the line stopped. Something was happening up ahead, at the front. There was an altercation of some kind. Arra made her way to the front of the line, pulling Imra along with her. She wanted to see what was going on.

Silanar was confronting two humans—the ones Elanil had let into the village, Jalnab and Martan. The Remnant boy she had a crush on. Arra felt her mouth twist as she saw them. Had *they* been responsible for the attack?

"We left before...cars...came," Jalnab was saying. His English was getting better.

"You knew they were coming?" Silanar asked. "Did you cause this?"

Jalnab shook his head violently. "No," he said. "Did not know."

"Then how did you know to leave?"

Jalnab tapped his ear. "Hear."

"You heard them?"

He nodded. "You...busy."

The Waychoice. The elves had been distracted by the cere-mony. They'd thought themselves safe, that the Remnant had been destroyed. They'd made themselves sitting ducks. Arra had pranced about on stage, in her tight leather outfit, while her people were about to be slaughtered.

She almost threw up right then. But she held it in, trying to remain calm, proud. Trying to keep her face straight. But inside, she was seething.

"Where do you...go?" Jalnab asked.

"Away," Silanar said. "We have nowhere to go. We'll find a Hunter cache and do what we can out in the forest. We're elves. We can manage."

"Listen," Jalnab said, leaning closer. "Remnant have...place."

"You have a place? What kind of place?"

"Remnant have...Splinter."

Silanar seemed flustered. "I don't know what you mean."

"We not first to...banish. To be banished. We...*were* not *the* first." He was getting better at adding all the extra words the language needed. Low Remnant didn't have any of those words, Arra knew. It was an economical language, an ugly one. But Jalnab really seemed to want to speak like the elves.

"Wait," Silanar said. "You're telling me there are others

like you? Other Remnant who don't live in Gulthurub? What did you call it—a Splinter?"

"Yes, yes," Jalnab said. "Splinter. We have place. Not...city. Small. But...rooms. Sleep. Food. We will...you come. You... *can* come to Splinter. You...save us. You...nice to us."

"Love," Martan suddenly said. Then he looked down, obviously embarrassed.

"Love," Jalnab said.

"Thank you," Silanar said. "We accept."

Jalnab nodded, and smiled, and turned in a different direction, striking out into the forest. Silanar followed, and the elves followed him.

They had a place to go now. These two Remnant, for whatever reason, had decided to shelter them.

She wondered what this Splinter would be like.

A DARK MAN stepped out from behind a tree, and Trey jumped. He'd been walking through the forest for ages, it seemed, alone with his thoughts. Where had this guy come from?

He recognized the man. It was the same elf he'd seen across the street, when he'd first gone back to Arra's place to look for the Book. Trey stood his ground, waiting to see what the stranger wanted.

"That storm," the man said, "that was you?" The man's voice sounded familiar. A dark memory stirred within Trey, indistinct.

He shook his head. "Mostly the others," he said. "My magic is weak. Who are you?"

The figure took a step forward. His features were typically elven—handsome and chiseled, vaguely feminine. His hair was dark, the same color as Trey's, and long. His eyes were blue.

"Did your friends survive?" the man asked, ignoring Trey's question.

"I don't know," Trey said. "Are you part of this attack?" Trey was unarmed, but he started thinking of ways he could escape. He realized how woefully unprepared he was for life on his own. He'd be totally unable to defend himself against this elf, whoever he was.

"I came to find you," the man said.

"But who *are* you?" Trey asked again.

"Let me ask you this," the man said, taking another step forward. He was only a few feet from Trey, but his hands were empty. Trey didn't see any obvious weapons on him. "Do you want to learn how to improve your magic? Maybe pick up a few new Talents?"

That wasn't the question Trey had expected. "I don't understand," he said. "They told me my Will was weak, and I'm missing half my powers."

"That *is* strange," the man said. "You can only access three of the Ways?"

Trey nodded.

"Very interesting," the man mused. "Still, my offer stands. I can train you, make you better. Teach you darkprime magic, if your Alignment holds."

"Thank you for the offer," Trey said, "but I still don't know who you are. If you'll excuse me, I'll be heading on my way now."

"I'd very much prefer it if you came with me," the man said, his voice getting colder.

"Mother taught me not to talk to strangers," Trey replied. It was a juvenile thing to say, but it was the first response he had thought of.

The man suddenly burst out laughing. The sound chilled Trey—it was too evil, too...wrong. "Trey," the man said, still laughing, "I'm not a stranger."

He pulled something from his pocket, then fiddled with his ear. When he took his hand away, Trey saw that the man had put on an earring of some kind. It was made of wood, shaped like a claw, with a crystalline blue jewel placed in the center.

Trey wasn't sure what was happening. Then the man's face started changing, subtly morphing into a different shape. The points of his ears shrank and rounded out, and his face filled in, growing rounder. His hair grew shorter and his lips grew slightly thicker. It only took moments, but soon Trey found himself looking at an entirely different man. A human.

It was his father.

"You knew me as Simon," his father said. "But you can call me Quynn."

PART
TWO

PART
TWO

FIFTEEN

JALNAB AND MARTAN led the elves through the forest. The procession wound around huge redwoods, across streams, up hills. This was a part of the vast forest that Arra had never been to, at least not recently. But Muir Woods was big—especially now that it had had time to regrow. Three hundred years was enough time for even saplings to grow large. And with no humans around to interfere—no humans except the Remnant, of course—nature had regained a foothold.

Arra and Imra were at the rear of the procession, so they couldn't see what transpired at the front of the line. Silanar and Jalnab had spoken with some other Remnant—still recognizable, even here, by their dirty, stringy hair and unkempt clothing. Then word passed down the line that they were being allowed in.

This was the Splinter, Arra had learned. Martan had walked with them, speaking haltingly in English she could barely understand. The Splinter, he had said, was the name of both the people and the place. They were a remnant of the Remnant, a fraction of humanity that *didn't* want to kill elves. People who actually wanted peace.

Arra wasn't sure the elves were entitled to it.

But right now they *needed* peace, more than anything. Arra sped up, overtaking Fenian on his stretcher, leaving Imra behind. He was sleeping fitfully as the stretcher bounced and moved, his skin pale and his brow drenched with sweat. She approached and laid a hand on him. His skin was cold. Arra felt her stomach tying itself in knots.

He didn't look good.

She wondered what would happen if he died. Could she go on? She blinked, willing tears away. No, she couldn't think like that. He would be fine. Elven magic would heal him. They would be together again soon, luxuriating in each other's presence, the attack on their village a distant memory.

A tear escaped, despite her best efforts, tracking a trail down her cheek. She walked along, trying not to jolt the stretcher, holding Fenian's hand. He *would* make it.

He had to.

The Splinter was a little town, if you could call it that. It looked a lot more like Sylrantheas than Gulthurub: predominantly wooden houses were scattered here and there in the grass, camouflaged in greens and browns. The whole settlement was hidden in a meadow surrounded by thick tree growth. Unless you were flying, you'd have a tough time locating the village.

That was the idea.

The Splinter was reviled by the Remnant, for obvious reasons. They had a semblance of normalcy, here: an actual system of government, a courthouse, even *doctors*. It was, Arra realized, a lot closer to the way things had been before the Sundering.

Except this village was small. Very small. Fewer than three hundred humans lived here, all banished or run away from various Remnant outposts. All were outlaws, technically. All would be killed on sight if the Remnant found them.

And now, thanks to Jalnab, they were opening their gates for the first time. They were letting elves in. Sheltering them. Feeding them.

After all the violence that had already occurred, Arra couldn't help but wonder if the Splinter were making a terrible mistake.

THEY SENT Arra to some kind of warehouse that had been converted into housing for the elves, where she and Imra dropped off the few belongings they had managed to take with them out of Sylrantheas. Rows and rows of displaced elves were there, rolling blankets out on the floors and using shirts or jackets for pillows. Arra saw tears on many faces, or burn marks, or blood. The Sylranthean elves had been reduced to a shadow of their former selves by the Cothellon.

And Arra still didn't know *why*.

She couldn't be there. She couldn't see her people like this, her friends and Mentors. She needed to get out. She needed to leave.

She needed to check on Fenian.

The little village in the middle of the meadow was neatly made, for humans. It was nothing like the Remnant she had known—humans stood in front of little wooden houses, staring at Arra and Imra as they passed. The humans of the Splinter didn't seem entirely happy to see them. Arra knew that even now, her father was meeting with Jalnab and the other leaders of the Splinter. They were concerned that whatever had prompted the Cothellon to attack Sylrantheas would also bring them here. Perhaps they had spies in the forest.

Even now, troops might be moving toward this hidden village in the woods. And the question on the Splinter's mind, Arra knew, was whether they should take up arms. Whether they should fight.

Because fighting was what the *Remnant* did. And the Splinter wanted none of it.

Arra saw uneasiness on their faces, too. Even though the Splinter wanted peace with elves, it didn't mean they *liked* elves. They were scared, and Arra couldn't blame them. The Sundering, those events three hundred years ago, had taught the survivors of humanity one thing.

Don't mess with elves.

It was perhaps not the lesson the Eldrim had intended to teach. Could they ever make it right? Could elves ever coexist with humans? Arra didn't know. But this, at least, was a step in that direction.

They had a hospital there, believe it or not. A hospital that relied on *human* medicine, not magic. And Fenian was there. He hadn't looked good. Arra didn't know whether he would live or die.

Especially if they weren't using magic.

Impulsively, she reached out for Imra's hand. "What would it have been like," she said, "if elves had made themselves known from the beginning? If instead of hiding from humans, seeking to control them, we'd just lived among them, together as friends?"

Imra looked at her, green eyes sad. "I think it would have been beautiful," she said. "Maybe things would have been different. Better."

Maybe the humans wouldn't have been so screwed up. Maybe the elves wouldn't have had to kill them.

Or maybe it would have been war from the very start.

But there was nothing she could do now. The past was the

past; it wasn't her fault. *She* hadn't made those decisions. She hadn't destroyed most of humanity and enslaved the rest. She hadn't even been born at that time. Let the sins of the fathers remain where they belonged: with her father.

At least there was a Splinter now. Perhaps eventually, some part of humanity would come to forgive them.

Or perhaps Arra was grasping at straws.

They arrived at the hospital. It was a small building, wooden like the others, with regularly spaced windows and squared-off walls. Humans built everything with right angles, unlike elves. It served the purpose, but it didn't have much visual appeal. There was even a sign outside, and Arra was startled to see it written in English. "Medicine," the sign read. Were the Splinter trying to revert to the language of their ancestors? Did communication with the elves matter that much to them? Arra found herself very impressed.

They went inside.

The woman at the front desk looked alarmed to see them. "Hello," she said, and then she started speaking quietly but furiously into a headset. What words Arra could make out sounded like English. Interesting.

"Room 107," she said, her voice clipped. "And uh...um." She didn't seem to know how to finish. "Twins...protect you?"

Arra was floored. This was a whole new level for humans to be operating on. Peaceful, English-speaking—and now they were learning the Eldrim religion? Incredible. How had Elanil not told her any of this?

Maybe she hadn't known.

Arra smiled at the woman, making the sign of the Twins: two fingers crossed together. "Thank you," she said. The receptionist smiled back, awkwardly.

They arrived at room 107 to see a flurry of activity. A doctor and two nurses were there, shouting at each other.

Their hair was cut short, unlike the other Remnant, but they had reverted to their old language in their haste. One nurse was frantically doing something with an intravenous device, while another prepared what Arra recognized as an AED. That didn't bode well. Had Fenian's heart stopped?

She stepped into the room.

"Wait outside," the doctor said in English, his tone making it clear that he would brook no argument from her. She stepped further into the room anyway, looking down at Fenian. He was lying motionless on his back, his skin completely white, his mouth slightly open. He wasn't breathing. She felt ice ripple down her spine.

No. This couldn't be happening.

"Can I help?" she asked, her voice coming out as a croak. Imra stood closer to her, her body lending support.

"*Kun!*" one of the nurses said, and the defibrillator pulsed loudly. Fenian's back arched up, his body bouncing in the bed. Nothing else happened. He still wasn't breathing. She heard a heart monitor wailing, its solid tone incessant.

"What happened?" Arra asked, trying to make sense of the situation. Where were the mages? Where was Eloen? Surely the Restoration Mentor had made it out of the city. Why was Fenian being subjected to human medicine? She looked at the doctor frantically. The human seemed to know what he was doing, but he also looked scared. He didn't want an elf to die on his watch.

"His heart...stopped," the doctor said in halting English. "Blood. Too much...loss."

This couldn't be happening.

"*Kun!*" the nurse said again, and the AED zapped Fenian. Still nothing. The doctor babbled something in Low Remnant, and the other nurse injected something else into

Fenian's IV. Arra's hearing had gone fuzzy, like she was underwater. She couldn't focus. She couldn't understand.

She could only look at Fenian, lying there on the stark white bed, lying perfectly still amidst the human chaos. Where were the elves? Where was the wood? Where was the Prime magic, the saving grace of the Twins?

She stood there, frozen. She was useless. Unable to act. Unable to help.

Her friend, her companion, her lover, was lying there on that bed.

And she could do nothing.

She was not a mage.

The room whirled around her. "Time of death," she heard the doctor say. It was as if she were standing at the end of a long tunnel, unable to hear except by echo. She found herself falling, her vision failing. She was in Imra's arms on the floor. Someone was screaming. The noise—the noise was terrible. The shriek of a woman who had just lost everything. The sound of pain. The sound of death. The sound of innocence and life forever destroyed.

After a moment, she realized the screaming was her own.

SIXTEEN

TREY'S FATHER WAS ALIVE. His father was standing in front of him. He was having trouble processing it. Where had the man been? Why had he left? *How was he an elf?*

But one question in particular interested him the most: why was the bastard here now?

"This attack," Trey said, motioning behind him to where Sylrantheas burned. "This was you?" He knew his father had been prone to violence, but he couldn't imagine he'd let it go this far.

Simon—Quynn—smirked. "It was time to bring you home."

It couldn't be. "Why didn't you just *take* me, then?" Trey asked. "Why kill all these people?"

"The Eldrim are a threat," he said. "I was ordered to lower that threat. I started with the Remnant, trying to reduce the elves' supply of primewood, but it wasn't enough. So I turned up the heat. And besides—the Eldrim have been living far too cozily for far too long. It was time for them to learn their place."

"But why did you need *me*?"

"You'll find that out soon enough."

But wait—if Quynn was an *elf*, then...

"I'm so confused," Trey said. His head was spinning.

"Of course you are," Quynn said. "You always have been, ever since I met you."

Met him? That was an odd way to put it. Didn't he mean when Trey was born?

"Was Mom an elf too?" he asked. His mother had never given him much attention, but she had been loving when she'd been around. She'd been good. Nothing like his father.

"No," Quynn said.

"So I'm half-elf?"

"No."

This was really making no sense at all.

"So what—" he started.

"You're an elf," Quynn said. "Full-blooded, near as I can tell."

"But..." he started reaching for his ears.

"We don't have time for this," Quynn interrupted. "Are you coming with me?"

"After you killed all those elves? All my *friends*? Just so you could—what—teach them their place? Fuck you." Trey turned away.

But a sound in the forest caught his attention. Footsteps. Trey stopped, turning back to Quynn. Did he have henchmen? More soldiers? Trey realized with a sinking feeling that he wasn't going to be able to simply walk away from his father.

Not without a fight.

"I can hear you, whoever you are," Quynn said, addressing the person in the forest. "Show yourself." So the unseen person *wasn't* one of Quynn's lackeys? Maybe Trey could get away after all. His muscles tensed as he prepared to bolt.

Then Callan stepped out from behind a tree.

Trey felt joy surge through him. Yes! Callan was a big man. He was good in a fight. Between the two of them, they could take Quynn on. They could—

"I brought you the Book," Callan said. He pulled the Book of Amplification out of his pack and handed it to Quynn.

Trey gaped.

Quynn took the Book, smiling that crooked smile he had. "Excellent. I really should thank you for all your help, by the way. Shooting you was an inspired idea—I should have tried it sooner."

"Wait," Trey said, "*you* shot Callan?"

Quynn eyed him. "Of course. You don't think this guy would get caught in the line of fire on his own, do you? Big strapping boy like him?" He slapped Callan's arm as if to emphasize the point. Callan towered over Quynn, but it didn't seem to matter—he looked scared.

"Callan," Trey said, "you *let* him shoot you?" None of this was making any sense. Callan was his best friend. They'd fallen from the city together. They'd both had loved ones taken from them by the Department. They'd known each other for a long time. How could Callan betray him?

Callan nodded soberly. "You got what you came for," he said, looking at Quynn. "You got Trey and the Book. Now I want to see my sister."

"You were in contact with my father?" Trey asked. The radio Orym had given him. Of course. He must have been using it to talk to Quynn. But Orym had given him that radio. Was Orym in on all this, too?

Callan ignored him. "I hate it down here," he said, still addressing Quynn. "Take me back to the city with you."

Quynn smirked at him. "Yes," he said, "all these trees do get a bit...repetitive. Do you have anything else for me?"

Callan looked confused. "I don't think so," he said. "Was I supposed to?"

"Just checking," Quynn said. "Once again, thank you for your help. With everything. But for now, I think your usefulness has ended." A knife had appeared in his hand. He stepped toward Callan, eyes narrow. Then the knife slashed upward, and Callan gasped. The gasp turned into a gurgle as a line of red appeared at his throat. Blood began pouring from the wound, and Callan tried to grasp at it.

Trey started forward, but it was already too late. Callan slumped, his mouth open, blood streaming down his chest. He fell to his knees on the hard dirt, then fell the rest of the way, landing face first on the ground. Blood formed a dark pool in the soil beneath him.

Trey lunged toward him. If he could get to his friend in time, maybe he could—

"I don't think so," Quynn said, grabbing Trey's shirt and pulling him up roughly. "You're too weak, and it's too late." He spit on Callan's corpse. "Humans disgust me."

Trey was frozen, unable to react. His friend had betrayed him. And now he was dead.

"I'll ask you one last time," Quynn said, his breath stinking in Trey's face. "Will you come with me willingly?"

Trey looked at his father, at the man he'd known and hated his entire life. At the murderer, the torturer, the destroyer he knew him to be.

"No," Trey breathed, "I will not."

"Fine," Quynn said, raising his hand.

Something darkly purple clamped down around Trey's mind.

SEVENTEEN

ALLAIN WALKED the streets of Splintertown. That's what he'd started calling it, since it didn't seem to have a name. They knew how to build things properly here, at least—everything was straight and orderly. He liked it.

He wished his father could have been here with him to see it.

He fought back tears, focusing instead on the carving in his hand. Not a stag this time—he was working on a raccoon, a rather difficult animal to get right. Not as difficult as a hummingbird, but still hard. Raccoons had a certain personality about them, a certain look to their face. You had to carve it very carefully to make it work.

He'd been carving ever since he could remember. It was something Orist had never been good at, but he'd encouraged Allain. His father had always supported him, no matter what.

Allain sniffed, struggling to stay calm. It was all Trey's fault—that maniac had arrived out of thin air, and suddenly the whole village was all over him like he was some kind of god. He'd sure captured Arra's attention, alright. Arra and the rest of the town. Maybe Fenian would kick the guy's ass, assuming Allain didn't get to him first.

But killing him probably wasn't the best option. Allain didn't know what had come over him earlier, trying to kill Trey—he wasn't a murderer. He *knew* he was a bully, and he was comfortable with that fact. But he wasn't a murderer. Something about the day had enraged him in a way he didn't truly understand.

Maybe his father would have known.

Allain stopped suddenly, leaning hard against a light post. He felt emotion overpower him—sadness, anger, hatred. He didn't know how to handle the surge of feelings. His hands started hurting, and he realized he was gripping his carving too tightly, the edges of the wood digging into his skin.

He took a deep breath. Orist was gone. His father was dead. He had died with honor, saving Kharis. He had sacrificed himself. He had died a hero, just as Allain had always known he was.

Allain sniffed again, wiping at his eye. Damn tears. He wasn't a crier. He wasn't a fool.

He couldn't have emotions like this.

He gritted his teeth, reflexively casting an illusion. He always did that when he was emotional. Sometimes it calmed him.

But something unexpected happened. Another Allain was standing in front of him, cast from the feet of the raccoon he'd been carving.

Illusion-Allain looked at him, his brow crooked with concern. Was the illusion thinking something? Was he making fun of him? Allain balled his fist.

But no, that couldn't be. Illusions weren't real—that's why they were called illusions. Why had he cast one of himself? He didn't know. Perhaps he had just wanted to escape, to be somebody else. Or maybe he wished he could be legion, his own army. That way he could destroy Trey once and for all, and take Arra for his own.

The illusion frowned at him.

What the hell? Allain took a step back, then tripped on something and fell. Illusion-Allain stepped forward, looming over him, a dissatisfied expression on his face. Like he was judging him.

"You don't know!" Allain shouted at himself. "You weren't there!" He felt tears coming again. What was he, a woman? Crying when things didn't go his way? He would *not cry*. He sniffed instead.

Stay focused. Stay cool.

You can handle this.

The illusion bent toward him. Real-Allain wasn't doing this—how could the illusion move on it's own? None of the others ever did that.

What was happening?

Then Illusion-Allain opened its mouth, and Allain saw that there was a fiery chasm inside. Flames spiraled down and down, roiling infinitely between the false man's teeth. He could hear the sound of hell itself, pulling him in, willing him onward, waiting to consume him.

Allain scuttled backwards, crawling on the ground, trying to get away from his own illusion. He dropped the half-formed raccoon carving, hearing it clatter in the dust. That should have ended the illusion instantly.

Except it didn't.

Illusion-Allain crossed its arms, and the fire went on and on. Allain was captivated by it, drawn in, spiraling downward into oblivion. The illusion of himself was *evil*, he instinctively knew. Dangerous. It could mean the end of life itself.

But what the hell was going on?

Suddenly the world swam. Real-Allain's vision went sideways, bits and pieces of the city jumping around like puzzle pieces tossed in the air. He couldn't...what was... Illusion-Allain stood there, an island in a storm, the only part of the world that wasn't spinning and cracking and breaking apart like the leaves in autumn.

His head started *hurting*. Why wouldn't the illusion stop? What was going on? Why did it hurt so much?

Then it all slammed home with an audible *smack*, and everything was back to normal.

The illusion was gone. The world was together, staying put as he turned his head. The headache was still there, though, pounding away like a builder at a construction site. The raccoon carving was on the ground where he had dropped it, the legs turned to dust.

Allain took a deep breath. What in the hell had all that been about? His father had warned him about projecting illusions of himself. He'd told him it was dangerous, but never why.

Maybe he should have heeded his dead father's advice.

Allain got to his feet shakily, picking up the partial raccoon. He set off down the street again, moving aimlessly, his thoughts a whirl.

EIGHTEEN

ELANIL WALKED THROUGH THE DINGY, dark corridors and tunnels, listening to the others talking quietly. She was still holding Rylan's hand—he seemed to need the physical contact now, despite him shying away at first. She didn't blame him. It couldn't be easy, living with what he'd just seen.

She'd never had to witness the death of a friend.

She didn't know what to think. From the moment she'd started that fire and run away, things had been crazy. She didn't know what she'd expected, exactly, when she'd decided to flee the scene with Rylan. She didn't know what she'd expected, but it hadn't been this.

She thought she understood now. Rylan made more sense to her now that she'd seen where he lived. The environment down here in the Under was harsh, dirty. Dismal. It was such a far cry from the home that she had known. But there was also a strange familiarity about it. This Crew—this Shock Crew—seemed like a team. It was a good fit for Rylan.

Would she ever see her home again? She didn't know. No, she could do better than that. She *would* see home again, she resolved. She'd go back. She'd own up to her mistakes, and she'd be better. Do better. Somehow.

Maybe Rylan would come with her.

She squeezed his hand, flashing him a smile. It was hard to see down here in the tunnels, but she thought he looked back at her, his expression sad. He squeezed her hand back.

"What if we crash the city?" Shot was saying.

Dill grunted. "And kill everyone in it? That's your plan?"

Shot seemed to think about that for a minute. "We need a forcefinder," he said. "I heard they can use their forcefields to bounce things, make them not crash."

"Phoenix could do that," Dill said softly. "She was really good."

"Well," Shot said, "without a forcefinder, I guess our only choice is to kill the entire government."

Small broke out laughing. "Your plans just keep getting better and better!"

They came to a branch in the tunnel, and Rylan stopped. "I can't..." he started. "Can someone else lead?" He was still emotional, still struggling.

Dill elbowed his way through. "Sorry. It's this way." He led on, taking the branch to the right. The rest of the group followed.

"I'm serious," Shot said.

"And how do you expect our Crew to take down the entire government?" Small asked. "There are only thirty of us."

"Simple," Shot said, "we ally with all the other Crews."

That really got Small laughing.

"Shh," Elanil said. She didn't particularly want to get spotted by more of those guards. Small eyed her briefly, then shut up.

"It's really not a bad plan," Dill said. "In fact, that's exactly the idea."

"What?" Shot said. "That was *your* plan?"

"Of course," Dill said. "Why else do you think I was gone so often? It takes a *lot* of work to unite the Under. Years. Decades."

"We had to recreate Queen's legacy," Small said.

"Wait—you *knew* about this?" Shot said.

"Small is a good talker," Dill said. But Shot looked crest-fallen. "Listen—I'm sorry I didn't tell you every detail of the plan. I've been up here a long time, okay? I've made a lot of mistakes. I realize now that Queen was probably my best chance of pulling everything together. We had the cars, back then. We could have done great things."

"Why didn't you?" Rylan asked.

Dill turned to him. "Frankly, I was scared. The Cothellon are a force to be reckoned with. Even the Eldrim on the surface, with all their resources and abilities, even *they* never managed to come up against the Cothellon. They're monstrous, and powerful, and—"

"And you like it up here," Small said.

Dill hung his head. "I'm a fool."

Rylan narrowed his eyes. "You let my mother die. She died saving this place—this world—and you could have stopped all this before she *needed* to?"

The tunnel was silent for a long moment. When Dill raised his head again, his expression was haunted. "I don't think there's any way to stop the Cothellon," he said. "And do you want to know the worst part? Do you want to know the truth? I never had a plan at all."

Elanil could see shock in everyone's eyes.

"Your father would be ashamed," Rylan whispered.

That seemed to hurt Dill more than anything that had gone before. His shoulders began to shake, tears welling in his eyes.

"We don't have much time," he said, trying to hold the tears back. "Before he left, Dad said the Conjunction was scheduled in just a few weeks."

Rylan was glaring at him. "And I suppose you're going to tell me what the Conjunction is?"

"It's when all seven cities connect together, forming the device. Fennas Elenathon."

"Which will destroy the planet," Small said.

"Yes," Dill said. "Come on—let's keep walking." He sniffed.

They continued down the tunnel, following him. Elanil watched Rylan, hoping he was okay.

"I was close," Dill said. "I had most of the Crews here ready to sign on. But now—I'm not sure we have the time."

"Why *didn't* you have more time?" Elanil asked.

"Dad and I don't talk that much anymore," Dill said, his flashlight moving erratically from side to side as he walked. "It's risky. If anyone caught him with me, it would be bad. Plus, I don't think he knew the exact timing. The Cothellon operate via a very strict command structure, and he's not exactly at the top of the food chain. Close, but not quite."

"Oh?" Elanil asked. She was used to how things were run in Sylrantheas. The Council there worked very effectively, if slowly.

"It all starts with the Cundu," Dill said. "That's the supreme leader—she has the final word on everything. Below that, we have the Conin—the Council. There's a Small Council and a Large Council, which they use to divide tasks up as needed. But ultimately, the Cundu has the final say."

"Orym told you all this?" Rylan asked.

"Yes. The Cundu has been the same for at least a thousand years, if not longer."

"Shouldn't she be dead? I thought elves only lived a thousand years at most."

"That's right," Dill said. "She *should* probably be dead by now. But she's not, and no one knows why. So she remains in charge."

"Who's the Cundu, again?" Small asked. "I know you told us this once."

"Her name is Lorelei," Dill said. His footsteps echoed loudly in the tunnel. "She's been the supreme leader for a very long time."

"So what's the bitch's deal?" Shot asked.

Dill shot him a glare. "Don't *ever* underestimate Lorelei," he said. "She is a very intelligent, capable woman. *Very* dangerous. Not like Den Boss was."

"Who?"

"Never mind."

"So why don't we just take her out?" Small asked.

Dill laughed. "Why don't pigs fly?"

The group was silent for a moment—apparently nobody understood the phrase.

"Guys," Dill said, "taking out Lorelei is not gonna happen. And besides, I have a better idea."

"Do tell, supreme leader," Small said, bowing showily to Dill as he walked.

"Dad is working on something of his own," Dill said. "I think he's trying to disable the whole device, somehow. Until that happens, I have a new plan: one that might actually work. We're going to destroy the darkprime forests. All of them."

"How many forests are there?" Rylan asked. His mood seemed to have lightened, at least. Elanil resolved to ask him about his mother when she got the chance. She wanted to know the story.

"Four, in this city," Dill said, "unless they somehow managed to hide one from us all these years. With our limited numbers, we'll have to hit them one at a time, as quickly as possible."

"I would have expected more," Rylan said. "The Under is *way* bigger than it needs to be. I figured all the extra space was for those forests."

"You mean the mystery rooms," Dill said. "Nobody knows what they are for."

"Really? Not even the Planners? Not even your father?"

"If my father knows, he hasn't told me," Dill said. "But I honestly don't think anybody knows. I've seen the blueprints —there are huge areas in the Under that are just blacked out, with nothing in them. It's either the best-kept secret in the city, or they're just plain empty."

"Maybe they made a mistake."

"It seems unlikely that the Cothellon built them by mistake, but I suppose anything is possible. We'll likely never find out what those areas are for."

"Mystery rooms are fine and all," Small said, "but how are we going to do it? How can we destroy an entire forest?"

"Darkprime trees burn just like any other tree," Dill said. "But it won't be as simple as that. There will be guards. With guns. We'll need everyone on hand to lend support, using whatever magical Talent they have."

"Or just pure ingenuity," Small said.

"That includes you, Elanil," Dill said. "If you're willing to help. Your magic would be very good to have along."

Elanil thought about that. Did she want to get caught up in this? The boys' crusade to free the city from tyranny was noble, if misguided. After what Dill had just told them, she didn't think they stood a chance. But she saw that Rylan was looking at her expectantly. He wanted her to help, she realized. She suddenly became conscious of his hand, still holding on to hers.

He stepped towards her. "Will you?" he asked. His dark brown eyes were captivating, even in the dimness of the tunnel. She felt her heart start beating faster.

"Yes," she whispered.

"Aw, come on, guys, get a room!" Small said from behind them. Shot whistled loudly.

Elanil blushed, stepping away from Rylan. She still held onto his hand, though—she wasn't letting him go any time soon.

Dill cleared his throat. "Well, then, that's settled."

"I would need more primewood," Elanil said.

Dill nodded. "Hopefully I'll have good news for you on that front soon."

"Alright, boss," Shot said, "we need details. Who's gonna do what?"

"We may have to improvise," Dill said. "I had hoped we would have more time than this." They took a turn, heading down yet another tunnel. Everything looked the same down here. Elanil didn't know how anyone could navigate in the Under.

"Are we going the right way?" Rylan asked, as if reading her mind.

NINETEEN

ARRA WAS numb to the world around her.

People were saying things, touching her, talking to her, but she couldn't hear. She blinked, her eyelids feeling like lead. The room spun slowly, wheels and shadows fluttering away like leaves in the wind. Her heart was cold.

Fenian was dead.

She struggled up, feeling as if her mind were swimming through thick mud. The sounds around her were muted, low. She tried to take a breath. Failed.

She should have seen it coming, should have been able to protect him. She was a Hunter *and* a Healer, dammit! She should have been able to help.

But she wasn't a mage.

All around her in her mind, the Eldrim Ways fell to the ground. Dead. Useless. Buried.

Neither magic nor Mundane could have saved Fenian, she realized then. The Twins had preordained his fate, and there was nothing she could have done.

He was gone.

She willed the tears to come. Failed.

She took a breath instead.

She felt a tugging at her hand. Sounds righted themselves in her ear, tuning upwards until she could understand. Her vision was next, sliding out of the mud and into the air. She could see; she could hear.

She could feel.

Imra was tugging at her, concern in her tear-filled eyes. Where was she sitting?

Oh, yes.

The Splinter. They had a courthouse, an oddly civilized thing in the middle of the forest. That's where Arra was now.

They were holding a public hearing, a meeting between human and elves. They were deciding what should be done, inasmuch as the language barrier allowed.

The Sylrantheas Council was down two members—both Orist and Eloen had died during the attack. Kharis was injured, but he was present. The other members—Silanar, Bellas, Daylor, Belstram, and Nuvian—were there and accounted for. Everyone was quieter than usual, still shocked from what they had just lived through.

"Surely you must know *something* about the attack," Bellas was saying to Orym. Orym was pacing back and forth in his usual way, a wire trailing from his ear to connect with something in his pocket. Was it a radio?

"I spoke with Greyson," Orym said. "He's a Supervisor in New San Francisco, my main human contact inside the government. Greyson said it was *Quynn* leading the attack."

"Quynn?" Bellas asked.

"My old boss. The man who recruited me. He can be quite...harsh. Greyson didn't know why he was attacking. It was something about a personal project Quynn had."

"What?" Bellas said. "That makes no sense. What project could he possibly have had down here?"

"Well," Orym said, pausing as if reluctant to continue. "I may not have told you everything about Trey."

"Now's the time," Silanar said, his voice cold. "Quynn killed hundreds of Eldrim today, and destroyed Sylrantheas. Tell us what you know."

"Trey is Quynn's son. At least, that's how I heard it."

"That's a strange way to put it," Silanar said. "Is he Quynn's son, or isn't he?"

"I'm not sure," Orym said. "They certainly look alike, but I've never seen two people be more opposite each other. I think there's something going on there beyond what we know."

"So Quynn was there to get Trey?"

"I believe so."

"Has anyone seen Trey since the attack?" Nobody in the room answered that. "So it's safe to say he got him, then," Silanar said. "But at what cost?" He blew out a breath. Her father sounded disgusted. Disgusted and sad.

Arra thought back to what Allain had said during the attack. "He's coming for Trey," he'd said as he'd run by her. It hadn't made sense then, but now she thought she understood. Quynn—a Cothellon, a man she'd never met—was behind all this.

And Trey was Quynn's son.

She felt a shiver run through her as she realized the implications. Trey was the son of her enemy. Had he been planning this with his father the whole time? Had they planned to infiltrate the elves, then destroy them? Why Sylrantheas? Why now?

Why her?

She remembered the look on his face, that day when he was crying on a log. She'd almost kissed him then, almost betrayed Fenian. She'd almost cheated on the love of her life right then with a stranger she barely knew. A stranger who was responsible for hundreds of deaths. Her people, slaughtered, and all for what? Some father-son vendetta?

She felt her heart grow cold.

The world was a much crueler place than Arra had thought. She felt despair growing within her, but she grabbed it and turned it. Turned it into anger. This was Trey's fault. Fenian was dead because of him and his father.

They would both be made to pay for this.

The decision made, her breathing slowed. She knew what needed to be done. She would kill Trey, somehow, and all would be right. Easy. She had a channel for her emotions now, a place to put them.

Good.

"Orym," Bellas said, "something has been bothering me ever since you told us your side of the story the other day. You said the Cothellon were trying to escape the planet in order to avoid an environmental catastrophe. Yet we—the Eldrim—still went ahead with the Sundering, in order to reset the balance of life. We succeeded, and by all accounts the planet is thriving. Why are the Cothellon still trying to leave?"

Orym pursed his lips. "I don't know," he said. "It's Lorelei, I think. She's the Cundu. She has always insisted the plan continue, has never wavered in her conviction. It's almost as if she...knows something we don't."

Silanar frowned. "So it may not be an environmental issue at all," he mused. "None of this makes sense."

"It's something about the gate technology, I think," Orym said. "That magic has long been rumored to have certain... side effects. People have come through the gates corrupted, or confused. It can do strange things to the mind. Some claim the gates can remove memories, or give them back. Quynn never put any stock in those rumors, and neither do I."

"Then why bring it up?"

"It's the only possibility I can think of. Lorelei is either hiding something, or something happened to her. We may never find out which."

"The question," Jalnab suddenly said, speaking up for the first time, "is if...Quynn...will attack us. The Splinter is...not ready."

"If Orym is correct," Silanar said, "then he already has Trey. He has no reason to come here."

"You do not...know," Jalnab said.

Silanar bowed his head. "No," he admitted.

Suddenly there was a loud, high-pitched whining sound, mixed with a low rumbling. The twin sounds pierced the air, vibrating the floor and shaking the walls and windows.

Bellas stuck his head out a window to see what was going on. "Uh, guys," he said, "you might want to see this."

ALLAIN WAS FEELING MAGNANIMOUS. It was a feeling he wasn't used to. Shouldn't he be burning with hatred, sadness, or fear? Any of those things would be normal after what he'd just been through. But he couldn't really bring himself to feel anything like that. Maybe it had been that strange illusion of himself—maybe it had sapped him of all negative emotion.

That was a neat trick, if so.

He started making his way down the street, heading in no direction in particular. Suddenly a loud, piercing sound cut through the air. The ground started rumbling strangely, in tune with the sound. What the—?

A massive city appeared above him then, its image fluttering and waving for an instant before solidifying. Allain could see a glowing, curving sphere around the bottom of the city for an instant, then it faded away.

Was that New San Francisco? It looked huge and ominous, hovering above them as it did. Why had it appeared after all these years? He'd always known it was there, floating and invisible.

He preferred it that way.

Then another sound cut in, this one much lower and thicker. It sounded like massive engines, heard from a long way away. Allain shielded his eyes against the setting sun, looking to the west, where the sound was coming from.

After a moment another city sprang into view, far in the distance, warping into shape as it appeared. The new city looked different, somehow. It was shaped differently, had different things underneath it. And it was bigger. Much, *much* bigger.

What was going on? Was this the beginning of another attack?

TWENTY

"IT'S THE CONJUNCTION," Orym said. "I told you it would be soon."

The room was bustling with an undercurrent of fear, everyone whispering to each other intensely. Arra wished she could be somewhere—anywhere—else, but she knew she should stay. She needed to hear what they were going to do. Thoughts of Fenian kept creeping into her mind, and she felt herself gripping Imra's hand tightly. She would avenge him if she could.

"Explain," Silanar said. "What is the Conjunction?"

"Fennas Elenathon—the Gateway to the Stars—was constructed in seven parts. Seven replica cities, meant to make it easier to house the millions of humans it takes to keep things running. The device was designed to amplify the seventh darkprime power. As I explained before, it taps into Earth's core to get the energy it needs to create a gate large enough to send the entire planet through. The seven cities are designed to fit together into one massive device. They're moving towards each other now, forming up. That is the Conjunction."

"Where will...Earth...be sent?" Jalnab asked.

"Lorelei was very specific about that bit," Orym said. "The gate points to a solar system roughly twenty thousand light years away from us."

"Why there?" Silanar asked.

"I don't know."

"How does Lorelei know to go there?"

"I don't know. She seems to know something we don't. Precisely what she knows, and how she knows it, is anyone's guess."

"So you mean to tell me your entire organization—these Cothellon—have been working for hundreds of years to transport the entire planet tens of thousands of light years away, all on the word of one individual?"

"It's not as simple as that," Orym said, "but in a nutshell, yes. The Cothellon initially just wanted to escape, to get off the planet. When it came time to pick a destination, Lorelei provided the answer."

"Surely *someone* among you must have asked her why?"

Orym thought about that for a moment. "No," he said, "not that I've ever heard. I never thought about it before."

"But you're the Scientist General! Isn't it your *job* to ask questions like that?"

"It is," Orym said. "And I didn't. I am sorry."

Silanar sighed. "Elves," he said. "What are we doing here? How did we get this far? I fear a lot of us made some pretty poor decisions over the years."

Jalnab cleared his throat. "Is that..." He paused, his mouth making motions in the air. "Is that...an...apology?"

Silanar hung his head. "There is no question that humanity did this world great harm," he said, "but we elves have been no better. We took free will away from your people,

Jalnab, and that was not our right. We are not the gods we made ourselves out to be."

"Twins guide us," Bellas murmured. Silanar looked at him but didn't respond.

"With the Conjunction begun," Orym said, "that means we have at best three days before they open the planetary gate. And that's if they go through all the safety checks properly—Lorelei has been known to get impatient."

"She waited almost three hundred years to try again," Silanar said. "Why would she be in a hurry now?"

Orym shrugged. "It wouldn't be the first time."

"Well," Bellas said, "we're still left without a plan. How can we stop them?"

"If only we still had the Prime Trees," Silanar said.

"Maybe more have appeared," Kharis said. It was the first time Arra had heard him speak since the meeting began. He was cradling his arm awkwardly, his face a mask of pain and grief.

"That's only happened a few times in recorded history," Belstram said. "No one knows why they sometimes appear spontaneously, and we would have heard if any had—someone's yearly survey would have found it. They would have sent word."

Kharis nodded soberly. "It must be possible to create more Trees somehow," he said. "Something must happen to create them."

"If it were ever possible to create Prime Trees," Belstram said, "the art has been lost to us for many millennia. We gave up trying a thousand years ago. Now is not the time to suddenly start trying again."

"I know," Kharis said. "I'm just thinking out loud."

"What would we do with the Trees, anyway?" Silanar asked. "If we had them."

"Well," Orym said, "if we did have all the Trees, we could probably soulsunder everyone in the cities."

"I don't know how controllable the magic is," Silanar said. "We might end up killing each and every living thing on board. But that ignores the other problem—the cities are thousands of feet above us, and protected by forcefields."

"Only on the bottom."

"Yes, but that's enough. Soulsundering is directional. It travels across the planet on the ground, only reaching up to a certain height. That's why everyone in airplanes during the Sundering survived. The magic couldn't touch them." He shivered, as if remembering back to how it had felt to manipulate the magic, to kill all those people.

"This discussion is pointless," Bellas said. "We have no Trees."

"Are we at least agreeing that action must be taken?" Orym asked. He stood still, which was unusual for him. He looked at everyone in the room with anticipation.

"Are we really down to three days?" Silanar asked.

"Yes."

"Then let's vote," Silanar said, "even if we don't know precisely what we're going to do about it, we need to do something. Jalnab, do you agree?"

Jalnab turned to address the Splinter representatives in the room. "We vote," he said in his characteristically rough English. "Help the elves?"

Every human raised their hand.

"Council," Silanar said, "I put the vote to you, too. All in favor of taking direct action against the Cothellon, raise your hands." The five remaining Council members, Silanar included, raised their hands. Arra raised her hand, too, from her position in the back of the room. Silanar saw her hand and nodded at her silently.

"Then it's unanimous," he said. "We—humans and elves —will do what we can to combat this threat. It is taking place on our doorstep—indeed, right above our heads. Therefore, it is up to us to fight it. We will do so."

His short speech was met with light applause. Jalnab and Silanar looked at each other, smiling tightly.

But what, Arra wondered, would their action be?

"I sent messengers after we met last," Bellas said. "Other Eldrim villages are being told of the impending threat as we speak. We called them to a High Council, but there's no time for that now."

Silanar clasped his hands together. "Send more messengers out to the nearby elven villages. Have them meet us here, bringing anyone who can fight, and all their mages. And primewood, as much as they can. Twins know we'll need it, but I fear there is no way they can reach us in time."

Bellas nodded briskly, making notes on a piece of paper.

"But the real question still remains," Silanar said. "What can we do about Fennas Elenathon?"

"The tunnel to the core is nearby," Orym said, resuming his pacing. "We can get there in just a few hours. I propose we go there and try to infiltrate it. Best case, we get in and disable the device from that end. That would only be a delaying tactic, though. Ultimately, we need to destroy everything—including the floating cities."

Silanar frowned. "That place Elanil found," he said. "That city in the forest, with the hole and the metal prongs. Is that what you're referring to?"

"Yes," Orym said. "That's the Fennas Elenathon receiver site. That's where they beam the planet's energy up to the device in the air."

"How long has it been there?"

"Since before the Sundering. It's protected by a powerful

forcefinder, keeping the area hidden and shielded at all times. The forcefield must have been down for some reason when she found it."

"Then how will *we* get in?"

"I do not know," Orym said. "Wait a minute." He pulled a square metal device from his pocket and fiddled with it for a moment. A wire trailed from the device up to his ear, where he had something inserted. Was it some kind of radio?

"Dillon?" Orym said, speaking into the device. "Dillon, do you copy?" He waited for a moment before repeating the question. "He's not at his radio," Orym said, addressing Silanar. "But I'll keep trying. Maybe he or Greyson can do something on their end. If they can get into Planner Central undetected, they might be able to travel through the gate and meet us on the other side."

"So what should we do?" Silanar asked.

"Send a team to the receiver site. I'll keep trying to contact my son. It's our only way to do any damage. One way or another, we need to get into that site."

Silanar nodded. "All in favor?" he asked the Council. Everyone raised their hand.

Arra nodded to herself. Finally, something was happening. This would be her way to fight back against the evil that had killed Fenian. She relished the opportunity.

She would make sure to get on that team.

TREY'S BRAIN wasn't working correctly. It was like a steel plate had slammed down around his thoughts, walling him in. He tried over and over to escape, but he was stuck. Trapped.

He thought he could hear laughter in his head.

He found himself following his father, unable to do anything else. They'd taken one of the flying cars—Quynn had called it a "fallcar"—and flown it through the forest, eventually arriving at some kind of metal city in the woods. A gigantic hole was in the middle of the city, with four huge metal prongs positioned around it, reaching to the sky.

The two pilots landed the fallcar, and Quynn and Trey got out. Quynn marched them over to a larger building that was positioned off to one side of the encampment. The guards at the building obviously recognized Quynn; they saluted him as he and Trey approached.

Trey tried again to move, to make his legs stop following his father. Why couldn't he just run away? But try as he might, nothing happened. Quynn turned to look at him, and he felt a darkness closing in on his mind. What had he just been doing? Oh yes, he was following his father, like a good little boy. Quynn smirked at him, then turned and led the way inside the building.

Trey found himself inside a large chamber filled with some kind of technology he'd never seen before. Wires and pipes snaked along the floor and up the walls, and racks of blinking equipment made up the left side of the room. In the center of the chamber was a large dais with what looked like a metal gate positioned in the center. It had a thick frame, and inside the frame light swirled. Trey thought he could see people moving in the image it held, along with buildings and cars. It looked like a doorway to a city. How strange.

Quynn started walking toward the dais, but a stern-looking elven woman dressed in dark blue swung out in front of him, blocking his path. She was carrying a small gun of some kind, and her blonde hair was clipped short. Her shirt had a white stripe across the heart.

"High Mindmaster," the woman said, "I didn't think to see you here."

"Yes?" Quynn said.

"Uh, how can I help you, sir?"

"We are going through the gate. Step aside, please."

"Of course, sir. May I ask—why not take your fallcar up?"

"Do you question every officer who comes through here?"

"Of course not, sir. I apologize."

"The Conjunction is beginning," Quynn said. "The cities are a moving target right now, as you should know. The gate is safer." He made as if to push past the woman.

"Even with the...side effects?" the woman asked. She looked at the gate. Was that fear in her eyes?

"When will people stop perpetrating that myth?" Quynn asked. "Let us through. We are going up."

"Yes, sir." The woman moved aside.

A piercing whine started up just then, and everything in the room started vibrating. A piece of Trey's mind grew alarmed, but it was immediately pushed aside. There was nothing to be afraid of.

"You see," Quynn said, brushing past the woman, "the Conjunction begins." He walked briskly up to the gate, Trey following along. They arrived at the dais. "You first," Quynn said, motioning to Trey.

He stepped through the gate.

It felt like ice washing over him, chilling his veins. Something unlocked in his mind, as if a previously-hidden door had just opened. Then he emerged onto a bustling city square, filled with uniformed men and women. The sun was setting, golden light casting long shadows in the square. It lent an eerie look to the scene.

Trey put a hand to his head. Had he been imagining it, or had something just happened in his mind?

Then Quynn stepped through the gate, eyes on him.

And suddenly Trey *remembered*.

Whirls, shapes. Things crashing down around him. Golden glow, yellow light. The screams of millions dying. A great city. Ships in the air.

And Quynn, reaching out his hand.

Slaps. Screams. A cloud of purple, fogging his brain. Darkness.

He was a child. No, he was a teenager. He hated his father. His father hated him.

He had no mother, not at first.

Adulthood. Fear. Tests. Something dark and shiny in his hand.

Pain.

Reset.

Childhood—no, he was a teenager. He didn't know his own age. His father was there again, still. Slaps and screams, tests again.

The dark wood.

Failure.

Reset.

An operating room. Needles and knives. The beeping of a machine. His father yelling something at him. Blood and pain.

Wood.

A woman—a mother. His father beating her.

Reset.

Trey stumbled in the city square, falling to the ground, his mind reeling. His thoughts were going in circles, round and round and...

He sat up suddenly. He *remembered* now. What had been so confusing just a moment ago became clear. His father— *was* he his father?—raising him, treating him like a child.

Testing him.

Over and over and over again.

Trey took a deep, shuddering breath. Quynn was standing in front of him, a look of alarm on his face.

"Who *are* you?" Trey asked.

TWENTY-ONE

RYLAN STILL HADN'T COME to grips with it. Con, his best friend, was dead. Killed in an insane ritual. Killed to make a magical tree.

She hadn't deserved it—no one did. How many thousands had died in ceremonies like that? How could these Cothellon kill so many people, and not even care?

Why had Rylan taken so long to go after her? He could have saved her. He could have found her. He was sure that if he'd just *tried*, his best friend would not be dead.

Rylan had failed.

But he had to move on. He had to. Everyone died in the Under. Everyone, even Con. Sooner or later, there was nothing you could do. So he *would* move on. He would live his life. Who knew when death would come for him? He could only do the best he could.

But there was one thing Rylan knew. One thing he was certain of. That ceremony with the trees—that ritual killing—he would stop it, somehow.

No more innocents would die for a tree.

"Do you know where we are?" he asked. They'd been traveling through the Under, following Dill, not really paying attention to where they were going. Rylan thought Dill had memorized the layout in this part of the city, but something wasn't right. They were supposed to be heading back to Shock Crew headquarters, but they were going the wrong way.

"Dammit," Dill said, "I took a wrong turn somewhere." He looked around, trying to get his bearings. "Wait a minute, I think I know where we are. Follow me."

He walked on into the tunnel, everyone following close behind. Rylan suddenly realized he was still holding Elanil's hand. Should he let go? Did she want him to let go? Were the other boys making fun of him?

Or did he actually *like* holding her hand?

They rounded a corner and found themselves in a new tunnel. Dill bent down and fiddled with the wall, drawing aside a hidden panel. He reached into the opening and pulled out a pouch and a note. He opened the note and read it aloud.

"Quick enough for you? This may be the last time I can get any. Device is activating. Greyson." Dill opened the pouch and looked inside, smiling. Then he handed it to Elanil.

"Just what the doctor ordered," he said. "Prime elm."

Elanil let go of Rylan's hand to accept the pouch, her face beaming as she looked inside.

"Woohoo!" she said, the sound echoing down the tunnel.

"Shh," Rylan said.

"Sorry," she whispered.

Dill closed the wall compartment. The panel fit so tightly that it looked like nothing was there. "Dead drop," Dill said by way of explanation—whatever that meant. "Follow me," he said, leading them further down the tunnel.

They walked for what seemed like hours. Something was missing, Rylan realized, something he had found himself needing. What was it? He looked at his hand, realizing how cold it was.

Elanil. He was actually missing her hand in his. What was coming over him? One week with these elves and he was like some undergirl, wanting attention! He stole a glance at Elanil as they walked in the dark. She seemed fine on her own. She didn't need any comforting now that she had her primewood. Her step seemed stronger, her expression firmer. Armed with magic, she looked ready to handle anything that came her way. She was strong. Like Con had been.

After a while, Small spoke. "Boss?" he said. "You sure you know where you're going?"

Dill sighed. "I don't know what's wrong with me," he said. "I need to get my bearings. Let's ascend to street level really quick. All these damn tunnels look the same."

Small frowned, but went along with it. They followed Dill through a series of turns and up several ladders, moving upwards from floor to floor until they reached a sewer pipe. These were always the best places to travel in the Under— assuming you loved the smell of shit. He saw Elanil wrinkling her nose as they sloshed through the dark liquid lining the bottom of the huge pipe, but she didn't say anything.

Her stomach must be stronger than he'd thought.

Eventually they reached a manhole, and Dill popped it open.

"I can't see anything," he whispered down at them. "Come up."

He slid the manhole to the side, careful to do it quietly. Then the group followed him up the ladder and out onto the street.

It was nighttime, and the area was pitch black. The moon must not have risen yet. Where were they? Rylan didn't recognize the area. Short buildings lined the streets, no light shining from any of them. There weren't even any streetlights in this part of the city.

"Come on," Dill said, motioning for them to follow.

THE ELDRIM SET OUT IMMEDIATELY. Silanar and Jalnab had agreed to send a team of Hunters—no surprise there. Hunters were best-equipped to deal with whatever they would find at the receiver site, after all. There had been no argument from the Splinter humans—none of them seemed interested in taking the risk.

Fine. The elves had gotten everyone into this mess, and they would get everyone out of it.

They set out into the forest, Arra and Imra taking up the rear, with Lhoris and Orym at the front. Kharis had declined to join the group—he was too broken up after losing Fenian. Arra had lost a lover, but Kharis had lost a son. Arra wished there was something she could have said to him to make it better, to let him know she understood his pain, but the words had died on her lips.

There was no comfort left in her.

"We should have brought a Healer," Orym said.

Lhoris shook his head. "They're all needed back with the Splinter," he said. "We're trained in field medicine. We'll be fine. I agree we should have brought more people, though. I mean, we're good Hunters and all—but who knows what we'll encounter out here?"

Arra agreed. More people would certainly have been better.

It was her first expedition as an adult. She had thought it would feel different, somehow. And it did, but not for the reasons she had expected. She looked ahead of her, at Orym and Lhoris as they trudged through the forest, talking quietly. The group of Hunters felt different—wrong.

It just wasn't the same without Fenian and Kharis.

Fenian. She missed him terribly. He'd been more than just a lover to her, more than just a pretty face. He'd been her friend, her companion, a strength she could rely on.

She didn't know if she could go on without him.

She'd imagined marrying him, having a daughter, enjoying life together. She'd imagined treks through the woods, arm in arm, competing for who could take down their prey in the fewest shots. She'd imagined nights with him underneath the stars, next to their favorite tree on the hill. She'd imagined life with him, and now that was gone.

Gone.

Tears rolled down her cheeks as she walked silently through the trees. Had there been enough death, yet? Sylrantheas was in flames—was that not enough?

She stomped through the forest, heedless of the noise she was making, ignoring the looks Imra was giving her. Yes, she knew her brow was furrowed. She knew her face was drawn. Branches and leaves whipped by as she glared at nothing, seeing only red.

Trey. This was his fault. One way or another, he would pay for what he'd done.

"THIS IS PLANNER CENTRAL, isn't it," Shot said.

Elanil looked around. Everything was so dark, it was hard to see anything. She'd been to Planner Central before, back when she and Rylan had gone through that gate. Was this the same place? She couldn't tell.

They walked a few blocks away from the manhole cover,

trying to get their bearings. Elanil had thought these boys would always know their way around, but they all seemed so confused.

She shivered in the cold night air.

The buildings—what she could see of them, anyway—were so stark. So unnatural. She missed the trees on the ground, the birds and flowers and insects. She didn't want to end up stuck here with these dirty boys in this frigid city. She looked down at herself and sniffed. She desperately needed a bath.

"Where are you *going?*" Small asked, but Shot grabbed him, clapping a hand over his mouth.

"Shh," he said, peering out at something. Then he motioned for everyone to get back against a nearby wall.

Elanil heard a click and a hissing sound. "There's someone down there," a strange voice said, and Elanil flattened herself against the wall. "I'll check it out." She heard footsteps coming from down the road. Nobody moved.

Dill motioned for them to follow.

He crept around the corner of the building they were up against, away from the footsteps, everyone else following close behind. They made their way around the building in the pitch black night, everyone staying as quiet as they could.

There was a sudden hiss of static right next to Elanil's ear. She shrieked, surprised. A man was there, reaching out for her, trying to grab her.

She ducked under his grasp and ran.

Then Rylan was beside her, and Dill, and they were all running. "Go, go!" Dill shouted. She heard a yell, saw the flash of a gun reflecting the moon. She felt a chill ripple through her, deeper than the cold.

This might be the end.

Everyone was running now, and Dill had a hand in his

pocket. The gun-bearing man was pointing his weapon at them wildly, trying to keep up with them as they sped down the street. He brought the muzzle up to bear as she watched, preparing to shoot.

But Dill, apparently, had other ideas.

Blue lightning shot out from his hand, hitting the guard in the chest and sending him flying, his gun clattering somewhere on the street. The lightning seared her retinas, spots covering her vision. She tried to keep running, tried to keep her balance. But she couldn't see a thing.

Shouts sounded from further away. The lightning must have drawn the attention of other guards.

"Where to, boss?" Shot said.

"Follow me," Dill said.

They followed.

His path took them through a narrow alley between two buildings, then a sharp right turn down another street. There weren't enough lights here, Twins damn it. How could anyone see anything?

Elanil could hear more guards gathering in the dark. Why were there so many of them? Why was she always drawing them out?

Why was she always in the wrong place at the wrong time?

"Where's that damn manhole?" Dill hissed.

Nobody knew—they'd gotten turned around in the dark. So they stopped running, finally, trying to get their bearings.

"Boss..." Small said, and Elanil looked to see where he was pointing.

Four men were converging on their location, dark uniforms just barely visible as shadows in the night. Two more were coming from the opposite direction.

Their options were rapidly diminishing.

Guns glittered, reflecting the faint moonlight from above. Elanil reached for the primewood in her pocket, getting ready to Invest.

But before she could do anything, four balls of brilliant blue light shot out from Dill's hands. Elanil shielded her eyes from the glare as the lightning balls flew at the guards, hitting them and sending them flying backwards ten feet. They landed on the ground in a clatter, dazed, light playing over them.

Now Elanil's night vision was truly gone. Next to her, the outline of Dill slumped, shivering as he fell to the ground. Shot caught him, holding him up.

"No more," Dill said, his voice shaky, his hands trembling. "That's all I can do. We have to go."

Shot nodded. "Come on."

He let Dill lean on him as they stumbled down the street, heading away from both sets of guards. They ducked into an alley, and Elanil could hear the remaining guards pursuing.

Soon they found themselves in a large, dark square. Dim lights ringed a circular platform in the center of the square, and a swirling oval of light was floating in the middle of the platform. It looked like the gate, the one she and Rylan had come through from the surface earlier.

Shouts sounded from all around, guards roused via radios. She could hear them converging on the square—they'd be surrounded in moments.

"What should we do?" Elanil asked.

"Through there," Rylan said, pointing at the swirling portal.

"I don't think that's a good idea," Small said.

"No time," Dill breathed, barely able to stand. Expending that much magic must have really taken it out of him. "We have to—" He stumbled, and Shot caught him, holding him up.

"Come on, guys," Shot said, supporting Dill as they made their way toward the gate. The sudden brightness hurt her eyes.

Elanil couldn't see Rylan's face. She wondered if he was as scared as she was. She could hear guards approaching from all around the square, shadows moving everywhere. Radio static hissed from somewhere nearby. Something glittered in the distance.

There was no other option—they had to go. There might be hundreds of Cothellon all around them, but they just couldn't see. So she ran, pulling Rylan along with her. The group crossed the open square quickly, Dill and Shot trailing close behind. Elanil swallowed as she approached the gate—it swirled in the night, looking like a portal to the Twins' true hell. What would be waiting on the other side? Would the guards follow them through? Would anyone survive the journey?

It didn't matter. They had to go. They had no choice.

She jumped through the gate.

Ice washed over her, sending shivers down her spine. She blinked, her eyes trying to adjust to the room she found herself in.

She'd been here before.

It was the gate chamber in Fennas Elenathon, on the surface of Earth. It was where she and Rylan had been tied up on the chairs, the place where Elanil had performed a little tap dance to Invest her wood. She smiled, remembering the look on that officer's face.

They were back. Which might be a problem.

Rylan looked at her strangely, as if he didn't know who she was. He put a hand to his head, blinking rapidly.

"Are you okay?" Elanil asked.

He tapped his head. "I'm fine, I think." He didn't sound very convincing. The gate seemed to affect him every time they passed through. How much more of it could he take?

The others came through one at a time, shivering as they appeared. Dill was last, still leaning on Shot for support.

"Get away from the gate!" Dill said. "They're coming after us!"

Sure enough, a shot rang out and a bullet flew through the gate, hitting the far wall. Everyone flinched, but at least the wall didn't explode. The gun wasn't a mergegun.

Thank the Twins for simple blessings.

"This way!" Rylan shouted, running toward the front door.

But the door burst open and three people strode in, and Rylan skidded to a stop. Elanil recognized one of them immediately—it was the woman officer, the one she'd danced in front of. She had a massive gun in her arms, looking for all the world as if it were her favorite possession. And two men were with her, each carrying guns of their own.

None of them looked very happy.

TWENTY-TWO

JUST AS ORYM HAD PROMISED, it didn't take Arra and the others long to reach their destination. Fennas Elenathon, Gateway to the Stars. The great hole in the earth.

Except they couldn't get in.

They couldn't even *see* it, actually. One moment they were walking through the forest, and the next they had run into an invisible wall. Beyond the wall was nothing—just more forest. And try as they might, they couldn't move any further.

"So this is the forcefield?" Arra asked.

Orym nodded, fiddling with his radio. He'd been trying for the past few hours, but he hadn't been able to get in contact with anyone.

"So now what?" Arra asked.

Orym looked around. "We wait, I guess, and hope I can get through to Dillon. They have to drop the forcefield any time they need to let someone in, so maybe we'll get lucky."

Get lucky? What kind of a plan was that? Arra set her things down. "I'm not just going to stand here doing nothing."

Then she heard the unmistakable sound of footsteps coming from somewhere out in the forest. It sounded like people—a lot of them.

"What was that?" she asked.

"We may have company," Orym said.

"I'm going to check it out."

She had scaled a nearby tree before anyone could object, balancing on a slender branch near the top. She'd been hoping the vantage point would let her see through the force-field to whatever lay beyond, but it didn't. There was nothing there—only forest extending out into the distance.

Orym had mentioned this before, but she hadn't realized just how powerful the forcefields were. They could render anything inside them completely invisible, yes, but it wasn't just that. They could also render new surroundings to take their place.

It must require a powerful mage to make it all possible.

Footsteps sounded again, all around her. She turned, jerking about so sharply that she almost lost her balance in the tree. Cursing at her stupidity, she looked in the other direction.

An army was approaching. Hundreds upon hundreds of Cothellon soldiers, just like the ones she'd seen in Sylranth-eas, were moving toward their location. How could they know she and the others were here? The little group had moved through the forest as silently as they always did, not drawing attention to themselves. They couldn't have been heard.

Were the soldiers here for some other reason?

She glanced upward at the city, noting that it seemed smaller. It had *risen*, she realized, but that wasn't all.

There were two more cities in the sky next to it.

They really were converging like Orym had said. How

many were there? Seven, he had said. Seven cities spread across the sky.

And soon all of them would be above this forest.

Arra shuddered. Time was drawing short.

But right now they had bigger problems. Arra climbed down the tree, taking care to be as quiet as possible.

"Orym," she whispered, "there's an army coming."

"Cothellon?" he asked, matching her whisper. Lhoris and Imra drew closer.

Arra nodded. "Hundreds of them."

Orym looked out at the forest, out at where she knew the enemy was approaching. What should they do? Surely Orym had some kind of a plan, a contingency for this kind of thing. He'd been working on this for years—centuries, in fact. He would certainly know what to do.

Orym took a breath. "We may be fucked," he said.

Arra frowned.

That was not the response she'd been expecting.

"WHY IS THIS MAN HERE?" Grathgor asked. He was looking at Trey with an annoyed expression. Trey didn't know how he knew Grathgor's name—it was just there in his mind, waiting for him. He winced as Quynn squeezed his arm tightly.

"He's here to show off," Morgian said. She was a stately looking elf, blonde hair perfectly coifed on top of her head.

"This is Trey," Quynn said. "My...son."

"Oh, he's *that* project," Argus said. "Did it finally work?"

"In a manner of speaking."

An elven woman strode into the room just then. She was of middling height, with long dark hair and green eyes and wearing a bright red dress. The fabric hugged her body tightly, showing off her curves. Like all elves, her ears were pointed. She wore no jewelry that Trey could see.

He found her strangely erotic, and familiar. Why would that be? He'd certainly never met a woman quite like *this* before. Still, there seemed to be something unusual about her. Something his foggy mind couldn't understand.

Suddenly her name popped into his head, unbidden. This was Lorelei. And with her name came more: she was the Cundu, the supreme leader of the Cothellon elves.

She was the lady in charge of everything.

She looked at him suddenly, green eyes narrowing. He could feel those eyes piercing into his very soul.

"What is the meaning of this?" she asked, still staring at him, eyes unblinking. Trey didn't know if she was talking to him or to somebody else.

Next to him, Quynn cleared his throat. "I have only recently reacquired the boy," he said. "He needs to remain on a short leash."

Lorelei walked forward, red high heels clicking on the Council Room floor. She approached Trey until she was standing mere inches from him, still staring deeply into his eyes. Trey found himself licking his lips. He felt an erection growing.

"Stop that," Quynn hissed.

"Fine," Lorelei said, spinning and marching back to the front of the room. Quynn relaxed his grip on Trey's arm.

"Does anyone know," Lorelei said, turning to face the Small Council again, "where Orym has gone?"

Nobody answered. The room was completely silent.

She sighed. "We must assume he has defected, then. He has managed to keep his intentions concealed for a very long time. I fear what his plan might be. Nevertheless, we must proceed. Grathgor, please report."

Grathgor stood. "The cities are converging on schedule," he said. "Initial diagnostics are being run as we speak, but the real tests must wait until the Conjunction is finalized. As of now"—he checked his watch—"we are forty-six hours from the event."

"And the planet bore?"

"The site has been well maintained. I do not anticipate any issues with the device."

"I trust there will not be," Lorelei said. "You all have your jobs to do. I suggest you get to it."

She stared daggers around the room.

"Just one more thing," she said, turning to Quynn. "Just what in the absolute *fuck* did you think you were doing today?"

Her voice wasn't any louder than it had been before, but there was a new intensity there.

She seemed *very* dangerous.

Quynn shifted uncomfortably. "My lady," he said, "are you referring to the incursion at Sylrantheas?"

"Yes, I'm referring to the *incursion*," she spat. "Just what in the name of the Twins did you think you were accomplishing there? We've avoided outright attacks against the Eldrim for our *entire* history, and you saw fit to break that two days before our plan is complete? Using the Remnant to hurt them is one thing—we've been doing that for centuries. But attacking them yourself? You crossed a line."

"The Eldrim are weak," Quynn said, his voice faltering slightly. "They barely fought back, and their little town is destroyed now. There will be no repercussions."

Lorelei stepped forward, approaching Quynn. Her glare looked like it could melt the wall. "You underestimate the Eldrim," she said. "Silanar in particular. You chose the wrong elves to antagonize. Now I've been forced to mobilize an army

—something the Cothellon have *never* had to utilize—all because of *you*." She closed her mouth, still glaring at Quynn. Trey found himself transfixed by her lips, full and red like her dress. She leaned in even closer. "You have no idea what is at stake. This plan cannot fail because of you."

Then, inexplicably, Lorelei kissed Quynn full on the lips. Trey could see that Quynn was as surprised as he was, but he leaned in, relishing the kiss. Trey could see their tongues working furiously together. He felt like he should look away, but he couldn't. His erection began again.

The grip inside Trey's mind loosened for a brief moment, while they were kissing. It felt like a breath of fresh air, like the sun coming out after a long storm. Then the kiss ended, and his mind returned to the way it had been—clutched by something malevolent.

His father.

Lorelei pulled away, the kiss over. The rest of the Council members were averting their eyes awkwardly.

"What is this?" Lorelei asked, pulling something from Quynn's hand. Quynn started forward as if to grab it back, but she turned her glare on him and he stood down.

"The Book of Amplification," Quynn said. "Silanar had been keeping it all these years. This one was using it." He gestured toward Trey.

Lorelei glanced at Trey, then looked down at the Book in her hand. "I'll be keeping this."

Quynn didn't look very happy about that.

Lorelei looked at Trey, then, and he felt the full weight of her stare. "Train him, if you can," she said. "Perhaps he can be of use to us if the Eldrim resist. Train him now—tonight."

"Yes, my lady," Quynn said, bowing.

Lorelei turned and made her way toward the exit at the front of the room.

"My army will wipe out the Eldrim in the area once and for all," she said. "It was not my wish to destroy so many fellow elves, but you forced my hand." She glanced at Quynn. "I hope you're satisfied."

She left, and Trey could feel everyone finally breathe.

TWENTY-THREE

THE WOMAN OFFICER raised her gun and pointed it at Elanil. "You," she said. "Get your hands up."

Elanil obliged—but first, she snagged a chip of prime-wood, hiding it between two fingers.

"Who are you?" the woman asked. "What's your name?"

"Who are *you*?" Elanil asked, feeling impertinent. She'd been shot at enough in the past week that she was growing decidedly tired of it.

"Her name is Marissa," Rylan said.

"What?" Elanil asked. "How do you know that?"

Rylan pointed. "Name tag."

Oh. He was right, Elanil saw. Marissa was wearing a black name tag affixed to the breast of her navy-blue shirt. What kind of evil Cothellon wore a *name tag*?

"You can read," Marissa said. "Very good. Now who the hell are *you*?"

"Well," Elanil said, shifting sideways so she would be closer to Rylan, "my name is Elanil. This is Rylan. We really enjoyed your hospitality last time, so we thought we'd come back!"

Marissa narrowed her eyes. "You've certainly developed a mouth since last we met."

Elanil glared at her and took another step to the right. "I saw a girl die today," she said. "One of you Cothellon killed her. There was a lot of blood."

Marissa frowned. "Which means you were in yet another place you should not have been. Who *are* you, and why were you there?"

Elanil glanced at Rylan, saw that he had a piece of dark-prime wood in his hand. He nodded ever so slightly, and she flashed him a smile.

"Now!" she shouted, dipping her knees in a plié. Investment powered up her primewood and she wasted no time, burning the wood and exerting her Will. Next to her, Rylan was doing the same thing. They weren't holding hands, this time.

There were three Cothellon in the room: Marissa and two men that were flanking her. Marissa seemed the most dangerous, so Elanil focused on her first. She Willed the woman backwards, hoping to fling her hard against the wall.

But nothing happened.

"What—" Elanil started, but Marissa's hand was tightening on the trigger of her gun.

"Didn't work," Rylan whispered. "I tried to raise her, but—"

"I tried to throw her back."

"So we—"

"We interfered with each other, somehow. Why? I thought our magic worked *together*."

"I don't know what you're blabbing about," Marissa said, "but if you don't shut up I *will* shoot you." She touched her ear. "Mission, I've got intruders through Gate 1A. It's those two kids again, but they brought friends this time." She listened for a moment. "Yes, sir." Then she returned her hand to her gun, addressing Elanil once again. "I'm bringing you in. Come with me."

As if to punctuate her words, more Cothellon men started filing into the gate room. Soon there were ten armed guards, or soldiers, or whatever they were—all with guns pointing at Elanil and her group.

"Okay," she said. "We'll come with you. Don't shoot." But she glanced at Rylan as she said it, then flicked her eyes toward the big gun in Marissa's hand.

Rylan took her meaning.

They both had wood chips in their hands in a flash, and Elanil twirled, infusing hers with power. Then she lashed out with leafrunning magic again. Except this time she didn't try to touch Marissa, or any of her lackeys. This time, she went for an inanimate object. Maybe the magic would work better this way. Maybe they wouldn't cancel each other out like they had before. She used her magic to pull at the thing that was standing between her and freedom.

She went for the guns.

All ten guns instantly flew out of everyone's hands, sailing upwards or sideways into the air. The Cothellon gaped as they watched their weapons fly away under the control of magic.

Elanil felt herself swell with pride as she exercised her Will, splitting it into ten tiny parts and using each to control a gun. Only, something wasn't right. Something about the movement was wrong.

The guns weren't doing *precisely* what she wanted them to do.

They moved erratically, zooming and flying about the room, hurtling over and over in the air. Elanil concentrated, trying to reign them in, trying to get them to follow her magical Will, but it didn't work.

Actually, it made it *worse.*

One of the guns fired. The loud *bang* startled everyone, most of all Elanil. She hadn't Willed the trigger to move. Why had it done that? Then her eyes widened in alarm as she saw what *else* the guns were doing.

They were going crazy, zipping around in random arcs. Several soldiers ducked as the guns came sailing through the air. One of them actually hit Marissa, but she shrugged the blow off and made a grab at it. The gun was going too quickly, though—it was gone before she could grasp it. All around the room, the guns were moving and moving. Elanil could feel them in her head, but the movements were incredibly wrong.

What was going on?

She tried to burn another piece of primewood, increasing the force of her Will to bring the guns under control. But that just made it worse—two of them fired, bullets hitting a pipe and a rack of electronics behind her. She could hear a hissing sound as the pipe began emitting steam. Next to her, Rylan had his teeth gritted. He was trying just as hard as she was to make the guns obey.

Was Rylan's magic interfering with her own? Instead of canceling it out, like it had when she'd tried to move Marissa, was it making it random, uncontrollable?

Yes. That must be it. But they'd used co-magic like this before, with the bucket and the fire. And again, getting out of jail. It had worked before. What was different this time?

Elanil jumped to the side to escape a rapidly moving firearm, narrowly avoiding being smacked in the face by a hunk of metal. Around her, more of the guns were firing, the sound deafening in the enclosed space. She dodged again, and this time she tripped over Rylan. She reached out reflexively, grabbing his arm to steady herself.

And just like that, the guns stopped careening about the room.

Elanil watched them go with an open mouth, unconsciously doing a little can-can kick to Invest another piece of wood. The ten bits of her mind were still connected to the guns, but something was different this time. There was a new power there, a second power. Rylan was there. Now that she was touching him, she could *feel* him.

And she could work *with* him.

Now the guns were spiraling in perfect arcs around the room, a beautiful ballet of steel. Elanil moved them side-to-side, as always, while Rylan was moving them up and down. The result was an intricate pattern of movement, a braid of metal, a helix of burnished steel. Elanil envisioned trails behind each gun, flying in the air behind them as they moved.

It was beautiful.

"We have to *touch* each other," Elanil breathed, and Rylan gave her an unreadable look. Was he *blushing*?

That was it, though. That was all it took. They could perform magic together, but only if they were touching. She remembered the bucket now. The magic had only failed when Rylan had fainted, dropping her hand.

It was all so simple.

But now that they had the guns under control, what should they *do* with them? The Cothellon were straightening now, no longer having to dodge bullets and errant guns. Now they were glaring at Elanil and the others. Now they were pulling knives out, or just plain fists. Now they were advancing on them, murderous intent in their eyes.

Now they were in trouble.

Elanil gestured with her left hand, the hand holding the

primewood. The gesture wasn't strictly necessary, but she found it helpful for guiding her Will. Plus it just looked cool. The ten soldiers were still approaching warily, hands and knives out, ready to attack. They were moving slowly, though. They didn't know what magic Elanil and her friends were capable of.

Well, then. It was time for a demonstration.

She flicked her fingers lazily, and all the Cothellon flew up into the air.

She heard shrieks and exclamations as the soldiers floated upwards, arms and legs mingling with the guns in an intricate pattern, rotating around and around the room about ten feet up. She saw fear in the Cothellon's eyes. Even Marissa was afraid. Being disarmed was one thing, but now they had no control of their bodies at all. Elanil could only imagine what must be going through their heads.

She made a fist and twisted it, and the rotation grew faster. She saw flashing eyes and teeth, steel and navy blue and hair and a few knives that had come loose. Everything was twirling quickly now, a whirlwind of things. She'd never done this with leafrunning, before. She hadn't thought of it before. Always she had moved herself, or maybe one other thing. Leafrunning for her had always been a joy, a dance, flying fleetly through the roofs of trees.

But now—now leafrunning was a *weapon*.

She was still holding Rylan's arm, and now she slid her fingers down to grasp his hand. It was warm, that hand, and she could feel his pulse. He flashed a grin at her, his face flushed, and she felt him exercise his magic.

That's when everything started moving *up*.

The maelstrom of bodies and guns and knives twirled faster and faster, rising higher and higher in the vast gate chamber. Their passage was forming a wind now, a tornado of elves and air. Elanil laughed as she increased the power, easily flexing her Will in a vortex of motion.

Faster.

Faster.

Faster.

She felt Rylan clenching her hand, and she kicked her feet out again, Investing yet another chip of wood. And just for a second, she caught a glare from Marissa, the Cothellon officer. The look in the woman's eyes was pure hate, pure evil. She wanted them dead. She wanted them captive. She wanted them *something*, anything but here. She hated Eldrim scum and humans and the world they lived in. Marissa hated everything.

All this Elanil saw in the brief meeting of their eyes.

And Elanil remembered. She pictured Con, saw the blood pouring from her skin. Saw the death in that girl's eyes. Saw the way the dark elves worshipped it. She remembered the senselessness of it. How much Rylan had loved that girl. How much pain the Cothellon had caused.

She remembered all of it, and she wanted it *done*.

And through her link with Rylan, she could feel him thinking the same thing.

The tornado above them whirled faster and faster, and a high-pitched whine entered the room, vibrating the metal and electronics and Elanil's teeth. Wind whipped through her hair, and she felt as if there was an electric charge to the air, flooding through her senses. The elves up above were just a blur now. They were moving hopelessly fast.

Then Elanil nodded at Rylan. Both of them gestured, their free hands making a flicking motion, as if trying to shake off excess water. The sound of shearing metal filled the room, and the ceiling burst apart into massive fragments. Steel and cement and rebar and plaster shredded upwards and out, revealing a star-swept sky. And the tornado of elves—those terrible Cothellon—blasted out of the chamber and into the vast space beyond, flying hundreds and hundreds of feet, flying as far as she could push them, propelled by Elanil's rage.

She listened to their screams diminish in the night, a sickly grin creasing her face.

The guards and their guns were gone.

The room was quiet. They were saved.

The wood ran out, then, flashing into dust and flying from her hand. Elanil drew in a deep breath, feeling suddenly very exhausted. Her emotions were wild—she felt elated, angry, weak, and...disgusted with herself.

She'd never killed anybody before.

She released Rylan's hand, saw her thoughts mirrored in his eyes. "We had to," he whispered. She nodded slowly. He was right.

It was self defense. Pure, powerful defense.

They'd had no choice.

"Holy shit," Dill said. "I've never seen anything like that before."

"Why didn't you tell us you could do that?" Small asked. The short boy was gaping.

"We didn't know," Elanil said. She was still picturing the soldiers, hearing their screams. Had they *needed* to die? Had she needed to be so violent? She shared another look with Rylan, unspoken communication passing between them.

Yes, she knew then. Yes. They had needed to deal with the Cothellon soldiers decisively. They had needed to make a stand.

And besides—there would be more Cothellon still to come.

"Well," she heard a voice say, and her eyes snapped to the

front door of the building. It was gaping open, and there was no ceiling above it—Elanil and Rylan had destroyed the ceiling. There was a man standing there. A very tall man. An almost *handsome* man, if she was being honest. The man took a step inside the shell of the building, his eyes bright with merriment. "Have little children come to play with me?"

Then his eyes got hard, and a silvery bubble snapped into place around Elanil. There was one around Rylan, too, and around Dill and Shot and Small.

They were all trapped.

It was a bubble of energy. A forcefield. Magic wrapped them in a silvery cocoon, and Elanil knew they were in very deep trouble.

The tall man took a step forward, and Elanil was suddenly cognizant of just how *big* he was. He towered over them, his hair slicked back and dark, his smile revealing perfect teeth. There was a power about him, an aura.

Elanil suddenly felt very, very afraid.

"Who the fuck are *you*?" Rylan shouted up at him from behind his silvery shell. Elanil shot him a glare. Why would he antagonize this obviously powerful person?

"Forcefinder Elion," the man said, his voice rich and elegant and strangely quiet. "I saw what you just did to Marissa. Very impressive, for such little ones."

Rylan didn't reply.

Elion took another step forward and gave a great rippling sigh. Then he flicked a finger to his ear. "Yes, Mission," he said. "I will be killing them now."

TWENTY-FOUR

TREY TRUDGED through endless white corridors, Quynn gripping his elbow tightly. His mind felt even foggier than before. He was unable to put coherent thoughts together. The unending whiteness of the corridors mesmerized him. He didn't think to wonder where they were going—he didn't care.

He lived to serve.

They reached their destination, walking through an unmarked door and entering what appeared to be a small apartment. It was austere—the walls were white, and the apartment was filled with clean, white furniture of a design Trey hadn't seen before. A bed was positioned against one corner, a chair against another. It was small, but it seemed functional. Everything looked like it belonged on a spaceship from one of his science fiction books. Trey was pleased to realize he could still recall his books through the fog in his mind.

Lorelei was sitting at a small white table on a small white chair, her legs crossed daintily. She looked resplendent in that form-fitting red dress of hers. She'd been eating something, and she pushed the plate aside when they entered, taking a drink of water and standing up.

"Quynn," she said, walking up to the man, "why do you make me chastise you in front of the others?"

Quynn hung his head. "It's these...urges," he said. "Sometimes I can't control them."

Lorelei clicked her tongue in disapproval. "You're better than that," she said, stepping forward and placing a hand on his crotch. "I know you can have *great* control when you want to."

Quynn swallowed uncomfortably, looking over at Trey. Trey just stared back, his mind swirling with purple fog. He was beyond caring.

"Is this...appropriate, my lady?" Quynn asked.

Lorelei sighed and stepped back, removing her hand. "No, I suppose it isn't," she said. "But when have you ever been concerned with propriety?" She sat back down in her chair and picked up her fork, toying with her unfinished food. Trey just stood there, Quynn's hand still on his elbow.

"Quynn," Lorelei said after a moment, "do you think the plan will succeed?"

"I do not know, my lady," Quynn said. He was standing very stiffly.

Lorelei eyed him. "But surely you *want* it to succeed. Do you not yearn to escape this dreadful world?"

Trey watched as Quynn nodded slowly. "Yes," his father said, baring his teeth in a rictus grin. "I very much want that."

"Aren't you at all curious about where we're going?" She picked up a piece of food—it looked like some kind of fish—and brought a bite of it to her mouth.

Quynn cleared his throat. "I trust my lady."

"You probably shouldn't," she said, taking the bite of fish. She chewed and swallowed and took a drink from her water glass, managing to look perfectly regal the entire time.

God, she was beautiful.

"Where we are going," she said, "you will be treated well."

Quynn bowed slightly, his body still stiff. Trey looked at the floor, suddenly bored by the whole thing. His mind was running in endless circles of nothing.

"This fish is quite good, you know," Lorelei said. "I have it brought up from the surface. Transmuted food has never quite agreed with me, you see. Something about it rings false. I can have the chef bring in more, if you two are hungry?"

Neither of them responded.

"Very well," Lorelei said, putting her fork down daintily.

She was gorgeous, in a haughty sort of way. And still so familiar. Trey couldn't put his finger on it. She stood up again, and Trey watched her dress slide perfectly over her body as she moved. She had ample hips, and her breasts—Trey found himself intensely wanting to touch them, to taste them.

He felt blood flowing to his groin.

Lorelei stepped over to Trey, looking up at him with piercing green eyes, her lips red and glistening. "Quynn," she said, still looking at Trey, "don't ever give me another reason to reprimand you." Her body was just inches away from Trey —he longed to reach out and touch her. Quynn cleared his throat to reply, but Lorelei continued. "If you do," she said to Quynn, "I'll be forced to kill you. I'm sure you understand."

Quynn opened his mouth, then shut it, bowing. "Yes, my lady," he said stiffly. He turned to go, pulling Trey along.

"Leave him," Lorelei said.

Quynn looked at Trey, then at Lorelei. "My lady?"

"You heard me."

Quynn swallowed, looking again at Trey, a confused expression on his face. Then he bowed. "Of course, my lady," he said. "But I will stay nearby. His leash must be maintained."

Lorelei nodded at him, and Trey's father left the room. Trey felt the cloud in his head dissipate as the man left, his hold loosening slightly. Trey took in a deep breath. He felt himself able to think again, at least a little. It was amazing.

"So, Trey," Lorelei said, still agonizingly close, "how do you find my apartment?" She looked up at him and quirked an eyebrow.

Trey's mind was still a bit fuzzy. "Um," he said, looking around the room. "It's...different, I guess. I like it."

Lorelei put a hand on his chest, toying with a button on his shirt. "And how do you find me?"

She stepped forward, her body pressing firmly against Trey. He could smell her, cinnamon mixed with the fresh fish she'd been eating. He ran his hand through his hair unconsciously, trying to look away, but unable to. He tried staring at her elven ears instead of her face, but even *they* were enough to turn him on.

What was wrong with him?

Lorelei stood up on tip-toes, her face inches away from his. She met his eyes, dark hair framing her face. She didn't seem dangerous now. She wasn't giving any orders. She wasn't threatening to kill anyone. She was just there, standing in front of him, beautiful.

She kissed him.

Trey found himself returning the kiss passionately. Her tongue entered his mouth, exploring. He delighted in tasting her, feeling himself growing larger with every moment. Lorelei had her hands inside his shirt, feeling his chest. He reached out for her, his hands around her waist, pulling her close. She rubbed her chest against him, her crotch against his. Her mouth tasted spicy and sweet.

The fog in his brain lifted a bit, but a different kind of cloud replaced it.

Pure lust.

His hands roamed over her body as they continued to kiss, and Lorelei stepped backwards toward the white bed. Trey didn't understand what was going on, why he was feeling this way around this person who he'd just met. He felt like he *knew* her, somehow. Then all he could think about was her breasts and her mouth and her tongue. He reached down, pulling the tight red dress up and over her head, revealing her incredible body. She had managed to undo his shirt without ripping any buttons, and she helped him out of it, her hands running along his arms and stomach.

Then they were falling onto the bed, a tangle of limbs and hair and breath. Lorelei reached into his pants, and his head felt like it was ready to explode. Distantly, a part of him knew that Quynn was still in his head, probably knew what was going on right now. Weren't he and Lorelei a couple? Hadn't she been kissing *him* just minutes ago? None of it made sense. But Lorelei had his pants off, and she was pushing him inside her, and he was lost to the ecstasy of the moment.

Her elven body was perfect, every curve beautiful as her back arched and she cried out with pleasure. He thrust into her, his hands on her breasts, his mind gone. Her red lips were open as she laid there under him.

When it was over, they lay together in her bed. Trey was still having trouble thinking. He couldn't remember what he'd been doing yesterday, or even an hour ago. All he could think of was this beautiful, dangerous woman lying next to him.

Her legs were intertwined with his, her breasts perfectly round, her eyes perfectly green. She kissed him again, lightly.

"I should have shown you this form long ago," she said. "It seems to have improved your performance markedly."

What?

Trey didn't understand what she had meant by that. He reached up and stroked her hair, thinking it over. "What do mean?"

Lorelei shifted, moving up to straddle him in the bed. He lay on his back under her, marveling at her beauty. Her long hair was rumpled, trailing over one shoulder to fall on her breast. "I think you know," she said, a faint smile on her lips.

But Trey didn't know. He scooted backward, trying to get out from under her, but she stayed put, grinding her pelvis against his stomach. He could feel her warmth and her wetness. "I really don't understand," he said, his breathing coming faster. What was she doing to him?

"Oh, alright," Lorelei said, "if you insist." She tilted her head to the side and quirked an eyebrow.

And then she *changed*.

Her features slowly melded into something else—still pretty, but not the same. Her lips were thinner, her hair a bit shorter, her eyes still green. Even her breasts and hips got smaller, and her skin tone changed, growing lighter. The points on her ears smoothed out. Trey felt his heart start to race, beating faster and faster as he witnessed the change.

No. It couldn't be.

It was.

"Lora?" Trey asked, his voice coming out sounding strangled. His hands were on her legs—her new, human legs. His *wife* was sitting on him, naked. His wife, the love of his life. His wife, who had been taken from him.

"I thought you were taken for Civil Service?" he asked. He felt like the world was spinning around him.

Lora—Lorelei—laughed, the sound familiar to him now. "Oh, that?" she said. "I suspect Orym set that up. I went along with it for appearances. We don't want to disrupt the *Citizens* now, do we?" She laughed again, gesturing to the white apartment. "They took me right back here, to my home. My *real* home. Now, where were we?"

She leaned over him, human breasts dangling tantalizingly.

"Wait, wait," Trey said, pushing himself back so he could sit against the headboard. Lorelei moved with him, still sitting naked in his lap. "You're an *elf?*"

"Oh, let's not turn this into a question-and-answer session," she said, pouting. "I just wanted to have some fun. We're not actually married, you know." She moved her face in closer. "It was annulled right after the ceremony." Her fingers trailed a line down his chest. "Quynn thought it might help if you had a wife, someone like me. And it seems to have worked." She squirmed against him, and Trey felt himself getting hard again.

Then she pulled back. "You *are* a Prime Mage, right?"

Trey frowned, nodding. "Yes," he said, "but I can only do half the magic. And I'm weak."

Lorelei laughed, the sound tinkling in the stark white room. "Not from where I'm sitting," she said, slipping him inside her again.

Trey gasped. What was this woman thinking?

"What about Quynn?" he asked as she ground her hips up and down against him. "It looked like you two were"—he gasped again—"a couple." His breathing was ragged.

Lorelei shrugged as she moved on him. "He amuses me,"

she said, "as do you. You two have a lot in common, you know."

Trey couldn't imagine how that could be. "But we love each other," he said. "You're my wife." The bed was bouncing now, and Lorelei's eyes were closed. She raked his chest with her nails as she rode him, her breasts bouncing. He needed to stop this. He needed to—

He climaxed suddenly, for the second time that night. His mind went away for a long moment, blissfully away. Just gone. No more worries or fears. No more complications. No more strange father and purple fog. No more—

He opened his eyes and beheld Lora's green eyes watching him. No—Lorelei. That was her name.

"You were just an experiment," she said, patting his chest, beads of sweat on her brow. She lifted herself off of him and tilted her head again. As he watched, her face and body transformed back into the elf.

Back into Lorelei.

Trey sat forward. "An...*experiment?*"

Lorelei looked back at him as she got off the bed, her elven ass distractingly close. "He tried very hard, you know," she said. "To make you. I'm happy to know I was part of the solution, in the end." She bent down to retrieve her dress.

Trey launched himself off the bed, grabbing Lorelei and slamming her back against the table. The plate of half-eaten fish clattered away, her dress falling to the floor. Trey's hand was around her neck. He was no longer aware of their nakedness.

He was only thinking of one thing.

"How could it all be a lie?" he asked, his voice quivering, his body pressing her to the table. "How could you not have loved me?"

Lorelei looked at him, something like alarm flashing

briefly in her eyes. She put a delicate hand to his wrist, as if wanting to ward him off, but unsure how. "Come now," she said quietly, "you're hardly the worst thing I've done in my life." She blinked demurely, concern gone from her face.

Trey felt rage take hold of him. He squeezed her neck, his muscles clenching tightly. She lay against the table, unable to take a breath, her eyes wide. She slapped at him, but he held her firmly.

His wife, his bride. His lover and his friend. He looked into her green eyes and knew her for what she truly was—a manipulator and a liar. A powerful enemy.

An elf.

First Callan, then Quynn, and now her. His entire life had been a lie. All of it.

He pressed his hand harder around her neck, wanting her to die. He imagined the breath seeping out of her lungs, her eyes glazing over. Blood rushed through his veins as he strangled her, wanting nothing more than to brutally kill this liar, this vixen. This elf. Lorelei struggled frantically against him, but he did not relent.

It was time to end this part of the story.

Suddenly the door to the room slammed open, and Quynn strode in, shoving Trey away with a powerful arm. Trey lost his grip and his balance, falling hard onto the bed behind him.

"What is the meaning of this?" Quynn said, looking from one of them to the other. Lorelei was gasping on the table, her hand to her neck, naked breasts heaving.

Trey felt the fog close in around his mind, stronger this time. He struggled against it, but he could do nothing to resist. Quynn was too strong.

He tried to reason, his thoughts thick. He lay on the bed mutely, hearing Quynn and Lorelei talking as if from far away. If Quynn and Lorelei were elves, did that mean they were his parents? Had Trey been married to his own mother? No, that didn't make sense. She had called him an experiment, and Quynn had alluded to that, too. Trey thought back to the memories that had unlocked as he passed through the gate.

Yes, he remembered it now.

He remembered Quynn experimented on him, raising him as his son. Trying to get something out of him, but failing. Then the man must have done something with his magic to wipe out Trey's memory, and the process had repeated. Over and over again. But what had Quynn wanted from him?

Suddenly Trey knew the answer. Quynn had wanted a Prime Mage. *That* had been Trey's purpose. The man had experimented on him, trying different things in an attempt to draw the magic out. And it had finally worked, at least in part. But how had Quynn known that the magic was inside of Trey to begin with? Was it some kind of intuition?

And if Quynn wasn't his father, and Lorelei wasn't his wife—or his mother—what *was* Trey? Where had he come from? And another sobering thought:

How *old* was he?

"Have you had enough now?" Quynn was saying to Lorelei. "Or would you prefer conjugal visits? I'm sure I can arrange attempted murder again, too, if you like." Quynn's tone was snide, his mouth curled into a sneer.

Lorelei got up off the table, suddenly regal in her nakedness. She slapped Quynn hard across the face. "Never speak that way to me again," she said, her voice cold. She looked at Trey, her gaze flat, hard. "He has strength," she said. "I admire him for that. Get his clothes back on and train him. Now."

Quynn opened his mouth as if to reply, but obviously

thought better of it. "You heard her, *son*," he said to Trey. "Let's go."

The purple fog came thicker through his mind, and Trey found himself standing. His movements were not his own. "Thank you for a wonderful time," he said to Lorelei, bowing, his limp cock dangling between his legs.

Lorelei burst out laughing. "Isn't he a darling?" she said.

Trey was too far gone to care.

TWENTY-FIVE

"WHAT SHOULD WE DO?" Arra asked. Orym was just standing there, a frown on his face. He seemed frozen. Was the man losing his nerve after all this time?

There was an army approaching all around them. This was the wrong time to lose their nerve.

Orym finally looked at her, as if snapping out of a reverie. "I don't know, dammit," he said, banging his fist on the invisible forcefield. It fuzzed and hissed under his fist. "Ow." He pulled his hand back. "Remind me not to do that again."

Arra glared at him. She needed action. She needed to be doing something. Surely they wouldn't just stand here in the forest with an army on the way?

"You guys are pretty good with a bow, right?" Orym asked.

She heard a loud sound, then, off in the distance, coming from somewhere beyond the forcefield. It sounded like metal ripping, mixed with—screams? And gunfire? What was going on?

Then there was a loud crack of a branch breaking, and a soldier stepped into view from behind a tree, carrying a large gun. He looked surprised to see them, but he didn't pause long.

He opened fire.

SO THERE ELANIL WAS, trapped inside a silvery bubble made of magical energy, inside a room with a swirling gate but no ceiling, stuck in an invisible city in the middle of the forest, surrounded by probably hundreds of armed guards, staring at a tall, dark mage who was really rather good-looking, but was clearly about to kill her.

Just another day in paradise.

Any time she touched the forcefield surrounding her, she got a little *zap*, as if electricity were coursing through her finger. It tingled. She didn't like it.

How would she get out of this?

Forcefinder Elion—who looked like he probably should be wearing a long, black cape and maybe twirling a cane—strode forward with powerful steps. He was advancing toward Rylan, who was incessantly tapping the edge of his forcefield. Elanil thought she saw panic in his eyes.

She turned to check on the others. Small and Shot and Dill were trapped in forcefields of their own, and some of them were awfully tight. Shot's bubble was so close to his body, he could barely move at all. She could see him trying, though. He was struggling to move his arm without getting zapped too hard. Then he caught her staring and winked at her. Winked! Was he planning something?

She turned back to Elion. He had said he'd kill them—but how? With the forcefields? Maybe he could shrink them, crushing everyone into little bits of pulp. Maybe he could use them to electrocute everybody. Or maybe he'd just do what Elanil had done, and throw the forcefields a thousand feet away.

So, by Elanil's count, there were at least three ways to die.

Great.

"Hey, Elion!" Elanil said, hoping to distract him.

It worked.

Elion turned to her. "Who might you be?" he asked, rich voice rolling towards her.

"Elanil," she said. "Are you really making *five* forcefields at once?"

Elion nodded. "Of course."

"But that's incredible!" He looked like the sort of man who craved compliments.

"Why thank you, little one," Elion said. "In fact, I can produce far more than five fields at one time. For example, at this very moment I am also producing a field half a mile in diameter, and three hundred feet tall!"

"Wow!" Elanil exclaimed. "What for?"

"To surround this complex, of course. We must prevent little elves from ruining our plans, after all."

"Aw," Elanil said, glancing at Shot. "We didn't mean anything. We'd heard there was a powerful mage in here, and we wanted to meet him!"

Only an idiot would believe that line, but Elanil needed to do *something* to buy time. Shot was still moving, trying to get his arm into his back pocket. She kept hearing little *zaps* as he touched the forcefield surrounding him, his face grimacing. Was there something in his pocket?

Elion strode towards her. "Do you want to see something else?"

She hoped he was talking about magic. "Sure!" she said, keeping her voice chipper.

The forcefinder held out both hands in front of him, palms up. Two bright bubbles appeared above each hand, perfectly spherical, floating maybe six inches above his palms. He made a tossing motion with his right hand, as if throwing one of the spheres into the air. Sure enough, the sphere flew upwards, arcing over to the left. As it moved, he tossed the sphere that was in his left hand over to his right, pretending to catch it. Then a third sphere appeared, and soon he was juggling them in the air. His grin widened, displaying large white teeth.

Actually, it *was* pretty impressive.

"Wow," Elanil said. "How did you learn to do that?" She looked again at Shot and saw him bringing a piece of wood out from his pocket. Was he about to do magic? Darkprime magic?

Elanil tried to remember what Shot's power was. He was always using a weird dark gun—a mergegun, they had called it. The gun could shoot through *anything* using a power they called mergemelding.

Mergemelding.

That was Shot's power. But what did it mean? She turned back to Elion, but the mage had tracked her gaze. He'd seen Shot. Even now, he was doing something with his hands, probably preparing to squish Shot to death inside his forcefield.

But Shot had other plans.

He appeared to *fuzz*, his very being becoming slightly transparent.

Then he walked through the forcefield.

Elanil blinked. Had she really just seen that? Yes—there he was, outside his forcefield, his body still kind of half-there. Was it a trick of the starlight, or was Shot a bunch of mist, able to pass *through* objects?

Mergemelding. If guns could do it, why couldn't a *person*? It made sense.

But he wasn't done. Before Elion could react, Shot bounded over to Dill's forcefield, reached inside it, and pulled Dill out. Dill's body also sort of *fuzzed* as he passed through the forcefield. Now they were both outside the bubbles, and moving quickly. Elion was bringing his hands up, clearly preparing to create more forcefields or something even worse.

But Shot was just too fast.

He ran over to Rylan's forcefield next, and then he just kept running right on through it, pushing Rylan through ahead of him. They both *fuzzed* as they escaped. And now Dill and Shot and Rylan were free, but Elanil and Small were still trapped.

And Elion was getting very angry.

"Little children," he rumbled, "do not play these games with me."

He cast a forcefield, finally, a bubble around Shot. But that, Elanil knew, had been a bad decision. Shot didn't even notice the field—he just *fuzzed* right through it and kept on running. Elion roared, infuriated. He cast bubble after bubble around Shot, but the boy just kept burning darkprime wood and running through.

You couldn't stop a mergemelder, Elanil realized. You couldn't trap them. You probably couldn't hurt them at all. They could easily be the most powerful mages in the world.

Elion finally seemed to realize his mistake. He turned, probably planning to encapsulate somebody else. He moved to face Rylan, and Rylan brought his hands up over his face, cringing.

"No!" Elanil screamed. Where was Dill? Why wasn't he helping? Why wasn't Shot freeing *her*?

Elion didn't make another forcefield this time. Instead, he picked Rylan up.

By his neck.

Rylan gurgled, gasping, trying to kick at the tall man and having no luck at all. Elion was angry. He was going to kill Rylan with his bare hands.

"Stop it!" Elanil shouted. She beat her fists against her forcefield, heedless of the pain shooting through her skin. "Let him go!"

Shot had gotten Small free now, and he was finally coming for her. But then Shot's body became solid again, and he dropped dust from his hand. And he looked at her, and shrugged.

And passed out on the floor.

Shit. Shot had overused his magic. She'd seen this before, up in Planner Central. Dill had used too much shockstriking magic, and he had almost fainted from it. There was a limit, she knew. And Shot had passed it by.

This wasn't good. What could she do? Rylan was choking now just kicking feebly, not even making any noise. Elion was growling at him like a dog on the prowl. Shot was out cold, and Small had run over to the wall, fiddling with some electronics. Dill was nowhere. He'd disappeared.

Rylan was about to die, and there was nothing Elanil could do. She screamed something unintelligible, but it did nothing to help.

But then she saw something. Something glittering on a shelf. Something she could barely see, but something she recognized nonetheless.

It was a knife.

It must have escaped her tornado of magic. It must have belonged to one of the Cothellon she had killed, but it hadn't made the trip. It was still there, just lying peacefully on a shelf, about twenty feet away.

Pointing directly at Elion's back.

Elanil went to grab a piece of primewood. If she could figure out a way to Invest it, she could use leafrunning magic to throw the knife at Elion. Maybe kill him. Rylan had only seconds to live, she knew. She could see his eyes already closing, his face going purple. So she reached for the wood she knew was there.

But right at that moment, her forcefield *shrank*.

It collapsed into her, pushing at her skin, sending jolting shocks of electricity all through her. She couldn't move. She couldn't think. She couldn't do *anything* now—the shock was just too much. She could feel the forcefield pressing in on her, pushing her, trying to squeeze her to a pulp. This was it. Her final moments. Rylan and Elanil, both killed by a handsome evil mage.

Just another day in paradise.

But then a knife appeared in Elion's back, blood already spurting from the perfectly stabbed artery. And Dill stepped away, a grim smile on his face.

The knife, Elanil saw, was his.

Instantly the forcefield around Elanil winked off. Elion stumbled, dropping Rylan, and Dill was there in a flash to catch the boy. Elanil ran over to them, glancing at the knife she had intended to throw. It was still there, just sitting on the shelf.

She had failed. She hadn't been able to stop Elion.

But Dill, luckily, had.

"You okay?" he asked Rylan, who was coughing and gasping.

Rylan nodded. "How—" he started, but another spasm of coughing overtook him. "How did you do it?"

"Knife in my pocket," Dill said. "Some things don't need a magical solution."

As if to punctuate his statement, Elion chose that moment to finally keel over.

The man was dead.

TWENTY-SIX

ARRA DOVE behind a tree as the soldier opened fire, the others with her doing the same. Bullets and bark went flying as the soldier let his automatic weapon go, blanketing the area. Arra was beginning to wish the Eldrim had approved of guns. They would certainly have come in handy right about now.

She grabbed her new recurve bow, careful to avoid accidentally running into the forcefield she knew was right next to her. Nocking an arrow, she stuck her head out from behind the tree. The soldier was advancing, gun still in hand. He had a helmet on, but his face was unprotected—it would be an easy shot. She loosed, and the man went down with an arrow in the face.

Good riddance.

Orym, Imra and Lhoris came out from behind various trees, looking at her gratefully. "Nice shot," Orym said.

But that had only been the beginning. Arra could hear more soldiers trampling through the woods, breaking branches and talking amongst themselves. They didn't seem like a very disciplined bunch, and they certainly didn't respect the forest properly.

She could use that to her advantage.

But still, it was guns against arrows. It was a fight they couldn't win. Arra looked around. What could they do? They could climb trees, but the advancing soldiers weren't dogs or wolves or bears. They were elves, with deadly long-range weapons. Treeing themselves wouldn't work. Arra felt panic rising as she realized they were trapped. They were going to die here in the forest, trapped against a magical, invisible forcefield.

Suddenly there was a fuzzing sound, and half the forest turned into a shimmering white mist that dissipated as quickly as it had appeared. Had that been the forcefield? Arra reached a hand out tentatively to where she knew it had been. Nothing. She pushed her whole arm in—still, nothing happened. So she walked through it.

The forcefield was gone.

She saw that Orym had made the same discovery. "Their forcefinder must have dropped the shield," he said.

Arra could hear the army of soldiers getting closer. The men would be on them at any moment. "Let's go," she hissed. They set out through the trees with soldiers right behind them.

The forest didn't last long. Now that they were inside where the forcefield had been, the invisibility illusion was gone. Arra saw that the forest opened up into a vast earthen pit, with metal buildings and a huge claw-like contraption taking up most of the space.

This was Fennas Elenathon. The receiver site, Orym had called it. The place where the great city device got its power from the core of the planet. Arra marveled that the Cothellon had managed to keep its existence a secret for so long. But with invisibility magic at their disposal, there was no limit to their deceptive power.

She motioned for the others to keep moving. They ran down the slope of the pit, sprinting through the open area until they encountered the first of the metal buildings. Arra thought she had seen people moving about in the area during their descent. Armed guards, or soldiers. Cothellon.

Gunfire erupted from somewhere further away. Yes, there were definitely guards down there. But why were they shooting? Someone else was clearly in this little city, and the Cothellon didn't like it.

She motioned for everyone to get behind one of the buildings, blocking as much line of sight as possible. She knew it was only a matter of time before the guards in this area found them.

"So what's your plan?" she asked Orym.

"We need to do as much damage as we can to the device," he said. "Not the buildings, necessarily." He motioned toward the huge claw that towered above everything else. "That. If we can destroy it, or even damage it significantly, it'll delay the mission. That'll give us time to figure out how to end the Cothellon threat once and for all."

Arra snorted. "I don't know if you noticed," she said, "but there are hundreds of Cothellon out there, and more in here. And they have *guns,* while we have..." She lifted her bow and glared at him.

Then she heard a scream, coming from the big claw device.

It sounded like her sister.

"Elanil?" Arra said. Without waiting for Orym to respond, she started running toward the big machine.

SHOT WAS STILL OUT COLD. Rylan had recovered now only coughing a little bit. Elanil was still jittery from having been shocked so much by her collapsing forcefield. Elion was laying on the floor, dead. And Small was over by the wall, playing with the electronics.

"What now?" Elanil asked.

"We should go back through the gate," Dill said. "Planner Central is safer than this place."

Elanil nodded—he was probably right. She reached down to Shot. "I'll help carry him."

But then footsteps sounded, and uniformed Cothellon men appeared through the gate.

With guns.

"Maybe I was wrong," Dill said. "Maybe Planner Central isn't such a good idea."

"Hands up," one of the new arrivals said. He was a big man, a little heavyset, and his gun was big like he was. He didn't look very nice.

"Distract them," Dill whispered to her. "I'll stay with Shot."

It was as good a plan as any.

A bunch of machines fell off the wall in a resounding crash just then, wires and metal cascading to the floor. The soldiers all scrambled, ducking behind pieces of machinery, finding places to hide.

Small laughed. "Sometimes you don't even need an *electrical* solution! Now, uh, we should probably run."

Elanil could see that he was right.

They ran, and the soldiers weren't quite quick enough to follow.

She *was* a good runner, after all. Movement was her Way.

She led Rylan out of the building, ducking immediately to the side. But then the Cothellon reacted—not by shooting at them, but by running in pursuit.

And *they* were pretty quick, too.

So Elanil moved. She took a turn at random, barreling down an alley, Rylan close behind. She saw more of the Cothellon further back, guns up.

She ducked low, trying to present as small a target as possible. Maybe if she could just—there. She darted to the left, angling down an even smaller alley. She didn't remember the layout of this place, but hopefully the soldiers didn't, either. They were from the floating city—they didn't work down here.

Maybe she could lose them.

But then there was some kind of blue glow above her, and Elanil heard a voice ring out.

"Mage children," the voice said. "How very interesting."

A man was standing on the roof. He was dressed all in black, with a black hood around his face, and his eyes were glowing an eerie blue. The man lifted his hands and they, too, were glowing, crackling with some kind of blue lightning.

Creepy.

But Elanil knew this magic. She'd seen it before. This was shockstriking, the power Dill had used up in Planner Central. This was a new mage, blocking their path. And he was, from the looks of it, *very* powerful.

Great. Guns behind, magic ahead.

How could they escape?

The shockstriker released his magic. A big blue ball of brilliant light shot towards them, and Rylan slammed into her just in time to push her out of the way. She felt the breath burst out of her lungs as the energy blasted into the cement wall to their right, obliterating it. A cloud of disintegrated dust filled the air, obscuring everything for just a moment.

"Come on!" Rylan shouted, pulling at her. She followed.

Through the hole in the wall.

Then they ran and ran, angling through streets and alleys, just running endlessly, trying to get as far away as possible from the gun-toting guards and the mysterious mage. They kept running, and kept running, and soon they found themselves staring at an impossible situation.

It was a hole. The big, infinitely deep hole in the ground at the edge of the installation. The hole with the hundred-foot claws rearing upwards from beside it, with little orange and blue lights ringing it and hanging from the claws above. The hole was very wide, and there was no cover next to it. If they skirted around it, they'd be exposed for far too long.

They were trapped.

Elanil looked behind her. The guards that had been chasing her were far behind now. They weren't the best runners, what with all the guns and gear they were carrying. But the mage, that glowing shockstriker, *was* fast.

He was almost upon them.

Elanil could see a glowing smile, see his hands raised with light surrounded them. He was going to blast them again, she knew. They were going to die out here beside a bottomless pit.

Not the way she had wanted to go.

She turned again, looking back at the hole. There was a catwalk on it. A very narrow catwalk made of metal, forming a bridge across the chasm. It was probably for maintenance— it looked temporary, rickety. The bridge was divided into three segments, and it led right across the hole. They could jump on it, run across, and escape this metal city and hide in the woods nearby. It was just a hundred foot run to the trees, once they crossed the pit.

Easy.

"Go," Rylan said, pointing at the bridge. "Let's get out of here."

"Be careful," Elanil said.

Rylan nodded, and she set out.

Surely nothing bad could happen as they crossed the bridge.

RYLAN WATCHED as Elanil got onto the bridge. It seemed fairly sturdy, at least, if a bit small. He began to follow her, watching the big pit below. There were lights, down there, twinkling, mesmerizing.

But before he could get on the bridge, a blast of lightning hit him in the leg. He went down, hitting the ground hard. His leg *hurt*, electricity making the muscles contract painfully.

He struggled to get up as another ball of lightning struck the bridge itself. The structure rattled and Elanil screamed, nearly losing her balance and falling into the pit. She grabbed the handholds on the bridge tightly, alarm growing in her eyes. She was already at the middle of the bridge, right in the center of the deep hole. She turned to look at him, and he could see the panic written on her face.

Rylan tried to get up, but his leg wasn't working very well. It looked like Elanil was trying to decide if she should return to him or continue on. He tried again and actually managed to stand, balancing poorly on the leg that had been hit.

Glancing behind him, he saw the shockstriker standing only a hundred feet away. The darkmage's face was glowing, making him look like some kind of demon.

The man raised his fist and sent another ball of lightning out. Rylan flinched, but the lightning wasn't aimed at him.

It was aimed at the bridge.

"No!" Rylan shouted, but it was too late.

The structure failed, its segments breaking apart from each other. And then it fell, with Elanil still on it.

Rylan watched as she dropped into the bottomless hole in the ground, screaming the whole way down.

TWENTY-SEVEN

TREY WAS SWEATING. Quynn had been working him hard, teaching him the basics of darkprime magic. It was a whole new set of things to learn—new rules, new techniques, new possibilities.

Except, as before, he could only do half of it. Darkprime used the same types of wood that regular lightprime magic used, except the wood was weird: dark and strangely shiny, almost like metal. Quynn had refused to go into detail about where it came from.

They had experimented at first, seeing what Trey could do. In the beginning, it had been difficult for Trey to follow along, or even communicate at all—the fog in his mind had been too thick. So Quynn had been forced to ease up until Trey had been able to participate in the training.

Birch and spruce, ash and hemlock, elm and fir. Those were the woodpairs Trey could use, the same as it had been with the Eldrim. It had only been a short while, but Quynn had already taught him what those woods could do. It was a lot to remember, and Quynn hadn't had a handy chart like Arra had given him.

Trey tried repeating it in his mind, hoping it would stick. The fog was making it hard to think. Birch and spruce were for transmuting—the ability to transform objects into food and water and other things. Trey didn't see how that would be very useful in a fight, which was clearly what Quynn was preparing him for.

Ash and hemlock were for forcefinding, which let him create forcefields. Trey had learned that this was what shielded the whole city, although that was done not by a single mage, but by many darkmages working together. Trey was so weak that it wasn't very useful—he could only create very small forcefields that winked out after a second.

So that left elm and fir. Shockstriker. This was the fun one, balls and bolts of lightning. Or at least, it was supposed to be balls and bolts. So far, Trey had only managed tiny little jolts of electricity.

He needed the Book of Amplification.

"You're really bad at this, aren't you?" Quynn said after they'd been at it for a while. They were practicing on the roof of a skyscraper, high above the city. The city lights glittered below and beyond, tantalizing Trey. He wondered what it would feel like to fall, to watch those lights rush up to meet him. To end this perpetual agony in his mind.

Trey realized Quynn had spoken to him. He was trying to stop thinking of the man as his father. Quynn had refused to answer any questions about himself or Lorelei, but Trey knew that he wasn't related to those two. He couldn't be.

"I can't help it," he said, finally responding to Quynn. "I guess I was born like this."

"You're not trying hard enough," Quynn said.

Just then, Lorelei stepped out onto the roof. She was wearing a different outfit than before: shiny leather pants and a tight-fitting leather jacket, all in red. She strode toward them confidently, no evidence of their prior encounter on her face. "There's been a disturbance on the ground," she said, addressing Quynn.

"What is it?" he asked.

"Eldrim," she said. "Just some kids. But they managed to take out the forcefinder on duty, so now the whole thing is unprotected. I'm going down there to take care of it myself."

"Wouldn't you prefer I go?" Quynn asked.

Lorelei eyed him. "You've done enough damage already. Before I left, I wanted to check on your progress."

Quynn looked at Trey. "He's weak, but he's improving with practice. We'll keep at it."

Trey hadn't realized he was improving. Maybe his lack of Will *was* something he could fix, with enough effort.

Maybe.

"Very well," Lorelei said, walking back to the door that led onto the roof. She opened it, then paused, turning back to Quynn. "Something about this timing is odd," she said. "Orym must be involved. Get Trey ready, and I don't mean just his power." She pointed to her head. "We may yet need him if this goes badly."

"Will you take the gate?" Quynn asked.

Lorelei shook her head. "No," she said, "never again."

Then she left.

Quynn turned and stared at Trey for a long moment, as if deciding how to proceed. Then he twisted his hand slightly, almost imperceptibly, and Trey felt the purple fog in his head increase a little bit. He suddenly felt very loyal. He would try harder. He would do better.

"Again," Quynn said.

RYLAN'S BREATH caught as he watched Elanil fall. Her hair was wild and her mouth was open as she screamed, falling faster than he would have believed possible. There was no bottom to this pit, not that he could see.

She was going to fall and fall and fall. And die.

He couldn't allow it.

Rylan didn't think—he just moved. A piece of wood was in his hand in a blink, and he was already exerting his Will through it.

The bridge stopped falling, already almost out of sight in the dimly lit pit. He could still hear Elanil screaming. He raised his hand, Willing the bridge to rise, and it did. It rose up and up, slowly but surely, until Elanil was above the hole in the ground.

Level with him.

She looked so scared. Tears were running down her face as she clutched the railing of the bridge, the metal segment spinning slowly in the air, no longer affected by gravity. The bridge itself had broken apart, and the segment she was on was short, not nearly wide enough to span the gap.

Rylan couldn't help any further. He couldn't move the bridge segment to him—he could only raise or lower it. His magic was too limited to save her on its own. There she was, floating above an impossibly deep hole in the ground, and he was the only thing stopping her from certain death. But he couldn't take her all the way.

Then he felt the wood starting to run out.

"Use your magic to move the bridge!" he yelled at her.

She shook her head. "I can't!" she shouted. "If we aren't holding hands, it doesn't work! You saw what happened earlier!"

He realized she was right. They couldn't work together to move the bridge unless they were physically touching each other. Rylan didn't know *why* it worked that way, but that's the way it was. He remembered the water bucket back in Sylrantheas, how it had veered wildly just as he was fainting. He remembered the guns in the gate chamber—they couldn't control them together, not unless they were touching each other.

It was a kind of co-magic, Rylan realized. There was some kind of connection, a blending of the souls. This was the only way pairs of mages could work together. They had to be in physical contact.

But Rylan couldn't reach Elanil.

So she was stuck.

"You have to jump!" he shouted.

"It's too far! I'll never make it!"

Suddenly a nearby sound caught his attention. He turned to see the shockstriker darkmage standing just ten feet away, blue lightning circling around his hands and arms.

The darkmage grinned.

ARRA AND IMRA sprinted through the metal city, heading toward where they'd heard the screams. They only had to stop twice to shoot guards as they went.

As they neared the device at the edge of the city, Arra saw that it was really a gigantic hole in the ground, with four metal claws jutting up above it, high into the air. The whole thing looked evil—evil and strange. Perhaps this was why the Eldrim had banned technology.

But where had that scream come from? They kept running, and soon Arra saw something she had never seen before.

It was a man wearing a hood, and he was glowing bright

blue. Strange lightning played across his features, lending him a menacing, demonic look. She glanced around, quickly taking in the scene. She saw Rylan standing against a metal railing, looking out at something in the pit she couldn't see. Then the strange blue man raised his arms, drawing her attention. Lightning crackled around his hands.

He seemed full of himself, as if his power were immeasurable. As if he alone would stop the onslaught of Eldrim into his hallowed sanctum. As if he would save the world with the power of his infinite magic.

So Arra shot him.

It only took a second. The arrow was on her bow and in the air without even a thought. And the arrow flew straight, of course, slamming into the man's heart. He dropped his arms, grunting, but the blue light didn't go out that easily. He regained his composure. His light flared even brighter.

Arra drew another arrow, but Imra was faster. She loosed an arrow of her own toward the man, and Arra could see it curving through the air, borne by Imra's bladedancing magic. The arrow quickly found its mark, embedding itself deeply in the man's head.

The blue light went out, and the man toppled backward, dead.

So much for infinite magic.

ELANIL SAW the arrows hit the shockstriker. It was too dark to make out faces from such a distance, but she thought she recognized Arra as one of the archers. Her sister was here!

But she couldn't focus on that now. She was standing awkwardly on a thin metal platform, slowly rotating in mid-air above a bottomless pit. Rylan had saved her in the nick of time, but it hadn't been enough. She was still stuck here, unless she could somehow get off this platform.

It was an impossible jump. She knew that. She'd been leafrunning since she was ten, and she knew what she could and couldn't do. It wasn't that she was afraid of heights, although this endless pit was a bit scary. No—she just knew she couldn't make the leap.

"You have to jump!" she heard Rylan repeating, shouting at her from across the pit. "My magic is running out!"

So she could jump, or she could fall. It was now or never. If she failed, at least she'd tried. It would be better than doing nothing.

It would be the jump of her life.

She pulled two pieces of prime elm from her pocket, going through the steps in her head. She'd need as much power as possible for the leap. That meant more Material, which she had. More Will, which her fear would help create. And more Investment.

Which meant she would have to *dance* on this floating piece of metal.

Well, there was nothing else for it.

She grabbed the chips of wood—she was almost out of it now—and stepped back to the far end of the bridge segment. She would have to time it right—the bridge was rotating in the air. She dipped into a plié, her customary first move, then followed it up with a pirouette. That was enough to send the bridge segment tilting and careening, and she almost lost her balance. She felt a little power Invest into the wood in her hand, but it wasn't enough. She didn't trust it. She had to do something else, a Movement that would be enough to grant her the power for this impossible jump.

Cartwheels were out. So was just about any other kind of dance step she could think of. Anything she did would throw the bridge off-balance, and she knew that Rylan wouldn't be able to keep it upright. He didn't have that kind of control.

What could she do? The *type* of Movement didn't matter, she knew. It was the skill at which the Movement was executed, the preciseness of its intent. She'd always danced or done gymnastics before, but that wouldn't work here.

She needed something new.

She looked at Rylan, seeing the frightened expression on his face. He was desperately trying to keep her from falling, looking so afraid he might lose her. She'd never had someone feel that way about her before, other than her parents. Nobody actually cared whether she lived or died. It felt good, knowing that she mattered to someone. That her life was important. That Rylan cared. She smiled to herself, thinking of him.

Movement was the leafrunning Way.

But Movement didn't *always* have to be about dancing.

She knew what she could do.

She blew Rylan a kiss.

Magic instantly flooded into the wood at her fingertips, Investment bringing the power to life in a flash. There was so *much* of it, so much magic. She could feel the strength of it, knew that everything was at her command.

All because of a simple kiss.

There was no time to waste. She ran, feet clanging against the metal bridge. She reached the edge of the bridge, and she didn't pause. She didn't think twice. She didn't blink.

She just *jumped*.

The prime elm in her hand flared to life, leafrunning magic taking control of her body. She sailed through the air in a shallow arc, moving faster and farther than she ever had before. She crossed the chasm below her, feet taking long strides in the air. Wind rushed by her as she flew, exhilaration taking hold. She was going to make it! She was going to survive! She was going to—

Oh, shit.

She landed in a heap, right on top of Rylan.

When the dust cleared, she was still lying on top of him, feeling his body underneath her. She was alive! She had made it! She couldn't quite believe it. Rylan had saved her.

"Ouch," he groaned.

And she kissed him.

The kiss only lasted for a moment, but it was a beautiful moment. It felt different than kissing Martan. It felt...better. More visceral, as if there was meaning beyond the kiss itself. As if all the corridors and jail cells and soldiers and flames had brought them together. As if they had brought them here.

And then the moment was over.

She pulled back awkwardly, saw Rylan looking at her with something like shock on his face. Oh, no, she shouldn't have done that. She shouldn't have kissed him. He didn't feel the same way. She shouldn't have—

He kissed her back.

TWENTY-EIGHT

ELANIL *WAS* HERE. It must have been her scream that Arra had heard earlier. And that *jump* her sister had made—it had been magnificent! Elanil had always been extremely Talented at leafrunning, but that jump had been far beyond what Arra had thought possible.

But now she was kissing that boy. Hadn't she just met him? Guards were crashing in all around them, an army was advancing toward their location, and all Elanil could do was make out with some *boy*? Arra growled to herself—her sister never did understand priorities. She was a great leafrunner, but that didn't necessarily make her *smart*.

She stalked over to them. "Is now really the time for that?" she asked.

Elanil broke off the kiss, looking up at Arra sheepishly. "Sorry," she said. "I almost died, you know."

"I know."

"That was a nice shot you made! That mage never knew what hit him!"

"He knew," Arra said. "And Imra was the one that killed him."

"It was still a good shot."

"We need to get out of here," Arra said, glancing around. She knew there were Cothellon everywhere, approaching their position. She just couldn't see any of them yet.

Just then, Imra jogged up. "Guards on both sides," she said, motioning to the nearest building. "They have swords."

Swords were good. That would make them far easier to deal with.

"Lani," Arra said, "you up for some sword fighting?"

Elanil nodded. "Only weapon I'm any good at."

"Great," Arra said. "Come on, let's get you one."

The kids stood, looking askance at Arra, as if she were their mother. But Arra was no mother—she just wanted to get out of there alive.

"Arra..." Imra said in warning.

Arra drew an arrow from her quiver, nocking it to her bowstring. This smaller bow had already proved far more useful than her old longbow had—it was much better in actual combat. She missed her longbow, but she was grateful for the extra maneuverability this little recurve gave her.

Three guards rounded the corner of the building—two on the right, one on the left. Imra and Arra immediately loosed their arrows, sending two of the guards crashing to the ground. As long as Arra could keep sufficient range on her enemies, she'd be able to dispatch them fairly easily.

The third guard came running at them, sword raised. The whole thing looked a bit silly, a swordsman charging two archers. Imra already had an arrow out. The poor guy didn't stand a chance.

Suddenly the man flew high up into the air, then slammed back down to the ground, his sword clattering away. He was dead from the impact, his eyes staring sightlessly up at the starry sky.

Arra looked over at Rylan, seeing dust trailing from his hand. "We had that guy," she said, brandishing an arrow. "Don't waste your magic on easy stuff."

Rylan looked embarrassed. "I was just trying to help."

Elanil darted forward, grabbing the fallen guard's sword. She hefted it, looking at it from all different angles, a smile on her face. "This'll work," she said. She seemed recovered already from her near-death experience.

Perhaps she was stronger than Arra had thought.

"Come on," Arra said, "we need to find Orym."

They set out through the city, threading their way between metal buildings and light posts. It really did feel like a small city, with the buildings arranged in neat rows with streets between. Arra could see a few trees here and there, standing out awkwardly against the straight metal lines of everything else. She wondered why the Cothellon had left them there.

The night was getting darker, somehow. How was that possible? Then Arra looked up and saw the reason. The entire night sky was blocked out, covered up by an immense black shape. The city: New San Francisco. It had moved into position directly over this place, this little city on the ground. It had been positioned off to the east before, but now it was right on top of them.

That probably wasn't good.

Suddenly there was a loud series of *clangs* from far above them, along with some kind of grinding noise. Then there was a screeching sound, like metal scraping hard against metal. More clangs sounded, then all was silent.

What had just happened?

Then there was light. Hundreds upon hundreds of bright lights flared out from the underside of the great floating city, shining down toward the ground. Most of them weren't bright enough to reach the ground, but they still hurt her eyes to look at. Arra shielded her gaze, squinting against the sudden brightness.

Then the city on the ground responded. Everywhere lights turned up and on, intensely illuminating the metal city. She looked at the massive claw-like device, standing far above the other buildings. It, too, was brighter, with hundreds of new lights shining from it, all white and blue and orange.

Was this the Conjunction? Arra looked up again, at the city above. It seemed bigger than it had been before, when it had first appeared over the Splinter. Then she realized what she was seeing: *two* of the cities had joined together, connecting together like a massive metal puzzle. And this was just the first pairing: Arra knew that there would eventually be seven of them up there, held tightly together, a massive monster in the sky.

Time was running out.

With everything suddenly so bright, Arra could see much further than she could before. She surveyed the area. Up ahead, a group of guards were marching toward them, swords out. To her right, down another street, she could see more guards.

Time to go to work. At least the light would make it easier to find her targets. With a glance at Imra, she nocked an arrow to her bow.

ELANIL FELT something whizz by her left cheek, flinging her hair aside as it passed. She put her hand to her cheek, feeling it sting. Had that been a *bullet*? Was someone trying to shoot her?

She turned around, looking for the source of the shot. Her

newly-bright surroundings made it easy to see: there was a shooter on the roof behind her, a block away and three stories up. She saw a second gunman setting up another sniper rifle next to the first. They'd be able to pick off nearly anyone from that position—the building was higher than anything else around it.

She turned towards Arra, hoping to grab her attention, but something else caught her eye first. Rylan. He was staring up at the building with the snipers, dark intent on his face. What was he about to do?

Suddenly the entire three-story building *ripped* out of the ground, pieces of foundation flying. The ground shook as the building pulled free, and Elanil stumbled, struggling to keep her balance. She could see the looks of surprise on the faces of the guards on the roof. One of them reflexively fired his weapon, but the aim was wild, harmless. She watched as the building continued to sail higher and higher, flying up into the sky.

Rylan was lifting an *entire building*. The power that must take! But what was his plan? Was he just going to drop it? She started backpedaling, moving further away from the building. She wasn't much for physics, but she didn't think letting a three-story building fall to the ground was a very good idea.

She had to get clear.

Sure enough, Rylan released his magic and the building dropped. Elanil shielded her face as it slammed into the ground, rocking the whole block and sending cracks through the pavement. The building crumbled as it hit, each floor falling into the next as it collapsed. A great wave of dust and debris flew out from the building, flying past her, whipping through her hair. Chunks of rock and metal hit her, cutting into her skin and clothes.

She peeked through her fingers. Rylan was on the ground,

dazed. He apparently hadn't thought his actions through. Dropping a building that size from that height wasn't exactly a smart plan.

Suddenly Orym appeared, bursting out from an alley next to Rylan. "Are you okay?" she heard him say. He helped the boy up, brushing dirt from his hair.

Rylan nodded sheepishly. "Sorry about that. I was trying to take out the guards on the roof."

"Nice piece of magic," Orym said, ruffling his hair, "but you might want to be a bit more careful."

"Sorry," Rylan said.

This was how the cities had been floating all this time, Elanil suddenly realized. This dark magic that Rylan could do —that's what made it all possible.

She turned and found herself face to face with another Cothellon.

She drew her sword.

GUARDS WERE ARRIVING by the dozen. Rylan was out of maple, having used it all up in that stupid move with the building. He saw Elanil with her sword, expertly fighting against two guards at once. She was a sword fighter, too? What else could she do?

Dill arrived just then, Shot and Small right behind.

"Dillon," Orym said, clasping his son's hand. "It's good to see you."

"It has been too long."

"You okay?" Rylan asked Shot.

The boy nodded. "Good to go."

"So what's the plan?"

"First," Orym said, "we need to get through all these

Cothellon guards. They've really stepped up patrols since I was here last. Then we destroy the device."

"Sounds good," Dill said.

"I'm out of darkprime wood," Rylan said.

Dill fished a knife out of his pocket and handed it to him. "Here—it's better than nothing. Nice job with that building, by the way."

Rylan blushed. "Thanks."

SWORD FIGHTING CAME EASILY to Elanil. It felt like an extension of dancing to her, all forms and movement, flowing from one thing to the next like an intricate performance.

An intricate performance where you could die at any moment.

The guard she was fighting was more awkward in his style, his movements rigid. It wasn't that he was bad with the sword—he just lacked refinement. Style. And he telegraphed his moves too obviously.

The guard feinted, moving his sword down as if to go for a thrust to her gut. But his body betrayed his true intentions—he was trying to draw her sword down in a parry. So she flicked her sword up instead, hitting the man's chin and drawing blood, leaving herself open. It was a risk—if he went through with his original thrust...

But he didn't. He flinched out of his move, instinctively bringing his sword up to where hers had just been, trying to parry her. She followed through with a slash across his midsection and he dropped his sword, clutching at his stomach, blood pouring from between his hands.

Elanil calmly stuck her sword through his neck.

She pulled the sword out, watching as the guard fell to the

ground, blood foaming from his mouth. These men were trying to kill her and her sister and everyone else she knew. So she would kill each and every one of them if she could, and not think twice about it. The thought was cold, different. She wasn't sure she liked it, but she needed it right now. She needed to be strong.

She spun, seeking out other attackers. Arra and Imra were still dispatching men one after another, their bows a blur. Elanil knew she would never be that good with a bow, but at least she could hold her own with a sword.

The Cothellon in her area seemed under control. But where was Rylan? There: two blocks away from her, fighting with a knife. The other boys were with him, too—Dill and Shot and Small. They were fighting together.

But something wasn't right. There was a sound nearby—what was it? It sounded like marching. Loud footsteps in unison. Elanil ran toward the sound, heading closer to Rylan. And as she rounded the next building, she saw it.

Men. Dozens of them. Armed to the teeth, marching in perfect rows. These weren't guards—these were true soldiers. An army was bearing down on Rylan and the others, and they didn't even see them yet.

Shit. What could she do? Elanil looked around frantically. Arra was still preoccupied with her bow. Imra was fighting, too. Sylrantheas had only sent a handful of people to this place—not *nearly* enough to fight an entire army. What options did they have?

Well, she had to at least *warn* him. "Ryl!" she shouted, trying to get his attention. She ran towards him, closing the distance, sword in hand. If nothing else, she would at least help him fight.

But then she had an impossible idea.

She skidded to a stop on the pavement, looking at the

army that was approaching quickly. Could she? It shouldn't be possible. Leafrunning magic was about jumping and leaping, about flitting through the trees. But at its heart, it was about pushing and pulling, moving things sideways. If she was strong enough, she just might be able to do what she had in mind.

Nothing for it but to try. The army would be impossible to defeat, not with so few on their side. She saw Rylan looking at her, a question on his face. Then he, too, saw the army. She saw horror dawning on his face.

"Dill!" he shouted. Dill looked up and saw it too, but he was embroiled in a bitter fight with another guard. They seemed evenly matched.

"Go!" Dill said, struggling with his knife. "Get out of here!"

"No," Rylan said, stepping back into the fray. "I won't leave you!"

The army was just seconds away, drawing swords and guns as Elanil watched. It was now or never.

It was up to her.

She heard a loud buzzing in her ears, but she ignored it. She had to focus. She started running.

Toward the army.

Rylan screamed something at her, but she ignored him, pulling the last of her primewood from her pocket. She only had two pieces. Two lousy pieces.

Hopefully it would be enough.

She stuck the primewood in her mouth and continued running, keeping her hands free. She needed Movement, Investment. She needed as much power for this as she could get.

She launched herself into a double handspring, flipping down the road at the army. Gymnastics—this was a *powerful*

Investment, something not many elves could do. She felt magic flooding into the primewood in her mouth, swelling with the soul of her Movement.

She was ready.

She bit down on the wood, landing smoothly on the ground. Her legs were splayed out and her body was low, her hands keeping herself balanced.

And she exerted her Will.

At first the earth just vibrated. She could feel it under her feet and hands, shaking slightly, but it wasn't enough. So she gritted her teeth and pushed harder.

Much harder.

The ground opened, stretching apart directly underneath the advancing soldiers. It split in a jagged line, yawning like the mouth of a whale. She used her Will to push the earth further apart, and the ground shook roughly, nearly knocking her over. The soldiers fell into the pit she had made, screaming as they went.

The chasm swallowed them up as if they were nothing, accepting their bodies deep into the earth like some kind of sacrifice. The abyss before her looked dark and deep, wide and menacing. She imagined flames at the bottom, roasting the men alive, searing the flesh from their bones. The image made her cringe.

Then the soldiers were gone, swallowed up by the earth itself.

The primewood in her mouth turned to dust. She spit it out, standing up and brushing her hands off. She hadn't thought it was possible, hadn't known she could move the ground like that. But she had done it! For the second time that night, she had done the impossible. She was a true mage. A strong mage. Not a Prime Mage, but at least she was a damn good leafrunner.

She smiled to herself.

Then she stumbled.

She suddenly felt incredibly tired. Handling that much power had exhausted her—she needed to sleep. Through bleary eyes, she saw Rylan looking at her from a block away, a look of concern on his face. She saw Arra run up to her, asking her something that she couldn't hear.

Then a bright light shone in her face, and there was a buzzing sound. She blinked, trying to clear her vision. What was that noise? She squinted, trying to see past the lights.

There was a vehicle in front of her, floating in the air, its lights pointed directly at her. The vehicle had a large, flat area on the back, and she could see men milling about on it. Some of them were shooting their guns at something she couldn't see.

Then somebody else stepped into view, standing there on the floating ship. It was a woman, dressed in red. She stood straight and tall, a gun in her hand.

"Enough!" the woman shouted.

TWENTY-NINE

"LORELEI," Orym breathed. The guards around them had stopped what they were doing when the droplift arrived. Now they were just standing at attention, looking like they were waiting for something.

"Who is that?" Rylan asked, watching the red woman step forward. He wasn't sure what was going on.

"That is Lorelei," Orym said. "The Cundu. The woman in charge."

"Is she a mage?"

"No. But don't let that fool you—she's still very dangerous."

"What should we do?"

"I don't know," Orym said. "I don't know."

Suddenly the soldiers on board the droplift opened fire. Rylan threw himself to the side and scrambled behind a building, seeing everyone else doing the same. The guards on the ground didn't respond—they just stood there, motionless.

"Enough!" Lorelei shouted.

ARRA DIDN'T LIKE the look of this. The woman in red was different from the other soldiers. She seemed more intelligent, somehow, more dangerous. Was she some kind of super mage? Arra wasn't sure she wanted to find out.

So she shot her.

The shot came easily, like it always did: pull an arrow, nock it, sight, and loose. She'd done it a million times before. Except this time her aim failed, the arrow sailing right by the woman in red. It hit one of the soldiers behind her instead, sending the man falling from the droplift, screaming.

"Very well," the woman said, aiming her gun at Arra. "If that's how you want to play."

Arra ran.

She weaved from side to side, trying to make herself a difficult target as she sped down the street. Elanil was running with her. She could tell her sister was tired—that display of raw power had been astounding, ripping the earth apart like that. But Elanil managed to keep up nonetheless, running down the street beside her. Bullets whizzed and pinged as the woman in red tried to hit them. Either their erratic running was working, or the woman wasn't a very good shot.

Arra heard a whirring sound, and she spared a glance behind her. The flying ship was moving closer. Shit. It could probably fly much faster than she could run. They had to do something.

Arra grabbed Elanil's hand and turned down a side street, pulling her sister with her. She didn't want to be responsible for the brat's death, even if the girl did deserve it sometimes.

But that had been a bad move. The alley she had turned down was narrow, and it ended abruptly. A tree stood at the far end, looking incongruous amidst the buildings. An elm tree. It wasn't big, but neither was the alley they were in. She might be able to squeeze by the tree if she tried, but she wasn't sure.

The droplift was right behind them, so there was no other choice. She and Elanil set out down the alley in single file, one behind the other. Arra heard the sound of feet landing hard on the pavement behind her, and she looked back to see the woman in red advancing down the alley towards her, eyes glittering.

RYLAN HEARD THE DROPLIFT MOVING, so he peered out of his hiding place. Sure enough, it was in motion, flying in the direction the girls had been. He took off after it. He wasn't sure what he could do to help, but he had to try. Orym appeared from somewhere, running alongside him. Maybe the two of them could make a difference.

"WHO *ARE* YOU?" Arra shouted. The woman in red was still advancing on them, gun trained at Arra's head. The woman walked steadily, purposefully, her expression deadly calm.

"My name is Lorelei," the woman said. "And who might you be?"

Arra looked behind her. They had reached the elm tree, and although it wasn't big, it still blocked most of the alley exit. With Lorelei holding a gun on her, Arra didn't think she could make it out safely. Elanil was next to her, looking scared. She'd lost her sword somewhere along the way, and she was breathing heavily, still tired from her magical exertion.

They were trapped in an alley against a tree.

It was a fitting end.

"My name is Arra," she said, hoping to delay the inevitable.

Lorelei walked forward until she was standing directly in front of them. She held the gun to Arra's head, just inches away.

"You people are interrupting my mission," Lorelei said. "So here's what's going to happen. I'm going to shoot you, then I'm going to shoot this person here." She nodded at Elanil. "After that, I'm going to find and kill every other Eldrim who has invaded this area."

Arra swallowed hard. There must be something she could do to escape this situation. Where was everyone else?

"When that is done," Lorelei continued, "I'm going to find your family, and everyone you've ever known. I'm going to kill them, too, and then I'm going to burn their homes. This will all happen tonight, you understand. I'm a very fast work-er." She flicked her hair back as she talked. Were all Cothellon this crazy?

"It's not that I'm vindictive," Lorelei continued. "Well, maybe it is. Truth be told, I'm just sick to death of all this. It isn't personal, you understand. It's just that you Eldrim have been nothing but trouble, and I've been waiting a long, *long* time to finish the mission. If Quynn hadn't gotten you involved, you might have lived your lives, blissfully unaware of what was going on around you. But that's not what happened, so here we are."

She clenched the grip of her gun tighter, a smile on her face. Arra shrank back, but there was nowhere else to go.

"So this is where you die, you pretty little thing," Lorelei said. "If it's any consolation, your family's deaths will be quick. I'm sure Sylrantheas will make an excellent bonfire."

Arra opened her mouth, but she didn't know what to say.

"When you meet the Twins," Lorelei said, her voice low, "tell your father I said hello."

She pulled the trigger.

IN ELANIL'S MIND, the scene paused.

How had they gotten here? What had transpired?

They were up against a tree, her sister and she, and a mean woman was pointing a gun at her. But that's not how they'd arrived here. That's not precisely why they were about to die.

Elanil had fled Sylrantheas. She'd run because she'd felt to blame. It had been *her* bucket that had started the fire, after all. She'd hit the Remnant's torch with it, her magic gone awry. She'd watched the flames arc and trail, flying in through the window.

Burning all their wood away.

She'd let Jalnab into the city, against her father's wishes. And it was *Jalnab* who had run into her bucket to begin with. If she hadn't let him in, none of this would have happened.

But that wasn't all.

The Remnant had only been there because of *her*. That's what Orym had said—they'd seen her, noticed her peeking at the edges of this terrible Cothellon city in the woods. They hadn't liked the intrusion, so they had finally attacked.

And they had killed and killed, all because *she* had wanted to *prove* herself. Because *she* had run away, again, flying through the woods.

And her father had told her *not* to fly.

But she'd done it anyway, because that's what she did! And she wasn't *supposed* to be following the Hunters, anyway, when they had found those humans from the sky. She wasn't supposed to be there at all.

She was supposed to be back home, minding her own business, maybe dancing or practicing leaps or drawing with her mother. Sword practice. *Something*.

But even that was not the true beginning of it all.

She'd *angered* the Remnant. She'd angered Jalnab by kissing his son—his poor, dirty, funny son. She was an elf— she wasn't supposed to be in Gulthurub. She was *supposed* to have been shot. Killed. Dead.

Not kissing the enemy.

Nor was she supposed to have been in Old San Francisco, chasing the Remnant, showing off. She just wanted to be like her sister. She just wanted Arra's hair, her feeling of authority, the way she walked. She just wanted Arra's *talent*, dammit. She was good at *everything*, and it wasn't fair. Everyone loved her.

And Elanil was just a nuisance.

It was her fault Fenian had fallen.

It was her fault Arra's love would never walk again.

She was to blame.

And now the moment had come. Now Elanil had proven her *true* uselessness. Now she was here, in this Cothellon stronghold, having brought hordes of soldiers and guards and guns to bear. She'd traveled through the Under in the sky. She'd been to Planner Central. She'd seen the death up there.

And she'd antagonized everyone along the way.

And now, at the end of it all, after everything Elanil had done, her sister was going to die.

No.

This, she could not allow.

It was time to *stop* being the one who screwed everything up.

It was time to stop doing whatever *she* wanted.

It was time to do something for *someone else*.

EVERYTHING HAPPENED IN SLOW MOTION.

Arra saw Lorelei's hand on the gun. She saw her finger move, saw the trigger pulling back. She saw the look on the woman's face, the expression of pure malice.

This was it, Arra knew.

The moment of her death.

But then something else happened. Elanil grabbed the gun, wrenching it to the side, pointing it at her own heart.

The gun fired, and Elanil went down in a spray of blood.

"*No!*" Arra screamed. She fell to her knees, leaning over her sister. Blood was seeping from the girl's body, mingling with the roots of the elm tree. "No," she repeated, "not like this."

"Arra," Elanil whispered. "Live...for me." Then the light went out of her eyes, and she died.

It had all happened in a moment.

Tears came to her eyes. Elanil had sacrificed herself to save Arra—but *why*? What could have possessed her to do such a terrible thing? Arra had done nothing but treat her badly her entire life. She had resented her, made fun of her. She had even wished her dead. What had Arra ever done to deserve her sister's sacrifice?

None of it made sense at all.

She heard a clicking sound. It was Lorelei's gun, cocked and ready to shoot. Pointed at her head.

But Arra didn't care. She stayed bent over Elanil's form, sobbing. Oh, Elanil. How could she have done this? And for what? How could she have been so selfless that she would put herself in harm's way for someone like Arra?

She didn't understand.

But she felt something new growing inside her. Something she hadn't known was there, hadn't expected. As she knelt there crying, Arra *knew* why her sister had done it. Why she had put her own life before Arra's. She understood the sacrifice and the power that it held. Her sister had been good —*truly* good. Her sister had loved her, and Arra had gone all this time without understanding that.

And for the first time in her life, Arra realized that she loved her sister, too.

Something lifted in her mind. It was like a weight falling away, a door opening. Something dark fell from her, then, the strength of its passing palpable. She felt something new entering her spirit, filling up dark passageways. Her blood ran hot and cold, alternating with the beating of her heart.

"I'm so sorry," she whispered, hot tears falling onto Elanil's face. "I was so terrible to you."

Lorelei pulled the trigger.

THIRTY

RYLAN'S EYES WERE WIDE. No. It couldn't be.

Elanil hadn't been shot. She wasn't dead. After everything he'd done to save her, it couldn't be true.

It couldn't be true.

He felt numb, unable to react. Orym stood next to him. The man placed a hand on Rylan's shoulder.

But the evil woman wasn't done. She pointed her gun at Arra's head and pulled the trigger.

The ground shook just as she did it, though, and the shot went wide. Then the ground kept shaking, harder and harder. Rylan couldn't keep his balance—he fell to his knees, still in shock. Next to him, Orym was also having a difficult time standing.

What was happening now?

Lorelei was thrown off her feet, the gun flying from her hand. What was going on? Was it an earthquake? How could this be happening so soon after Elanil's death? Rylan wanted to grieve. He wanted to cry. Anything but this constant conflict, this endless sequence of violence.

He wanted to mourn the girl he'd grown to love in such a short time. But the ground just kept on shaking.

Then the tree at the end of the alley *changed*.

The shaking continued, harder now, and the tree grew. It's trunk rippled and twisted as it did, becoming wider and wider. It pushed Arra and Lorelei along with it, shoving them further down the alley. It kept growing, slamming into nearby buildings, ripping them apart as if they were made of twigs.

It was getting taller, too. The ground shook, and a great crunching sound reached his ears as the tree rippled, reshaping itself into a huge, towering, monumental form. Rylan staggered back, scrambling on all fours as the tree continued to expand. Soon it was hundreds of feet above the buildings, and it just kept getting bigger. It's color began to change, growing greener and stronger in the harsh light of the cities above and below.

Arra was riding the change, her feet planted around one of the roots as it got larger and larger, rippling through the earth and shattering nearby windows and walls. Her head was bowed and her hand was touching the tree, maintaining contact with the wood. She seemed devastated by the loss of her sister, oblivious to everything around her. She just stood there, resolute, while the tree grew and changed around her.

Then, at long last, the tree stopped growing. Its trunk took up the entire block, and its crown was far, far above them, maybe a thousand feet tall.

"Twins," Orym said, a look of pure shock on his face. "I can't believe my eyes. It's a Prime Tree. A new Prime Tree."

Rylan looked again at the Tree. It certainly fit the description he'd heard. But how could it be? What had caused it to exist?

"True sacrifice," Orym said as if in answer to his question. "That's what we've been missing this entire time."

Elanil's body was gone. Perhaps it had been consumed by the Tree as it grew into its new form. Rylan felt tears coming to his eyes. After everything that had happened, he wouldn't even be able to bury her. It was a travesty. He felt his heart break.

Arra knelt under the tree, her hand on one of the roots, her head bowed. He could see her crying, her back shaking as sobs racked her body. Her silhouette brought fresh tears to his eyes.

Then he saw Lorelei, stumbling in the alley, trying to find her gun. Rylan started to get up, preparing to do something—anything—to prevent Lorelei from hurting Arra. But then he heard a click and he felt the cold barrel of a gun against his temple.

"Don't move," a voice said.

Rylan put his hands up, daring to turn his head slightly. A soldier had a gun on him, and another had one pointed at Orym. Down the street, he could see more soldiers appearing by the dozens. Dill and Shot were already captured, and Small was nowhere to be seen.

"Arra!" he heard a voice shout, and he saw Imra, off to his left. Her hands were up, and she was being paraded by a group of soldiers with guns in their hands. Where had all these men come from?

Rylan felt all the energy go out of him. After everything, after all they'd done, it was over. They'd finally been captured. They were finally done.

There was no way out this time.

He watched as Lorelei picked her gun up from where it had fallen in the street. The woman leveled it at Arra, walking shakily toward the Tree, her shoes clicking starkly on the torn pavement.

"You and I have unfinished business," Lorelei said, the

gun pointed right at Arra's head. Her voice echoed strangely in the night.

Arra looked up at the woman slowly, coldly, all emotion gone from her face. She had one hand still on the Tree, her long hair slung back over one shoulder. She was beautiful, Rylan realized, with the lights shining on her, her back straight and proud. She was beautiful, and she was dangerous.

And she was angry.

Arra flicked her hand as if brushing away something distasteful. The motion was casual, effortless, like she didn't even care.

The air rippled around Arra, a circle of distortion flexing out around her, blasting outward impossibly fast. Rylan felt it blow past him, but it didn't touch him. Instead, every Cothellon soldier and guard flew back, hurtling through the air. Then the buildings around them crumpled, blowing out in a circle of incredible destruction.

Wind and debris blew past him as the ripple of wreckage spread outwards, further and further away, destroying everything it touched, until more than half the city had been demolished. The city cracked and tore, ripping apart as Arra's magic did its work, slamming into buildings, shredding them as if they were paper. Walls and windows fell by the hundreds, blown apart as if they were child's toys. The circle of destruction continued onward, everything shattering before Arra's horrible magic.

Every guard or soldier he could see was down, crumpled or battered or oozing blood. Limbs and body parts were everywhere, blood spattering the ground. But his friends were untouched, standing upright amidst the carnage.

Rylan took a ragged breath. What the hell had just happened?

Then Arra stood, slowly, confidently. She looked around, tears drying on her face. He saw her reach into the pouch at her waist, then she flicked her fingers again. Her expression was disdainful.

A gust of powerful wind blew in, and Arra launched into the sky, arcing out of the city and into the forest, flying effortlessly through the air.

And just like that, she was gone.

Rylan looked around. He could see dead soldiers and guards everywhere, but Lorelei was nowhere to be found. He stepped forward, picking through the wreckage on the street. Most of the city had been flattened, metal and bodies strewn everywhere. Ahead of him, the new Prime Tree swayed slightly in the breeze. Rylan drew in a deep, unsteady breath. So much had just happened. He had lost a dear friend. Everyone had almost died.

"What's this?" he asked aloud, bending to retrieve something from the ground. It was a book. It was dirty and a bit burnt around the edges, but it was a book.

"The Book of Amplification," Orym said, coming to stand beside him. "I wonder where that came from." He laid a hand on Rylan's shoulder.

They looked out at the city, at the destruction Arra had caused. Elanil was dead. Arra was gone. And the world was about to end.

"What now?" Rylan asked. The big claw in the background was still there—it had escaped Arra's wrath, somehow. "Do we still need to destroy that machine?"

Orym shook his head slowly. "We know how to make Prime Trees now," he said. "This changes everything."

PART THREE

THIRTY-ONE

"IS THE DEVICE STILL FUNCTIONAL?" Lorelei asked. She seemed harried, her clothes in disarray.

Trey slumped in his chair, struggling to keep his eyes open. It had been a long night of training. Long, but fruitful.

"It is, my lady," someone replied. "The mage only destroyed the outbuildings. The primary function is still operational."

"Good," Lorelei said, turning to face Quynn. "And why is this one here?" She gestured to Trey as she said it, a look of disdain on her face. Something had clearly riled her up. Her hair was all messy, her makeup smudged.

"I came to present him to you," Quynn said. "He has progressed quickly. He is ours now."

Lorelei strode over to where Trey was sitting, bending to look him in the eye. Apparently satisfied with what she saw, she clicked her tongue. "Fine," she said. "Now get him out of here. I have a mission to run."

"Yes, my lady."

QUYNN TOOK him back to the roof. "We have one more lesson," he said. "I didn't want to show you this, but Lorelei insisted. Here."

He handed Trey a wooden staff.

Trey recognized the staff. It was the same one that had been in his bookstore, in the display case in the Back Room. But as quickly as the thought had come, it disappeared, fluttering away behind the purple mist shrouding his mind.

He took the staff from Quynn. The wood felt warm to his touch, as all primewood did—or at least half of it, anyway. The staff was constructed of six wide bands of wood, each a slightly different color and grain. The six parts were joined together with a seventh, darker wood, itself worked into thin strips between each of the six larger segments.

He wanted to ask questions, but he was not allowed to. So instead, he just held the staff and looked at Quynn expectantly.

"This," Quynn said, "is the Tree Ring Staff. The elves created it long ago, back in an age when creating artifacts like this was an everyday occurrence. Now? Not so much. We lost the art of creating things like this thousands of years ago, and only a few remain. Like this one, and this." He fingered the earring in his ear. Trey had learned that the earring was called the Earring of Mist, and it provided Quynn with a constant human illusion if he wanted it, even without being near any kind of Prime Tree.

"The Staff is *very* powerful," Quynn continued. "It provides an infinite source of primewood that never depletes, never lessens. Mages that wield the Staff are still limited by their Will and their physical stamina, of course. I told Lorelei the Staff wouldn't help you, but she wanted me to try it anyway." His lip curled at Trey as he spoke. "You have the weakest Will of any mage I've ever known. You probably won't even be able to *use* the Staff."

Trey stood there, smiling beatifically at the man. He enjoyed these discussions. Learning about magic was fun. Yes, he was terrible at it, but he would get better. He would try *very* hard.

Anything to please his mindmaster.

The larger sections of the Staff were familiar to him. It was made out of the deciduous woods of the Ways: maple, birch, poplar, ash, and oak. And the seventh wood, the one in little strips between the others, was willow. But what was the willow for? Trey had been taught which magical power was associated with each of the woods. All of them, that is, except for willow.

He opened his mouth to ask, but his brain immediately shut the thought down. Questions were forbidden. He'd just have to hope Quynn explained it to him at some point.

"Well?" Quynn said. "Are you just going to stand there?"

Trey found that he knew what he was supposed to do. He hadn't known a moment ago, but the thought was there now, appearing from the dark recesses of his mind. Any time Trey needed to know what to do, a command was waiting for him. It gave him a sense of security.

Following directions. This, he could do.

Trey grasped the Staff, feeling its warmth exude into his palm. The wood felt good, almost like there was life within it. He moved his hand until it was touching the ash segment of the Staff. Time to see if it could do any magic.

He summoned a storm.

At first nothing happened. Then a cloud appeared, white tendrils, just wisps. But Trey kept concentrating, watching as the cloud grew. And grew. And soon it was huge and gray, pregnant with impending rain. A wind whipped up, blowing across the roof, whistling in the little crevices along the walls.

It had actually worked! There was no rain or lightning—not yet, anyway. Maybe he still wasn't strong enough for that. But this was still a big improvement. Alone, without the Staff or the Book, Trey couldn't have done as much as this. Apparently the Staff acted as a kind of conduit, making it easier to touch the magic.

Cool.

He flipped the Staff, twirling it so the end that had been resting on the roof was now on top. This made the other end of the Staff easier to reach. He found the elm segment and wrapped his hand around it.

Then he sailed away, flying across the roof in a shallow arc. He came to rest right on the edge of the platform, wheeling his arms to keep from falling. Oops. He'd have to be more careful than that. No sense in falling to his death!

He stepped back from the edge of the roof, leaving his hand where it was, on the elm, and tried the *other* side of the magic.

The Darkprime magic.

Lightning shot out from his hand, blasting a spot on the roof. Quynn jumped back in alarm, and Trey laughed out loud. This was awesome! He could finally do magic. Sure, the lightning had been a little weak. But it was better than nothing!

He flipped the Staff again, grabbing the ash end. Instantly he was enveloped in a forcefield, a big sphere of fuzzing white light surrounding him. He took a step forward, using his Will to move the forcefield, and was pleased to see that it took almost no effort. The shield moved with him as he walked, stepping over toward Quynn.

"Give me that," Quynn snapped, his expression angry.

What had Trey done this time? It seemed the man was never happy, and Trey desperately wanted to please him. Hadn't Quynn *wanted* him to be powerful? Wasn't that the point?

The forcefield snapped off, and Trey obediently handed the Staff to Quynn. Then he heard a little beeping sound coming from Quynn's shirt. Quynn pulled his communicator out and flicked it on.

"Yes?" he asked, listening for a moment. "I'll be right there." He flicked the communicator off. "I have to go. You stay here."

Trey nodded, and Quynn left, carrying the Staff with him. Trey felt himself missing it already, his magical potential fading as it left.

Trey didn't feel any change as Quynn exited. The comforting purple cloud in his mind stayed right where it was, buoying his thoughts. His mind spun uselessly, no commands to occupy it. He just stared out at the city skyline, his thoughts nowhere at all.

A few minutes later, Lorelei walked out onto the roof. Her hair looked better. "You," she said, "come with me."

Trey's mind accepted the command. "Yes, my lady," he said, and followed her inside.

THEY LAY TOGETHER in her white bed, Lorelei idly playing with Trey's hair. Trey's breathing was slow, contented. Life was simple. Happy.

Lorelei took a deep breath and let it out slowly. "How old would you say you are, Trey?" she asked.

"Thirty-two," Trey answered without thinking.

Lorelei looked at him oddly, but she didn't question him. "Not me," she said, laying back and staring at the ceiling. Trey watched her full lips as she continued. "I remember bits and pieces, you know. Shapes and colors. People. I think I was one of the Fourteen." She turned to him. "You were there, too."

Trey just smiled at her. He was happy to listen to her speak, to watch her chest rise and fall with every breath.

"But somewhere along the way," Lorelei continued, "I lost the power. I lost it all." She flexed her hand, inspecting her fingers as if there were something wrong with them. "I don't know why. Do you know?"

Trey shook his head.

"Of course you don't." She patted his bare chest. "Maybe I'm just blocked, like you were."

"Maybe you should shoot your best friend," Trey said. He wasn't sure why he had said that.

Lorelei grinned at him. "Still some spunk left in you, I see. Good. But there's one problem with your idea, you see: I don't have any friends." She sighed. "I can almost remember, but the memories are so dim. Incomplete. I know we came here for a reason, but for the *life* of me I just can't remember what it was."

Trey waited to see if she would say more, but she just laid there, silently looking up at the white ceiling. A single tear fell from the corner of her eye. He felt like she needed comforting, so he started kissing her. She allowed it.

Suddenly the door to her apartment burst open and Quynn strode in, carrying the Staff. He looked surprised to see them in bed together. His mouth opened soundlessly, eyes wide.

"What?" he asked. "Again?"

Trey just looked at him from his position straddling Lorelei. It was awkward with his head twisted around like that. The mist in his mind was flowing, swirling around. What was it doing?

Then he felt something snap. It hadn't happened *to* Trey, but he could still feel it in his mind. He saw a murderous expression on Quynn's face, and Trey realized that something about his mindmaster had just changed.

"Lorelei is *mine*, asshole," Quynn growled.

He flung his hand up, and Trey was ripped off of Lorelei, flying upwards and crunching against the ceiling. Hard. It hurt like hell.

Then he fell back down onto the bed, Lorelei hastily rolling out of the way underneath him.

"Quynn!" Lorelei snapped. "Stop it this instant!"

But Quynn ignored her, stepping up to the bed and grabbing Trey's arm roughly. Suddenly there was a connection, a link between Trey's mind and Quynn's. Trey could almost—but not quite—feel what the other man was thinking.

It wasn't good.

Quynn flipped the Staff end-over-end in the air, grabbing onto the oak end. His eyes glinted dangerously, and Trey knew what was about to happen.

Shit.

He felt magic surging through the link, and Quynn threw him upwards again. Quynn was *strong*—he was using the Staff for strengthshaping. Trey flew up to the ceiling, throwing his hands in front of his face and cringing.

Then something strange happened. Instead of hitting the ceiling, Trey flew right *through* it. The experience was bewildering—his own body fuzzed, becoming slightly transparent for a brief second. Then he passed through the ceiling tiles, insulation, pipes and electrical, and on up through the subfloor and floor in the apartment above. He kept going another few feet before gravity finally took over, and he fell back down to the floor.

"Ow," Trey said, looking around. He was in someone else's

apartment, very different from Lorelei's. Night and day different, in fact. Where Lorelei had all white furniture, walls, and fabrics, this apartment was all black. Like Lorelei's apartment, it was small, with a tiny table and a bed taking up most of the space.

Trey sat up, rubbing his arm where Quynn had grabbed him. He could feel a nasty bruise forming there. The purple mist in his mind hadn't lessened, and he thought he could hear pounding and screaming from Lorelei's apartment down below.

Something about Quynn had changed, though. Something had unlocked, almost like a block had lifted. Trey thought he knew what it was—it had happened to him, too. He counted on his fingers as he thought back to what had just happened. Quynn had used fallfoiling, strengthshaping, and mergemelding—at least three different types of magic. That could only mean one thing.

Quynn was a Prime Mage.

A young woman sat up in the bed, peering over her black sheets at Trey, who was still sitting on the floor, naked.

"Who are *you?*" she asked, a sultry smile on her face.

THIRTY-TWO

ARRA FLEW DOWN OUT of the sky, alighting easily on a sequoia branch. Her head was a jumble. Something had taken over back there, some kind of primal instinct. Something long forgotten. She didn't recognize it, didn't understand it. It just *was*.

She was a mage. After all this time. Finally a mage.

But she was more than that. She'd instinctively used leafrunning, back there in the city of metal—leafrunning to push everything away, to crush it and destroy it, pulverizing everything in her anguished path.

Then she'd called out to the heavens, and the wind had arrived, carrying her away. Giving her the power to fly.

Two powers, then. Two Talents. Which could only mean one thing.

She was a Prime Mage.

But how? Why? Clearly it had something to do with her sister's tragic death. Her sacrifice. Something had broken through in Arra's mind, then. A wall had come down. But at what cost?

Arra brushed a tear from her eye. Elanil was gone. It was

such a waste. Arra had always wanted to be a mage, but not like this. She hung her head, tears flowing freely.

Not like this.

She looked down at her hand. The flying had come naturally, as if she'd known how to do it her entire life. It was a combination of stormwarding and leafrunning. Instead of pulling in a whole storm, she just summoned enough wind to keep herself aloft. Leafrunning did the rest. It was startlingly easy.

She flexed her fingers, remembering how it had felt to have the magic flowing through her. She'd long imagined it, long wondered what it was like. Now she knew, and it was better than she had ever thought it could be.

The feeling, however, was bittersweet.

She wiped her nose with the back of her hand. That woman—Lorelei—was to blame. She had fired the gun that had killed her sister. She was undoubtedly on her way now to finish the job, burning Sylrantheas and tracking down all the Eldrim in the area.

Lorelei had mentioned Quynn, that his involvement had triggered all this. Where had she heard that name before? It was during the last Council meeting. Orym had said the name. He'd also said that Trey was Quynn's son. That Quynn had sent his soldiers into Sylrantheas in order to get him.

Lorelei had said that none of this would have happened without them, without Quynn getting the Eldrim involved. She wouldn't have been there, wouldn't have tried to shoot Arra. Elanil wouldn't have died.

This was all Trey's fault. He had come upon them, visiting where he was unwanted, bringing his weak magic and strange headaches.

Fenian and Elanil were dead because of him, along with Twins-only-knew how many others.

Trey must not be allowed to survive this.

But first, she needed to see her village. She needed to view the destruction Trey had caused. Arra summoned the storm again and flew away, heading toward Sylrantheas.

"HAVE THEY ARRIVED?" Lorelei asked into her communicator. "Tell them to speed it up. This night has already gone to shit, and I don't want any more mistakes. I'm going to sleep for a few hours, and I want Sylrantheas gone from the map by the time I wake up. And Grathgor? Activate all the troops. Yes, *all* of them. Yes, I know the cities are still joining. Just send them out as they become available. And setup more gates. I have a feeling this night isn't over yet."

She clicked off her communicator.

Quynn and Trey were sitting in Lorelei's apartment, appropriately clothed and mollified. Quynn was idly stroking the Tree Ring Staff, and Trey was sitting still, thinking of nothing. The mindmaster next to him allowed nothing else.

"You two," Lorelei said, "are my aces in this fight. If the Eldrim put up more resistance, I want you both out there, dealing with it." She leaned forward, displaying a tantalizing amount of cleavage. "And I want you both to get along."

Quynn grunted. Trey said nothing.

"And to get things started," she continued, "I want Trey down there now, on the ground. Quynn, give him the Staff."

Quynn looked at her as if she were insane.

"Now, Quynn."

Quynn looked at the Staff for a long moment, his fingers playing over the wood. Then, with a grimace, he handed it to Trey.

Trey took the Staff obediently, paying no attention to the

235

glare Quynn was giving him. The man was acting like a spoiled child who'd just had his favorite toy taken away.

"The Remnant have been hiding something," Lorelei said. "Or at least, they *think* they've hidden it, but it's been there for years. Nobody can hide that long."

"What is it?" Quynn asked.

"They call it the 'Splinter.' A stupid name for a stupid little faction of people. The humans there won't listen to us—they don't even speak their own language, half the time. They're completely unlike the Remnant. They're wimps, just like the Eldrim. So if I had to guess where Silanar is going, that'd be the place."

"We should destroy it," Quynn said.

Lorelei appraised him. "Your penchant for destruction does not always become you," she said. "But in this case, you're right. Do what you need to do."

She left.

And Trey followed, obedient until the end.

Perhaps this "Splinter" would be a welcome distraction.

SYLRANTHEAS WAS STILL BURNING.

Arra could see hundreds of Cothellon troops filing through the forest, marching systematically down every street and passage, checking for survivors. There were none to be found—all had gone to the Splinter.

So the Cothellon set the buildings on fire instead.

Arra thought about going down and fighting them, but she was just one person. Even with her new powers, there was only so much she could do. So she gritted her teeth and watched them from her perch high up in the trees.

She heard the whirring sound of an engine, and a large

droplift flew into view below her. It was similar to the one Lorelei had been on—a wide, flat platform made up most of the vehicle, and a boxy cockpit took up the front. Loud fan-like engines propelled the machine, pushing it through the air. There must be mages inside, she realized, keeping it afloat. Like the cities.

Arra dropped down a few branches, trying to get a closer look as the droplift floated over the city. There was someone on the back of it—someone she recognized. She squinted her eyes.

It was Trey.

She felt her heart drop. This was it, her moment of opportunity. There he was, surrounded by only a few soldiers. She could fly over to the droplift and take him out. And just like that, she would have vengeance for Elanil and Fenian. Could it really be that easy?

She reached for her primewood pouch.

But something exploded beneath her.

A blast of heat and smoke rushed up at her from below, sending her hair flying and ripping through her clothes. She pulled storm power to her as quickly as she could, trying to fly upwards. But the explosion had left a raging fire below, and the wind wasn't responding right. She was having trouble getting away.

Below her, she could see that nothing was left. Several blocks of buildings had been completely obliterated, nearby trees and plants destroyed along with them. Smoke poured upwards at her, and her eyes stung. She couldn't breathe.

She pulled at the storm frantically, Willing the wind to help her, but it wasn't working. So she relied instead on pure leafrunning, pushing her body forward through the trees. She felt a primewood chip turn to dust in her hand as she sailed through the air, flames towering up below her as if to lick at her feet. Thank the Twins for the primewood Silanar had given her earlier.

Had he known she would become a mage?

No. That was impossible.

Another explosion suddenly rocked the ground, and another. The Cothellon were pummeling the city with bombs of some kind, indiscriminately destroying everything. Trees and houses alike were destroyed, fragments of wood and stone hurtling through the air in every direction. The sky filled with smoke, and Arra choked as she flew, struggling to keep aloft despite the destruction.

She alighted on one tree, only to have it immediately begin tipping away from her. The whole base of the trunk had been fractured, a bomb eating into it and destroying the thick bark. Redwoods were resilient to fire, but they couldn't survive this.

The forest was being destroyed.

Arra screamed, pulling another piece of elm from her pouch and continuing her flight from Sylrantheas. Her bow clattered against her back as she moved. The droplift with Trey on it was nowhere to be seen.

Twins!

Still more explosions sounded in the distance, and fire leapt from every part of the city. Arra made her way to the edge of Sylrantheas and flew beyond it, taking shelter high up in a redwood that was outside the city bounds.

She stood there, perched on the branch, tears streaming down her face.

Sylrantheas was gone.

THIRTY-THREE

THEY FOUND LHORIS' body on the way out. He had been shot twice, then badly beaten. Rylan averted his eyes. He couldn't take more death, not now.

Every time he closed his eyes he saw them. Con and Elanil. Dark blood dripping from them, their eyes staring, sightless.

Dead.

Rylan knew that those visions would haunt him for the rest of his life.

He could still taste her. That kiss Elanil had given him, after making the impossible leap from the floating bridge. It had been magical. The kiss, not the jump. Well, the jump, too. Both.

But the kiss had been better.

He licked his lips, remembering the moment. Savoring it. He sniffed. Was he crying? No, that wasn't something under-kids did. Underkids *never* cried.

He wiped his eyes.

He missed her so much.

Shot and Small and Dillon were fine, as were Orym and

Imra. The six of them buried Lhoris as well as they could, then made the slow trek out of the flattened city, heading back into the forest.

Orym had a plan.

RYLAN SAT in the courthouse in the Splinter, his feet swinging off the end of his chair. They built things differently here, he noticed. More like they did topside in New San Francisco. Must be the human influence.

He yawned. How long had it been since he had slept last? Far too long. The night wasn't over yet, but it would be dawn soon. He yawned again, trying to pay attention as the elven Council debated.

Silanar was standing at the front of the room. His eyes were red, and his face looked haggard. He had taken the news of Elanil's death stoically, never one to show emotion. Still, Rylan could see it, buried there beneath the surface. The man had been crying, and he'd obviously gotten no sleep.

Rylan shifted in his seat. He felt as if he should do something, say something to Silanar. Tell him how much Elanil had meant to him, in the end. Tell him how brave she was, how selfless. But Rylan didn't really know Silanar. And he didn't know what to say.

Besides, the adults were busy.

"Tell us again," Silanar was saying.

Orym sighed. "We don't have much time," he said. "The device is powering up."

"Please," Silanar replied, "humor me." There was an edge to his voice that hadn't been there before.

Orym bowed his head. "Lorelei had them cornered—Arra and Elanil—and she had a gun up to Arra's head. At the last second, Elanil pulled the gun to herself instead of Arra. She sacrificed herself to save Arra."

He wrung his hands as if reliving the memory. "As Elanil's blood mixed with the tree's roots, it transformed. Not into a Darkprime Tree, as the Cothellon have been making all these years, but into a true Prime Tree. We'd been going about it the wrong way all this time, you see. We—the Cothellon, that is—have been killing humans for centuries, slaughtering them and letting their blood mix with the roots of trees. And it worked, after a fashion, but the magic it created was dark, twisted. Darkprime.

"The difference is the willingness. The person has to *want* to die, I assume for some greater good, or possibly to save someone they love. And when they do, a Prime Tree is born."

Silanar grimaced. "This is macabre," he said. "I can't believe we're even discussing this." He looked out at the room, tears flooding his eyes. "My daughter. My flesh and blood. That she had to die for...for *this*."

"The Twins work in mysterious ways," Orym said. "I am sorry for your loss."

The look Silanar gave him made Rylan's blood curdle. The two men stared at each other murderously, tears streaming down Silanar's face.

After a moment, he relented.

"I can't believe the magic even works like that," he said. "It doesn't make sense. The Twins are supposed to be loving, benign gods. I can't believe the source of magic involves so much...killing."

"Do you even *believe* in the Twins?" Orym asked.

Silanar shook his head. "There are days when I do," he said. "But most days, no. If the Twins *were* real, I'd expect to have some kind of indication. Some way to know."

"Human religions don't work like that, you know. Everything relies on blind faith, faith in a power they can't see."

"I know. And I suppose it makes sense that elven religion would be the same. But it's been so long since we arrived, and our records are so murky. I guess I just feel like somewhere, somehow, there is proof that the Twins exist. If they exist."

"The power must come from somewhere."

"Yes," Silanar said, "it must. Death creates it, and it becomes death. The elven magic of death and destruction." He stared at the floor sadly. "I always thought the elves were a noble people, a pure people. I thought we were good." He glanced at Orym. "Most of us, anyway. But now—now I'm not so sure. We've slaughtered billions, and for what? This planet is about to die, anyway."

"Not if I have anything to say about it."

"Your plan is to create more Prime Trees? Enact another Sundering?"

"Yes."

"Death begets death. It is a circle that *must* be broken."

"Surely the survival of the planet is more important than your sudden morality?"

"No," Silanar said. "No, I will not do it. I will not order the death of fourteen individuals, just so we have a small chance to save the planet. And besides, you said it yourself: we need *willing* sacrifices. Nobody will accept that challenge. Nobody is willing to die for this."

He looked around the room. "There has been too much death already," he whispered, bowing his head and sitting down at his small desk.

The room was silent for a long moment. Rylan swung his feet in the air, thinking about what he had learned. Con had died to power a tree, to create Darkprime magic. It hadn't been murder just for murder's sake, it had been a ritual killing, intended to produce a result. It was terrible. It was senseless. But at least Con's life had gone for something. Her life, such as it was, had been useless down in the Under. As had his. He thought she'd be happy to know that her death had created power—even a dark power.

Rylan, however, was not happy about it at all.

Movement caught his eye. Something was happening in the courtroom. People—elves and humans—were standing, getting up from their seats and shuffling to the front of the room. Silanar was still sitting, slumped forward in his chair, eyes on his desk, tears drying on his face. He didn't even notice what was going on.

The people formed a line at the front of the room, and Rylan counted how many there were. Thirteen. There were thirteen people standing, and he recognized two Council members and several Mentors. The rest of the group was made up of humans whom he hadn't met.

What were they doing?

Orym cleared his throat, and Silanar looked up.

"No," he said. "No, no, you can't do this!" He stood, his movements shaky.

"We want this planet to survive," Nuvian said. He was one of the thirteen standing, and Rylan recognized him as the Movement Mentor.

He had been Elanil's favorite.

Belstram was next to him in line. "If our sacrifice can save the millions that are left on Earth," he said, "it is worth it. Don't we owe it to the ones we've wronged? Don't we owe it to *them*?" He looked at Jalnab.

Jalnab stood. "I should...do...this," he said. "I see thirteen. One more...is needed."

"No!" someone said from the back of the room. Rylan looked over to see a boy there, sitting next to Allain. A dirty boy, wearing the familiar Remnant dreadlocks. It was Martan, Rylan realized. Jalnab's son.

Hadn't Elanil had a thing for him?

"No," another voice said. It was a female voice, cool and calm. Rylan looked around the room, unsure who had spoken. "I will volunteer," the woman said, and Rylan saw Melenora stand. She walked calmly over to the end of the line. Melenora, Arra and Elanil's mother. Silanar's wife.

"Not you," Silanar breathed. "I can't lose you, too." He stepped around his desk, coming to stand in front of his wife.

She took his hands in her own. "You will not sway me," she said. "This planet needs us now, more than ever. We did not have to pay the price before. But now—now we shall. It is poetic, is it not?"

Rylan saw tears in Silanar's eyes. "My wife," he said. "We must survive this together!"

"No," Melenora said. "We *all* must survive. We all must do our part."

Orym moved to stand in front of the group of volunteers. He bowed before them, clasping his hands. "Your bravery will be recounted for all time," he said.

"If you are wrong about any of this," Silanar said to him, his tone biting, "I swear to the Twins, I will kill you myself."

Orym lowered his eyes, unable to meet Silanar's gaze. "I wish to the Twins that I was wrong," he said. "I wish it with all my heart."

THIRTY-FOUR

TEARS WERE STREAMING from Arra's face as she watched the trees burn. The redwood forest had survived for centuries. It was no stranger to fire, which often strengthened the forest, clearing out the underbrush and recycling nutrients into the soil. But this was not a regular forest fire.

This was a Cothellon inferno.

Arra watched as the trees smoked and burned. In the distance, a great, tall redwood began to fall, its trunk cracking audibly. Sparks flew from its leaves and branches as it moved, tipping ponderously before crashing down. That tree had stood for hundreds of years. It had grown tall and strong, its bark thick, its branches many.

And now it was dead.

Arra gripped a branch above her, fingers digging into the rough wood. The trees had been like a family to her. They'd always been there, seeing her through thick and thin. The buildings? They could be rebuilt.

It would take a long, long time to replace the trees.

She peered down at the edge of Sylrantheas. The Cothellon had burned it and bombed it, then left. She could still see some of them retreating into the forest, heading in the direction of the Splinter. Out for more bloodshed, no doubt.

Curiously, there was a patch of forest up ahead that wasn't burning. It was at the edge of Tarwa Matso, the gardens. Perhaps the Cothellon had missed it. Perhaps they hadn't realized it was part of the village.

Arra swung closer to take a look. She could see the garden fence, and just inside it were trees. Fourteen of them, somehow safe from the fire that had destroyed everything else.

It was Nuala's Grove of Fourteen.

Her aunt had always loved those trees. They were special to her, for reasons no one knew. She'd been determined to grow them, to bring them here and keep them alive at all costs. And despite all the destruction and the chaos and the death, they had somehow managed to survive.

Nuala would be pleased.

Arra pulled more elm out of her pouch, shooting away through the forest toward Splinter territory. She had to warn them about the army's approach. As she left, she took one last look at the grove, saying a little prayer to the Twins that the Fourteen would continue to survive.

MORNING HAD ARRIVED, and the meeting in the Splinter courthouse continued. The humans brought in food to keep everyone fed, luckily. Rylan's stomach grumbled loudly when he smelled it—it was some kind of meat he'd never had before, and it smelled *wonderful*.

Once the room got settled again, the discussion continued. Rylan listened intently—he had a feeling he would have some part to play in what was to come. He was a mage who could literally throw buildings around.

Who wouldn't want that?

"We have our volunteers," Orym said around a bite of cheese. "That means we can make new Prime Trees."

"But will it work?" Silanar asked, taking a sip of wine. The rest of the elven Council was staying quiet, letting Silanar and Orym do all the talking. Jalnab and the other Splinter humans were similarly silent, heads down and eating. Rylan wasn't sure just how much of the discussion they were following.

"What do you mean?" Orym asked.

"The soulsundering. Last time, we used it to kill humans. What's our goal this time?"

"Our best bet is if we can take out the Cothellon aboard the sky cities. If we can kill them all, this will be over."

"But won't that cause the cities to fall?"

"Most of the mages keeping the cities running are actually human," Orym said. "Enslaved. Every few weeks, the Department of Civil Service rounds up new humans and tests them. Those without magical Talent go to the Darkprime forests. Those who do have Talent get assigned to one of the mage teams. If we wipe out the Cothellon, the cities will instantly lose their system of government. Everyone in Mission Control will die. But the mages will live, and the cities will survive."

Silanar swallowed a piece of meat. "But will the ritual work?"

"You tell me," Orym said. "You were the one who led the soulsundering last time. How does the magic work?"

"Nothing is certain," Silanar said. "So much about all this is still shrouded in mystery. But thinking back to how the magic felt...yes, I think it can be done. I can turn it around on the elves, leaving the humans alone."

"Good."

"But that still leaves us with our original problem: how can we get the magic high enough into the sky? It won't reach to the cities."

"I've got a plan for that," Orym said. He turned to look squarely at Rylan. "First, we'll create a Prime Forest, the first the world's seen in millennia. Then, Rylan will lift the entire thing into the air."

The room erupted into noise.

What? Rylan was going to lift an *entire forest*? He looked down at his hands, still greasy from the meat he'd been served. Could he do it? Then he glanced at the Book of Amplification, lying on the seat next to him. Orym had told him to keep it safe, to keep it close. Was the Book the secret? He looked up at Orym, and the man smiled.

Silanar raised his hand, gesturing for silence. "Is he strong enough?"

"You should have seen him at the receiver site," Orym said. "The boy lifted an entire building and threw it into the air. And that was *without* the Book."

"Tell me again how the Book fell back into our hands?"

"Good fortune," Orym said. "That's all I know."

Silanar sighed. "There are still problems. Where will we get the trees? We need all fourteen of them. We don't have time to travel around the world."

Orym turned in his chair, scanning through the audience. Then he spotted what he was looking for. "Nuala," he said, gesturing toward where she was sitting. "I believe she's been saving something for exactly this moment."

"Is this true?" Silanar asked.

Nuala stood, blushing. "Long ago," she said, "the Twins spoke to me. They told me to grow the Fourteen, to keep them safe and strong. I did not know for what purpose."

Silanar pursed his lips. "Sylrantheas was burning when we left. Your Fourteen may be nothing but ash."

Suddenly there was a sound in the room—something unexpected, a kind of rustling. Then Rylan felt his hair start to move about on his head. He stopped swinging his feet, looking around the room with alarm. What was happening?

A wind picked up, swirling through the courtroom. The wind grew stronger and stronger, until papers began flying off desks and everyone's hair and clothing was fluttering about. One of the courtroom windows shattered, the shards of glass flying out of the room, away from everyone. A shadow appeared in the window, rays of light from the rising sun shooting around the figure and streaming into the room.

"The Fourteen still live," the figure said, "at least for now. The fire grows strong around them. There is not much time left."

Then the figure came in through the window. She floated in, actually, legs and arms motionless as she entered the courthouse. When she'd come all the way in, she just hovered there, hands out and facing up, wind blowing through her long hair. Everyone in the room gasped when they saw her.

It was Arra.

THIRTY-FIVE

RYLAN WAS surprised that Arra had come back. She had been angry when he'd last seen her—*very* angry, and powerful.

Elanil had just been killed.

Rylan thought Arra had run away.

But Silanar didn't look surprised to see her. He walked over to Arra calmly, gazing at her for a moment with a smile on his face.

Then he grabbed her in a fierce hug.

"Welcome, daughter," he said. "It is good to see you safe."

Arra dropped her hands, returning the hug. The wind stopped and she sank to the floor, dust falling from around her as she did. "Father," she said. "Elanil is dead." There were tears in her eyes.

"I know," Silanar said, holding her. "I know."

They stayed like that for a little while, then Silanar pulled back, holding her at arm's length. "So it *is* true. You're a Prime Mage."

"Did you know?" Arra asked. "Before it happened, I mean?"

"I suspected," Silanar said. He was smiling, but there was still pain behind his eyes. "I always knew you were destined for great things, somehow."

Arra didn't respond. She just looked at her father as if settling her thoughts. Then she pulled away, looking around at the rest of the room.

"There is an army marching on this area," she said. "Cothellon soldiers. They have flying ships and guns. And bombs. Somehow they know about the Splinter. It isn't safe here anymore."

"We need those Prime Trees," Orym said. "Can we skirt around the Cothellon? Get to Nuala's grove without being seen?"

"They march through the forest like humans," Arra said. "No offense."

Jalnab frowned at her.

"What I mean is," Arra said, "You can easily get around them. But heed my warning: this area needs to be evacuated, because the Cothellon *are* coming. Unless you think you can stay and fight?"

Jalnab spoke up.

"We fight," he said. "We stay. We not let...Cothellon... take us."

Then he turned to the row of Splinter humans sitting beside him.

"*Wa kag bandag wa!*" he said in Low Remnant. "*Wa kag canta fuun galag! Wa kag kun wa bantalag!*"

He switched back to English. "Silanar, we have...work. Many work. We leave...sky cities...to you. We fight on ground."

"Thank you, Jalnab," Silanar said. "You're a good man."

Jalnab bowed slightly. "Let us...go," he said, and he and the other humans left the building.

Nuala came up to Arra. She looked shy, almost reverent. "Are they really okay?" she asked. "My trees?"

Arra looked down at her. "For now. We should send stormwardens to the grove to keep the fire away." She turned to Silanar. "They destroyed Sylrantheas. All of it."

"I feared as much," Silanar said. "But we're fighting for the planet's survival here. We can rebuild the city."

"Can we rebuild the trees?"

"They will grow again, in time. Arra, what is your role in all of this?"

Arra seemed taken aback by the question. "You mean you'll let me decide?"

Silanar nodded. "You are a Prime Mage, my dear, and by the looks of it a very strong one. This is your fight as much as ours. It is not my place to order you around."

Arra opened her mouth, then closed it. Rylan could see her brain working, trying to figure out what to say. Clearly this reaction from her father had been unexpected.

"Thank you, Father," she said at long last. Silanar squeezed her hands.

"Mages," Orym said, appearing behind them. "We need fourteen mages to activate the Trees."

"Do we have enough?" Silanar asked.

"I've been absent too long," Orym said. "This is no longer my village."

"It is still your people, Orym."

"Not until I make amends."

"If we get through this, consider yourself an Eldrim once again," Silanar said, putting a hand on Orym's shoulder.

"Thank you, my friend," Orym said. "Now, about those mages..."

"We have enough," Belstram said from his seat nearby. The Instruction Mentor had been silent until now. He was one of the fourteen volunteers, one of the people who would die to save the planet. He was also a Council member, and apparently he'd been doing the math. "We have mages Aligned with every woodpair. More than two of them, in every case except for maple and pine. Only Allain and Chasianna are Aligned with that woodpair now that Aolis is dead."

Silanar swung his head around to look at Allain, who was sitting sullenly in the back of the room, about five seats over from Rylan. "Good," he said. "And we have mages for willow/cypress?"

"Exactly one of each," Belstram said. "The Twins are smiling on us."

"Perhaps they are," Silanar said, "but this is still a shitty plan."

"It'll work," Orym said.

"I need to replenish my primewood," Arra said, and she suddenly laughed. "It sounds so funny to say that. I've gone my whole life shunning the stuff, wishing it didn't exist. But I need more now. A *lot* more. Do you know where I can get some? The Primestore in Sylrantheas is gone."

Silanar nodded. "We brought as much with us as we could," he said. "It's two buildings south of us. Take as much as you need. But Arra, you haven't told me what your part is in this, yet."

"There's someone I need to kill," she said, before spinning and heading toward the window. "Stay safe, Father. I'll do my best to ensure we survive."

She lifted her hands and the wind picked up again, carrying her body up into the air. Rylan saw her look over at Allain briefly, and some kind of moment passed between them. Then she turned in the air and flew through the window.

She looked so *cool*.

"I wonder where she's going," Orym said.

RYLAN GOT a few hours of sleep after the meeting. It wasn't enough, but it sure helped. Dill shook him awake at noon.

"We need to practice with that Book," Dill said.

"I've got no more wood," Rylan mumbled, still groggy. When this was all over, he vowed, he would sleep for a week straight.

"Dad had some," Dill said. "Here." He thrust a handful of darkprime maple at Rylan.

Rylan rolled out of bed.

SOME MINUTES LATER, Rylan was standing in the forest just outside the Splinter. Dill, Small, and Shot were gathered with him to test out the Book of Amplification.

The Book was unassuming. Not that Rylan had handled many books before, but he knew what they looked like. He'd seen rich topsiders with them from time to time. This one was hard-bound, with thick leather covers and browned, crinkly pages with inscrutable writing on them.

"So this is some kind of magical artifact?" he asked.

Dill nodded. "Elves haven't been able to make these for millennia," he said. "Silanar must have been keeping this one safe for a long time."

"How does it work?"

Dill shrugged. "How do computers work?"

What the hell was he talking about? Rylan didn't know how to respond.

"Never mind. Bad example. Point is, nobody knows how it works. It just does."

"Whatever," Rylan said. "What is it supposed to do?"

"It amplifies."

"Good explanation," Small said. He'd been playing around with some equipment the humans had here in the city—something involving electricity.

"Seriously," Dill said, "the Book of Amplification makes your magic stronger. *Much* stronger. The Book enables your Will to do crazy things. Remember that building you lifted? Which, by the way, was pretty damn impressive. But you could lift a hell of a lot more than that with this thing."

"Okay," Rylan said. "Let's give it a shot."

THE BOOK TURNED out to be incredibly simple to work with. Just hold the damn thing, do some magic, and boom! Amplified. Rylan quickly used up all the darkprime maple Dill had given him, but he was satisfied. He'd be able to lift the forest. Probably. He hoped.

Maybe he should get some more sleep.

"The army's probably close," Shot mused. "I wonder how long we have?"

"Not long, I'd imagine," Dill said. "We should get back to the courthouse. That's where they've setup the base of operations. They should be ready to head to the Fourteen soon."

"I still think we should get all the Under Crews together," Shot said.

"Even if we could do that," Small said, "we'd also need some way to get them down here."

"All those guns Smoke was making would be nice to have, too," Dill said. "He was really tearing through them. We could have done it, you know. Taken out the forests. Taken back the city."

"Not now," Shot said. "With the cities joined like that, you know they probably increased patrols. Everything is probably different now, and there are a lot more than four forests."

"What did they do with the Unders?" Small asked. "Hell, they must be right up against the topsiders, or even the Upper Apartments. What'd they do, just jam seven cities together? Like some kind of puzzle?"

"Apparently so," Dill said. "Just like that. The Unders from the other cities are probably up in the air, or lined up next to each other."

"Do you think the other cities even *have* underkids?" Rylan asked.

"I would think so," Dill said. "It would stand to reason that with all that space available, every city would have developed similar...residents...in the Under."

"We should get all their Crews, too, boss," Small said.

"If only we could get back up there."

Rylan looked up at the massive city structure floating above them. The sun was behind the cities now, casting a great shadow on the ground. Everything was darker than it should be. He found himself shivering.

"Time's up, boys," Orym said, appearing at the edge of the park. "We're heading to the grove of the Fourteen."

It was time to go to work.

THIRTY-SIX

IT DIDN'T TAKE Arra long to find Trey. She had filled up on primewood, taking as much with her as she could hold. She'd even added a second pouch before flying back out into the forest.

The Cothellon army was still hours away from the Splinter. She could see that the soldiers had no idea how to move through the forest. They were trampling everything in sight, but this actually made them slower, constantly hung up in the undergrowth. Arra snorted in derision. If they simply worked *with* the forest, taking the little animal trails that were scattered here and there, they would make far better time. How long had it been since the Cothellon had lived in a forest? How could they so easily have forgotten the Ways?

Why weren't they taking their stupid flying cars, anyway? Wouldn't that be faster than this march? Maybe Lorelei hadn't wanted to waste the equipment on what would surely be a slaughter. Maybe she was complacent after all the killing she had already done.

There he was.

She saw him.

Trey.

He was taking up the rear, carrying some kind of staff. He was his usual self, unsure of what was going on, unable to take the lead. She found herself smirking at him from her position in the tops of the trees. He seemed more dense than usual, if his body language was any guide. He was subdued, almost moving like a machine.

Even if there was something wrong with him, it didn't absolve him. Fenian and Elanil's deaths could be traced directly to him, so he would pay. It was really that simple. Life could be boiled down to the choices one made, and Arra had made hers.

Trey would die.

She alighted on a tree branch behind him, unslinging her bow. This would be the first time she'd use bladedancing magic to aid her arrows, and she felt a little thrill of anticipation. She wondered how it would feel to kill Trey. Would it be enough to assuage her feelings of guilt over Elanil's death? Would it be enough to end her grief over Fenian?

Probably not, but it didn't matter. The man would die either way.

She nocked an arrow and shot it, burning yew. The arrow sailed through the air, taking a straight line toward its target. Wind did not affect it. Leaves did not stop it. Her aim had been a few inches off, but she corrected for it with her mind. She was a mage now.

Her shots would never miss again.

The arrow slammed into Trey's back and he went down.

And the army just kept walking, leaving him behind in the dirt.

THIRTY-SEVEN

TREY FELT the arrow pierce his back, and the world tilted as he fell face-first to the forest floor.

It hurt like hell.

Luckily, his hand was already touching the birch section of the Tree Ring Staff. The arrow had gone straight through his heart, piercing the organ. It should have killed him. It *would* have, if he hadn't already been instinctively burning birch.

It still hurt. He gritted his teeth as the soulsoothing took effect, pushing the arrow out of him on its own, sealing up the hole and repairing his damaged heart. It only took a second, and the bloody arrow was back on the ground where it belonged.

Trey took a deep, shuddering breath.

He was healed.

But who the hell had shot him?

He turned, and there she was. Arra, with another arrow pointed inches away from his head. Damn, she was gorgeous, even when she was trying to kill him. Wait—*why* was she trying to kill him, exactly? Had he insulted her on accident at some point? Had he—

The thought was interrupted as a purple cloud flowed in through his mind. A new command unlocked:

Kill the bitch.

So be it.

They both moved at the same time. Trey flipped the Staff, hitting Arra's bow with it as it moved. But she maintained her hold on the bow, moving it quickly back into position, still pointed at his head.

She loosed the arrow.

But now Trey was gripping elm. He threw himself backward and to the side using leafrunning. He wasn't as fast as he should have been, but it was good enough to dodge the arrow. It sailed by him, nothing but wood and wind.

Then he used the dark side of elm to send a ball of lightning shooting at Arra.

She flinched, but she wasn't fast enough. He saw her hand dipping into her primewood pouch as the ball of lightning struck her in the chest, and she went down.

Then the arrow that he had dodged hit him solidly in the back.

How the hell—?

It wasn't a kill shot that time—the arrow had missed any vital organs. Still, it was enough to send him to the ground, writhing in agony. He felt his head start to whirl as he frantically moved his hand down on the Staff, down until it was touching birch. Then he sighed in relief as the healing took effect. Like before, the arrow slid right out of his body as the hole patched up.

Where had the arrow come from?

But Arra was up again, standing over him, bow in hand. He'd seen her take the lightning blast full-on. She should be dead, or at least unconscious. What was going on? She wasn't a mage. How had she survived?

"Why are you trying to kill me?" he asked.

Arra lowered the bow a notch, glaring at him. "Quynn," she said. "That's your father, right? He was coming for you that day, the day he attacked Sylrantheas. The day Fenian died." A look of pure hatred crossed her face, and she pulled the arrow back another few inches. "Everyone died because of you. My *entire village was destroyed.*"

Trey opened his mouth to reply, but his mindmaster would have none of it—he felt darkness closing in around his thoughts. So instead of saying what he was about to say, this is what came out:

"Fenian deserved what he got. Now you'll die, too."

The words resounded in the air.

Neither of them moved.

Then the purple gave its next command, and Trey slid his hand back to elm. He launched Arra away from him, trying to slam her against a tree. The arrow fell from her bow as she moved, surprise on her face.

But then something strange happened. Arra *resisted* his magic. She flew back several feet, then stopped, hovering in mid-air. He could almost feel her Will, pushing back against his, two leafrunners at war.

That could only mean one thing.

Arra *was* a mage.

Well, shit. She was probably stronger than him, too. Sure enough, she began inching towards him, hovering a few feet off the ground.

Her Will was stronger than his.

Trey started to summon a lightning blast, but Arra slung her bow onto her back and raised her hands.

Wind picked up, strong and fast and cold. The wind was

really powerful, whipping through the trees like a hurricane. Clouds rolled in, flowing in underneath the floating cities, dark and ominous. Was Arra summoning this storm? Was she a leafrunner *and* a stormwarden?

Was she a *Prime Mage*?

Trey knew he was in trouble. He stood awkwardly, trying to brace himself against the wind. It was impossible to do, since the wind was coming in circles through the forest, constantly changing directions. He could almost see it spiraling through the leaves and branches, whipping through his hair. It was getting hard to breathe.

Well. Two could play at this game.

Trey gripped the Tree Ring Staff on the ash end, holding it tightly so he wouldn't lose it in the wind. He stared at Arra with hatred in his eyes, staring at her as the clouds grew darker and the air grew colder.

And he summoned a storm of his own.

THIRTY-EIGHT

ARRA ROSE WITH THE WIND.

Clouds roiled around her, pummeling against each other, constantly in motion. The wind swirled like a great whirlpool, buffeting against her and buoying her into the air.

She saw Trey rising with her.

He held his staff in front of him like a quarterstaff, both hands gripping the wood, intent written darkly on his face.

Lightning crashed nearby, flashing brightly. Thunder pealed, rocking across the forest, a deafening avalanche of sound.

Trey and Arra faced each other, floating high above the tree tops, the thunderstorm swirling around them.

Trey struck first.

Lightning crackled around him, shooting out in sparkling segments to slash at Arra. She dodged, elm magic flipping her sideways. The lightning shot past her and burst into a cloud, and it started to rain.

Arra pulled out chips of oak and poplar, burning them both at once. The oak lent her strength, and the poplar gave her bladedancing, the ability to control arrows with her mind.

Without pausing, she grabbed three arrows from her quiver, shooting them one after another at Trey.

But Trey had a forcefield up around him, and the arrows bounced off. Grimacing, Arra burned poplar again, retrieving the fallen arrows and shooting them back at Trey with her Will alone. Again and again she did this, but his forcefield was impenetrable. She could see a wicked grin on his face, and she found herself roaring with anger.

She tried burning elm, using leafrunning to push against his forcefield. It worked! His forcefield slammed into his body, sending him careening through the storm. But the magic caused her to lose focus—she flew backwards in the storm, flying into thick, gray clouds.

She lost sight of him.

Then he was there, teeth flashing as lightning struck, coming at her fast. He had one hand on the staff, his other hand holding a knife, flying towards her quickly. She scrambled in her primewood pouch, but it was too late.

Trey plunged the knife into her breast.

Arra screamed, hot pain slicing through her chest. She grappled with Trey, trying to pull the knife from her. She felt life ebbing out of her, but she also felt something else. A connection, a momentary flash of something when she touched Trey. For an instant, purple clouds dominated her vision. Then she felt herself slipping away, her magic weakening.

She began to fall, the clouds closing in around her.

She released her grip on Trey's hand, feeling him pummel her with his fist and the wooden staff he was carrying. Blows pounded against her, wind and rain ripping across her skin. The staff hit her in the jaw, and she saw spots. Lightning crashed, mere feet away from her. The world was chaos and death.

"No!" she screamed, frantically reaching into her prime-wood pouch, burning everything she touched. The knife flew out of her chest, the wound closing. Strength flooded into her body, her vision improving. She no longer needed to breathe —the wood gave her life. The storm around her strengthened, but it was *her* storm. It gave way before her, carrying her, shielding her.

She pulled back a strengthened hand and slapped Trey.

Hard.

The man reeled from the blow, flying backwards, flipping end-over-end as he floated through the air. His clothes were soaking wet, and she could see blood flying from his mouth. But he righted himself, shaking his head, his hands still firmly gripping that staff of his. He spit at her, thick blood flying darkly through the air and scattering in the wind. Then he grinned, his teeth red.

Snarling, Trey leapt towards her.

She whipped her bow around from where she had slung it on her back, just in time to hit him in the face with it. But Trey had a forcefield up already, a flat shield across his face. He swung the staff, lightning crackling across its length.

Arra wasn't quick enough to get out of the way. The staff connected with her arm, electricity flowing out of it and into her. She jolted, feeling her muscles clench uncontrollably. Her hand was already touching birch, and she used its magic to continually heal herself as the lightning ravaged her.

The shock continued for a long moment until Trey pulled the staff away, his hands moving to a different wood. But Arra burned more ash, calling the storm to fight for her. An unbe-lievably strong gust of wind burst into Trey, catapulting him hundreds of feet through the air and into the clouds. Arra sped after him, rain pelting against her face.

She flew through the clouds, searching for him. Shouldn't

he be right there? Shouldn't he be chasing her? The wind had just been a ploy to push him away—it wouldn't have done any real damage. She needed to find him so she could finish the job.

But Trey was nowhere to be found.

TREY CIRCLED IN THE AIR, flying above Arra. He hadn't thought of this use for the magic before—it was quite intoxicating, being able to fly like this. He could just barely do it. Even though his Will was weak, so far he'd been able to keep up with Arra. She was strong, though. Very strong. It was only a matter of time before she got through to him.

The girl could definitely carry a grudge.

So Trey had to do something, anything, to maintain an advantage. His best bet seemed to be trickery. If he could just sneak up on her, catch her unawares, he could take her out. It was a slim chance, but it was a chance nonetheless.

Had she been a Prime Mage this whole time? Had she been keeping it from him? It didn't make sense. That was three of them now, by his count: himself, Quynn, and Arra. They were sprouting up like flies—at this rate, soon everyone would be a Prime Mage. He wasn't the special one anymore.

Oh, well. Time to kill her.

But it was too late—he'd been thinking for too long. He heard something behind him and he ducked instinctively, just in time to see an arrow slice through the air where his head had been.

Arra was back.

Trey spun awkwardly in the air, trying to keep all his magic going at once. He was maintaining a storm, using the wind to keep his body aloft. He was using leafrunning to move, shockstriking to blast out at her. Three types of wood, but he only had two hands. He had to keep shifting them around on the Tree Ring Staff—it provided an unlimited source of wood, but you had to *touch* the wood to make it happen.

It was a lot of work.

Another arrow shot through the air at him, but he was already grasping elm. Instead of dodging it, he plucked the arrow out of the sky with his mind. The arrow seemed flimsy, hard to hang on to with the leafrunning magic. It kept wanting to slip from his mental grip. He could tell he wouldn't be able to do anything with the arrow other than drop it. There must be yet another kind of magic associated with weaponry like this. Something he couldn't do.

But Arra clearly had that power. She just kept shooting him, the arrows flying through the air. Some of them came at him straight on; others took an arcing path. One of them even bent all the way around in a half-circle until it was approaching him from behind, at deadly speed.

She was getting good.

It was all Trey could do to keep his forcefield and the storm up. The arrows couldn't get through the shield, at least, but it also trapped him inside a bubble. He couldn't strike back at her. There must be some other way to approach this.

Oh. Yes. Of course there was.

He turned off his forcefield, ducking to avoid another arrow. Then he clamped the shield around Arra.

The wind still kept her aloft, but otherwise she was trapped. He could see her shocked expression as she realized what had happened. She couldn't strike at him, couldn't shoot that pesky bow. All she could do was stare at him helplessly, her lips slightly parted.

Trey came in closer, staying just outside the forcefield,

inspecting her. Her back was arched as she pounded against the forcefield. He could see it sending little zaps of electricity into her, and she grimaced with the pain of it. But she didn't stop. She was ferocious, like a tiger in a cage—something else he'd only read about in books. Tigers had been beautiful animals. Beautiful and deadly.

Like Arra.

He licked his lips, undressing her with his mind. He had her now. He could kill her, but perhaps he should play with her first? The purple mist flew across his vision, engorging his thoughts.

But then everything flicked off—his wind, his forcefield, everything. Trey felt himself falling, and his hand felt suddenly cold.

He had dropped the Staff.

Shit.

THIRTY-NINE

THE FORCEFIELD DISAPPEARED, and Arra drew in a deep breath. It hadn't prevented her from breathing, but it was still scary, being trapped inside an electric magical bubble. She was glad to be rid of it.

And now the idiot had dropped his staff.

Arra swooped down, following him. This was her chance, her opportunity to kill the man. Once and for all.

TREY FUMBLED in his pockets as he fell. There was darkprime wood in there somewhere, he knew. The Staff was out of sight now, having doubtlessly landed somewhere on the forest floor. Which, in a few seconds, would be where he was. Landed, and very much dead.

Ah! Wood. As he touched the wood chip, his brain immediately identified it. It was a skill he just *had*—he didn't know why. The chip of wood was ash, he knew. Darkprime ash. Forcefinder material.

Well, that wouldn't help. Not in a fall. Forcefields were

good for blocking arrows, or for trapping people. They weren't any good when you were falling from a thousand feet in the air.

Right?

But it was the only wood he had. Might as well try it.

He burned the dark ash, and a forcefield sprang into existence around him. It took just a fraction of his Will to keep the forcefield around him as he fell—he had to keep moving it so he stayed in the center.

Wait—what if he *didn't* move it?

He tried that, and instantly his body slammed into the side of the forcefield, raw energy coursing through his body.

And he kept on falling, forcefield and all.

Well shit, that didn't work. And it hurt like hell. Trey moved the forcefield away, keeping himself positioned in the center of it. Treetops started flying by as he fell. He probably had something like two seconds before he died. There was nothing else to do.

But his mind was curious—it quested into the forcefield itself, his Will meandering into the little grains of light that made up the shield. Wait—there was something there. If he twisted his mind *just right...*

He hit the ground.

But the forcefield *bended*, absorbing some of the shock of the impact. Trey could feel it affecting him, too, even though he wasn't touching the shield. Then it broke, splattering briefly across the landscape before fizzling out into thin air. And Trey hit the ground with all of the remaining force.

It hurt. Badly. He felt bones crunching. Then, as if to add insult to injury, something hit him hard in the head. He blinked, trying to clear his vision. Then he saw it, lying there on the ground.

It was the Staff.

ARRA TRIED to follow Trey as he fell, but he was going too fast. It was too dangerous for her to follow at that speed—she'd lose control of the wind. She knew that, somehow. Like she'd done this kind of magic before.

Even though she hadn't.

So she fell slowly, keeping her movement controlled. It didn't matter, anyway. Trey had dropped his source of magic. He was doubtlessly already lying lifeless on the ground, having fallen to his death.

She reached the trees, her magic carrying her between branches and needles and leaves. She was almost there. She was about to witness the death of the man who was responsible for her loved ones' deaths. Her only regret was that the murder had not come by her hand. She peered down at the ground as the clouds and fog blew away, revealing the forest floor.

Nothing was there.

Suddenly she felt cold steel between her ribs. Blood spewed from the wound, trickling down her torso, hot and wet. She gasped, turning.

It was Trey. He was grinning that wicked grin of his, the Staff in his hands. She kept turning until they were face to face, inches apart in the swirling maelstrom. Teeth gritted, she reached behind her and pulled the knife out, brandishing it in front of her, blood still dripping from the blade.

Trey was looking at her, not at the knife. He had eyes only for her, those deep, blue eyes. She looked into them and saw something for a second. Something deep, something haunted. She saw the whirling of solar systems and the passage of millennia. She saw the agony of millions and the death of Trees. She saw power. She saw Time.

She struck with the knife.

THEY CONTINUED like this for what seemed like ages.

Arra was stronger, but Trey had nearly infinite power. Trey only had half the Talents, but he had access to both sides of them: dark and light. Trey's Will was lacking, but he made up for it with impenetrable forcefields and bolts of lightning, magic Arra couldn't do. Arra's arrows were deadly, but her supply was limited.

It was a match made in hell.

And so they fought, whirling across space and time, the storm their ever-present guardian. Their chase ranged all over the Muir Forest and the mountains beyond. Fueled by rage, propelled by wood, Trey and Arra flew over the land. Thoughts of the deadly machine in the sky had fled. Arra had only thoughts of revenge.

The fight continued for what seemed like days, but it had only been an hour. For Prime Mages are powerful indeed, but their magic is driven by Will alone. And the Will of even the greatest mage is not infinite. Soon they tire and fall.

And so it was that Arra found herself at the top of a cliff, high up on Mount Tamalpais. The storm had developed a life of its own—it swirled and spattered, lightning rippling across the sky. It had grown and grown until it was no longer under her control. She was weak, tired.

She could no longer fly.

Trey looked as tired as she felt, but his face still held grim determination. He wanted to kill her, and she didn't know why. It wasn't just self-defense. There was more.

There had been a moment, earlier, when she saw him looking at her differently. She'd seen that look before—back when Fenian had caught them sitting on that log. Trey had wanted to kiss her, then, she was sure. And for just a moment, he'd looked like that again.

But then the moment had passed.

Now he pursued her relentlessly, hanging tightly to that staff of his.

Arra wondered what was driving him. Where had he gone after the attack on Sylrantheas? Had he been siding with the enemy this whole time, or was there something else at work?

She staggered backwards, away from Trey. He had a knife in one hand, the staff in the other. He must have secreted knives all over his person, somehow—he kept coming up with more of them. Arra dug into her primewood pouch, wearily pulling out a piece of elm. She had tried every trick, every power at her disposal. Trey managed to counter them all. Now her energy was low—dreadfully low. She didn't have the strength to fight on.

She was going to die here on the mountain.

TREY SMILED AS HE APPROACHED. Arra had backed herself into a corner. More of a deadly drop than a corner, really, but it amounted to the same thing. He could feel weariness coursing through him. It had been terribly difficult to keep the magic going for this long. He brandished his knife and his Staff, trying to get up the energy for one final attack.

He could feel the mindmaster in his head, urging him on.

He pressed Arra back until she was on the edge of the cliff, seeing the exhaustion in her eyes as he approached. It was at least a hundred foot drop off the edge of the cliff. It would surely be fatal unless she managed one final, desperate leafrunning. Trey didn't think she had it in her.

He could kill her with a simple push.

But he hesitated. Why was he here? How had he gotten to this place? He didn't hate Arra, and he didn't think she hated him. *Something* was driving her, though. She truly wanted to kill him, for reasons he could only guess at. Something about Quynn, she had said, and Fenian's death.

Fenian's death.

He felt a moment of sadness as he thought about the man. He had been good—a strong, loyal companion to Arra. Sure, Trey had been jealous of him, but who wouldn't be? He was tall, handsome, athletic—everything Trey was not. He had been perfect for Arra, and Trey was sad to hear of his passing.

Then the purple mist shrouded his thoughts, clamping down yet again over his mind. But the connection to his mindmaster was getting tenuous, somehow. He felt that it might snap at any moment.

Yet Trey was weak—too weak to resist.

He could do nothing to stop the flow.

And so it took hold, fully enveloping him. And Trey thought no more thoughts of his own.

"How long have you been a Prime Mage?" he asked as he approached. The words were almost lost in the blustering wind, but he knew that Arra had heard him.

She didn't answer. He stepped towards her and she took a step back, away from him. Then she slipped, her feet failing to find purchase on the slippery ground. The wind whipped at her hair as she fell.

Trey lunged forward, his movement propelled by leafrunning. He managed to grab her arm, arresting her fall in the nick of time. He lay prone on the ground, his hand reaching over the edge to hold her as she dangled over the hundred foot drop.

Something about the situation seemed familiar.

Lightning flashed around them, illuminating the storm-ridden landscape. Trey saw fear in her eyes: fear of dying, fear of abandoning her people.

Fear of what she'd become.

But the purple storm closed in again, fracturing his thoughts. And Trey had no choice but to obey.

He opened his hand.

Arra fell, screaming. Mist and fog and clouds obscured her as she fell. Trey did not see her hit the ground, but he knew she could not have survived.

Arra was dead.

Trey lay there on the ground, shivering as cold rain sliced into him. The purple mist was strong inside him, whirling in his mind like a tempest in a bottle. But something else was there, too, some kind of understanding. Trey's mind froze, suddenly sure that something was dreadfully wrong.

Everything that had just happened—the fight, the storm, her fall—felt familiar. This had all happened before.

Trey felt ice enter his veins as realization dawned.

The mist in his mind started shrieking, unintelligible words chanting around and around inside his thoughts. But Trey wrestled it down, fighting with every last piece of raw energy he had left.

He would *not* be controlled. He was *not* a pawn. He would not be a slave any longer.

No. More.

He shouted, his voice garbled and strange, the sound lost immediately in the storm. He felt the wind grow stronger around him, buffeting him as the fight continued inside his head. He clamped his hands against his temples, screaming with every last bit of energy he had.

"NO MORE!"

Thunder pealed, the sound shaking Trey to his very

bones. And with every scrap of feeling he held within him, he renounced the magic that had taken hold of his mind. He pushed against it, peeling it back, forcing it out of him, giving it no quarter.

He would be a puppet no more.

He would no longer be a slave.

And suddenly everything was clear.

He felt it lifting, the purple clouds parting in his mind. He felt it ripping apart, fading into nothing.

Nothing.

The mindmaster was gone.

It was gone! And Trey felt something rushing through him—it felt like Will, strong and pure. As if a part of him had been missing, a small fraction of his brain that had not been his. But it was back now—his mind was finally his own. He finally had control. His destiny was in his hands.

And Arra was dead.

Something new flooded through him, then. Remorse. Grief. Awareness.

Shame.

He had *killed* her. Arra. The strong, vibrant woman was gone, fallen to her death. He'd fought her and raged at her and used his magic and his mind against her. He'd done his best to end her beautiful life, and all for what?

Because *Quynn* had demanded it.

And Trey had not resisted until it was far too late.

Now there was nothing he could do. He lay there, peering down the cliff, tears streaming down his face and mingling with the rain. He lay there, crying for what had been lost. For the mistakes he had made, for the lives he had lived. For the death he had caused.

"Koranaar!" Trey cried, and the storm howled in response.

FORTY

QUYNN STUMBLED INTO MISSION CONTROL, his head pounding, his breathing quick. Technicians and support staff looked up from checklists and screens, watching him as he entered. Lorelei stood, concern written on her face.

"He broke my control," Quynn said, gasping. That had never happened before, not in hundreds of years of using the magic—except for Phoenix. She had been the only other one to resist. "I've lost him," he said. "And he has the Staff."

Lorelei frowned, then spun and addressed the Mission Commander. "Sylvis, we need to move the timetable up."

Sylvis took off her headset. "Testing is still in process," she said. "We cannot activate the device until it is complete."

"I've got a Prime Mage loose on the surface," Lorelei said, "and who knows how many Eldrim about to wreak havoc on our plan. We need to go now. We don't have time for tests."

"If we don't complete the tests," Sylvis said, "this whole thing could fail. Or worse, explode. We need to take the time to get it right."

"Abort the tests," Lorelei said. "That's an order."

Sylvis nodded briskly, turning back to her desk and replacing her headset. "Engine Room," she said.

"Engine Room," came the response over the room's loudspeakers.

"Begin orientation procedures."

"Aye, sir."

"Timekeeper, set mission clock to T-minus 12 hours, in 3, 2, 1...mark."

"Clock synchronized."

"Is twelve hours the best you can do?" Lorelei asked.

"Yes," Sylvis said, holding her gaze for a moment as if daring her to argue further. Then she returned to her procedure. "Gate Control."

"Gate Control here."

"Be advised mission timetable has moved forward. Have your mages on standby."

"Roger that, Mission."

"Receiver."

"Receiver here."

"Mission timetable has advanced. Give me go or no go for core drill."

"Core drill is go, Mission."

"Roger. Fallfoilers."

"Fallfoilers."

"Get ready for altitude calibration in T-minus sixty seconds...mark."

"Roger, Mission."

Sylvis turned in her seat to look at Lorelei. "Let's hope it works," she said.

Lorelei nodded. "I'm going to mobilize everything we have," she said. "If the ground puts up resistance, we'll neutralize it."

Sylvis nodded.

This was it. The end of the mission was nearly at hand. Quynn's head was still hurting terribly. He trudged out of the room, looking for some Aspirin.

RYLAN WAS SOAKED. He and a few dozen other elves and humans were traipsing through the forest, heading toward Nuala's mysterious Grove of Fourteen. They had to take the long way around, though, because of the Cothellon army in the woods. Then a storm had sprung up unexpectedly, and now everyone was cold and miserable. They hadn't been prepared for weather like this.

"I don't like this storm," Orym said, hiking alongside Dill. "There's something strange about it."

"You think it's a mage?" Dill asked.

"I don't know, but it wouldn't surprise me. At least it probably put the fires out in Sylrantheas."

Dill shivered, crossing his arms as he trudged through the woods. "No rain in the Under," he said, looking miserable. "I'd forgotten how much it sucked."

Suddenly there was a loud whirring sound from above them. It sounded like engines—really big engines. Rylan craned his neck, trying to see what was going on, but the sky was covered with dark clouds. It was the middle of the day, but it might as well have been dusk for the amount of light they were getting. He couldn't even see the cluster of floating cities he knew were there.

"What is that sound?" Rylan asked.

Orym frowned, looking up at the clouds. "Docking procedures were already done last night," he said, "so this is probably final positioning. They have to get the cities in exactly the right place over the receiver site."

"You mean the hole in the ground?"

"Just so. They'll breach the core and funnel energy from it to make the gate. If they get that far, the planet will probably only have minutes left before the black hole forms and we all die."

"I thought we had three days until they started it?" Rylan asked.

"I thought so, too. They must have skipped the diagnostics." Orym clucked his tongue. "Not a good idea, Lorelei."

Rylan looked again at the clouds roiling overhead. He jumped as lightning flashed suddenly, scaring him. If a mage *was* causing this storm, he hoped they would come to give them some assistance. There was an entire army out there, and it was only a matter of time before they reached the Splinter.

They were going to need all the help they could get.

TREY GRIEVED. He hadn't wanted to kill Arra. It hadn't been *him* doing those things, fighting her. It had been that goddamn Quynn and his magic. He hadn't wanted to see her fall to her death.

Her. Koranaar. Arra. Trey didn't know why that name had entered his head. Koranaar. He'd never heard it before. But something about the whole situation was familiar to him, as if he'd lived through it once before, or something very much like it.

What was happening to him? Everything he thought he'd known was gone. He had no father. No mother. No wife. He had no idea what his origin was, in fact. No idea how *old* he even was.

Normally his head would start hurting at this point,

thinking these thoughts, but this time it felt strangely clear. Despite his utter confusion, despite his sadness, his mind was fine. He took a deep breath, relishing the smell of rain. It felt so good to be free of Quynn.

Something hit him *hard* on the side of the head.

He rolled over, seeing stars. *Now* his head was hurting, dammit. Rain fell into his eyes, and lightning struck nearby, illuminating something. Someone. Someone he hadn't expected to see again.

Arra.

She looked resplendent, standing there over him, wind rippling through her hair, wet clothes plastered to her body. Another lightning bolt struck, flashing across her face, and Trey could see her expression.

It was murderous.

She flung her bow and quiver down and stepped forward, grabbing Trey by his shirt collar and hauling him up with incredible strength. He was still holding onto the Staff, luckily. He just needed to—

She slapped him, hard. Then she slapped him again. He felt something break in his nose, and he knew blood was flying from his face. He couldn't see. It hurt *so much*. Then he felt the Staff being taken away from him, and Arra kneed him in the stomach. He doubled over, falling roughly to the muddy ground. He crawled on his hands and knees, trying weakly to get away from her. But she kicked him again and again, anger pulsing through her fists. He collapsed, all strength gone, his body racked with pain. Arra was going to kill him. She was going to win.

After all this time.

"You bastard!" Arra shrieked as she continued hitting him, beating him with the Staff. "Fenian and Elanil are dead because of you!"

He rolled onto his back, holding his hands in front of his face to shield himself from her continued strikes. She was relentless, hitting him over and over again. She was mad with rage. She was unstoppable.

He opened his eyes to look at her, squinting at her through blood and water. There must be *something* he could do, some way to stop her. But she had the Staff, and he was out of wood. He was weak and soaked, and she had already hurt him so badly. There was nothing he could do.

Lightning struck again, and something in the flash caught his eye. The Staff lashed out at him, beating against him mercilessly. He could feel that it was only a matter of seconds before he succumbed. But something had caught his attention—what was it? He felt consciousness slipping away.

There it was, illuminated again by a bolt of lightning in the darkness. The Staff was made of six segments of wood, powering the six pairs of magic. But there was a seventh wood, in little strips between all the others. It was willow, he knew.

But no one had ever told him what it was for.

Arra swung the Staff at him again, going for his face this time, trying for a killing blow. But Trey reached out and caught the Staff, just for an instant. As Arra pulled it back, out of his reach, his fingers slipped over one of the willow segments in the Staff.

And, quick as a thought, he activated the magic.

Instantly a circular plane snapped into being, a flat circle of light bounded by swirling wisps. The circle surrounded them in a flash, slipping over both Arra and Trey, sliding over their bodies entirely before disappearing.

And just like that, in a fraction of a moment, Arra and Trey were somewhere *else*.

FORTY-ONE

ARRA FELT a momentary sense of displacement, of *otherness*. She blinked, losing her balance and collapsing on top of Trey. The Staff fell to the side with Trey's fingers still touching it. Arra felt the breath rush out of her lungs as she landed, Trey grunting underneath her. Something clicked inside her head, then, like a door unlocking.

She made as if to get up, but she was so tired. So very tired.

Then the door inside her mind opened.

ARRA STOOD on the Sending platform. It was nighttime, and the moons were out, shining on the gathered elves and illuminating their faces. This was it—their final moments on Valaralda. All around them, the cityscape of Ilyrion glittered in the night, graceful spires and flowing lines fanning out around them as if embracing them. As if to say goodbye.

Trey wrapped his strong arms around her, pulling her

close. "Whatever happens," he said, "know this: we will always be together."

Arra looked into his blue eyes and saw his love for her. The lines on his face had gotten stronger, more pronounced, as the Sending had drawn closer. As he battled with the Senate and worked furiously on his research. She had felt for him, had tried to support him as best she could, bringing him meals when he worked late, being there for him when he came home, exhausted. Now the time had finally come, and her husband looked tired beyond words. Tired, but pleased. It was finally happening. She thought the lines and wrinkles on his face made him look distinguished.

She leaned into him, their lips touching. All around them, elves were saying their final goodbyes, reaching out to loved ones, shedding tears. Arra pulled back from the kiss, seeking out Trey's eyes one final time.

"This will be an awfully big adventure," she whispered.

"I love you," Trey replied.

ARRA'S EYES opened and she drew in a deep, shuddering breath. Then she gagged. It *stunk* in here. She looked around. Where the hell was she?

Trey wriggled underneath her, and she became aware of her position. She was lying on top of him in some kind of dim room. He looked dreadful, although the worst of the damage had been healed. His face was bloody and his hair bedraggled. They were both soaking wet.

Everything from the past few hours came back to her, all at once. She remembered fighting Trey. She remembered killing him over and over, but he had always been able to heal his way through it. Even now, his fingers touched the birch segment of his staff, and she could see him concentrating, weakly trying to use soulsoothing to repair the damage she had caused.

He opened his eyes, then, and the world changed.

She remembered him now. It was only fragments, memories here and there scattered across time, but she remembered. She had *loved* this man, somewhere in the distant past. But who was he? Why did she know these things? Why did she feel this way?

Who was *she?*

"What?" Trey asked. He seemed confused.

Arra shook her head, the motion sending droplets of rainwater cascading down on him. He spluttered. "I'm not sure," she said. "Something happened just now. I remember... things. Things I don't understand. I remember you."

Trey frowned. "But that's impossible."

"I agree." But she couldn't shake the feeling, couldn't unknow what she now understood. Trey was not a bad man. He was not to blame for what had happened to Fenian and Elanil, for what was about to happen to the planet. She lay on him, their faces inches apart, and she saw the look in his eyes. Fear, bewilderment, betrayal. And behind it all, behind the pain and exhaustion, there was something else.

"I'm sorry I tried to kill you," she whispered.

Trey smiled, baring bloody teeth. "Likewise," he said.

Arra held his gaze for a long moment, then rolled off of him and got up. Her muscles were sore, stretched almost to their breaking point. Weariness overtook her as she stood, getting shakily to her feet. She swayed, her vision swimming before her. She took a deep breath, steadying herself. Digging into her primewood pouch, she found a remnant of birch and burned it. The healing that burst through her body felt incredible, but it further tired her. She almost blacked out from the effort. She opened her eyes, carefully, slowly, and looked around.

Hundreds of people were looking at her.

Rows and rows of people—humans, by the looks of it—sat together, chained to metal benches in long lines. Baskets filled with something—wood?—sat in front of them. The people were dirty, disheveled, and they looked malnourished. What *was* this place?

Beside her, Trey got up slowly. He swayed and almost fell, but Arra reached out to him. They supported each other, standing there staring at the sea of downtrodden faces.

The faces stared back.

FORTY-TWO

RYLAN PACED BACK AND FORTH, heedless of the rain. He couldn't be there for this. He couldn't watch.

There were no screams or cries, no sounds of agony. The fourteen volunteers had stayed firm. They *wanted* this, wanted to be part of this new phase. This new life, if one could call it that. This new death.

Prime Trees.

But Rylan didn't want to watch. Not after what he'd already seen. His mind kept flashing back to Con. Blood filled his thoughts, and he wanted to scream, but he resisted the urge. Instead he just paced, thinking dark things, willing the rain to wash away the blood in his head.

The actual transition, though, could not be ignored.

The ground shook roughly, horribly, and Rylan was instantly thrown off his feet. He tumbled, managing to land without hurting himself too terribly, looking in the direction of the grove as the ground underneath him trembled.

As they rose, the Trees pushed everything around them aside. They slid and moved, making room for each other as they grew. Anyone near them at the moment of transition was thrown back, pushed away like unwanted refuse. The change was smooth, as it had been for Elanil's Tree. The trees grew taller and wider, thicker and more robust, their branches and leaves thrusting out, grasping at the sky. The colors grew stronger, even in the dim light. And the *power* they exuded...it was palpable.

When it was over, Rylan found it hard to breathe. Fourteen massive Prime Trees towered over the forest. They were so large that Rylan couldn't even look at them all at once, not from this close a vantage point. He wondered if anyone had been hurt during the transition. Those things were *big*.

As if in answer to his question, yips and yells burst out from around him in the forest. Elves started streaming in, some of them falling to their knees, beaming, gazing upwards at the glorious trees. It seemed like they were having a religious experience.

Rylan couldn't blame them.

The Trees were incredible, waving in the wind: majestic, serene. Powerful. He could see why the elves worshipped them. But as he stood there, gazing up at the giant, leafy verdure, only one thought crossed his mind.

Just how in the *hell* was he going to lift all these Trees into the sky?

SOME TIME LATER, Rylan was standing inside the Prime Forest, watching the proceedings. He had taken to keeping the Book of Amplification with him at all times. By all accounts, it was the only way out of the pickle they were in.

The Prime Forest—he'd started calling it that, for lack of a better name—was incredible. Fourteen majestic Trees towered over them, easily ten times bigger than any ordinary tree. There was a feeling of *life* emanating from them, even down here on the ground. There was a feeling of great happiness. Of power.

Silanar was pacing back and forth. Everyone was gathered in the Forest, coordinating their next move. People were moving into position, forming up into a cluster in front of Silanar. Finally, the former leader of Sylrantheas stopped, turning to face the group. Rylan stood behind him, observing. His job was to lift the Forest—nothing else. This first part was up to the elves.

Silanar cleared his throat, ready to address the elves. "We few are witnesses," he began, "to the first full set of new Prime Trees the world has seen in many millennia. The magic gathered here is incredible—with it, we can power our civilization for many millennia to come. But we face a grave peril, a threat to our very existence. The Cothellon device above us, if left unchecked, will destroy this planet.

"It is up to us, then, to combat this nightmare. To prevent this calamity from destroying our people, our homes, our lives. We must stand and fight! For we—we elves—are the only ones who can."

He turned suddenly, and looked at Rylan. "No," he said quietly, looking down at him. Rylan felt himself shrinking under that gaze. "I misspoke. It is not just the elves who are fighting here today." He smiled, turning back to the gathered group. "We have created Prime Trees," he said, "at great cost and sacrifice. Now we need fourteen mages, fourteen souls Aligned to the very wood itself, to see this through. You are here, and you are called. This is your moment. Will you answer that call?"

The Forest was silent for a minute. Only the sound of rain pattering through the Trees could be heard, wind rustling through the leaves overhead.

"No," somebody said, and Rylan wondered if he'd heard correctly. After that great speech, someone was going to decline?

"Who said that?" Silanar asked. "Come forward."

"No," Allain said, louder this time. He stepped forward, out of the group of mages. "I will not help."

Silanar's brow furrowed. "Son," he said, "we need you. You are one of our last two remaining mistweavers. Without you, we cannot continue. This is your duty."

"I am not *your* son," Allain spit, "and this is not *my* duty." He turned and started to leave.

"Wait!" Silanar called. "Where are you going?"

"I've got someone to kill," Allain said, his face dark. He strode out of the Forest.

"What is up with everyone having someone to kill today?" Orym asked.

Silanar shook his head. "I have no idea what's come over the lad," he said. "But without him, we're all going to die. I can't force him to help, but we need him. Someone is going to have to convince him."

"Any bright ideas?" Orym asked.

"He won't listen to me," Silanar said. "How much time do you think we have?"

Orym looked up in the direction of the sky cities. "Mere hours," he said.

"Well, fuck," was Silanar's reply.

"ALTITUDE HOLDING STEADY WITHIN TOLERANCE," a voice said over the loudspeaker.

"Roger," Sylvis said into her headset.

Quynn was sitting in the back of Mission Control,

dejected. His one purpose, his one success, was gone. Lost. And his head was still hurting like a motherfucker. Painkillers weren't helping.

"Receiver," Sylvis said.

"Go for Receiver."

"Prepare for core breach in T-minus 10 hours...mark."

"Roger, Mission. Clock synchronized."

"Too slow," Lorelei muttered. Then she swiveled in her chair, turning to glare at Quynn. "Are you just going to sit there uselessly?"

Quynn held up his hands. "What do you want me to do?"

"Do *something*," she said, but was interrupted by the loud-speaker.

"Mission, this is Grounds."

"Go ahead, Grounds," Sylvis responded.

"We have...something happening down here. Check your seismograph."

Sylvis turned to look at the seismology station. The man at that desk had his headset on and was speaking rapidly into it. He stopped when he saw Sylvis looking at him.

"Um," he said, "major...seismic disturbance...underneath us." He seemed to be having trouble getting the words out.

"Is it an earthquake?" Sylvis asked. "Another volcano?"

"Um, no," the man said, "I don't think so."

"Then what is it?"

"I don't know, sir."

Sylvis turned in her chair, exasperated. "Can anyone get me a visual on the surface?" she asked.

"Hang on," another elf said, tapping rapidly on his touch-screen. "On-screen," he said after a moment.

A large center portion of the screen across the front wall flicked to a video feed. Quynn had trouble making sense of what he was seeing, at first. It looked like...no. It couldn't be.

"Well fuck me with a broken stick," Lorelei said. "Those are Prime Trees."

"How did they..." Sylvis said, trailing off.

Lorelei turned to Quynn. "You," she said. "You and all those fancy powers you have now. This is your job. *Get down there and fix this!*"

"Yes, my lady," Quynn said, closing his primewood pouch and standing.

It was time to kill more elves.

THE DIRTY HUMANS just stared at Trey. Chains led from around their waists to the benches they were sitting on, and they clutched something in their hands. They looked like how he imagined ship slaves would look, chained in a galley, forced to row.

Then, as one, the humans turned away from him, going back to what they were doing. They shut their eyes, concentrating.

"You, over there!" a voice shouted. Trey looked around to see an angry-looking elf heading towards him. He had a whip in his hands. An actual whip.

"What are you doing down here out of uniform?" the man asked as he approached. Next to him, Trey could feel Arra tensing. Trey saw that she had one hand in her primewood pouch.

He thought quickly. What normally happened in books? What would be a good response?

"Inspection," he said. "A...surprise inspection. No uniforms." Trey knew the story probably wouldn't work, but it was the best he had at a moment's notice.

"You two look like you've been through hell," the man

said, coming up to stand in front of them. "A very *wet* hell." He smiled. "See, the problem is, there's no such thing as a surprise inspection down here in Forcefinder Corps. And uniforms are required at all times." He stood there, flicking his whip into his other hand.

"Well," Arra said, "that's bad news for you, then."

She struck. It wasn't so much of a physical motion as a mental one. The man with the whip flew back suddenly, flying through the air, sailing over the heads of the slaves, slamming against the far wall. Then he fell in a crumpled heap, unconscious or dead.

Probably dead.

"Nice one," Trey said.

"Thanks," Arra said, flashing him a weak smile.

They stepped forward, approaching the dirty humans on their dirty benches. "What do you think is going on here?" Trey asked.

Arra shrugged. "He said 'Forcefinder Corps.' Does that mean anything to you?"

"Forcefields," he said. "Like the ones you saw me make. That must be what they're here for."

"What, enslaved down here? Is that—" she stopped, her hand to her mouth. "Is that what all the humans are *for*, up here in the sky cities?"

Trey nodded grimly, looking at her. "I think so," he said. "They use something called Civil Service to round up the population. This must be part of it. It's how they keep the city running, I guess."

"That's...terrible," Arra said. "Why don't they resist?"

Trey shrugged. "It's ingrained into us from a very young age," he said. "It's just part of life up here. No one questions it."

"Ugh," Arra said. "Cothellon make me sick."

"What should we do?"

"We need to free them, somehow."

"I agree, but how?"

"I don't know," Arra said. "How did we even *get* here? Are we inside one of the cities?"

Trey looked at the Staff he was holding. "The Tree Ring Staff," he said, holding it up for Arra to look at. "It provides an unlimited source of primewood. See the little rings between the larger sections?"

"Willow," Arra said, realization dawning on her face. "You made a gate."

Trey nodded. "I guess that's what it was."

"Can you do it again?"

ALLAIN RAN THROUGH THE FOREST, heedless of the wind and rain. He was angry again, the emotion familiar, almost welcome. He contemplated shedding the feeling, channeling it into an illusion of himself like he had before, but he decided not to. He liked the feel of rage boiling through his blood. He liked the anticipation of death.

He was going to kill Trey.

If he could find him, at least. It was a stupid plan, he knew. But something about it felt right. Oh, sure, Silanar wanted him to *help*, to do what was *right*. But Allain was still so angry. Trey had been responsible for his father's death. He needed to die. Allain didn't care about anything else.

But Allain was lost. Lost in the vast Muir Forest, the place he'd called home all his life. It looked different in the rain. Dark. Frightening. The tall redwoods, normally so graceful and serene, rose before him, threatening and severe. They were watching him, even now. Watching his every move, waiting to strike.

Lightning crashed, and Allain jumped. Then he chastised himself. Who was he, some kind of child, jumping at lightning? He was a *man* now. A powerful mistweaver. Trey would never even see him coming.

If, that is, he could find the bastard.

Thunder rumbled through the forest, and Allain found himself shivering.

"I DON'T KNOW how the magic works," Trey said, "but I think I can make another gate. What are you thinking?"

Arra was still leaning against him, dripping. "These poor humans," she said. "Can we free them?"

Trey shook his head. "I don't see how," he said. "Not by ourselves. We need help." He turned to her, gripping her elbow. "You're a mage now."

Arra looked at him, sodden hair hanging limply around her face. Even so, she was still beautiful. She shrugged. "It just happened," she said. "When Elanil died. Something broke in my head, like a wall that had been blocking my mind." She flexed her fingers. "And now I'm a Prime Mage."

But Trey was taken aback by the first thing she had said. "Elanil is...*dead?*"

Arra hung her head. "Some Cothellon killed her. The woman was aiming for me, but Lani pulled the gun to herself, instead. She died trying to save me, and I still don't know why."

Trey could see her eyes watering, and he pulled her into a hug. "I'm so sorry," he said. "That's terrible." They stood like that for a moment, Arra crying softly into his shoulder.

After a few minutes, she pulled back. "I don't know why I was so bent on killing you," she said, "when I should have been trying to find the woman who shot Elanil."

"Who was she?" Trey asked.

"She said her name was Lorelei."

"Oh," Trey said, suddenly remembering the events of the past few days. He had slept with Lorelei—several times, in fact. She had manipulated him, toyed with him. He shuddered, thinking about it, but a part of him was already picturing her naked. He shook his head, trying to clear his thoughts.

"You know her?" Arra asked, eyes narrowing.

"I'm afraid so," Trey said. "Remember my wife? Up in the city?"

"Yes," Arra said, "although you didn't talk about her very much. What was her name, again?"

"Lora," Trey said.

"Remind me what happened to her?"

"She was taken for Civil Service," Trey said, motioning at the rows of mage slaves in the room. "Except that was all a lie. Lora herself was a lie."

"What do you mean?"

"She was playing me. Her and Quynn were trying to get me to turn into a Prime Mage. Somehow they knew I had it in me, they just didn't know how to get it out."

"But that's...that makes no sense."

"I know. I'm not Quynn's son, and Lora was not my wife. She had the marriage annulled. And it gets worse. It turns out Lora isn't who she said she was at all. She's actually an elf, and her real name is Lorelei."

"So you were married to the woman who killed my sister." Her tone was flat.

"I'm afraid so. At least for a few hours, I guess."

Arra opened her mouth, but she didn't say anything. Trey watched her expression, trying to read what she was thinking. He could tell she was working through it, thinking through the connections. Reevaluating the past few days.

"It's starting to make sense," she said. "But I still don't understand one thing."

"Yes?"

"Who are *you*? Where did you come from?"

Trey sighed. "I wish I knew. I think I've forgotten who I am. Lost the memory. But you're familiar to me, somehow. I feel like I know you."

Arra stepped closer. "I remember you too, but the memory makes no sense. It's like it was from another life."

Trey pursed his lips, unsure how to proceed. There was something there between them, but he didn't know what it was.

Not yet.

"What should we do now?" he asked.

"Can you take us back to the surface? This city—this device—it's powering up. We don't have much time. Orym has a plan to defeat it. He's going to try another soulsundering. But Trey, there's an army in the woods, heading towards them. They need help."

"Then that's where we should be." Trey took her arm, pulling her up against him. "Let me try something. I'm not sure if this will work."

He took one last look at the humans, chained to their benches. They were a pathetic lot, and he wanted to help them, but he wasn't sure how. Maybe somebody in the Splinter would know what to do.

He held Arra tightly with his right arm. With his left arm, he held the Tree Ring Staff, his hand wrapped around one of the willow segments. Then he exercised his Will, questing into the Staff with his mind.

He could feel it there, the wood. It was almost like it was alive, sentient, waiting for him. Waiting for a command. *Can you take me where I want to go?* he thought into the willow.

YES, he felt in reply. He almost dropped the Staff then, he was so surprised. He hadn't expected the wood to actually talk to him. Or had he been imagining it?

Are you there? he asked it.

Nothing came back. The wood was silent. Perhaps it had all been in his head.

Well, there was nothing else for it. He had to try. He reached out again to the wood, Willing it to respond. His mind felt stronger now, more in control. He felt more powerful than before. Perhaps breaking Quynn's control on him had improved his strength. Perhaps Quynn had been controlling him his entire life. Whatever the case, that part of his mind was his, again.

It was time to put it to use.

He Willed the willow to open a gate. With his mind, he pictured Sylrantheas, the beautiful elven village built amongst the trees. One thought in particular entered his mind: the garden. Tarwa Matso. He pictured the rows of vegetables he had seen as he walked by. The little grove of fourteen trees. He pictured the tranquility, the beauty of it.

Take me there, he commanded the Staff. And a gate opened—not on top of them, but in front of them, a great oval sliding open like a sleeper waking. Through the gate, he could see swirling pictures, but it was too dark to make anything out. He hoped the gate was pointing in the right direction. He could feel it there, channeling out from the Staff. He made a little *twist* in his mind, snapping off the invisible flow of power. The gate stayed where it was, wisps of light spinning off it merrily.

He looked down at Arra, still held tightly in his arms. "I guess this wasn't necessary," he said, releasing his grip.

"I don't mind," she said, looking at the gate he had made. "How long will it last?"

"I don't know," Trey said. "It's the first time I've made one on purpose."

"We'd better go through before it disappears, then."

"Yes." He walked toward the gate, pulling Arra along with him.

"Do you think it's safe?" she asked.

"Only one way to find out."

FORTY-THREE

THEY STEPPED OUT INTO A NIGHTMARE.

Smoke was everywhere, and Trey immediately started coughing. Everywhere he looked, the forest had burned. The rows of beautiful plants he had pictured were gone, leaving dark ash in their place. The trees—the beautiful trees that had been so much a part of Sylrantheas—were dead now, burned, broken, fallen. The storm seemed to have let up for the moment; everything was dripping and black.

Arra stepped through the gate behind him, holding her sleeve across her mouth.

"What happened here?" Trey asked.

"The Cothellon happened," Arra said. "They came here with bombs and fire, burning everything they saw. It was terrible."

"Your beautiful city," Trey said. "Your poor, beautiful city. It's all gone."

"Yes."

"I'm so sorry."

"Don't apologize," Arra said, her tone bitter, "help me get the bastards that did this."

"I will," Trey said, squeezing her arm. Then he turned around, and his jaw dropped. "What the..."

Arra turned around to see what he was looking at. "Wow," she breathed. "They did it. They actually did it!"

"Those are Prime Trees, aren't they?" Trey asked.

"Yes," Arra said, "aren't they beautiful?"

"Beautiful," Trey echoed. They stood side by side, admiring the Trees. They were so peaceful, so majestic, standing out amongst the burnt landscape. Trey found himself reaching out and taking Arra's hand. She didn't resist.

"Done with your killing?" a voice said, and Trey turned to see Silanar striding toward them. He was accompanied by Rylan, and some other boys Trey didn't recognize.

Trey looked over to see Arra blushing. "I was going after him," she said, nodding at Trey, "but I was misguided. He's not the real enemy here."

Silanar looked at the two of them, his gaze alternating between Trey and Arra. He seemed to note that they were holding hands, but he didn't comment on it. "So, the prodigal son returns," he said, his gaze settling on Trey. "Not the best parable for the moment, I admit, but it was the first thing that came to mind. Where did you disappear to, Trey?"

"It's a long story."

Silanar nodded. "I imagine it is. Are you with us?"

"I am. How can I help?"

"There's an army marching on the Splinter," Silanar said. "We could use any help you can give us to take them out."

"I'll see what I can do," Trey said.

"Hey," Rylan said, "does that lead back to the city?" He was pointing at the gate Trey had made. It was still there, swirling brightly in the dark forest.

How had Rylan known what it was?

"It does," Trey said. "To somewhere in the Under, I think. It's a room full of human mages. Slaves."

Rylan looked at the boys standing next to him. "What do you think?" he asked. "Back to the original plan?"

"What plan?" one of the boys asked.

"The one where we take back the city," Rylan said.

"I'm in," said the other boy.

"Me too," said a second boy.

"Are you sure it's safe?" a third boy asked. He seemed older, more mature. Like he was used to leading. Trey realized he recognized him. It was the boy with the pickle on his shirt, the one from the meeting that had started everything. Dill.

"It's safe," Trey said, "I think. We took out some kind of officer while we were up there. I think he's dead, but there may be others."

Rylan shrugged. "We'll have to risk it."

"You need to stay here," Silanar said. "To lift this Forest."

Rylan hung his head. "I always miss all the fun," he said, but there was a twinkle in his eye. He wasn't actually mad, Trey could tell. He was happy to have a part to play.

Dill stepped forward. "Let's see what's on the other side," he said. "I've been feeling a bit useless down here, anyway. It'll be good to have something to do."

The other boys muttered their agreement.

"You made this gate?" Dill asked Trey. Trey nodded. "Can you make another one? One leading to the Splinter?"

"I think so," Trey said. "But I've never been to the Splinter before. I think I need to go there, first."

"That's where the army is heading," Silanar said. "You and Arra should go. They could use your help. She can take you there."

"Will you be alright here?" Arra asked.

"We've got it under control," Silanar said, although his

face looked worried. "If you see Allain, can you send him here? He's gone missing, and we need him for the soul-sundering."

"Sure," Arra said. "If we see him, we'll tell him."

"Thank you."

"Well," Dill said, "I guess this is goodbye. Good luck, Rylan." The boy slapped Rylan hard on the back, and he coughed.

"Good luck yourself," Rylan said.

"Ready?" Dill asked, turning to the other two boys.

"Ready!" they responded.

Trey watched as the three of them stepped through the gate he had made. Soon they disappeared, swallowed by the swirling circle of light.

"Hey," Rylan said, addressing Trey. "You guys fighting together now?"

Trey glanced at Arra. "I guess so," he said.

Rylan took a step forward, speaking quietly. "There's something you should know," he said, "something Elanil and I almost died finding out. If you try to do magic together, on the same thing, it won't work. It'll go crazy. You have to touch her"—he nodded toward Arra—"when you do it. That's the only way it works."

Arra's eyes narrowed. "How do you know this?" she asked. "What did you do with my sister?"

"That fire?" Rylan said. "The one in the Primestore building? It was our fault. We didn't know it yet, but if you don't touch each other while you work the magic, bad things tend to happen." His voice got sad. "I think that bucket of water was the first time it happened for us. Maybe if we'd learned more quickly..."

Trey put a hand on his shoulder. "Elanil dying wasn't your fault," he said quietly.

Rylan sighed.

"That girl was always getting into trouble," Arra said. "I miss her."

"So do I," Rylan said. "So do I."

"I'M SO TIRED," Arra said after Rylan left. "You put up quite a fight."

Trey grinned at her. She found the look endearing. "You weren't so bad yourself," he said. His gaze lingered on her before moving back up to the Trees. "These really are something, you know."

She followed his gaze. They *were* impressive. Better than the paintings, up close like this. But she was having trouble focusing on it. She was just so tired. She sighed. "We should get to the Splinter," she said. "Maybe we can catch a few hours of sleep."

"Do you think we have that much time?"

"I don't know." She turned to Silanar. "Did Orym say anything about how long we have?"

"Maybe only a matter of hours."

"Where was the army? Did you pass them on your way here?"

"They are probably almost to the Splinter by now," Silanar said. "They were easy to avoid in the forest. Jalnab is mounting some kind of defense there, but I don't know if it will be enough."

"Why were you there, anyway?" Trey asked. "Lorelei said it was a Remnant faction. Why did they let you in?"

"It was Elanil," Silanar said. "She showed kindness to Jalnab and Martan. She let them into Sylrantheas while we were fighting the Remnant. I argued with her, but she was determined—and she was right. Jalnab is a good man. What he has done with the Splinter...I would never have thought it possible."

Arra's stomach was in knots. The elves had a place to stay, a place to heal and regroup—and it was *Elanil* who had made it possible? Without her sister, where would the Eldrim have gone? They would have been wandering, scared and alone.

Nobody would have been there to try to heal Fenian.

It didn't matter that they had failed—Fenian had been terribly wounded. Only magic would have saved him, and the elves didn't have enough of that. The fact was, the Splinter had *tried*.

And all because of her poor, dead sister.

Arra felt a tear trickle down her cheek. How had she been so wrong about the girl? Now there was nothing she could do. She couldn't apologize. She couldn't explain herself.

She would never have a moment with Elanil again.

She found herself leaning on Trey for support. "We have to go see what we can do," she said. "If we can save the Splinter, we should try."

"Can you show me the way?" Trey asked.

"It will be faster if we leafrun," she said. "Do you have the energy for it?"

Trey nodded. "I'll try."

THEY MADE it to the Splinter ten minutes later. Their flight through the trees had been swift, but it had taken the last of Arra's waning strength. Her eyelids drooped, and her muscles wouldn't respond. She had to get some sleep.

Next to her, Trey alighted on the ground, stumbling as he

landed. "Shit," he said, "doing this much magic really takes it out of you."

Arra nodded. "We need to rest."

The village was in an uproar. Hordes of people—mostly humans—were milling about, trying to organize weapons and positions. They were far more orderly than any Remnant she had ever seen.

Jalnab saw them approaching and walked over to meet them. "Hello," he said. "You look...bad."

Arra laughed weakly. Jalnab's command of English definitely left something to be desired. "We used too much magic. We need some rest."

"Why magic?" Jalnab asked. "No fighting...yet."

Arra gave Trey a sidelong glance. "Uh," she said, "it's a long story."

Jalnab frowned. "Scouts say army...almost here. You see... them?"

"We passed over them," Trey said. "They'll be here soon."

"We must...defend. Fight. I must...work. Prepare." He motioned toward an older woman who was standing nearby. "Kantag will...show you...bed. You sleep. Sleep fast. Fight... soon. Need you."

"Thank you," Arra said. "Thank you for your help."

ARRA AWOKE to someone pounding on her door. She looked around blearily. How long had she been asleep? It couldn't have been more than an hour. Sounds started coming to her —distant gunfire and shouts.

The fighting had begun.

She yawned, getting slowly out of bed. She and Trey had

been put up in two rooms of somebody's house. She'd been too tired to say much to their host.

The pounding continued, louder this time.

"I'm coming!" she called, standing and walking unsteadily toward the bedroom door. It opened to reveal the frantic face of Kantag.

"Run," she said breathlessly. "All...must run."

"What?" Arra asked. "But the fighting has just begun."

"We die," Kantag said. "Half...dead. Cannot...fight."

Across the hall, Arra saw another door open, and Trey's sleepy head poked out. "What's going on?"

"They're being overrun," Arra said. "Kantag says everyone is leaving."

"Shit," Trey said. "We need to help them, if we can."

Arra yawned, nodding. "Let me get my things."

She went back into her room and put on her outer shirt, slung her quiver and bow over her back, and strapped on her primewood pouch. The pouch was getting low, as were her arrows. She would need to refill both before they left the city.

"I'm ready," she said, leaving the room. Trey was emerging from his room as well, the Tree Ring Staff in his hand.

"I don't know if I can do this," he said. "I'm still so tired."

"We have to try," Arra said.

"I'll do my best."

"Come," Kantag said, leading the way out of the house.

Then there was a garbled scream, and Kantag was falling to the ground, blood flying from a terrible slash across her throat.

"What—" Arra began, looking up to see an elf standing in front of her, wielding a knife.

The elf grinned. "Who's next?" he asked.

"Quynn," Trey breathed.

Quynn struck.

FORTY-FOUR

TREY FLUNG up a forcefield around Arra, blocking Quynn's strike. It was a reflexive action, something he'd gotten good at during his battle with Arra.

But it didn't work.

The knife went right *through* the forcefield, and so did Quynn's arm, becoming slightly transparent as it did. Trey watched as the knife headed straight for Arra's chest.

Luckily, she had good reflexes. She dodged, throwing her body to the side to avoid the knife. Her movement took her right through Trey's forcefield, leaving her unprotected. How had she gotten through?

Then Trey realized his mistake. In his haste, he'd made the forcefield one-sided—Arra could leave the forcefield any time she wanted. A one-sided forcefield was supposed to keep other objects out, but anything could leave it. Of course, none of it had worked against Quynn.

Because Quynn was a mergemelder.

Trey sprung forward, intending to help Arra, but she got to her feet remarkably quickly, her eyes alert.

"Wow," she said, raising her hand and burning elm, flinging Quynn away from her casually. The man flew backwards dozens of feet, landing in a sprawl further down the road. "That was *amazing*," she said, looking at Trey and pulling her bow from her shoulder. "Going through that forcefield, it was like getting a jolt of energy all at once! I feel *great* now!"

As if to emphasize her point, she quickly drew two arrows and shot them toward Quynn. Trey could see her burning poplar as she did, focusing the arrows toward her target.

"So who's this guy attacking us?" she asked.

"That's Quynn," Trey said. "He was my father."

"I see."

"He's the one who attacked Sylrantheas."

"And I'm guessing he's incredibly dangerous?"

"Well," Trey said, "the arrows you just shot appear to have gone right through him."

"What?" He could see Arra scrutinizing Quynn. It was true—her arrows hadn't touched the man at all. "How?"

"He's a mergemelder," Trey said. "And a mindmaster, and who knows what else." Quynn was getting to his feet, still holding a knife. He had a nasty look on his face.

"So he's a Prime Mage?" Arra asked.

"Guess so," Trey said.

Arra whistled quietly. "This will be fun." She pulled two more arrows from her quiver, then glanced at Trey. "Do that forcefield thing on yourself," she said. "It will help."

"Okay."

He made a one-sided forcefield, a bubble of energy surrounding himself. Then he walked through it.

It was like waking up after a long, refreshing sleep. Like taking a cold shower. Like drinking your sixth cup of coffee, your brain alive with possibilities.

Arra was right: it felt *great*.

Trey spun, hands gripping the Tree Ring Staff, suddenly full of energy. Quynn had recovered and was stalking down the street towards them, his face murderous. Arra was shooting arrow after arrow at him, but they just passed right through the man, fuzzing a little bit as they did.

"Arrows are useless!" Trey shouted at her.

"I can see that," Arra returned, digging in her pouch.

Quynn focused on Trey as he approached, darkprime wood visible in his hand. Trey saw him burn the wood, and suddenly fingers of purple mist reached out to him, filtering toward his brain.

"Not this time!" Trey shouted, exerting his Will to combat the mindmaster. Trey felt the purple clouds shrink away from him, shrieking in his mind as he forced them out. Quynn looked like he was visibly in pain from the effort.

"How are you *doing* that?" Quynn yelled.

Trey didn't bother to respond.

The rain started up again, cold drops splattering hard against his face. "Great," Trey muttered, swinging his Staff around to grab the elm end. Next to him, Arra was preparing an offense of her own.

"Try to keep him distracted," she said.

Trey nodded. That shouldn't be too difficult. Quynn seemed most interested in him, anyway. "Hey *Dad*," he yelled, taunting, "did Lorelei throw you out of bed again?"

Quynn's face twisted with hatred, and he came running at Trey, knife out. Trey blinked, suddenly indecisive. What should he do? He had so many powers to choose from, and now that he wasn't so tired, the sky was the limit. He found himself reaching for one of the willow segments on the Staff. This new power he had found would be perfect. He could take Quynn and gate him somewhere far away. Easy!

Quynn rushed toward him as he activated the magic, Willing a gate to form around Quynn. But Quynn must have anticipated the move—he already had a piece of wood in his hand, and he burned it. Trey felt his gate fizzle before it could form, blocked by something he couldn't see. Was Quynn burning willow, too?

Apparently he was. A gate started forming, in the air above Trey. He didn't see it so much as *feel* it start to appear, cutting into the energies of the world above him. Well, two could play at that game. Trey activated the willow under his fingers again and slashed mentally at the gate, Willing it to disappear. And sure enough, it did.

But it had just been a distraction. Quynn barreled into Trey, momentum carrying them both to the ground in a heap. Trey's hand was on the wrong side of the Staff to get a force-field up, and he was forced to take a deep gash from Quynn's knife. Trey bellowed with pain, scrambling to find the birch segment toward the middle of the Staff. Quynn reared back, swinging his hand in a mighty punch that connected solidly with Trey's face. Trey saw stars, losing his grip on the Staff. He could feel blood streaming from his body as Quynn punched him again and again. Trey put his hands in front of his face, trying to ward off the blows, but it was no use. Quynn was strong, and he was mad.

Suddenly a massive gust of wind slammed into Quynn, ripping him away from Trey and carrying him up into the air. Arra stood under Quynn with her hands on her hips, burning primewood. She had put her bow away and was glaring at Quynn as the man spun in the air, whipping back and forth as Arra exerted her power.

Trey scrambled for his Staff, grabbing the birch section. He felt soulsoothing instantly surge through him, healing him, and he took in a shuddering breath.

That had been close.

But something was happening with Quynn. He was struggling with Arra, grappling with her on the muddy ground. They were both using magic, but Trey couldn't tell what kinds.

Rain pelted his face as he watched them fight.

Then Quynn roared, pulling a chip of wood from his pocket and burning it. The man fell to the ground as he did, air rippling around him as he wrenched himself from Arra's grasp. It was gravity magic, Trey realized.

Quynn was also a fallfoiler.

As Quynn hit the ground, Trey got to his feet. He could already feel the energy from the forcefield wearing off, weariness setting in again. Around him, the wind picked up, blowing harshly through the Splinter, carrying with it the scents of gunpowder and blood. The shouts and screams from around the little city were growing louder, echoing in his ears.

Quynn turned to Arra, an angry look on his face. "Die," he growled, flinging his hand out in front of him.

Arra flew up into the sky, faster than Trey could track. Quynn stood in the street, concentrating on his magic and Arra.

But Trey smiled—apparently Quynn didn't know about the tricks they could play with the storm. Arra would be safe, assuming she didn't fly high enough to actually hit the forcefield around the cities.

But Quynn didn't know any of that.

Trey stalked up to him, pulling a knife from its holster at his side. He had almost reached the man when his feet crunched loudly on the gravel underfoot, and Quynn turned. Trey followed through with the knife, throwing himself at Quynn. But the knife was just a feint—Trey had his other hand on the Staff, gripping elm, and he used the magic to throw Quynn violently to the ground.

Then Trey landed on Quynn, burying his knife to the hilt in the man's chest.

FORTY-FIVE

ARRA FELT Quynn's magical grip suddenly loosen, and she began to fall. She was thousands of feet up in the air, higher than she'd ever been before. She felt her stomach drop as she fell, picking up speed, the wind whistling by her ears.

Arra fished around in her primewood pouch. There was only one way she knew of to survive a drop like this: use the storm. She just needed some prime ash, and she could call the winds to her aid. It was a technique she'd used over and over again during her battle with Trey. She knew it would work, if she could find the wood.

She fell faster and faster, the ground rushing up to meet her. Arra felt a chill as she moved her hand through her pouch, frantically looking for the right wood. "Shit," she whispered as she fell headlong toward the earth, her legs flailing.

She was out of ash.

THE KNIFE FIZZLED as it went through Quynn's chest, meeting no resistance. Quynn had activated his damn mergemelding magic again, burning oak. Trey cursed, dropping the knife and rolling away as Quynn swung at him. Trey would have to catch the man unawares. Either that, or find a way to get rid of all his oak.

Until then, Quynn was nigh unstoppable.

Trey heard screaming from overhead. Arra! He looked up to see her hurtling toward the ground, hair streaming out behind her as she fell headfirst. But something was wrong. Why wasn't she using the storm to halt her fall? She shouldn't be out of control like that.

Out of the corner of his eye, Trey saw Quynn getting up from the ground, preparing to strike. He had drawn a knife, and he was heading for Trey.

But Arra was more important.

Trey flipped the Tree Ring Staff so the ash end was up. Then he he planted his feet, concentrating hard. The storm around him strengthened under his command, wind whipping wildly around the street. Trey used his Will to cancel the rain, forcing all his energy into it, putting everything into the air at his command. Arra continued screaming as she fell, plummeting toward certain death, and nothing was stopping her—nothing but the wind.

Trey just needed to make the wind strong enough.

Not for the first time, Trey wished he was a full Prime Mage instead of this bastardized half version. Fallfoiling, the magic of gravity control, would have been perfect here. But it was not one of his Talents. So he gritted his teeth, putting everything he had into the storm, hoping against hope that Arra would be alright.

Suddenly Trey gasped as he felt cold steel slice into him between his ribs. Heat spread from the wound as blood poured down his chest, and Trey found himself unable to breathe.

Still, he focused on the magic, Willing the storm to buoy Arra up, to prevent her from falling. He wanted her to live, wanted it more than anything he had ever wanted before in his life. She *would* live!

Trey felt his life dripping away as he continued channeling the storm. His vision dimmed and he slipped on the Staff, falling to his knees. Still he continued, pushing every last bit of energy he possessed into the wind.

In the background, he could hear Quynn laughing.

ARRA COULDN'T HELP SCREAMING as she dropped, moving impossibly fast. There was nothing that could arrest her fall.

But then she saw Trey there, a tiny figure on the ground. She saw him clutch the Staff, and suddenly the wind was there, whipping up underneath her, pushing against her fall.

Her speed slowed, but it wasn't enough. She was still going to hit the ground, hard enough to die. Trey didn't have enough power. The wind was not strong enough.

She rushed toward him, falling through the air. The rain had stopped, and the wind was coming much stronger now, pushing against her with reckless abandon. She slowed even further, and details began to resolve on the ground.

She saw Quynn approaching Trey, saw him stab him in the back.

She saw Trey fall, still clutching the Staff, blood pooling at his feet.

She saw Quynn step back, a wide smile taking over his face.

And still she fell.

She held her hands out in front of her, as if to embrace the world that was about to be her death.

TREY FELL TO THE GROUND, the Staff clattering down on top of him. The recharge from the forcefield had fully run out, his exertions over the past day catching up with him. He had no energy. He couldn't breathe.

He was done.

But as he fell, his fingers slipped over the willow in the Staff. And as his body gave up the fight, his mind battled on. It flailed out, reaching for something—anything—that could save him.

As Trey sank into nothingness, a massive gate sprang into existence. The gate swallowed them all up—Trey, Quynn, and Arra, as she hurtled to the ground—and transported them somewhere else.

PART
FOUR

PART

FOUR

FORTY-SIX

THE PASSAGE WAS much quicker than Arra had expected. She stood, clutching Trey close, as she took her last look at Valaralda. She felt tears coming to her eyes one final time as she looked away.

Through the gate.

The transfer took less than a second. Less than a blink. It was over before she knew it had even begun, feeling like ice water rushing over her, leaving her gasping for breath.

And then they were there, on the world their group had been assigned to.

Mar.

Earth.

It was different. Savage. Strange. But beautiful, with great green trees and insects and birds. She could see towering pedestals of rock, billowy clouds, and the sky—the sky was a shade of blue unlike anything she'd ever seen before. The sun shone down on her and the others in the group, and she took in her first breath on the new world.

The world that would be her home.

Only for a short time, of course—as long as it took to

locate the Mechanism. Then she would be away, her soul reclaimed, her body transferred back to Valaralda with the others.

She hoped it wouldn't take too long.

TREY STOOD on the mountain in mainland China with the others. He did not know the mountain's name. He did not even speak the language of the natives they had found there. He had not had time to marvel at this new planet's beauty, to make drawings of the strange animals he had already seen.

The elves needed magic. And he had volunteered, as he knew he would.

As Arra had.

That, he had *not* expected.

He squeezed her, feeling the warmth of her body next to his. He looked out at the rest of the Fourteen, gathered there to commit their ultimate sacrifice. He bowed his head as the ritual words were uttered.

He barely felt it when the knife slashed his throat, spraying hot blood onto the tree. And as he died, he uttered one final prayer to the Twins.

He held Arra's hand until the end.

QUYNN FELT rage course through his body. These people, these *senators*, could be so idiotic! They were willingly blind to the truth, unwilling to accept what he had tried so hard to explain.

The Fall was coming, and not for the first time.

Why wouldn't they listen to him? He stamped his foot, the

sound ringing out in the vast acropolis, echoing against the chill marble floor.

All around the room, senators looked at him, their expressions varying from snide to worried. Quynn knew he had been appearing unhinged of late, but time was growing short. They *had* to listen to him!

"Does the senator from Errenmel wish to speak?" a voice said in a cool, husky tone. It was Leriaar, that raven-haired bitch. How she had ever become the Speaker was beyond him. But he was not ready to address the Council. Not tonight.

"No, Speaker," Quynn said, trying to keep his tone gracious. "I apologize for my outburst."

"Your apology is noted," Leriaar said.

Quynn ground his teeth.

FORTY-SEVEN

ARRA BLINKED as the sounds of the storm crashed down around her. She was lying on the ground, and her entire body hurt like hell. She sat up painfully, looking around. She was in the forest, and the storm was still raging. Wind whistled through the trees as rain fell, percolating down between the leaves and branches overhead. She blinked, trying to clear her thoughts. What was that vision she had just seen? Unfamiliar names and places came to her mind, unbidden. Passing through that gate had done something to her, had unlocked memories she didn't know she had.

Trey.

Suddenly she remembered that Trey was dying when she had seen him last, had probably already died by now. She looked around and saw him lying a few feet away in a puddle. The Staff was next to him, but he didn't seem to be breathing.

Arra scrambled over to him on all fours, her body aching. Somehow her passage through the gate must have dampened her velocity. Nothing seemed broken after that fall from the sky, but everything hurt.

She grabbed the Staff, quickly finding the birch section in the middle. Placing a hand on Trey, she activated the magic.

Rivers of ice washed through her and into Trey. She arched her back as it coursed through her veins, her head angled up to the sky. She held that position as the soul-soothing magic did its work, healing both her and Trey, absolving them of their injuries.

She hoped she wasn't too late to save him.

TREY AWOKE, gasping for air. He was soaked, and his body hurt all over, but he was alive. He looked up to see Arra hovering over him, a worried expression on her face.

"Oh, thank the Twins," she said. "I thought I'd lost you."

Trey struggled to sit up. He was in a puddle, and it was *cold*. The storm was raging on around them, and he found himself shivering.

"So...cold," he said, his teeth chattering.

Then he remembered—they'd been fighting Quynn. Trey turned sharply, trying to see where Quynn was, but the motion made his vision swim and his head hurt.

"Where's..." he started.

"I don't know," Arra said. "He wasn't here when I woke up. We went through another gate, and now we're here. And he's not."

Trey suddenly felt like throwing up. His exertions over the past day had been too much for his body to handle. "Need...to sleep," he muttered, slumping over. His eyes wouldn't focus.

Arra pulled at him. "Come on," she said, "there's a hollowed-out tree over there. We can take shelter in it. Get some rest."

"Okay," Trey said, drooling into the puddle. He had to get it together. He didn't want her to see him like this.

"Try another forcefield," she said.

"I don't...think that's a good idea." The rush from the first one had faded precipitously, leaving him in even worse shape than before. Trey didn't think they could keep using the force-fields for energy.

"Here, I'll help you," Arra said, scrabbling under him. He felt her supporting him under his arm, and he made the effort to stand. It was incredibly difficult; he felt like his body weighed a thousand pounds, and his head was clamped inside a vice. But he managed it. He was shivering uncontrol-lably. "Come on," Arra said, helping him balance. He leaned against her as she led the way to the tree hollow.

IT WAS terrible seeing Trey like this. Arra's heart wrenched as she helped him into the hollow tree. It was an old redwood that had survived a forest fire years ago, the flames carving a hollow cavity into the massive trunk. Her people used hollows like this frequently—they made great camping spots when out on hunting expeditions. It would shelter them from the rain, and give them a modicum of protection from the wind.

There was just room enough for the two of them in the hollow. She helped Trey lie down, and he closed his eyes, out immediately. Arra settled down next to him, huddling up against him for warmth. They couldn't start a fire, not with the storm still out of control, not with Cothellon forces ranging through the forest. All they had was each other.

It felt awkward being this close to him, after everything. But the energy from the forcefield was gone now, and her body responded in kind. She needed to sleep. So she wrapped an arm around Trey and closed her eyes.

They shivered together as sleep overtook them.

ARRA AWOKE TO STRANGE SOUNDS. Footsteps, rough voices, sounds of clanking and clicking. Trey was already awake, and he put a finger up to his mouth, indicating quiet. They waited there, huddled together, as the sounds continued all around them.

After about ten minutes, the footsteps faded.

"Soldiers," Trey whispered. "Cothellon, I think. Good thing they didn't see us in here."

Arra shifted, moving away from Trey in the small space. It was still raining outside, and the wind was howling. She could still hear footsteps and shouts in the forest, but they were further away now.

She rested her head on her hand and looked at Trey. "How do you feel?"

"A bit better," he said. "I don't think we slept very long, although it's hard to tell."

"I feel like I could sleep for a week."

"I know how you feel. I lost count of how many times I've died in the past day, always brought back from the brink. That last time thanks to you."

"You've saved me your fair share of times, too," Arra said, smiling at him.

Trey bowed his head. "This mage business is something, isn't it?"

"It's certainly something."

They were silent for a minute.

"How long do you think we should stay in here?" Trey asked.

Arra tried flexing her legs. Her muscles were sore; she could barely move. "Let's at least wait until the soldiers are gone," she said. "I don't think I have the strength to battle an army."

"Quynn's out there, somewhere," Trey said. "We'll have to face him again, sooner or later."

"Later, I hope."

They rested there in the tree, listening to the sounds of the rain and the movements of the troops.

"Trey?" Arra asked after a moment.

"Yes?"

"Do you remember anything about me?"

"What do you mean?"

"Have you had any...visions, or anything? Like memories from another life?"

Trey turned to look at her, his expression guarded. "Yes," he said, "but I assumed I was just delusional. Do you... remember me?"

Arra lay back, looking up at the top of the tree hollow, picturing what she'd seen. "It happens whenever we go through one of those gates. It's like the gate unlocks a new memory that I'd lost. I remember you—us—together. We were...married." She glanced at Trey to see how he was taking it, but his expression was unreadable. "We were in love," she whispered.

"But how is that possible?" Trey asked.

"I don't know. How is *any* of this possible? We're both mages, you and I. Prime Mages. We're both doing things no one has done for millennia. Why is it happening?"

"And why is it happening to *us*?"

"Exactly."

"I don't know," Trey said. "The past few weeks have been like a dream for me. Or like a nightmare. I've lost everything I knew. I've learned that nothing about my life was true. I..." He stopped, suddenly awkward. "I met you."

Arra looked at him. "What did you think about me when we first met?"

"You seemed...nice," Trey said.

"Nice?" Arra laughed. "That's all?"

"Well, yes! I mean, you *were* nice. And..."

"And what?"

"Well," Trey said, seeming unwilling to continue.

"Say it!" Arra poked him in the ribs, and he flinched away, smiling. Then he turned to face her, their bodies inches away in the hollow tree.

"You're the most beautiful woman I've ever seen," Trey said. "And the most intelligent. The most fierce. The most strong."

Arra was caught a little off guard. She'd suspected he had a thing for her, but she hadn't realized how deep it went. The memories of him confused her. She remembered having deep love for him, but that wasn't *now*. That wasn't the present. Her eyes traced his face as he looked at her. That face that was at once so familiar and so strange. She did remember him, but something wasn't right. There was something different about him. Something missing.

He started to turn away, but she caught him, her hand on his arm. "Fenian's death is still so fresh," she said, feeling those emotions starting to return.

"I know," Trey said, "and that's why I didn't want to say anything. I understand. And I'm so, so sorry he died."

Arra fell back, her hand twirling her hair. It had been ages since she'd done that. She lay on the ground next to Trey and closed her eyes, thinking.

She had loved Fenian, it was true. And she was devastated by his death. She had been so sure she would spend the rest of her life with him, would grow old with him. And all of that had been taken away from her in a flash.

Even for an elf, she realized, moments could be fleeting. Time could be so short.

She opened her eyes, turning back to Trey. "You remind me of him in some ways," she said.

"Fenian?"

"Yes. You are strong, even though you won't admit it to yourself. And you're talented, both in the magical sense and the Mundane, even though you don't realize it. You're a good man, Trey. Don't ask me how I know that—it's just something I feel. Maybe it's something I remember."

Trey was staring at her, blue eyes shining. "Thank you," he said. "That means a lot."

"You're pretty handsome, too," Arra said, then she blushed. Why had she said that? "Even if you're not an elf."

"But I *am* an elf," Trey said.

"*What*? But your ears—"

"I asked Quynn about that, but he wouldn't tell me. So I thought it over. And really, when you think about it, the ears are the only thing that separates elves physically from humans. It would be pretty easy to change, say, with surgery."

"But why would you want to?"

Trey shrugged. "Ask the man who raised me. All of this was his doing. And I still don't know why."

"He told you you were an elf?"

"Yes."

"Maybe he was lying. And besides, it's not just *ears* that distinguish elves. Our faces are also different, and our eyes. Honestly, you can usually tell an elf when you see one, even if you can't see their ears."

Then she looked at Trey, really *looked* at him. It was all there, the features she knew to look for. The slightly angled face, the smaller eyes. The hair that fell in just such a way. She had been blind not to notice it before. "Twins," she breathed, "you really *are* an elf!"

Trey laughed. "Does this mean I get to live forever?" he asked, poking her in the stomach.

"Hey," she said, poking him back. "We don't live forever. At least..." She paused, thinking about the flashback she'd had earlier. Had that actually been *her*? Something about the memory felt ancient, like it had happened millennia ago. But that was impossible. She was about to turn fifty. She was Silanar's daughter. She couldn't have those memories.

"At least what?" Trey prompted, looking at her with a worried expression.

"I don't know," Arra said. "It's just that those memories I have, it feels like they happened such a long time ago."

"I know what you mean," Trey said.

But it couldn't be. She was still young. She had her whole life ahead of her, while so many others did not. Fenian. Eloen. Elanil. Her vision swam as her eyes suddenly brimmed with tears. So many had already been lost, thanks to the arrogance of elves.

"Hey," Trey said, seeing her tears. She started to turn away, not wanting him to see her cry, but he reached out to her, pulling her into an embrace. He held her there as she cried, her body racked with sobs. The rain fell around them as she thought about her lost loved ones, and the life they'd never live. She cried for Fenian, for her sister, for her friends.

Trey held her tightly as she eventually drifted back to sleep.

SHE AWOKE some time later to find him still holding her, his breathing slow. She turned in his arms and found him asleep, a peaceful expression on his face. She felt warm in his arms. Part of her felt terrible to be this close to another man this soon after Fenian's death. But another part of her responded to those deeply-buried memories. That part of her mind *felt* something for Trey, something deep, something strong. It was still developing, that feeling. She wasn't sure what it was.

She turned all the way over until she was facing him. He looked so peaceful, lying there in the dim light. He *was* a handsome man, she had to admit, even when he was dirty and disheveled and plainly worn out. She fought back a sudden urge to kiss him. It wasn't right. It was too soon. She barely knew the man.

But part of her, that part that remembered, *did* know him. It was an uncanny feeling, being of two minds like that. She wondered if there was a way to reconcile her thoughts, to blend the memories of what was with the reality of what is. As she continued to think it over, Trey opened his eyes.

Those beautiful blue eyes.

He was still sleepy, she could tell, still waking up. Something about the moment felt different, felt right. This wasn't the first time she'd lain with this man in the hollow of a tree. This was not the first time he had looked at her like that, with love in his eyes. And a part of her mind cracked open further, allowing something in. Not memories, exactly, but feelings. Emotions.

And the moment still seemed right.

She moved forward, her lips inches away from his. She watched his expression as she did, waiting to see how he would react. He looked at her for a long moment, just staring into her eyes. Then he came forward the rest of the way.

Their kiss was like nothing she'd ever felt before. Oh, the

part of her brain that *remembered* had definitely felt it before. But to her waking mind, this was new. This was brilliant. This was incredible. Her guilt and her sadness swept away as the two halves of her memory collided, relishing in this perfect moment.

She didn't know how long they lay there, just kissing in the tree. The storm blustered around them, rain and wind mixing with the feelings in her head, in her body. Thoughts of armies and magic fell aside as she explored Trey's mouth, his tongue, his face. The emotions and exertions of the day came to a crest there in his arms, and she poured them away like water in a stream. She melted in his embrace, and for a long moment she knew nothing else.

It seemed like hours had passed when she finally pulled away, breathless. She opened her mouth to say something, but words just seemed so wrong after that incredible kiss. So instead she just snuggled up against Trey, seeking his warmth. She at once barely knew him, and had known him all her life. It was an unsettling feeling, but she accepted it. Made peace with it.

Somehow she knew this perfect moment would not last.

THE NEXT TIME THEY AWOKE, the rain had finally stopped. Arra listened for the sounds of soldiers, but all she heard were a few birds. The light was noticeably brighter outside their tree hollow, although the vast cities in the sky still blotted out most of the sunlight.

She nudged Trey. "I'm starving," she said. "How long have we been here?"

Trey shrugged. "No idea," he said, sitting up. "Hopefully the world didn't go to hell while we were gone."

Arra smiled at him shyly, remembering their kiss. Had it been a bad idea? She looked at him, trying to read his thoughts from his expression. It proved largely unsuccessful.

Trey reached out and took her hand. "Thank you." That was all he said.

She squeezed his hand.

"We should go," she said. "Our people need us." It felt strange, thinking of the elves as *their* people, not just hers. But Trey was an elf, so they were his people as much as they were hers. Even if he hadn't lived among them. She would have to start thinking of him as someone like her. An elf.

Trey stretched his legs out, yawning. "I feel better, at least."

"Good enough to kill some Cothellon?"

"I think so. How do you feel?"

She looked at him, hearing an undertone to the question. "Good," she said, squeezing his hand again. "I feel good."

Trey nodded. "Good."

They were both suddenly so awkward.

Arra couldn't help but laugh. There was something fresh about this experience, something new. She opened her mouth to say something, but she was interrupted.

"*There* you are," a voice said from just outside the hollow tree.

Arra jumped, startled. She peered outside the tree and found Allain staring back at her.

"Did you sleep with him?" Allain asked, his tone bitter.

"What?" Arra said. "No! What kind of a question is that? Why are you here?"

Allain grinned widely, tossing a knife up and down in his hand. "Nothing you need to concern yourself with," he said. "I'm just here to kill Trey."

FORTY-EIGHT

"YOU MIGHT WANT to get in line," Trey said, standing behind Arra. He watched as Allain's eyes flicked from him to her, back and forth, flipping a knife in his hand. "Haven't you done enough already, Allain?"

"You killed my father and took my girl," Allain said. "I came here to kill you."

"First of all," Trey said, "I didn't kill Orist—he died saving Kharis. We were both there. We both saw it."

"I could have *saved* him," Allain said. Trey could see the pain in his eyes.

"It wasn't your fault," Trey said, placing his hands on Arra's shoulders. She was holding her body tensely, ready to spring into action should it become necessary.

"I could have saved him," Allain repeated.

"Secondly," Arra said, "I am *not* your girl. Where did you even get that idea?"

Allain hung his head. "I know," he said. "I just..." He sighed, putting the knife away. "It's stupid."

"What's really wrong, Allain?" Arra asked. "You can tell us."

Allain looked up, his eyes narrow, as if he expected a trick.

"It's okay," Trey said. "No hard feelings about trying to kill me."

Allain seemed like a powder keg of emotions ready to explode. "I just wanted to be *good* at something," he said. "I wanted Arra to like me."

"But I *do* like you," Arra said, "just not that way. And you are good at things. Lots of things!"

"You're a damn good mistweaver," Trey said. "Arra, you should have seen the bear he did. He literally had me convinced a grizzly bear was about to eat me!"

"What?" Arra asked. "I didn't even know you could *do* that!"

Allain grinned. "That was nothing—you should see my dragon."

"I really hope that wasn't a euphemism," Trey said.

Allain at least had the decency to blush. "Father always loved my dragon illusions, when he wasn't scolding me for them."

Arra reached out, placing a hand on Allain's shoulder. "Your father was a great man," she said. "He left us too soon."

"Allain," Trey said, "you do know we need you, right?"

Allain frowned. "No one ever needs me."

"The soulsundering," Arra said. "We need you for that. To activate one of the Trees."

"Oh, *that*," Allain said, rolling his eyes.

Arra withdrew her hand. "It's important, Allain."

"It's our best plan for getting rid of the Cothellon," Trey said.

Allain huffed. "I want to do something *cool*, like you guys do."

"We're just running defense," Trey said. "You get the cool

job. A real soulsundering. One of those doesn't come around every day."

It sure as hell *better* not, anyway.

"But it's a stupid tree!"

"Those Trees," Arra said, "are going to save us. *You* are going to save us. Don't you realize how important that is?"

Allain shuffled his feet, his eyes on the ground.

"Fine," he said after a moment. "I'll do it." He gave Arra a sidelong look. "So...are you two a thing now?"

Trey looked at Arra, seeing the uncertainty in her eyes. Should he say something, or would she? He didn't want to ruin the moment they'd shared. That incredible kiss.

"I think," Arra said, sounding out the words slowly, "that Trey and I have been a thing for a very long time."

FORTY-NINE

QUYNN SLIPPED THROUGH THE GATE, stumbling against a desk in Mission Control. Everything was a blur of pain.

"What happened to you?" Lorelei asked. "The gatemonitors barely got you in time."

Quynn pulled Trey's knife out, gasping as pain lanced upward through his body. He had already lost a lot of blood. He was dimly aware of Lorelei shouting at someone to get a medic.

THEY FIXED him up right there in Mission Control, giving him bandages and something for the pain. There was no prime birch here, not up in the cities, so there would be no healing magic. His body would have to heal on its own.

What had happened back there? One moment he'd been burning dark oak, impervious to knives and arrows, and the next he'd felt the blade piercing into him. He was probably just out of practice, had stopped the burn too soon. Or maybe the wood just gave out on its own. Whatever the case, he would have to be more careful in the future. Maybe actually wear some armor.

"Sylvis," Lorelei was saying, "what's the soonest we can pull the trigger?"

"Three more hours," Sylvis answered, her fingers flying over the touchscreen in front of her. "Alignment still isn't perfect. We're going as fast as we can."

Lorelei turned to Quynn. "The Eldrim are planning something, and they have an entire Prime Forest to back them up. We need to hold out for three more hours. Can you get back down there?"

Quynn nodded hesitantly. He needed rest. He needed healing. But this was the final moment. Now was not the time to back down. "I can."

"Good," Lorelei said. She picked up a headset lying on a desk and spoke into it. "Gate Control?"

"Go for Gate Control," a voice said over the loudspeaker.

"How many gatesenders can you spare for me without jeopardizing the operation?"

"Um," the voice said, pausing for a moment. "You can have three of them."

"Good," Lorelei said. "Send them up here to Mission Control."

"Aye, sir."

A minute later, three gates materialized in Mission Control, lined up neatly along the back wall. Three dark-mages walked through the gates, heads held high, haughty expressions on their faces. They were wearing sumptuous violet robes and carrying satchels of wood.

Dark willow.

"Mages," Lorelei said, bowing her head slightly. Even *she* treated them with respect! "Thank you for coming. We have work to do."

TREY FOLLOWED Arra to a Hunter's stash she knew about near their hollowed-out tree. The Sylranthean Hunters hid caches like this throughout the forest, filling them with basic supplies: dried fruit and nuts, cured meat, fresh water, arrows and fletching materials. Normally, in an emergency, Hunters could live off the land. But in times of bad weather, or if food was scarce for some reason, the stashes were a good emergency backup. All the Hunters knew where they were.

Full and largely refreshed, it was time to get back to the fight. They swung over to the Splinter, using leafrunning to speed their journey, but taking care not to over-expend the magic. They'd both learned the hard way that burning too much wood too fast was not sustainable.

The village was in ruins when they arrived. They found no living souls there—only the charred and battered remains of the dead. Splinter humans were scattered everywhere, burned and dying on the ground. Most of them were unarmed.

Trey felt like retching. So much violence! The Cothellon soldiers were heartless and brutal. Didn't they know that the Splinter was full of peaceful people?

"We should have been here," Trey said quietly. He and Arra were perched on the courthouse roof, one of the last remaining large buildings in the city. Destruction was spread out below them, death on a massive scale. Trey couldn't help but feel responsible for it all, somehow. Had anyone survived?

"We had our hands full with Quynn," Arra said. "Is this it? Are they done? Have they had their fill of blood?"

"I doubt it," Trey said. "You saw Lorelei. She is ruthless. As long as anyone is living down here, she'll hunt them down and destroy them." He looked up at the cities, still hovering there in the sky. "At least until her plan is complete."

"Then where are they?" Arra said. "Where did the army go?"

With a sinking feeling, Trey realized he knew. "The Prime Forest," he said.

"Shit," Arra said. "You're probably right. We have to get there. We have to help."

Trey nodded his agreement, clutching the Tree Ring Staff tightly. They sped off, heading back into the forest.

RYLAN WAS out of darkprime wood. It was his one skill, really, the only thing he could reliably do: lift things with magic. It was cool to have that power, but he was out of wood.

He was useless.

He watched as elves scaled the new Prime Trees, expertly sawing through massive branches, then cutting them into tiny segments. Within minutes of losing a branch, the Trees regrew it, spinning another one out from the trunk in a new shape.

"Got to replenish while we can," Orym said, walking over to where Rylan was standing. "This might be the only chance we get for a long time."

"Why?" Rylan asked.

"Once the soulsundering activates, the Trees die. It happened during the Sundering three hundred years ago. We didn't expect it then, and we lost all the Trees, even the ones that weren't involved in the ritual. They all died at once. This time, we'll be ready for it."

"Too bad that wood doesn't work for my magic."

"I asked Dillon to bring you some. I hope it makes it in time."

"You think of everything, don't you?"

Orym smiled. "I try, I really do. But even I make mistakes." He looked around at the bustling elves, cutting and hauling lumber and shouting instructions to each other. "I hope this isn't one of those times."

"When will it happen?" Rylan asked.

"The soulsundering?"

Rylan nodded.

"As soon as you get your dark maple, we can start."

"When will that be?"

"I don't know," Orym said. "I don't know."

Suddenly there were shouts from further away, at the edge of the Forest. Rylan heard gunfire.

Allain appeared out of nowhere, running quickly towards them. "They're here!" he shouted. "Take cover!"

"Out of time," Orym observed.

The Cothellon had arrived.

THERE WERE gates spawning around the edges of the Prime Forest. Trey watched them from his perch in a Tree, edges of whirling light clearly visible against the wood.

Soldiers were streaming out of the gates.

"What are we going to do?" Arra asked. She was crouched on the branch next to him, balancing easily.

They watched as the soldiers gathered at the edge of the Forest, wielding guns and swords and knives and even bows and arrows. These were Cothellon soldiers—not Remnant—which meant they were undoubtedly better trained.

Which meant the Eldrim were probably screwed.

"What else *can* we do?" Trey said. "We fight."

Arra grasped his hand, squeezing it tightly. "We'll do it together."

"Remember what Rylan said: we need to touch if we want to do magic together."

Arra looked up at him, eyes glinting in the fading sunlight. "Somehow I don't think that will be a problem."

Trey looked down from his perch in the Tree. Where were the Eldrim? Surely they were aware of the approaching army.

"There!" Arra whispered, pointing.

Trey saw elves appearing, coming out from hiding places in the Forest. They moved toward each other until they were standing in a line, palms raised in front of them, facing upward toward the sky.

Like a line of pigs waiting to be slaughtered.

He didn't know where that idea had come from. He'd never seen a pig before. But why were they just *standing* there? Shouldn't they—

The elves attacked.

Not with weapons, but with magic.

Cothellon soldiers flew backwards, hurtling through the air, screaming as they slammed into trees and rocks. Some of them crashed into branches, wood impaling them. Others flew out of sight at breakneck speed.

None of them survived.

"Leafrunners," Arra breathed. "I had hoped to never see this again."

"They know how to fight?"

"Not with weapons. But yes—all leafrunners train for this, starting at a certain age."

Trey watched the leafrunners work, using their magic to throw soldiers around as if they were nothing more than kindling. "The Cothellon don't stand a chance," he said.

But then the remaining Cothellon opened fire.

The line of leafrunners did their best to avoid the bullets, using their magic to move themselves sideways or backwards. But soldiers kept pouring in through the gates, vastly outnumbering the Sylranthean mages, and there was only so much they could do. Trey watched as one leafrunner went down in a spray of blood.

"We have to help," Trey said. Arra nodded.

They swung down from the Tree, using leafrunning to jump from branch to branch. Trey was grasping the Staff with one hand, touching elm: the wood that powered leafrunning and shockstriking.

Perfect.

He sent his Will into the Staff, sending lightning strikes spraying into the Cothellon army. He kept going as he moved, pummeling the soldiers with shock after shock.

Next to him, Arra was doing what she did best. She was a whirl of action, shooting arrow after arrow into the enemy army, bladedancing magic warping and bending their flight, never missing a shot. Elf after elf went down before her onslaught, caught unaware by the fury of it.

Trey switched tactics as he reached the ground. Arra was a killing machine, but she was vulnerable—any errant shot could take her down. So he flipped the Staff over to the ash end, activating a one-sided forcefield around her.

It fizzed into existence, shimmering as her arrows shot through it. Bullets pinged off the outer edge, ricocheting into the woods and embedding into the thick trunks of Trees.

It was a good thing the Cothellon didn't have any mergeguns.

Trey saw six more Eldrim appear nearby, intent on the Cothellon. He recognized a few of them—Kharis and Imra. And there was Allain! They all had bows out, and soon they were matching Arra shot for shot, arrows flying with deadly precision.

But they, too, were unprotected. So Trey split his mind seven ways, putting forcefields around each of them. It was more difficult than he'd expected—he had to really concentrate to keep them in place. He could feel his energy dropping, too—he wouldn't be able to keep this up for long.

The only problem was, he had forgotten to shield himself.

A bullet slammed into him, knocking him to the ground, the Staff falling from his grasp. His forcefields all winked out instantly, leaving everyone unprotected.

Bullets were flying everywhere.

Trey rolled over, grunting as the pain from the bullet hit him. But he managed to grab the birch segment of the Staff, channeling soulsoothing magic through his body.

The bullet left him as quickly as it had come.

Arra had taken shelter behind a massive Tree, watching him with concern. Trey gave her a thumbs-up sign and staggered to his feet. Cothellon soldiers were advancing all around him, guns blazing.

He popped a forcefield up around himself and sprinted out of the way, heading towards a Tree. He winced as two of the archers went down, blood flying in the air. There weren't enough Eldrim for this. The Cothellon had the advantage.

More Eldrim appeared, just then—Guardians, by the looks of it. They screamed as they ran, holding swords and axes and bows high. "For Sylrantheas!" he heard them shout as they approached the Cothellon army. The battle cry echoed throughout the Forest as other elves took up the call, and Trey found himself smiling. Everything was just as it should be, as it had been in his books.

Except this was real life, and real life could kill you.

He ducked as a bullet flew past him, cutting chunks of

bark off the Tree he was standing behind. Then he jumped out, lightning spewing from his hands. The Cothellon who had shot at him went down, his body jolting spasmodically from the torrents of electricity showering through him.

Another soldier took his place, and Trey shot him too, snarling. Then he advanced, blasting soldier after soldier, but they just kept coming.

There were too many.

The sounds of battle swept through the Forest all around him: screams and cries, gunshots and the clashing of swords. Eldrim were dying everywhere he looked, their faces staring sightlessly at the Trees. Trey popped up another forcefield as a squadron of soldiers pelted him with bullets. He almost tripped over a body, the gruesome sight of blood and bones causing him to gag.

It was all too much.

Where were the mages? Where were the Guardians? Surely Sylrantheas had enough people left to beat these Cothellon scum.

Trey cast about, looking for anyone he knew. Arra was there, far away, battling with a group of soldiers. She had a sword now, and she used it expertly, dispatching soldier after soldier, long hair flying out behind her as she moved. She was a deadly vision of beauty.

Trey turned as more soldiers approached, turning off his forcefield and flipping the Staff back to elm. He tried leafrunning this time, using it to clear the way. Soldiers flew backwards at his gesture, screaming as they slammed into Trees. Trey felt adrenaline coursing through him as he swept the Forest from side to side, heading towards Arra. None could stand before him.

Except his energy was ebbing. The power he was expending was too much—he would not be able to maintain it for long. He gestured toward the last few elves fighting Arra and they flipped backwards, flying off and disappearing somewhere into the Forest.

He felt weariness overtaking him.

Arra grinned as he arrived. "Having fun?" she asked, her eyes bright.

Trey grabbed her and kissed her, shaking away the tiredness. "Yes," he said.

But then an arrow hit him in the back, and a second one in the leg. A third arrow shot into Arra's hip, and both of them went down.

FIFTY

TREY CURSED, inspecting the two arrows jutting from his skin. Getting shot *hurt*. Arra rolled over next to him, grunting.

She grabbed his hand.

"Together," she said, pain filling her eyes. Trey nodded, clutching her. They held the Staff between them, touching birch.

He channeled the magic, soulsoothing bursting out from the Staff like an icy blast. The healing rippled through them, making them whole in a flash, the arrows sliding out of his wounds and falling to the ground.

He took a deep breath as the magic ran its course.

Then they were whole, sitting together underneath a Tree. "I'll never get used to that," Trey said.

"Neither will I," Arra said. "Come on."

They scrambled away, trying to get to cover. Cothellon were everywhere, continuing to arrive as new gates opened and closed around them.

Trey stood slowly, leaning on Arra for support. Soul-soothing magic always left him shaken, not quite good as new. It was like the body knew it had been mortally wounded, and it couldn't shake off the feeling.

He looked around, hoping for some kind of solution, some way to win. If the soldiers kept coming like this, there was no hope. They would slaughter everyone in the Forest—might already have done so, in fact—he didn't see anyone up and about nearby. Trey and Arra, powerful as they were, would not be enough to stop the army on their own.

Then Trey spied something else. It was a gate, but there weren't any soldiers coming out of it.

It was full of children.

They came screaming out, wearing ratty t-shirts and ripped jeans, brandishing rudimentary weapons, their hair wild and their faces dirty.

"Newfris!" some of them shouted as they ran, hurtling headlong toward the Cothellon force. Another group appeared next, their hair dyed wild shades of pink and purple and green. "New Paris!" they shouted in accented English. "New Sydney!" a group of girls screamed as they exited the swirling gate. Their cries mingled with the cries of the fallen and the oncoming army, until Trey couldn't keep the sounds and faces straight any more.

It seemed that the entire Under had come to help.

All of them.

Rylan and Orym jogged up just as Dill sauntered through the gate. Orym gave him a quick hug.

"You made good time," he said.

"Turns out my plan was closer than I thought," Dill said. "Just took Smoke to put in the finishing touches. He had all this ready by the time we got back."

He gestured to an older, hunched man with wild gray hair

who was walking through the gate behind them. Orym clapped the old man on the back. "Luthar!" he said. "You old bag. Glad to see you came around to the right side, eventually." He frowned. "You've aged."

"You haven't," Luthar said, peering up at Orym curiously.

"Must be good genes," Orym said, turning to face Trey. "This is Luthar."

"My undername is Smoke," Luthar said.

Two more boys came through the gate.

"And this," Orym said, gesturing to Dill, "is my son, Dillon. Here's Shot—he's a mergemelder, and Small. He's—"

"I'm the smart one," Small said, throwing a bundle of little black boxes and wires at Trey. Trey caught the bundle, unsure what it was. "Power cells," Small said. "Can you charge them up?"

"Sure," Trey said. Shockstriking should do the trick.

"Did you bring it?" Orym asked Dillon.

The boy nodded, unshouldering a pack and pulling out a handful of dark wood chips. "All the dark maple you can eat. Or...burn, or whatever it is you do with it."

Orym took the pack. "Thank you, son. You saved the day."

"Don't thank me just yet," Dillon said, eyeing the surrounding Forest. Underkids were everywhere, doing their best to kill as many Cothellon as they could. It seemed like the tides had turned.

"Will this be enough?" Rylan asked, looking inside the darkprime backpack.

Orym nodded. "It better be."

"Now what?" Trey asked.

"Now we mop up this army," Orym said, turning to Dillon. "You brought the guns?"

"We did. Not many of them, but it will help."

"That it will," Orym said. "That it will."

"Arra," Trey said, "I've been thinking. Our magic is powerful, but it can only do so much on its own. I've been thinking we should join together, like Rylan said."

"What's your idea?" she asked.

As he told her, he saw Orym's smile widening.

"T-MINUS TEN MINUTES," the timekeeper said over the loudspeaker. Quynn winced as he stood, wishing they had access to soulsoothers up in the city.

Lorelei swung around in her chair, slim legs crossed underneath her tight-fitting red dress. "You ready?" she asked.

Quynn nodded.

"THIS WILL BE HARDER than anything you've done before," Orym said, his hand on Rylan's shoulder. Rylan was stroking the Book of Amplification idly, listening to the sounds of battle all around. Orym had assured him he would be safe here, underneath the Prime Maple in the center of the Forest.

"The biggest danger is burning yourself out," Orym said. "They call it soulburning. It happens when you channel too much power. For example, if I were to touch this Tree"—he reached out and placed a hand on the Maple, as if to illustrate his point—"and burned the entire thing at once, I'd instantly soulburn myself. It's too much power for a single mage to handle. The same thing can happen with some artifacts, like this Book."

"What happens when you soulburn?" Rylan asked.

"You die," Orym said. "And worse—according to ancient elven mysticism, your soul also dies. Permanently."

"Why does that matter?"

Orym's eyes were veiled. "I don't know," he said, "but I have some theories."

Rylan had a sudden memory. "My mother," he said. "That's how Phoenix died."

Orym's face got sad. "I'm afraid so."

Rylan tried to hold back the tears that were threatening to come. He'd been holding them back for five long years—now was not the time.

When this was all over, he'd have himself a good cry.

Phoenix deserved that.

"How can I avoid her fate?" he asked. "There must be a way."

"Start out slowly," Orym said. "Ramp up your power level bit by bit. Be careful, though—it can be addicting, like a drug. Darkprime magic feels *good* when you use it, and the more you use, the better it feels. That's the biggest danger, here. I like to pay attention to my breathing. When I start breathing too quickly, I know it's time to back off."

"Sounds simple enough," Rylan said.

"It's anything but simple," Orym said. "But I'm sure you'll do fine."

"Why don't *you* lift the Forest? Why make me do it?"

"Because I'm weak," Orym said. There was something in his eyes, some kind of sadness. "No, you're the one best suited for this job. Do us proud, Rylan."

"I'll try."

ARRA HELD Trey's hand tightly, perched atop a Tree. They'd risked some wind to get up there, but it put them out of range of most arrows and made them a much harder target to hit with a gun.

"You ready?" Trey asked, holding the Staff in front of them. Cothellon soldiers were arrayed beneath them, continuing to pour out from gates that kept popping up around the Forest. There had been a few darkmages in the group, but they weren't very powerful; Arra and Trey had dispatched them easily. Arra wondered if Lorelei was holding anything in reserve.

Anything stronger.

But for now, their focus was on the soldiers. The underkids were quickly being overrun, their enthusiasm not enough to make up for the Cothellon's superior firepower and training.

"Here we go," Trey said, clutching ash. He was about to use darkprime magic—something she couldn't do.

So Arra burned elm—leafrunning—and Trey activated ash, a connection springing up between them. It was as if Arra could see into Trey's mind, peer into his very soul. It was heady stuff—intoxicating. She felt connected to him in a way she'd never felt with another person. Not even with Fenian. He held her tightly, Willing the magic to do as he planned. And she felt her own magic following him, guided by his mind and hers, working together in perfect harmony.

So *this* is what Rylan had meant.

It was beautiful.

They worked together, shaping the twin powers into one. Forcefields sprang into being—not spherical, but flat planes, like big pieces of fizzling paper. Trey manufactured them by the dozens, flicking them out from his mind and into the world. And Arra took them, using leafrunning magic to fling them against soldiers on the ground. The forcefields smacked into soldiers, sending them flying. It caused two things to happen: the electric shock from the forcefield stunned the soldiers, while the impact from the shield hit them hard, breaking noses and arms and sending many of them unconscious. It certainly caught them by surprise—Arra doubted if any of them had seen this use of magic before. She smiled as she continued throwing flat forcefields at them.

But the Cothellon learned quickly. They started dodging the forcefields, or bracing themselves against them, gritting their teeth as the electricity discharged into them. There was a limit to what Arra could do with leafrunning, and Trey couldn't keep the forcefields going forever.

"Let's try something else!" Arra yelled at him, and he nodded. He relaxed his grip on her hand slightly, and all the forcefields snapped out of existence. "Do you have any bright ideas?"

"Plan B," Trey said, flipping the Staff over. His hand was now holding the elm segment. Shockstriking. "I need both hands for this."

He let go of her.

Arra pulled elm and poplar from her pouch—leafrunning and bladedancing. Next to her, Trey had his other hand on ash—forcefinding.

"Ready?" Trey called, and Arra put her arms around his waist. His body felt tense.

"Ready!" she said, feeling the mental connection begin again.

In her mind, she could feel Trey's magic. He formed a series of little forcefields, small spheres bounded by light. Then he used shockstriking magic to fill them up with raw, electric power—lightning in a bottle.

Arra took them as they formed, capturing them with

leafrunning and floating them in the air. But leafrunning wasn't good with tiny objects—bullets and arrows couldn't be controlled that way. So she also burned poplar, using the power she had wanted all her life but never had.

Bladedancing.

Bladedancing was bullet magic.

One by one, the little balls of concentrated energy burst forth, propelled by bladedancing, shooting at the Cothellon soldiers like bright bullets from a magical gun.

The first soldier to be hit flew to the ground instantly, his body shaking uncontrollably, a dark hole visible in his body where the shockbullet had struck. The next one screamed, the bullet taking him right between the eyes.

So much energy in so small a space—it was *very* effective.

Arra smiled.

Trey was making them at a faster rate now. Part of Arra's mind was devoted to capturing the shockbullets, floating them in front of her using leafrunning. But the majority of her Will focused on shooting them at the Cothellon. Her mind split into fragments, powering bullets by the dozens, then by the hundreds, shooting them off in all directions, each one a deadly projectile heading unerringly toward its target.

The Cothellon died. Arra and Trey swept through them, hybrid magic cascading across their ranks. The electricity and the forcefields pierced through everything—armor, shields, even Trees. Nothing could stop them.

Arra laughed as she propelled another flurry of shockbullets into the enemy elves. And Trey laughed with her, the sound of their glee merging into one.

And by the hundreds, the Cothellon died.

QUYNN STOOD in front of the gate, taking deep breaths, steeling himself. He was strong. He was determined. He could do this.

"T-minus fifteen seconds," Sylvis said, taking over from the timekeeper.

This was it, the moment of his destiny. The final execution of the Cothellon plan.

"10...9...8...7...6..."

Quynn hitched up his pants, checking his darkprime supply. Dark maple, poplar, oak, and willow. All there. He was ready.

"5...4...3...2...1..."

Quynn stepped through the gate.

RYLAN STUMBLED, almost losing his balance, as the Earth shook. Overhead, a brilliant white light shot out from the center of the floating cities, piercing straight down into the planet below. The sound was deafening, a high-pitched scream paired with a loud rumble. Rylan struggled to stay on his feet as the ground pitched and yawed underneath him.

"What's happening?" he shouted at Orym, barely able to hear himself speak.

"It's begun," Orym shouted, his eyes dark. "This planet will be gone soon."

FIFTY-ONE

ARRA YELPED as the Tree shook beneath her. Trey reached out to steady himself against the trunk, dropping one hand off the Tree Ring Staff in the process. The forcefields encapsulating the shockbullets disappeared, causing the lightning inside to flail around wildly, out of control.

Arra stopped burning primewood and concentrated on keeping her balance. "What's going on?" she shouted.

A loud piercing sound took over her senses. She could see a bright light in the distance, shooting down in a straight line from the center of the sky cities.

"No idea," Trey shouted. "It's probably the Device. They've turned it on."

"Shit," Arra said.

Suddenly more gates opened on the ground beneath them, and more soldiers appeared.

"Where are they all *coming* from?" Arra asked.

Trey shrugged. "They have millions and millions of people up there. There's probably no end to this army."

"What should we do?"

Then a gate opened on the branch they were on, and Quynn stepped through.

"Fancy meeting you here," he said, a dark smile on his face.

"IT'S NOW OR NEVER!" Silanar shouted, running toward where Rylan and Orym were standing. The ground was still shaking, making it hard to stand.

"Are all the mages in their places?" Orym shouted.

"Yes!"

"Even Allain?"

"He is!"

"Then let's do it. Rylan, this is it, buddy!" Orym placed a hand on Rylan's shoulder. "Time to get this Forest up into the sky where it belongs!"

Rylan held the Book of Amplification tightly in one hand, his other hand buried in the backpack full of dark maple. He wanted to be strong, like Phoenix. He wanted to do his part to save the world.

It was now or never.

Now.

He closed his eyes and activated the magic, burning the first few pieces of dark maple in his hands. He could already feel the Book at work, making the magic more powerful—*far* more powerful. Good. This was going to take everything he had, and then some.

He continued on, burning more maple. The pieces of wood vaporized, turning into dust as he went through them, collecting the power in his mind. He could feel the Book in his hand—it was anxious, excited. Eager to burst forth. Good. It would need to be ready, if this was going to work.

Rylan opened his eyes, looking out at the Forest all around him. Fourteen Prime Trees, each monstrously huge, each incredibly majestic and powerful. And, undoubtedly, *heavy*. But he couldn't think about that. He had to focus on the magic.

He ramped up the power, doing as Orym had said, taking care not to go too fast. The air around him started to vibrate as he did, humming with a low, insistent sound. He was dimly aware of Orym and Silanar next to him, cheering him on. Silanar had his hand on the Tree in front of Rylan, ready to begin the soulsundering ritual once the Forest had been raised.

Time to go.

Rylan ratcheted up the magic, Willing it to spread, visualizing it floating underneath all the Trees.

Floating.

He burned more wood, channeling more power through the Book of Amplification, shaping it with his mind. Suddenly there was an audible *buzz* and the air rippled visibly, shooting out in a circle around him, filtering through the Trees. The ground was still shaking from the Cothellon's Device, but Rylan wasn't focused on that.

He was focused on the Trees.

A rumble sprang up, different from the sound of the Device. It was deeper, nearer. Louder.

Rylan pushed harder.

With a great cracking sound, the Trees pulled free, their roots ripping right out of the ground, spraying dirt and brush everywhere.

The entire Prime Forest lifted into the air, great green canopy waving.

TREY DIRECTED LIGHTNING AT QUYNN, but it did no good. The man was already burning oak, that cursed mergemelding magic, making him impervious to everything.

"What do you want?" Trey shouted, trying to maintain his balance on the great Prime branch as he flipped the Staff to its ash end.

"Just to kill you," Quynn said, flinging his hand out and burning dark maple. The fallfoiling magic pushed Trey off the branch, and then he was falling into mid-air, at least a hundred feet up. He could hear Arra screaming as he fell.

But then a funny thing happened. The entire Forest lifted up, rising into the air as if by magic.

And Trey stopped falling.

But of course, it *was* magic. He caught a glimpse of Rylan far below, concentrating fiercely, using his magic to raise *everything*. He had pulled up not just the Trees, but also a thick layer of soil and every single person in the area. All of it was caught in his embrace, his powerful fallfoiling magic.

Rising inexorably to the sky.

Trey looked up as he hovered, trying to get a glimpse through the leafy canopy above. The floating cities weren't there anymore—the Device had moved while he wasn't paying attention. It was off to the north now, just barely out of their way.

As the Forest continued to lift, Trey began to fall again. He wasn't sure how the magic worked, precisely, but he figured physics would eventually come into play.

And he didn't want to die just now.

So he conjured up a storm, activating the ash side of the Tree Ring Staff, begging the wind to greet him. It did, and he regained some modicum of control over his movement. His hands on ash and elm, he flew over to Arra and Quynn, still fighting on the great Tree branch.

"Die!" Arra shrieked, flinging arrows at Quynn without even bothering to use a bow. She just grabbed them from her quiver using her mind, shooting them at deadly speed toward the man.

But the arrows shot right through him.

He was invincible, his mergemelding power making everything *fuzz* when it should have hit him. As long as he was burning oak, nothing could kill the man.

Not unless he could be taken by surprise.

Trey swooped in, hoping to do just that. But Quynn turned, hearing him come, a sword flashing in his hand and arcing through the air.

Trey dodged to the side just before it sliced his arm off.

Where had he gotten a sword? Trey didn't have a weapon. Sure, he had *magic*, but he was getting very tired.

He alighted on the branch, trying desperately to catch his breath.

Quynn grinned, brandishing his sword.

ALLAIN STOOD BESIDE HIS TREE, a beautiful Prime Maple. He and Chasianna were the only mages left in the area that could activate the mistweaving woodpair. He was assigned to Maple, she to Pine. They were part of the Fourteen, the mages destined to change the fate of the planet. He stood next to his Tree, strong and proud.

Well, he wasn't *standing*, exactly. Technically, he was floating. Rylan had succeeded in raising the Forest, temporarily suspending the law of gravity. Allain struggled to maintain his position as he found his body hovering weightlessly in the air.

Then gravity reasserted itself, and Allain thumped down

onto the ground. The...ground? Allain looked out and saw that they were hundreds and hundreds of feet up in the air, yet there was still solid ground beneath his feet. Apparently Rylan hadn't been satisfied with raising just the Trees—he'd taken the Forest floor with him, as well.

That was probably a good thing, come to think of it. Otherwise, how would Allain still be standing there? He wouldn't be, that's how. He'd be dead, having fallen face-first to the ground far below.

Good job, Rylan.

ARRA SCREAMED as Quynn sliced his sword at Trey. She burned oak, feeling powerful strengthshaping magic flowing through her body. Her skin became hard as rock, her muscles growing strong. Her senses improved, sight and hearing and smell all sharpening.

Trey floated through the air toward Quynn, his Staff brandished out in front of him like a weapon. And Quynn was focused on him, holding his sword and burning oak, keeping his body impervious to impacts.

But mergemelding *must* have a weakness.

Arra realized there was one magic she'd never used yet, not once since she'd become a Prime Mage. She could have used it against Trey; it could have meant the difference in that epic battle. Cursing her stupidity, she grabbed a piece of prime maple. There was still one thing she'd never tried.

Mistweaving.

She looked at the maple in her hand, envisioning what she could do, a smile growing on her face.

Arrows flew out of the sky toward Quynn. Dozens of them. They pelted him from every angle, shooting toward him with impossible speed. She could see Quynn turn from Trey, intent on avoiding the deadly arrows. He pulled more oak from his pouch, burning chip after chip in a reckless attempt to keep his body melded into nothing. And sure enough, the arrows went right through him.

Because they were all illusions.

She heard Trey cursing as he alighted on the branch behind Quynn. He thought the arrows were real—she could see him shrink back, trying to avoid them. But she just smiled, burning maple and oak.

The arrows multiplied. Soon there were hundreds of them, filling the Forest with streaks of wood and stone. Arra laughed as Quynn flinched, steeling himself to remain still, trusting on his mergemelding magic to keep him safe. How much oak did he have?

Then a shot rang out on the ground nearby, startling her. She flinched, and a cluster of arrows accidentally merged together, flying through each other like the light they were made of. They flew erratically, flying in directions they shouldn't have been able to go. It only lasted for a second before she got it under control.

But Quynn turned towards her, eyes narrow. He had seen her mistake, had seen the arrows that didn't move correctly. He was beginning to suspect.

ALLAIN STOOD on the floating ground, trying not to be afraid of heights. There was nothing to be afraid of, really. Assuming Rylan didn't drop them. Assuming he wasn't killed, and the Forest didn't fall a few thousand feet to the *real* ground. Assuming Allain didn't accidentally walk off the edge of this floating nightmare, didn't fall through the thin veneer of soil.

That was a lot of assumptions.

He clung to his Tree, trying not to be afraid.

But then gates opened up all around him suddenly, appearing as big white circles in the air. And soldiers—more damn soldiers—ran through, guns trained on him.

Shit.

Not knowing what else to do, Allain pulled a half-formed stag and a carving knife from his pocket.

FIFTY-TWO

"WE'RE THERE!" Orym shouted.

Rylan was still concentrating, channeling immense amounts of power through the Book, keeping the Forest afloat three thousand feet in the air. He felt energy flooding through him, threatening to overwhelm him. He felt giddiness encroaching in his brain, the euphoria of the dark magic taking hold. But he held it back, viciously pushing it aside. He was the master, here. He was in control. The Book worked with him, helping him stay sane. He could feel it there, just under his fingers, pulsating to the rhythm of the world.

The setting sun was clearly visible now, out on the horizon. Clouds were *underneath* them, as they should be. And just to the north, behind Rylan, were the cities.

He turned to look at them, taking care to keep the magic going. New San Francisco had blossomed into something else, something far larger. Seven great, floating cities had come together, an intricate puzzle formed of glass and metal. The great Device, Fennas Elenathon, hovered there in the sky, steel spires reflecting the sunlight, its straight, solid lines a blinding contrast to the Prime Forest. Great stacks of the

Under thrust down from below street level, dredging the sky. Rylan's breath caught in his throat as he admired it. The city had finally reached its true potential.

And they were about to kill it.

"Here we go!" Silanar called, his hand placed firmly on the Prime Maple in front of Rylan. Rylan watched as the older elf concentrated, performing the ritual.

He had no idea how it worked, but he could see sweat beading on Silanar's brow. He imagined what it must be like, connecting all Fourteen Trees together as one, preparing a magical storm that would destroy all elves in the floating cities. He imagined the looks on their faces as the righteous indignation of the Eldrim flew through the city streets, decimating the Cothellon evil, killing everything it touched. He imagined the happiness he would feel when the world was saved, when the elves would thank him for the part he played. He imagined the souls of the dead, traveling into the sky, never to be heard from again.

And as he imagined it, Silanar continued the ritual.

The Trees began to glow.

ALLAIN WAS SCREWED. There were three soldiers approaching from around the left side of the Tree he was standing beside. They had guns out, and they looked ready to shoot. And Allain didn't have any weapons—not now. He was supposed to be participating in the soulsunder ritual. It had, in fact, already begun. Part of his mind was focused on the Maple Tree, feeling it connect to the others in the Forest. It was starting to glow, golden light shining out from its bark and leaves.

But Allain was about to get shot, and that would mean the end of the soulsundering.

So he kept his elbow on the Tree, hoping it would be enough to keep the ritual going. With his hands, he rapidly carved at the stag he had pulled from his pocket.

He felt the wood Invest almost immediately. This was child's play, something he'd been doing all his life. It was easy.

The magic of illusion.

"Hey!" a voice shouted from a dozen yards away, further off in the Forest. "Hey, you!" It was Other-Allain to the rescue, summoned from the mist of Allain's mind.

And he had a gun of his own.

The Cothellon soldiers turned like the idiots they were, attempting to meet this new threat. Allain continued working the stag, keeping the mistweaving magic flowing. His illusion was good—it looked just like him, except Other-Allain was meaner, and armed. Allain had never tried an actual *fight* with an illusion. It probably wouldn't be convincing enough, considering illusions didn't actually have any presence in the real world.

But the soldiers seemed convinced. They crept toward the illusion, hands on their guns. Real-Allain took the opportunity to edge around the Tree, trying to get out of their line of sight, taking care to maintain contact with the Tree at all times. He didn't want to screw up the soulsundering.

His first indication of trouble was when his head started hurting.

That didn't usually happen when he was playing with magic. Before he fully rounded the Tree, he glanced over at Other-Allain. The illusion was flickering strangely, and the soldiers were growing suspicious. That wouldn't do. So Allain strengthened the magic, sending flows of mistweaving out to form the image, planting it firmly in place. He needed these soldiers to *believe* in Other-Allain. It was his only chance.

Then Other-Allain looked at him, and everything went insane.

The world shifted, colors growing strange, depth perception changing. Allain's vision seemed to elongate, as if everything were growing longer, deeper, further away. Sounds around him grew muffled as the mistweaving magic spun out of control, flying outside the bounds of his imagination.

Other-Allain was staring at him, eyes aflame. The illusion had his hand up, motioning for him to stop. It was mouthing a word at him, over and over, but there was no sound to go with it. Allain didn't understand what the mist was saying.

He tried to halt the flow of magic, but it was no good. The stag wasn't even part of it anymore. It had fallen to the ground, Investment faded. Instead, the mistweaving had taken on a mind of its own, channeling power on and on from within Allain's very soul. The illusion kept repeating the word, and Allain shook his head, still not understanding. He lost his balance, falling to the ground, his knee crunching painfully on the wooden stag. His vision was still changing, mutating, and a buzzing sound rose up inside his ears.

Other-Allain was walking toward him now, and the Cothellon soldiers had had enough. They ran away from whatever was happening, cursing. But Allain was barely aware of them—his attention was focused solely on the illusion. Wasn't *he* the master, here? Shouldn't *he* be in control of his magic? Illusions had never taken on a mind of their own before.

A mind of their own.

Suddenly he knew what Other-Allain was saying. He understood the word the strangely solid illusion was trying to speak.

In the rush of the moment, in the strangeness of the magic gone awry, Allain realized the illusion was *actually* speaking. It stood in front of him, reaching out to him, fully solid and real, giving voice to the vision.

"No," it said, in a tone that sounded exactly like his.

Allain felt half of his mind rip apart in that instant, shrieking away into mist. Half his dreams, half his goals, half his interests and talents, half his life. Gone. He could feel it slipping through the air, merging like the ghost of a thought, integrating into this new Allain. This illusion that was no longer an illusion.

Allain felt a hole in his soul, then, and he knew no more.

GOLDEN GLOW EMANATED from the Trees, dazzling Rylan with its effervescent light. He could see bright little particles in the glow, like bits of dust, swirling about, just waiting to be put into action.

Soulsundering may be brutal, but it was also beautiful to behold.

But then something went wrong. He heard Silanar crying out, saw the elf jerk as he touched the Prime Cedar Tree, a look of profound concern on his face. What was going on?

It was all Rylan could do to keep the Forest afloat. He was churning through dark maple at an alarming rate, burning chip after chip of it. He hoped the backpack would last enough for this to be done.

And he was growing tired.

The Book of Amplification felt warm in his hand, lending its heat to the glow of the magic. The dark euphoria was still there, just outside, waiting to come in. Rylan just needed to let down his guard, to take a breath, and he'd be consumed by it.

He'd be dead.

But the Book was protecting him.

For now.

Out of the corner of his eye, he saw Orym lurch forward, heading towards Silanar. Something was definitely wrong, but Rylan didn't know what to do. He could only stand there, hoping he would be able to keep the Forest aloft. Hoping he wouldn't be consumed by the magic.

Then, all of a sudden, the glowing stopped.

The soulsundering had failed.

ALLAIN LOOKED UP, bewildered. The Forest was spinning, green canopy and golden fading sun and dark brown earth and Trees. He put a hand to his head, willing it to stop. It seemed to help somewhat—his vision became a bit clearer, less confusing.

He put a hand underneath himself and tried to get up, but he was too weak. Something was wrong. Something had happened, but he couldn't quite remember what. It had been something unexpected. Shaking his head, he tried again, but he just couldn't do it.

Then a hand reached down in front of him, palm out, fingers up. Whoever was on the other side of that hand wanted to help him up. Allain grabbed the hand and it gripped him tightly, helping him to his feet. He stood, staggering slightly, trying to get his wits about him. The golden rays of the setting sun blinded him momentarily, but he blinked and turned, trying to get a clearer look at the man who had helped him. But when he saw who it was, he almost fell again.

It was himself.

"Hi," the other Allain said. "Who are you?"

"Uh…" Allain said, still trying to see straight, "I'm Allain."

"That's funny," the other person said. "*I'm* Allain."

"I don't understand," Allain said.

The other Allain put a hand to his head, mimicking him. "I don't understand," he echoed.

"But who *are* you?" Allain asked.

"I'm you."

"How?"

"You tell me," the other Allain said. "You're the idiot who made me."

What? Allain had made a *copy* of himself? It had felt like a split, as if part of his very soul had been ripped away. Could mistweaving magic *do* that?

Other-Allain needed a name. Perhaps something simple.

Allain2.

"Not very nice, are you?" Allain asked.

Allain2 grinned at him. "No," he said. "You're not very nice at all."

This was getting them nowhere. Allain2 was clearly stupid—but was he real? He certainly seemed to be. He had helped Allain up, after all.

Illusions couldn't do that.

But what had happened? He looked around the Forest and saw that it was still floating, thousands of feet up in the air. But the Trees weren't glowing anymore. That meant the ritual had stopped, had possibly failed. Which was probably Allain's fault.

Silanar came bounding up suddenly, out of breath. "Are you okay?" he asked, but then he saw the two Allains standing there, looking at him. "More tricks?" he asked. "Now is *not* the time."

"No trick," Allain and Allain2 said together. Then they looked at each other. "Jinx," they both said.

"What..." Silanar started.

"I don't know what happened," the original Allain said to Silanar. "I was projecting an illusion of myself, and then I... *split*. And now this. It isn't an illusion."

Silanar stepped forward, as if he was about to touch Allain2. But apparently he thought better of it, turning instead back to Allain. "The ritual," he said. "We lost it. Your Tree dropped out. Do you feel well enough to continue? We don't have much time."

Allain looked at his double, and his double looked back. "We're good," they both said in unison.

"This is going to get old *really* fast," Allain muttered.

Allain2 nodded in agreement.

TREY DUCKED to the side as Quynn slashed at him, sword gleaming in the golden sunlight. The Trees had been glowing a moment before, but now they had stopped. He wondered why that was. Arrows continued shooting at Quynn, flying in from everywhere, but the man ignored them. The dark oak he was burning made him invincible.

Trey grew tired of this. It was a standoff—none of the mages could touch each other. Each was too powerful. There was no winning this fight.

Perhaps a change of venue was in order.

Trey darted over to Arra, taking care not to slip off the branch, and grabbed her arm. She was still concentrating on her magic, fabricating arrows out of thin air.

"Let's move," he whispered into her ear.

"I've almost got him," she hissed, burning maple furiously.

"He knows what you're doing," Trey said.

"No he doesn't!"

Trey shook his head. Now was not the time for an argument. He wrapped one arm around Arra's waist, holding the ash segment of the Staff with his other hand. Quynn was approaching, sword out.

The wind swept up suddenly, called by Trey's magic. It was a very strong wind, cold and harsh, carrying the scent of the sea. Trey stepped off of the branch, carrying Arra with him. She tried to protest, but he gripped her strongly, confidently. Quynn watched as they floated down to the ground, borne by the wind.

Then Quynn stepped out into mid-air as well. He burned dark maple, lowering himself slowly to the ground. "I went to a lot of trouble to create you," he said as he alighted, approaching Trey.

Trey was still holding onto Arra, still holding onto ash. He switched magic sides, putting up a forcefield around them both. He didn't want to take any chances.

"It took almost three hundred years to unlock your potential," Quynn continued, stepping forward. "And now Lorelei wants me to kill you!"

"So, spare me!" Trey shouted back at him. "If I'm your little *project*, why not let me live?"

"Because you're a failure," Quynn said. "If you can't be controlled, you're useless to me."

"So all you want is some lackey to be your slave? A *son* who does nothing but your bidding? What kind of a man are you, Quynn?"

"I'm the man who saw this through," Quynn said. "The man who knows this needs to happen."

"What needs to happen? The Cothellon mission? The great plan?"

"Yes!" Quynn spit, his face twisting. "We need to escape, to get out of this solar system. It's the only way!"

"But why? Because of the word of one woman? One lecherous woman?"

Quynn snarled. "How *dare* you speak of her that way!" he shouted. "Lorelei is a strong, beautiful woman. She knows the truth."

"The truth about what? That you're a liar? That you manipulated me? That you made me believe I was someone else, some*thing* else, just so you could get some kind of satisfaction out of knowing that I was a mage? All so you could control my mind, make me do your bidding? I'm not your son, Quynn. I won't kill for you."

Arra was looking at him with sadness on her face, but he ignored it for the time being. It was enough to touch her, to be in contact with her while this scene played out. How many times had he read it? The hero shouts at the villain. They duel. They fight. The hero wins, and the villain dies.

Is that how it would end? Was that the book his life intended to write?

"You're nothing without me," Quynn said, drawing closer. He was standing just inches away from Trey, but he withheld his sword. The two men stared each other down, with Arra right beside. All around them leaves whirled, caught up in the vestiges of the storm Trey had called.

"Wrong," Trey said. He noticed something on Quynn's chest. A red blotch, like blood. Were those bandages on his chest? Had Quynn been wounded?

"I'm *everything* without you," Trey said, shockstriking into Quynn with everything he had, aiming for the wound.

Lightning flashed between them, and Quynn froze for a long moment, his muscles contracting uncontrollably from the electricity coursing through his body. The wound in his chest burst open, blood flowing freely down his shirt. Quynn cried out in pain, his sword held awkwardly at his side. Trey continued the blast for as long as he could, before he felt himself growing tired. Quynn's shirt was smoking from the barrage, and Trey could smell the scent of burning flesh.

Enough.

Trey ended the assault, deactivating the elm. The electricity disappeared, leaving Quynn breathless, staggering.

But then, as Trey watched, Quynn's eyes grew clear. His breathing slowed. He straightened. "Is that the best you can do?" he asked, stepping toward Trey once again. Trey had read that line before so many times, but it felt different coming from Quynn. More real.

Then Trey caught sight of Silanar bursting in, carrying a sword of his own. The man swiped at Quynn, yelling loudly.

"GET AWAY..." Silanar said, swinging his sword around, "...FROM MY DAUGHTER!"

He must have caught Quynn by surprise, for the sword actually sliced through Quynn. A deep gash appeared across his side, and Quynn screamed in pain. Quicker than a flash, Quynn retaliated, whipping his sword around and stabbing it into Silanar's heart.

The men stood together for a long moment, staring at each other. Then Quynn pulled his sword out with a grunt, channeling willow. A gate swept over Quynn and he was gone.

Silanar fell to the ground, gasping.

ARRA SCREAMED as she saw her father go down. Blood was coursing from his body and his mouth. He was gasping and coughing.

He didn't look good.

She dropped down beside him, her hand touching his hand. She only needed to channel birch, and she could heal him.

Silanar would be fine.

Trey knelt with her, obviously thinking the same thing. He put his hand on her shoulder, activating the birch on the Tree Ring Staff. Together they tried to heal Silanar, the leader of Sylrantheas.

But it wasn't working.

Silanar coughed, spraying blood everywhere. Arra felt some of it hit her face, and she hunched over him, tears coming to her eyes. "Why won't it work?" she cried, her hand on his face.

"Arra," Silanar said, his mouth full of blood, his eyes unfocused. "Arra."

"No!" Arra said, trying again to heal her father. The birch wasn't responding to her for some reason. It felt like it was resisting, as if it were refusing to heal the man. But that made no sense! She tried harder, but it was no use.

The magic would not respond.

"My daughter," Silanar said, struggling to get the words out. "I have lived a...long and...fruitful life." He coughed. "I am not afraid of what lies next."

"I'll save you," Arra said. "I'm a mage now! I can *heal* you!"

She sobbed, fumbling with her pouch, drawing forth more wood. But Silanar took her hand, drawing her close. His touch was strangely steady, even as more coughing racked his body. His skin was growing pale.

"My daughter," Silanar said again, "there is one thing yet which I must tell you."

"What is it, Father?" Arra asked, tears dripping down her face.

"You are not...my daughter."

Arra felt a chill run through her. What was he talking about? Of course she was his daughter. Yet something about this was familiar to her. This had happened before. Visions swirled wildly around her brain, but she clamped them down. "What is this?" she exclaimed. "Why are you telling me this lie?"

"It is not a lie, Arra," Silanar said. "You weren't born to us by birth. We found you in the woods, all alone, as if by magic. I discovered you that day and raised you as my own. Your mother and I have loved you with everything we had." He started coughing again, uncontrollably.

Arra gripped her father's hand. "I don't believe you," she said, tears filling her vision. "It can't be true."

Why wouldn't the magic work?

"We told the others that we had hidden you," he said, his breathing shallow. "That we did not want you to grow up amongst the elves. When you came to us, we said you were a teenager, and the villagers believed us. But we knew not what age you truly were. You were ageless. You were an enigma."

Arra tried again to heal him, but something was blocking her. Something dark. Something vile. A shape in black and gold obstructed her vision, preventing her magic from working. It was like cancer, which soulsoothing could not heal. And yet it was different. More obscure.

More malevolent.

"I always knew," Silanar said, "that you were destined for

great things. I'm proud of you, Arra. You have always been my daughter, if not in fact, at least in love."

Arra held her father's hand, crying bitter tears as he slipped away.

"This is payment," Silanar whispered, "for my sins."

And just for a moment, she thought she saw something in the Trees. A golden light, but just a glimmer. A face, an eye. She thought she caught a wisp of something, a strand of essence, floating near her father's head. It was as if the Sundering magic had come to root inside him.

As if the magic itself was what prevented him from being healed.

Arra bent forward, kissing him softly on his forehead. Silanar's eyes were closed, and he was no longer breathing. She tried one last time, Willing birch to come alive, but it did no good.

Silanar was dead.

FIFTY-THREE

QUYNN FELL through the gate into Mission Control, clutching at his side. Pain lanced through his body as he grasped at the wound. Blood spilled out, seeping between his fingers.

"Core breach successful," the loudspeaker was saying. Quynn crawled away from the gate. Was anybody going to help him?

The main screen was filled with live camera feeds showing various angles on the Prime Forest, which was floating up in the sky, level with the cities. It was quite possibly the strangest thing Quynn had ever seen. Floating cities were one thing—but a floating Forest? He'd never thought it possible.

"What *was* that?" Sylvis asked.

"That," Lorelei said, "was the beginning of a soul-sundering."

"What happened to it?"

"I don't know."

"Do you think they could take us out with it?"

Lorelei pursed her lips. "Silanar is behind this. I'd stake

my life on it. I'd bet he could take us out, if he can get it to work."

"Will they try again?"

"I'm sure they will. How long until the gate is ready?"

"Gate Control, status update," Sylvis said.

"This is Gate Control. Energy dispersal in process. Level is on-screen."

A bar appeared on the main screen. As Quynn watched, still clutching his side, the bar begin to slowly fill.

"How long until we can get this planet out of here?" Lorelei asked again.

"If energy levels stay steady," Sylvis said, "it looks like we need about ten more minutes."

"Is anybody going to help me?" Quynn asked, his voice sounding more plaintive than he'd have liked.

Lorelei spared him a disgusted look. "You," she said, motioning to one of the gatesenders, "get a forcefinder up here. We'll use forcefields as a bandage."

"Aye, sir," the gatesender said, creating a gate and stepping through.

"Will that even work?" Quynn asked.

"It'll hurt like hell," Lorelei said, "but it'll work. You just need to delay them for ten more minutes. Ten more minutes. Can you do that?"

The gatesender reappeared, bringing another mage with him. That mage quickly set about creating a forcefield, a tight band around Quynn's waist, covering the wound. He could feel the forcefield digging into his flesh, electricity pulsing through his body. She was right—it hurt like hell.

"*Can you do that?*" Lorelei repeated.

"Yes," Quynn managed, getting awkwardly to his feet, teeth gritted against the pain. "Yes, my lady. But how will this forcefield stay with me?"

"Like this," Lorelei said, pinning a locator onto his shirt. "The mage can track you with this. Now go!"

"Your wish is my command."

"HOW LONG UNTIL THE PLANET DIES?" Rylan asked. He was still burning dark maple, keeping the Forest afloat. His energy was getting low, but he could last a while longer. The darkness eating at his thoughts had pulled back for a moment.

The Forest was floating, but the soulsundering had failed.

"About ten more minutes," Orym said, "assuming my calculations are correct. And my calculations are *always* correct."

"Where'd Silanar go?" Rylan asked. The man had grabbed a sword and ran off, leaving them behind.

"I don't know," Orym said. "Something must have gone wrong with the ritual. Maybe one of the mages got hurt."

"If we only have ten minutes, shouldn't we try again?"

Orym looked around, anxiety betraying his normal calm. Then he appeared to have made a decision. "Yes," he said, "we should try again. If we don't do it in the next few minutes, we won't be able to try again for a year." He stepped over to the Prime Cedar near to Rylan, placing his hands on the trunk.

"What are you doing?" Rylan asked.

"Soulsundering," Orym said, "I hope."

"Can you do it? I thought Silanar was the only one. Is that even the right kind of Tree for you?"

"Only one way to find out."

A GATE SLICED OPEN, and Trey saw Quynn stepping through. He stood quickly, taking his eyes off of Silanar and Arra. She was clearly distraught, but there was no time for mourning.

Not now.

Silanar wasn't even her father, apparently, if the man's last words could be believed. Trey shook his head, unsure what to think. But if what he remembered about Arra was true, then they had a history going back a long, *long* time. It made sense that Silanar wasn't her father.

He'd have to puzzle it through later.

Quynn approached them, unarmed. What was his plan—more magic? Another battle? Trey wasn't sure they had time for it—the world was about to die. The sounds of fighting continued all around him, underkids and elves dying to protect the Forest. They were fighting for one reason: to complete the soulsundering, to defeat the Cothellon.

The ritual must be protected.

And Quynn thought he could stop them. Trey's eyes narrowed as the man stepped closer. He was wincing as he walked, one hand touching his waist, then jerking back suddenly as if in pain. Was that a *forcefield* around him?

Suddenly Quynn lunged forward toward Trey. It wasn't a punch or a kick; there was no weapon in his hand. Trey flinched instinctively, but he didn't know how to react. There was nothing to dodge, nothing to block. Quynn wasn't attacking him.

Instead, Quynn just put a hand on Trey's shoulder.

"You know," he said, "you made a terrible son."

"And you were a terrible father," Trey said.

Were they really going to have this conversation now?

Then he felt Quynn burning oak. Mergemelding? But Trey wasn't attacking him. What was he doing?

Oh.

Trey's entire body went semi-transparent, and the Tree Ring Staff fell, his hand *fuzzing* as the Staff passed through. Quynn caught the Staff, releasing Trey's shoulder.

Then he swung the Staff at Trey's face, *hard*.

The blow caught Trey on the temple and he went down, ears ringing.

Quynn backed away, laughing. "Now what, little man? Are you going to cry because I took away your favorite toy?"

Trey snarled, staggering to his feet. He grasped for the Staff but Quynn danced away, keeping it out of his reach. The bastard was having far too much fun with the situation.

Then Arra darted in, hand out, prime elm ready. She twisted her fist and the Tree Ring Staff flew out of Quynn's grip, flying through the air toward Trey. Quynn tried to grab it as it flew, but he was too slow. Arra's leafrunning magic was too quick.

Trey caught it.

"Thanks!" he said, reaching for ash and elm. Quynn backed up a few steps, hands dipping into his pocket.

"Touch me," Arra said.

Now, that was a request that should never be denied—not coming from a woman such as Arra. But Trey could tell she hadn't meant it in that way: she had her bow out, three arrows already nocked to the string.

She wanted them to combine their powers.

"Okay," he said, stepping forward.

"Keep your hands on the Staff," she said, "and touch me."

"Sure."

Quynn was pulling a gun from his pocket. It glittered darkly in the waning sun, obviously made of darkprime oak. It was a mergegun, and it could shoot through anything.

Anything.

Shit.

Trey did as Arra had bid, keeping his hands where they were on the staff—on ash and elm—and leaning against her with one elbow. It did the trick—they were touching now, and Trey still had full access to the magic.

Instantly a connection bloomed in his mind, a merge between Arra and him.

Arra took the lead.

Quynn's finger was tightening on the trigger. The bullet from that gun would tear through anything Trey could put up—forcefields, wind, wood—*anything*. Short of dodging the damn thing, there would be nothing he could do. He started to close his eyes, dreading what was about to happen.

Then Arra went into action, controlling them both.

Trey felt shockstriker magic flowing out from the Staff he was holding, followed by forcefinding. Then he felt Arra burning everything she had—ash, maple, birch, poplar, elm, and oak—all six deciduous woods. He could feel the three arrows in her hand, knew their precise position on the bowstring and the tautness of the bow.

She loosed it all in a torrent of magic.

A massive form appeared in the air next to them, all reptilian scales and teeth and wings and fire. Trey turned his head to watch as it flew toward Quynn, roaring.

It was a dragon.

Quynn balked, stepping back and falling to the ground, clearly afraid. The dragon was enormous, its claws and teeth deadly sharp. It breathed fire at Quynn as it flew towards him, great wings flapping in the air. Quynn scrambled back in fear, dropping the gun.

Then the dragon fizzled into dust, and Trey felt strengthshaping taking over Arra's body. She drew her bow back, pulling it tighter than she normally could, nearly to the breaking point.

Then she loosed the arrows.

She had wrapped them with forcefields, shaping Trey's power using the connection between them. And inside the forcefields, Trey could see electricity bound up tightly inside. The shockbullets they had made earlier had been great, but these were something else. Something better.

Shockarrows.

The arrows flew through the air, propelled by bladedancing—but they weren't aimed at Quynn. Instead, Arra had aimed them up, far above them.

Toward the Tree.

He felt a storm surge suddenly. Wind sprang up, but it was blowing *down*, which was not a direction wind usually blew. A lightning bolt from the storm crashed into the Tree—not at its trunk, but at a large branch above them. The lightning cracked the branch, but it wasn't enough to break it. The branch was *big*.

Then the shockarrows hit the Tree. They exploded on impact, shattering the massive branch, sending wood shrapnel flying everywhere. The fragments ripped into Arra, Trey, and Quynn, flaying their skin. But Arra was burning birch, and soulsoothing magic quickly healed her wounds as well as Trey's.

Quynn was on the ground, bloody and scared, reaching for his gun. The branch cracked loudly overhead, and Quynn swept his head upwards, bringing his arms up to shield himself.

Arra used her final power, then: leafrunning. She pulled *hard* on the branch, wrenching it free from the Prime Tree.

The branch finally fell.

It sailed downward, hurtling with deadly force, flying

through the air like a meteor heading straight for Quynn. The branch was *huge*, more than big enough to hit Trey and Arra too.

He flung a forcefield up as quickly as he could, shielding the two of them. And the huge branch hit the ground, crunching against their forcefield, flattening an entire section of the hovering Forest floor. He could feel the weight of it, the vibration in his feet as hundreds of pounds of wood slammed into Quynn's body with its full force.

Quynn's body died with a sickening crunch.

When the dust cleared, the man was nowhere to be found. The massive branch was too big to see anything under. He was dead.

The whole thing had only taken seconds.

"Yes!" Arra shouted, her fist in the air.

Trey grinned at her. "That was awesome!"

They embraced, suddenly awkward. Trey felt like he was a kid again, caught up with the girl he liked. Her face was excited, flushed. She was happy, for the moment.

"That was a nice bit of magic," he said. "Especially the dragon."

"Thank Allain for the idea," she said.

"Maybe I will."

But it seemed the Cothellon weren't quite done. More gates appeared in the Forest, and still more soldiers arrived. Quynn might have been gone, but the battle continued.

Trey and Arra watched as the kids from the Under met the incoming horde.

Shot ran across the Forest floor, mergeguns in both hands. He fired them one after another, strafing and shooting, keeping a low profile. The bullets ripped through the oncoming Cothellon troops, piercing body after body, going right through wood and stone and armor, a cascade of unstoppable death. Troops went down by the dozen. Shot quickly ran out of bullets, but Luthar was nearby, ready to help. He threw the boy two more guns, and the killing continued unabated.

Then Trey caught sight of Small. The boy tossed a power cell at a soldier, and the man grabbed it instinctively. The power cell instantly shot electricity through him, sending him to the ground, convulsing. Small caught Trey looking and cheered at him.

"Shock Crew!" he shouted.

Trey gave him a thumbs-up.

Dillon was right behind Small, shooting balls of lightning from his hands. Luthar had activated an unfamiliar machine, an automatic weapon of some kind. It blazed, firing hundreds of bullets rapidly into the Cothellon army. Blood and screams were everywhere.

Trey realized then that it was a bad idea to underestimate underkids.

They could surprise you.

But even still, it wasn't enough. Gates continued opening, Cothellon forces flowing through them by the hundreds. The kids were running out of magic, running out of ammo. If soldiers kept coming, they'd be overrun soon.

Trey looked around, gauging the situation. He could see hundreds of soldiers from his position, and more were arriving by the second. It was only a matter of time before they were all killed.

Then Trey had an idea.

"My turn to be the hero," he said, flashing Arra a smile.

RYLAN WAS STARTING to lose his grip. The magic pouring through him was too much, too strong. He couldn't keep the Forest in the air for much longer. Darkness was encroaching, the euphoria almost too much to bear. Soon it would consume him, and the Forest would fall. He struggled against it, his mind at war, matching it strength for strength. An eye looked out at him, malevolent and strange, peering out from a pitch black Tree on a purple hill.

Something was awakening.

Rylan took a deep breath. The visions were coming faster now, threatening to break his concentration. His hand in the backpack was shaking, and the wood was almost gone.

There wasn't much time left.

He didn't want to meet his mother's fate.

Orym was focused, his hands pressed firmly against the Tree. Rylan was starting to think the man didn't know what he was doing.

But then the Cedar Tree started to glow, golden light shining out from the bark. The ritual was working! Silanar was still nowhere to be found, but Orym was managing it in his place. Perhaps he was more powerful than he had thought.

Rylan heard gunshots nearby—the soldiers were approaching his position. He had no choice but to stand there, shivering as magic washed through him.

He really didn't want to get shot today.

TREY GRASPED the Tree Ring Staff, his eyes tracking the movements of all the Cothellon troops arrayed within his sight. He and Arra were perched up on a Prime Tree branch again, giving him a better vantage point.

He'd only get one shot at this.

He shifted his grip on the Staff until he was touching one of the five willow slices. Then he concentrated.

He tapped into the willow, invoking its power. Then he split his mind, over and over, again and again, until there were hundreds of fragments of him, each connected to the prime willow in the Staff. He tensed, suddenly nervous. He'd never tried to do this much at once before. Would it work?

It didn't matter. The time had come. This was his moment. It was now or never, and various other cliches from books gone by. Trey suddenly had a mental vision of his bookstore, of Callan dusting the shelves, rearranging the titles. Trey wondered what had become of that life—it seemed so far away now. He missed his days in The Pig and Whistle, a beer in one hand and a book in the other.

His life had been so much simpler, then.

But now was not the time for reminiscing.

Trey activated the magic.

Hundreds upon hundreds of gates swept out from the Staff, directed by fragments of Trey's Will. He assigned each one to a soldier, intending to warp them all away to somewhere high in the sky, sending them falling to their death. It was cruel, but it was the best idea he had.

Except the magic didn't work.

The gates responded, splitting into reality, shining with orange-white bursts of light. But they didn't obey his Will precisely. They spawned into existence all at once, crazy and malformed.

Out of control.

Trey tried to reign them in, tried to control the gates' wild gyrations, but it was no good. His Will could not make it work. Perhaps he was still weak, as before. Perhaps gate-sending was not meant to be controlled in this way. The gates spun erratically, moving of their own accord. Trey watched, unable to take his hands away from the Staff, unable to stop the magic.

And as he watched, the gates converged on a single point.

Him.

He gasped as hundreds and hundreds of gates sliced over his body, rippling across him over and over and over and over and—

FIFTY-FOUR

TREY RUBBED HIS EYES. It was late, and he was tired. Tired of squinting by candlelight, hoping to avoid waking Arra. Tired of the long hours, of the arguments. It had put a strain on his marriage—Arra had been distant of late, cold and unemotional. He knew her, and he knew that her coldness was an indication of her displeasure. She was mad at him, and he hadn't had the time to talk to her about it.

But the archaeological dig had been a success, at long last. The Anthropological Society had initially forbade the expedition, and it was only after months of pleading, lobbying, and outright bribery that Trey had been allowed to proceed.

But it had been worth the effort, even if his marriage was suffering as a result. He was close to something, he knew. Something that would change his life, and the lives of everyone on Valaralda, forever.

Arra tossed in their bed, turning over and groaning softly. She had been sleeping poorly of late, and he knew it was his fault. He just had a little more work to do, and all of this would come to an end.

THE SOCIETY DIDN'T BELIEVE him. Trey had presented his results to them as he was expected to do, submitting the paper for peer review and all the usual approvals. The discovery he had made was important—far too important for this bureaucratic nightmare—but he had no choice. Systems were systems. And the elves were nothing if not rigorously formal.

Trey sighed, beating his hand against his desk. Arra was preparing dinner in the kitchen, the smells permeating their small house. Trey's stomach rumbling.

How could he convince them?

THE SECOND EXPEDITION had been an even greater success than the first. And now Trey knew the solution to the problem. The Fall was coming, but now he knew how to stop it.

The ancients had already shown them the way. They'd just needed to discover the beginning of the path.

Trey rubbed his eyes, exhaustion overtaking him. All he had to do now was write up the plans, detailing the seven worlds and the defense system they made up. He had all the evidence right here, although translating the ancient language was proving cumbersome. If only he had some research assistants...

Then he'd have to convince the Society to mount an expedition. And not just any expedition—one that involved gate-sending across tens of thousands of lightyears. Powerful magic. He knew the High Council would get involved, and then he'd have to convince them, too. Trey sighed, knowing the amount of trouble the next few months or years would be.

But the Fall was coming, and they had to be prepared.

LUCKILY, the Fall was slow. Trey had picked that up from one of his recent translations. How had the ancients known about the threat to their galaxy? Simple: the Fall had been here before. It had decimated everything, but some small remnant had survived. So the ancients had resolved to do something about it next time.

The Fall operated on galactic time—eons, not years. So Valaralda still had time. They could prepare. They could rediscover the massive Defense Mechanism the ancients had left behind. They could activate it.

They could be safe.

But even though they had plenty of time, they had to get started now.

TREY—HIS original name was Tarathiel, of course, but his mind preferred his latest name—stood on the Sending platform, looking at the moons. They were nestled together in the sky: one blue, one gold. Like two lovers. Like the Twins. Ilyrion sparkled underneath them, glittering spires and verdant treetops giving way to the sea beyond. It was peaceful. Beautiful.

It was about to be destroyed.

He dropped his gaze to the volunteers, their faces lit by pallid moonglow. They were about to leave Valaralda—possibly forever—in service of an ancient call. They were looking at him, waiting for his word. He was their leader. He was their death. But the Mechanism must be rebuilt, and there was no one better to do it than him.

He had discovered it, after all.

Trey gathered Arra close. "Whatever happens," he said, "know this: we will always be together." It was a line, a cliche.

It was a lie.

Trey knew that he would volunteer. He would be one of the Fourteen, would seed the planet with Prime Trees. He would become wood and leaf and pine and branch. He would become magic.

And he would never see Arra again.

But she needed to hear it, needed to know that everything would be okay. That they were doing this for a *reason*. That if they didn't—if the Sending failed—everything would be undone. This, Ilyrion—it would all be gone. As it had been before, so many eons ago.

He felt tears come to his eyes as Arra met his gaze. She was still incredibly beautiful, even after all these years. She leaned towards him, kissing him. All around them, Trey could hear the elves saying their last goodbyes. He could hear their words, sense their tears. The expedition would return here, if all went well. But Trey knew that something might— *must*—go wrong.

"This will be an awfully big adventure," Arra whispered.

"I love you," Trey replied.

He feared that the adventure would be bigger than she could possibly imagine.

FIFTY-FIVE

"I KNOW what we have to do," Trey said, opening his eyes. Arra was looking at him, her expression worried. The gates hadn't moved him anywhere, but they *had* unlocked his memory. Some of it, anyway. Enough to remember the purpose of everything.

The purpose of the planet.

"What?" Arra asked, but Trey grabbed her, pulling her close.

"Trust me," he said, and activated a gate.

Lorelei had been right the entire time.

RYLAN STRUGGLED to maintain his grip on the Forest. Cothcllon soldiers were everywhere, and he was growing weak. Carrying this much weight, even with the Book of Amplification, was hard. He couldn't keep it up forever.

He felt it slipping away. He felt himself succumbing to the darkness inside the wood. He felt the Coke-bright sweetness of it, the allure and the denial, the feeling that he was in control, that he could handle so much more. The eye on the purple hill opened for him, and he knew what Phoenix had faced. He saw her there, in his mind's eye, standing braced against the volcano, the fierceness of preservation in her soul.

She had been a woman for the ages.

But the Trees were glowing brightly now. The magic was almost ready to activate. He could see it beginning, stretching out from the Trees themselves, reaching out with tendrils of power, ready to murder and kill.

But then a gate opened right next to him, and Trey and Arra stepped out.

"Stop," Trey said.

"What?" Rylan managed weakly, his energy almost gone.

A shot rang out, and Rylan felt a bullet pierce his chest.

He fell, the world lurching beneath him. And with him went the Trees, the fallfoiler magic gone.

The Forest dropped.

He was dimly aware of Orym, grabbing the Book and the pack of wood, face grim. Orym groaned as he lashed out with the magic, trying desperately to maintain a hold on the Forest. To prevent it from falling.

It almost worked.

But Orym wasn't as strong as Rylan. Rylan struggled to get up, but there was warmth in his chest, a shooting pain that hadn't been there before. He felt himself slipping away as Orym took control.

Rylan watched as the golden glow from the Trees faded. The soulsundering had failed. Again. And Rylan knew that there would be no further attempts.

The Forest was falling.

Wind whipped by his face. His ears popped as the air pressure increased, clouds and wind and birds flashing past as the entire Forest fell, flying ponderously to the ground. Orym strained against it, channeling as much magic as possible, keeping the velocity as slow as he could.

He saw Trey and Arra looking at him, their expressions worried. They actually cared about him, he saw. Him, a kid from the Under. It would have warmed his heart, if he hadn't been bleeding out.

But then Trey reached down, the Tree Ring Staff in his hand, and invoked soulsoothing magic. Rylan felt it course through him, freeing the bullet from his body, repairing the hole it had made. He gasped as the healing finished.

"Wow!" he said, sitting up. He felt better. Much, much better.

Then the Forest crashed into the ground.

TREY BRACED himself as the Forest hit the ground, holding Arra close. Orym had done the job well, luckily—he had managed to slow their descent enough to keep the impact from being fatal.

Still, it was a rough landing. Trey lurched forward, nearly falling, feeling pain in his knees as the Forest hit. Arra gave a little cry as it happened, her fingers digging into his back. Leaves and dust flew up into the air everywhere, making it difficult to breathe.

But Trey knew there was little time left.

"Orym," he said, "I know."

"What?" Orym asked, dazed.

"I know what this planet is for."

"We don't have time for this, Trey."

"I know. You have to come with me. And I need the Book of Amplification. Can you get us to Gate Control?"

"What? Why?"

Trey explained as quickly as he could.

Right before they left, Luthar showed up, looking bedraggled. "Can I come?" he asked, his curly gray hair wild. "You might need my help."

"Sure," Trey said. "Come on."

THEY GATED TO GATE CONTROL, deep in the heart of the conjoined Under. Trey had been there once, he now remembered, long ago. There were no flashbacks as he passed through the gate this time—apparently it didn't always happen. Trey knew now that the gates were dangerous—truly dangerous—for they could eliminate memory as easily as giving it back. If that had not been the case, so much would have played out differently. But it was as it was, and gate-sending must be used very carefully.

Right now, Trey couldn't afford caution. He only had minutes left to save the planet.

Arra, Trey, Orym and Luthar arrived in Gate Control, stumbling as they stepped out of the gate. The room was tall and dim. They found themselves on a metal grate, overlooking a bottomless drop. It wasn't truly bottomless, Trey knew, but the light didn't reach all the way down, so he couldn't see where it ended. He shuddered. Heights again. After all the storm flying, gatesending, and magic using, he figured he should be immune to fear of heights by this point. Sadly, that didn't seem to be the case.

Gate Control technicians looked up as they entered, alarmed expressions on their faces. None of them had weapons, though—they were just scientists. Harmless.

"Gate opening in T-minus 30 seconds," a voice said over the loudspeakers in the room.

"Make the changes," Trey said. Orym and Luthar sped over to the consoles that ringed the deck, pushing harried technicians out of the way.

"What are you doing?" one of them asked.

"Saving you," Orym said, his hands flying over the console. Next to him, Luthar was flipping switches and pressing buttons. The room was abuzz with talking as everyone tried to figure out what was going on.

"He might be right," one of the technicians said. He was staring over Orym's shoulder. The screen in front of him was flashing with warnings. "There's a problem. Some kind of anomaly. The core..." the technician stopped, eyes wide with alarm.

"You almost wiped out the entire planet," Orym said.

"How could we have missed this?" another technician asked. "Our simulations were perfect!"

"You didn't miss it," Orym said, his fingers flying over the controls. "You were just overruled."

"20 seconds," the loudspeaker proclaimed.

"This is it," Trey said, grabbing Arra's hand.

A beam of light suddenly shot through the chamber, piercing upwards from far below. The white light cast a straight, bright line toward the ceiling, where it disappeared into a complicated-looking device.

Trey led Arra onto an alcove, a piece of platform that jutted out towards the light. Trey felt his stomach lurch, and he tried to ignore the perilous drop. Arra's hand was warm in his own. He could feel her heart beating rapidly.

"Ready?" he asked. She nodded, seeming confused. "Just trust me," he whispered, and she nodded again more emphatically, squeezing his hand.

Trey held the Tree Ring Staff and the Book of Amplification in his left hand, barely managing to hold them both together. He held Arra's hand in his right, and ahead of him was the brilliant white light.

His hand was wrapped around a willow segment in the Staff.

"Ready!" Luthar shouted. The other technicians were talking rapidly amongst themselves.

"Ready!" Orym reported, looking over at Trey. He felt his breath catch in his chest, his heart pause. This was it, the point of no return.

Orym flipped a final switch, and the brilliant beam of white light disappeared.

"10..." said the voice over the loudspeaker.

Trey channeled willow, activating gatesending magic. He felt the Book of Amplification respond, bringing the power level up to an almost unbearable level.

"9..."

His brain—no, his very *soul*—connected to Arra's, pulling her strength into his. Her Talent flooded through the Book and the Staff, adding power to the magic. Trey felt the increase and he smiled.

"8..."

He cast out with his mind, visualizing where the white pillar of light had been. It was the power from the planet's core, the energy that would have spelled the doom of the entire world.

"7..."

Orym and Luthar had turned it off, had deactivated the feed from the core. Yet Trey knew that the planet's purpose was this—it *needed* to travel through space, needed to pass through a gate. Needed to join a new solar system, as strange as that sounded.

Lorelei had been right.

She'd just been wrong about the method.

"6…"

Orym had been right, as well. Tapping into the planet's core would destabilize it, causing the destruction of Earth. And with Earth gone, the Defense Mechanism would be destroyed. The Fall would come, wreaking havoc upon the galaxy.

Luckily, Trey had another plan.

"5…"

Trey activated the magic, twisting his Will, controlling the willow. Arra's power flew through his own, twining with him, forming a new strand of light. Trey shot their twin power upwards, aiming it at the device overhead. A substitute for the planet's energy.

It was all so simple.

"4…"

But something was wrong. The magic wasn't complete. Trey could see it all in his head, knew what was missing. But he didn't know *why*. Arra was there, her magic full and pure and strong. And he was there, threading through her, contributing his Talents to the spectrum of magic.

"3…"

That was it. It was *his* fault. His Talent, his half-Talent. It wasn't enough. His power wasn't complete. He was only *half* a Prime Mage, and it wasn't enough.

His plan was going to fail.

"2…"

Suddenly a gate opened behind them, and he caught sight of Quynn stumbling through. The man was bent and bloodied, a rictus grin upon his face. He spared no glance for everyone else in the room—he had eyes only for Trey.

Snarling, Quynn leapt at them, trying to wrench the Staff away.

"The Staff is mine!" he yelled.

"1…"

But as soon as Quynn touched the Staff, his soul mingled with the others. Trey recoiled instinctively, not wanting Quynn's thoughts touching his own, but something felt *right* about it. Quynn's Talent matched up neatly against his own.

Filling all the gaps.

"Opening now," the loudspeaker said.

And Trey and Arra and Quynn, their souls wrapped up and flowing together, channeling willow magic through the Book and the Staff, opened a gate.

FIFTY-SIX

HAEMIR SNORTED, coming awake suddenly. The room was dark, the usual lights and letters blinking across the vast array of dusty consoles. He wiped his nose, smacking his lips. What had awakened him? He was the only one left here in this old room, monitoring these old machines. It was a boring job, but someone had to do it. Haemir had done it his whole life.

Normally the machines let him sleep.

An insistent beeping called to him, and Haemir noticed a red light blinking on one of the small consoles to his right. That was odd. The lights were never red in here. He pulled himself over to the machine, the wheels of his rusty chair squeaking on the floor. He read the label that was affixed to the blinking light.

EXTRASOLAR INCURSION
DEFMECH DETECTION CIRCUIT 1

Well, that was no use. Haemir had no idea what the label meant. He sighed, looking across the screens and lights in the room. He was accustomed to them, knew how they looked. He had guarded this chamber for decades, truth be told, although he didn't want his grandchildren to know that. They thought he had an important job at the Anthropological Society, something involving Research and Expeditions. They'd be dismayed if they learned he was just a night guard in a dusty old room full of ancient electronics.

One of the screens caught his eye. It held a diagram of the solar system. Valaralda was there, pictured fourth in line orbiting the star Persephone. Old Persey was bright and strong, as usual. Valaralda was depicted with its two moons, orbiting the star during the planet's winter phase. Haemir counted seven planets in total—all there as normal.

Wait a minute. *Seven?* There were six planets in the Persephone system, not seven. Where had the new planet come from? Haemir examined the screen more closely, trying to ignore the low-quality green rasterization of the ancient monitor. Honestly, it was amazing these things worked at all.

Sure enough, there was a new planet there, orbiting just slightly inward from Valaralda, closer to the star. The planet was a bit smaller than Valaralda, if the clunky screen could be believed. Yet there it was, orbiting happily, nearly in conjunction with Valaralda. How could it have appeared? Planets didn't just materialize out of thin air.

Haemir sighed, checking his coffee. Empty, of course. He flicked a finger across the point of his ear—a nervous habit he had developed over the years—and picked up the phone.

His superiors needed to be informed of this development.

ORYM ADJUSTED HIS SUIT, checking to make sure the collar was straight. He hadn't worn an outfit like this for hundreds of years.

The gate passage had been smooth, his solar transference calculations working as well as he had expected. Trey's alternate power source—drawing from the Twins themselves—had worked perfectly.

Orym was just mad he hadn't thought of it himself.

It got worse, though. The massive planetary gate had unlocked visions in his head, memories he hadn't known were there. If his calculations were correct—and they always were—Orym was 20,415 years old.

That was *far* too old for his tastes.

He looked over at Trey, who was fussing with Arra's hair. She had insisted on looking like an Eldrim, with a long, flowing dress and flowers in her hair. Orym had to admit she was a vision, even if her fashion sense wasn't always the best. He preferred her in that tight archer's outfit, all leather and...

He stopped himself, grinning. Trey sure was a lucky one. And Orym could remember them now. They had been a happy couple on Valaralda, long before any of this began. It had been Trey's discovery that had made this all possible, in fact. Trey's expedition had discovered the Defense Mechanism. He'd found out about the Fall, about the certain doom heading towards the Milky Way Galaxy.

He smiled as he watched Trey and Arra flirt and play, trying their best to look professional. They deserved as much happiness as they could get.

Orym was proud of them.

They looked younger now, as if something had smoothed away the wrinkles he remembered them having on Valaralda. What could have caused that?

How were they still alive after all this time?

He felt as if for every question answered, ten more sprouted in its place.

But now the moment was approaching. The Valaraldans had radioed ahead, notifying them of their intent to land starships on Earth. Gatesending was strictly outlawed by modern Valaraldan culture, owing to the inherent dangers. Orym smiled wryly to himself. If only they had known about those dangers sooner, so much could have been prevented.

Luckily, the Valaraldans possessed good spacefaring technology. Not faster-than-light travel, of course—that was impossible. But they could at least shuttle from planet to planet very efficiently, especially since Earth had inserted itself so closely to Valaralda in the new solar system.

Orym's calculations had proved correct, as usual.

ALL HER LIFE, Arra had wanted to have something important to do. To have Talent. To *matter*.

Now she mattered far more than she'd ever expected.

It had all been such a whirlwind. Only weeks had passed, but it already felt like years. Passage through the gate had retrieved many of her memories, but there were still vast swaths of time unaccounted for: thousands of years at once, completely empty. It was unsettling, to say the least. The gates giveth, and the gates taketh away. She understood now why her new friends on Valaralda had outlawed gatesending magic.

It was far too dangerous to use.

She shifted uncomfortably in her high-necked gown, her hand in Trey's. They were sitting on the Council in New Paris in the sky. Her outfit had been made in the current Valaraldan fashion, of course.

She hated it.

She hated being here in the sky cities, amidst the technology and the culture the Cothellon had created. But she did have to admit that New Paris was beautiful. The New Eiffel

Tower glimmered at night, a towering spire of hope. It shone against the backdrop of the city, full of inspiration and light.

The Cothellon had been rounded up in the weeks immediately after the gatesending. After the planet had gated, the army had just stopped coming. So the Eldrim had gone up to the cities to seek them out, and the Cothellon had not resisted. Their job was done, their great purpose satisfied. Their device had worked, thanks to Trey's help.

Apparently that was enough for them.

Quynn had been imprisoned, along with all the Cothellon leadership they could find. The humans living in the cities had been given a choice: come back to the Earth's surface, or maintain the cities, living out their lives without Cothellon rule.

Some of the humans had gone to the surface, wanting to fill out new cities and villages. Many of them had been entranced by the elves, wanting to join their way of life. And this time, the elves had actually been welcoming. For the first time in history, elves and humans had been willing to live together.

But it had only been a few weeks. Arra knew that before long, sparks would fly. It was only a matter of time.

In Silanar's absence, Arra had been asked to lead the Eldrim. But she had declined. Her father and sister and mother were dead, killed by Cothellon or sacrificed to the Trees. She knew now that they weren't *really* her family, but it hurt like they were.

She missed them terribly.

So she couldn't return to her people. There was just too much pain there. She chose instead to explore her new life with Trey—or perhaps it was an old life, revisited. Her mind was still swimming from it all. She didn't know what to think.

The cities in the sky had remained. The elves from Valaralda had promised the humans new technology, enough to keep the cities afloat without resorting to ritual murder and slavery. Mages and forcefields and dark forests would no longer be necessary—instead, people would come and go as they pleased, traveling to and from the cities and the ground, carrying goods and people and new memories.

So much bloodshed could have been saved, if the Cothellon had had the technology. But Valaralda was ages beyond Earth—eons, it felt. Society was very old on that planet, the line between magic and technology blurring and shifting, indiscernible.

They'd scoured the cities, searching for anyone who'd been in charge. But Lorelei was nowhere to be found, much to Arra's chagrin. The woman needed to pay for what she'd done to Elanil.

Arra grimaced at the thought of Lorelei, and the High Senator frowned at her.

"Does the senator from Pano Sylrantheas have something to add?" he asked.

Pano Sylrantheas. Reborn from the ashes of Sylrantheas, it was the first city of its kind. *Pano* meant "a piece of shaped wood" in the Eldrim tongue. It was a reference to the Splinter.

Yes, the Splinter would live there, side-by-side with elves. They were already rebuilding in the forest, planting new trees and forging new bonds. Humans and elves would live together there as equals, without illusions or prejudice. That was the theory, anyway.

Arra doubted it would be as easy as all that. The Remnant were still down there, after all. Gulthurub had been wiped out, but there were other cities—many others. And she was sure they wouldn't understand anything that was going on.

She realized the High Senator was still waiting for her to

respond. "My apologies, High Senator," she said. "I am still recovering from gatesickness, as I'm sure you understand. My expression was involuntary."

"Of course, Lady Alleria," the High Senator said, bowing to her slightly. Her original name, first given to her over twenty thousand years ago. So long. How could anyone exist for so many years? Arra grimaced again, hoping the High Senator didn't notice this time. She preferred her current name, Arra. It was less pretentious.

Trey shifted in his seat next to her, obviously as uncomfortable as she was. The sudden transition to this stuffy Valaraldan court was awkward. Strange. She longed for the forests and the Trees, for the home she'd used to have. So much had changed in so short a time. So much was different from what she'd thought. She couldn't keep up. She couldn't understand. She felt lost, adrift.

She missed her sister.

"YOU DID GOOD," Dill said, reaching out to shake Rylan's hand. They were standing on the New Golden Gate Bridge— or at least the beginnings of it. The bridge was set to span between New San Francisco and New Paris, forever linking the two floating cities. A new time of prosperity was coming, or so everyone said.

Rylan wasn't so sure.

Trey had healed his bullet wound, but it still hurt sometimes. He put a hand on his chest, remembering.

"I failed," he said. "I couldn't keep the Forest afloat."

"Nonsense," Dill said. "You did the best you could."

"It was incredible," Small said, clapping Rylan on the back. The short boy had a backpack full of electronics. He'd been playing with them ever since the Valaraldans had landed.

"This world owes you a great debt," Smoke said, stepping forward, his back hunched. "Even if the soulsundering was misguided, you did what was right. You fought for our survival."

"Thanks," Rylan said.

"So we've been thinking," Dill said. "It's high time you earned your undername."

"Uh," Rylan said, suddenly uncomfortable. He'd been wanting this for a long time. He'd thought the moment would never come.

"We want to call you Fall," Dill said. "You know, because of the magic you did."

Rylan shuffled his feet.

"What?" Dill asked. "You don't like it?"

"I mean," Rylan said, "it's great. It's a good name."

"But you don't want it."

"I want an undername. I do. It's just..."

There was silence for a long moment.

"You miss her," Dill said.

"Yes." The word came out as a whisper.

Dill put his hand on Rylan's shoulder. It was an uncharacteristically kind gesture, coming from him. "You two were a good match."

"Ryl," Rylan said, quietly.

"What?"

"I think you should call me Ryl. It's what Elanil would have wanted." He wiped a tear from the corner of his eye. Underkids didn't cry.

Dill watched him silently, then he shared a glance with Small. The kid nodded.

"Everyone!" Dill shouted suddenly. "Meet Ryl!"

The boys around him cheered.

Rylan looked out at the beginnings of the bridge. He wished Elanil could have been there to see it.

He wished Phoenix could have been there too.

SOME TIME LATER, Arra and Trey made their way to Valaralda. Trey held her in his arms as the two moons bathed them in silver light.

"What are you thinking?" Trey asked, searching her blue eyes.

Arra put her arms around his neck. "It seems so sudden," she said, "and yet so sure. I feel as if I've always lived this life, and also that I just began it."

"Gatesickness," Trey said.

"Yes, I suppose so. These new terms, these new places— sometimes I just want to be under the trees again, with nothing but the stars and the sky to worry about."

"With nothing but schoolchildren and tests and archery. I know," Trey said, laughing. "I feel the same way."

"You long for books and dreams?"

"Books, yes. And as for dreams, I think mine came true."

"You know those cliched lines won't work with me," Arra said.

Trey laughed again. It felt good to laugh, to not be afraid of what was to come. "Alright," he said. "I had to try. Still, you have to admit the world was a much simpler place before the Valaraldans came. Back when all we had was dreams."

"Yes," Arra agreed. "But their planet *is* a beautiful one."

Trey looked out at their surroundings, at the great city of Ilyrion. The city was gorgeous, every building and monument a work of art. Lights and colors and shapes filled every horizon, at once beautiful and strange. He liked it here, Trey realized. And yet he missed his old home, the floating city of New San Francisco.

"Some day," he said, pulling Arra close, "I want to take you to where I used to live. To my bookstore, to the pub I once visited. I think you'd like it there, even if it isn't a forest."

"I'd like that," Arra said. "They have beer there, right?"

Trey laughed. "Of course they do! It wouldn't be a pub without it."

"Do you ever miss your wife?"

Trey stopped cold. That question had been unexpected. "You mean Lora?"

Arra nodded. "She was a part of your life, whether you want to admit it or not."

She was right, of course. But Lora had proven to be a false hope, a dead end. "She wasn't you," Trey said, as if that were enough. He squeezed Arra, pulling her tightly against him. She looked up into his eyes, and he knew she could feel his love for her. They stood like that for a long moment, breathing in the unfamiliar air.

"What happens next?" Arra asked after a while.

"We need to find the other pieces," Trey said. "The other parts of the Defense Mechanism. Earth was the first. It only took us twenty thousand years to bring her in. How long will it take to find the others?"

"We'll get through it," Arra said. "Together." She smiled, standing on tip-toes to kiss him.

He returned the kiss. Her lips tasted of strawberries. The moons flew lazily across the sky, and the lights of Ilyrion shone and sparkled.

"I remember I loved you," Arra said as she pulled away.

"And what do you think now?"

"I don't know. It's so confusing. I have all these memories, all these visions in my head. I remember being with you, loving you, all across the years. But part of me just met you a few weeks ago. And part of me still grieves."

"For Fenian."

"For Fenian, and for Silanar and Melenora. For Lhoris and Eloen and Orist and all the others who died. For Elanil. It's too soon. We just met."

"I know," Trey said quietly. He was content just to be with her, to hold her here underneath the twin moons of their new —old—world. He would always have that little bookstore back home in the city. He would always have his memories of that time, as few and as dark as they had been. But now was the time for looking forward. For thinking new thoughts, having new dreams. Making new memories. He looked out at the glittering nighttime city and smiled.

This was going to be an awfully big adventure.

FIFTY-SEVEN

QUYNN PACED INSIDE HIS CELL, fuming. The Eldrim hadn't
had the decency to let him die. No, they'd repaired his
wounds, fixed him up—then slammed him into a jail cell to
rot. If that was justice, he didn't want it. He'd lost everything
—his palatial penthouse, his fallcars, his Staff. Lorelei. Everything was gone, and now all he had was a stinking cement
hellhole somewhere in the Under of New San Francisco.

At least they'd left him in the city. He was sick of trees.

Quynn heard a clinking sound. He looked around, trying
to find what had made the noise. It came again, and he realized it was coming from somewhere above him. He
looked up.

One of the small ceiling tiles slid aside, and something
dropped through it. Then the tile slid back into place.

What the hell?

Quynn crouched down, searching for the object that had
fallen. It was dark in the cell, and the object had been small.
He scrambled around on the floor. Where had it gone?

Then he found it. He picked up a piece of wood, roughly
square, with jagged edges. Oddly, the wood felt warm to the

touch. It wasn't darkprime wood—boy, would *that* have been something! It was just regular wood. Maple, unless he missed his guess. Just regular maple.

Or was it?

He turned the maple chip over and over in his hand, feeling its warmth. Even if it were prime maple, he couldn't do anything with it. His powers were only Aligned with dark-prime wood. He still didn't understand what the cruel gods were thinking when they assigned Talents—it always seemed so haphazard, so random. Quynn had three Talents, but they were all on the dark side of the magical equation.

Somewhere, he knew the Twins were laughing at him.

He sighed, sitting on the floor of his cold cell, leaning back against the wall. The wood was still warm, and he almost thought he could feel it pulsating in his hand. So strange.

His thoughts turned elsewhere: idle fantasies of leaving his cell, of getting out and exploring the world. He wanted to see this Valaralda everyone was talking about. Hell, if he ever got out, he might even get a telescope and look at all the new stars and planets.

It would have been nice to be free. Free from Lorelei's clutches, free from the oppressive Cothellon regime. It wasn't that he particularly begrudged Lorelei what she'd done, it was just that he liked the idea of doing what *he* wanted to do for a change.

He heard a scraping sound outside his cell, and a shadowy figure stepped up to the bars. Startled, Quynn got to his feet. Who could it be? He hadn't had any visitors since his imprisonment a few months ago. Why would someone suddenly want to see him now?

The figure stepped forward and its features resolved in the dim light. Quynn gasped as he saw who it was.

It was him. It was Quynn.

"Hello," the figure said. "I thought I might find you here."

"Wh-who are you?" Quynn asked. Was he hallucinating? Had they been putting something in his food?

The figure shrugged. "I'm Quynn," he said. "Or do you prefer Simon? Or Usunaar? I can give you others."

"B-but, that makes no sense," Quynn said. "*I'm* Quynn."

The figure shrugged again. "As you wish," he said, disappearing in a puff of light.

The chip of maple in Quynn's hand suddenly turned to dust.

SCIENCE HAD PROGRESSED QUITE FAR on Valaralda since Orym was there last. The memories were dim from that time, but he was pretty sure they hadn't had flying cars and spaceships and all these global network ocular implants. The elves had been much more reliant on magic twenty thousand years ago, as he remembered it.

He should be happy, he knew. The whole reason he'd joined the Cothellon in the first place was to get closer to the cutting edge—to *define* the cutting edge. But instead, he had invented a new type of magic. A magic that required murdering millions of innocent humans, their blood collecting on the roots of dark trees.

That wasn't science. That was playing god. And Orym didn't much like his chances in that arena.

Ilyrion boasted the largest university on the planet, and their research facilities were top notch. The astrophysicists there had been happy to give him a tour of their campus. So here he was, following a group of modern elven eggheads, trying to soak it all in.

The room they were standing in was bristling with tech—holoscreens and haptic touch devices and other things he couldn't name. It was the control center for something called the Ieahanea Telescope. It had just come online recently, and it was intended to peer into deep space, reaching outside the edges of the galaxy itself. It was state of the art technology, and the elves were quite proud of it.

He was listening to the scientists drone on and on about how the telescope worked, what types of light they could detect, how they filtered it and looked at the ionic polarization to detect early universe epochs. Normally this stuff would interest him greatly, but Orym was having trouble focusing.

Suddenly one of the holoscreens started flashing, and he could hear an insistent beeping sound. Even with all their knowledge and all their gear, sometimes there was just no substitute for a good beep.

"What's going on?" Orym asked. The scientists were suddenly excited, peering anxiously at the screens. One of them used fist gestures to manipulate the screen, translating the view and zooming in.

"What the hell...?" one of the scientists muttered.

"What *is* that?" another one exclaimed.

"It's heading right for us."

"It's still in intergalactic space. It could be millions of years before it even enters the Milky Way."

"That depends on how fast it's going."

"Of course it depends on its speed. I'm not an idiot."

"We need more measurements."

Director Lathanil took charge. "Get the rest of team in here," he said. "We need analysis on this phenomenon immediately." The rest of the group began speaking urgently into thin air, implants directing their voices to various recipients scattered around the city.

"What's going on?" Orym repeated. Were they just going to ignore him?

"I apologize," Lathanil said, coming over to him. "We're going to need you to leave now. We can continue the tour at a later date."

"But what *is* it?" Orym asked, motioning toward the screen.

"I fear it may be something worse than any of us anticipated," Lathanil said, his face grim.

ALLAIN WALKED through the streets of western New San Francisco, his twin walking beside him. Allain2 looked and sounded exactly like Allain in every way, but the two of them couldn't have been more different if they had tried.

"Do you remember anything from before?" Allain asked.

"Before I existed, you mean?" Allain2 replied.

"Well, yes, I guess," Allain said. "I mean, I didn't want to offend you or anything."

"None taken," Allain2 said. "And yes, I can remember most of it, though it is a bit murky. You really ought to shut up about this at some point."

"Sorry," Allain grunted. He'd asked the same questions every day, hoping to figure out the answer as to how his twin had formed. Hoping one day the answer would be different. But every day, Allain2 was his usual self—a bit surly, kind of mean. Allain himself felt better since his twin had arrived. His head felt clearer, happier. It was almost as if Allain2 had taken the worst parts of him and formed them into a real person.

Maybe it had something to do with mistweaving. His father *had* always told him not to project an illusion of himself. But in the stories, Koranaar had done it. Surely it couldn't be *that* bad of a thing.

He put the thought aside as they rounded the corner. Their path had been aimless. They were just exploring the city by foot, seeing what they could see. Trey had given him some human money before he left for Valaralda, telling him not to spend it all in one place.

Allain had never been in a city like this before. Everything was so tall, and big, and kind of dirty. And loud. There were people everywhere, bustling and talking and nearly running into each other on the street. There was a lot of life here, and Allain found himself liking it. It was a different kind of life, different from the trees and gardens he had grown up with. It was harder, more bitter. Faster paced.

It seemed to fit.

"I'm thirsty," Allain2 said.

"You're always thirsty."

"So?"

"So nothing. What about that?" Allain pointed at a sign hanging just down the street. The Pig and Whistle, it advertised, with a picture of a mug of beer.

"Looks like my kind of place," Allain2 said.

They found Kharis inside, nursing a beer. Allains walked over to him, pulling up two chairs. Kharis barely acknowledged them as they arrived. He seemed miserable, or drunk. Or both.

"What are you doing here?" Allain asked.

Kharis took a long pull from his mug. "What does it look like?" he said. "I'm drowning my sorrows."

"What sorrows?" Allain2 asked.

Kharis glared at him. "Well, let's see. My brother and my

son are dead. My home is destroyed, and all my students are scattered. We're in a new fucking solar system, in case you hadn't noticed."

"Why does that matter?" Allain2 prodded.

"It just does," Kharis said. "But that's not even the worst part." He took another drink.

Allain tapped the table. "What's the worst part?" he asked.

Kharis leaned forward, looking at the two of them. His expression was dark, his voice low. "I lost my bow," he said. Then he burst into tears.

Allain looked at his twin and they both rolled their eyes. "Hunters," Allain2 said.

"Didn't we always want to be a Hunter?" Allain asked.

"Bows and arrows are for sissies," Allain2 said, waving his hand at the bartender.

There was an unfamiliar sound from the corner of the room, drawing Allain's attention. He looked over to see a flatscreen television coming to life, displaying some kind of news program. Allain had seen his first TV not long ago, and he was still having trouble getting used to the idea. Apparently the Valaraldans were piping video signals over to Earth. Televisions, long extinct on the planet, were rapidly becoming a new form of entertainment for everyone.

The bartender brought some beers over, and Allain watched the screen.

"Talks between the United Sky Cities on Mar and the Ilyrion High Senate continue into their fifth week," the reporter was saying. Mar was Earth, the way the Valaraldans called it. Allain thought it sounded stupid.

"The two worlds are struggling to hammer out an alliance, bringing our two great peoples together for the first time."

The camera angle changed, and the reporter moved on to

her next story. She was kind of cute, Allain thought. He took a sip of beer.

"In other news, rumors are swirling of a scientific discovery brought about by the brand new Ieahanea Telescope. Scientists have not released their findings, but sources indicate that it may be a momentous occasion. For more on that, we turn to our reporter in the field. Ellarian?"

The screen cut to a shot of a professional-looking elven woman surrounded by a bunch of technological machines. She was holding a microphone and standing next to another man. "Thanks, Sarya," the woman said. "I'm here with Lathanil, Director of Technology for the Ieahanea Program. Director."

"Thanks for having me, Ellarian," the man said.

"Can you comment on the rumors related to the incursion that was recently detected outside our galaxy? People are calling it the Fall."

"We're not yet ready to release our findings, Ellarian," Lathanil said, his tone polished and precise. "I assure you, once we've fully vetted the results, you'll be the first to know."

"I'm sure we will, Director. But humor me for a minute. People out there are saying that the Fall is a real, unprecedented danger for the solar system. Some are calling it the Galaxy Eater. Others refer to it as Guruthos, the ancient specter of Death himself. Do you care to comment on these rumors?"

"The Space Agency cannot comment on rumors and speculation," Lathanil said, clearly trying to maintain his patience. "I should warn viewers that ancient myths and religions are not grounded in science. We will do our best to investigate this incursion and report back with the results as soon as we are able. Until then, there is no cause for concern. That is all."

"Thank you for your time, Director."

"Always a pleasure, Ellarian."

Allain took another drink of beer. This was a curious situation they were in. Had the planet just moved *towards* a greater danger? Why had the gate been necessary in the first place? Why did the planet have to move? Allain didn't have the answers, and he was beginning to realize he might not be able to trust the ones who did.

"Why is it," Kharis said, holding up his empty beer glass, "that I'm always getting drunk in a bar when the world ends?"

ILYRION WAS a lot to take in. After everything he'd experienced, Rylan thought he'd be ready to tackle another city. He craved adventure, wanted to fill the hole left behind by Con and Elanil. But Ilyrion was unlike anything he had ever expected to see.

Dillon and Small were with him, and they seemed equally impressed. Ilyrion was vast, combining modern technology with organic, natural aesthetics. It was as if the elves had taken what they loved of the Prime Trees and made buildings that captured their essence and form. Everything was curves and branches and leaves, interspersed with graceful spires and elegant arches. At night, the city was amazing—glittering lights spread for miles in every direction, a natural extension of the stars.

There were Prime Trees on Valaralda, of course. But instead of being invisible, the Trees were celebrated, integrated into the fabric of the city. They built their parks around them, vast open spaces dedicated to reading and picnics and the usual pleasures of a bright sunny day.

The Under was becoming more of a distant memory to Rylan. Dillon had said that he was done with it, having achieved his purpose. There would always be a soft spot in his heart for the underkids, he had said, but it was time to move on. He had encouraged Rylan to come with him, and Rylan had agreed.

Small was apparently fascinated by the new world. The technology here was far beyond anything Rylan had ever seen on Earth, and Small was drawn to it, wanting to participate in everything, to learn everything. But he was still just a kid, and a small one at that. The elves on Valaralda were still adjusting to this sudden influx of humans. So Small had to content himself with roaming and exploring.

They'd chartered transportation for the day, wanting to take a trip outside the city. The eastern edge of Ilyrion was bounded by water: a beautiful expanse of ocean, frequented by sailors and fishermen and yachtsmen in their rakish boats. But in the other direction, beyond the ragged western border of the city, there was a desert. Rylan had heard that there was a great city out there, a city of wonders such as the eye had never seen.

That was where they were going today.

The coachman was pleasant enough, driving an archaic looking cart pulled by two big animals Rylan didn't have a name for. They looked kind of like horses, but wider, with flat heads and thick lower legs.

"Don't they have cars here?" Rylan asked.

"Don't nobody get me where I want to go but George and Bessie," the driver said. George and Bessie? They sounded like names a human would use. How strange.

"Can you take us out to the desert?" Rylan asked.

"What you wanna go out there for?" the man asked. "You

chillen visiting old Mirra?" He seemed excited about the prospect.

"Um," Rylan started, but Dillon interrupted.

"That's right," he said, stepping up to the cart. The driver looked down at them, chewing some kind of grass-like thing. "We're visiting Mirra." He turned to Rylan, whispering. "We got anything better to do?"

"I thought we were going to Nekhrumet," Rylan said.

"Maybe this is more interesting."

Rylan shook his head. It didn't make any difference to him. If this Mirra was important enough for the driver to know, they should probably check it out.

They hopped on and held tight as the cart bounced and rattled out of the city. It took hours before they finally crossed into the edge of the desert. Luckily, Small had had the foresight to pack food and water. They lunched on cheese and bread as they heaved and bounced toward their destination.

Mirra's house turned out to be nowhere near civilization. It was just on its own, with nothing but sand for miles around. Rylan wondered where she got her food and water. The boys got out of the cart, looking at the house apprehensively.

"Will you wait for us?" Rylan asked the driver.

The driver flipped a metal thing at Rylan, and he caught it out of the air reflexively. It had a little button on it. It looked a little bit like the communicator Orym had given them earlier.

"Hit that button when ya chillen be ready to go on," the driver said.

"Can't you just wait?" Rylan didn't want to be stuck at this strange house.

"Will wait for a spell," the driver said, chewing another piece of grass. "But Mirra be right entertaining, she be. If I be gone when you return, jus' hit that button, an' I be here in a jif." He smiled as if he'd just told a joke.

Rylan looked up at Dillon questioningly, and Dillon shrugged. "Let's see what all the fuss is about."

"I'm game," Small said.

Rylan had a bad feeling about all this.

There was a little stone path leading up to the house—which was more of a shack, really—and the boys took it. An old lady was standing at the door when they arrived. Her face was wrinkled, her skin sagging. Her hair was white and scraggly, hanging in a thick braid down her back. She wore some kind of robe made out of purple fabric, with little faded patterns sewn into it. The front of the house was lined with open windows, and little pots were placed on the window sill. Rylan counted fourteen pots, and each one contained what looked to be a tiny tree.

"Come here, little ones," the woman said as they approached. "It be a pleasure to meet ya. Ya have the look of Mar about ya. I be Mirra."

She bustled back into the house, not waiting for them to acknowledge her. She seemed like a strange one, this Mirra.

The inside of the house was cluttered, filled mostly with plants and herbs that Rylan didn't recognize. A scent filled the air—musty, with a spicy edge to it. And there was something sweet behind all that, something that tickled Rylan's nose. He sneezed.

"Come, let me look at ya, child," Mirra said, walking up to Rylan and holding his face in wrinkled hands that were hot and dry. Rylan felt himself growing uncomfortable, but he humored the woman. She held his face steady, but she didn't seem to be looking directly at him. He couldn't see her eyes in the darkness of the room.

"Oh," the woman said. "Oh!"

"What?" Rylan asked.

"Ya soul is intact," Mirra said, "that much be true. But I feel da energies from da planet within. Oh, da souls of da dead are crying, it be true! Da forest be crying!" She pulled her hands back rapidly, growing visibly distressed. He felt a twinge of something as she pulled away, like something had just changed in his mind.

"What is it?" Rylan asked. "What's wrong?" Next to him, he could see Dillon frowning. Small was fiddling with something on a shelf. A mangy cat jumped up onto the table in the center of the room, looking at Rylan strangely.

"Don' touch that!" Mirra said, spinning to Small and smacking him on the back of the head.

"Ow," Small said, rubbing his head. "Sorry. What *are* these things?" He was looking at the little plants in the windows, the ones that looked like trees.

"Those be mine, child. Me own little Forest."

"Those are…Prime Trees?" Small asked.

"Ah, so the little ones be smart, as well! Come," Mirra said, shepherding them away from the little Trees in the window, "let old Mirra tell ya a story."

NEW SAN FRANCISCO WAS DIFFERENT.

It wasn't cleaner than before. It was actually dirtier. Part of that could be down to the repeal of the Clean Up The Streets Act. It had been one of the first actions of the new United Sky Cities government. As a result, underkids weren't forced to live in the Under anymore, even though many of them still preferred it. So there were vagrants, and homeless, and drug addicts—all the usual suspects—out on the streets. It gave the city a slightly more gritty vibe. More real. These were real people living out their lives, no longer forced to exist under Cothellon rule.

Trey was just here for old times' sake. He had checked up on the old bookstore, wiping down its accumulation of dust. There still weren't any customers, especially now that TVs were popping up everywhere in the cities. So Trey had closed up shop, shuttering the windows and barring the door. He had said a few words for Callan as he left. His best friend would have liked to have been there, to see the end.

Then he left, walking the streets, watching the electric cars and pedestrians. There were more dogs now, and even some fledgling trees that had been planted on some of the streets. There were no more Monitors, no more Planners. The Citizens were trying to survive, trying to blossom. Trey wished them luck.

Up ahead, there was a woman on the street, walking back and forth erratically, shouting at everyone that passed. People were avoiding her, crossing to the other side of the street as she shrieked at them. Something about the woman seemed familiar as Trey approached.

She had raven-dark hair, long and wild and ratty. Her clothes were tattered and soiled, but Trey could see that at one point they had been red. The woman looked at him as he neared, her eyes wild.

It was Lorelei.

"The city of doom has arrived!" she shouted at him, her hands curled into strange shapes. "The Specters of Death are upon us! Fear for your children, for your lives!"

"Lorelei?" Trey said, reaching out a hand hesitantly. She seemed unhinged, insane. What had happened to her?

"All dust, all dust, all dust," she chanted, her eyes on the pavement, her arms clutched inward as if she were cold. "The Trees are no more. The passage has been denied!"

"Can I help?" Trey asked, feeling helpless. "Are you okay?"

"The Twins will damn us for our sins!" Lorelei shouted, spittle flying in his face. "For all eternity we shall be damned, for we have killed the righteous! The souls of the dead cry out to be redeemed!"

This was getting him nowhere. But Trey felt bad just leaving her out here, to be ridiculed or ignored by passersby.

"Do you have anywhere to stay?" he asked.

"Can you feel them?" Lorelei responded, grabbing his arm suddenly. "They are close—so close. The Twins will be reunited at last, their battle for eternity rejoined! The purple mountains lay claim to them no longer!"

He reached down, trying to pry her hand off his arm, but she was gripping him too tightly. He could see her eyes moving, darting rapidly around as if she were seeing visions. "Our souls are not our own," she said, this time in a whisper. Trey had to strain to make her out. "The Fall is coming!"

Then she subsided into gibberish, drool escaping her mouth. Her head lolled and she swayed back and forth. Trey looked around, unsure what to do. Arra would have known.

He left Lorelei there in the end, raving at the world, mad as a hatter. Maybe the strain had been too much for her.

Or maybe she was right, and death really was headed for them.

Trey shivered, and walked on.

ARRA SAT beneath the Prime Elm Tree, just staring at the destruction she had caused. The city around Fennas Elenathon was rubble, ruins.

All because of her.

She had reacted out of rage, out of anger. She had leveled the whole thing with a glance. Even now, she had trouble believing that much power was within her, waiting to come out. After so much time as a Mundane, she still sometimes forgot that those days were over.

She was a Prime Mage now.

But her sister was dead. Elanil had died for *her*, to save *her*. It was an unfathomable sacrifice, a true gift unasked for. Arra could still picture the look on her face as Elanil had died. Her eyes had been clear as she gazed at Arra, love and respect and admiration on her face. Her sister had not been the troublemaker Arra took her for. She could have been a friend, rather than an enemy. The two of them could have been a pair, could have taken the world by storm.

But instead, Elanil was dead.

And Arra was alive.

She wiped a tear from her eye, laying her head back against the Tree Elanil had made.

She missed her sister so much.

She felt the wood underneath her pulsate slightly as she leaned against it. Had the Tree gotten warmer, or was that her imagination? She opened her eyes to look.

There was a face looking back at her.

Arra shrieked, blinking her eyes rapidly, trying to clear her vision. And just like that, the face was gone, back to whatever void it had sprung from. Arra took a deep, shuddering breath and leaned back against the Tree.

"Arra," she heard a voice whisper.

She started, looking around again. What was going on here? Had the Cothellon left some kind of deadly technology behind? Or was she finally going insane after all these years?

"Arra," the whisper said again. "It's me."

"Hello?" Arra said, querying the wind. The whisper

sounded like it was coming from...but no, that couldn't be possible.

She placed a hand against the Tree trunk, feeling its pulse, feeling its warmth. There was no mistaking it this time. The Tree was alive, like something was inside.

"Arra," the voice said again. "Can you find me?"

Arra's eyes narrowed as she looked at the Tree. She knew that voice.

"Elanil?" she said, still touching the Tree. "Is that you?"

THE
END

TO BE CONTINUED...

SEASON TWO BEGINS

Excerpt from THE ABSENT MEMORY, book six of The Metalwood Saga:

Kythaela sat on her storyteller's log, looking around the fire. Elven children stared back at her, their gazes calm and respectful. Kids were still raised well, here in the great city of Ilyrion. The elves hadn't lost that, at least, after all this time.

She raised her eyes above the fire, looking at the city that was visible in the distance. At night, Ilyrion shone with thousands of glittering lights, its own firmament below the sky. Kythaela took a deep breath, letting it out slowly. The silence around the campfire was palpable.

Her memories were returning.

"The Twins," she began. "Long worshipped by elves, these mysterious deities have been part of life on Valaralda for tens of thousands of years.

"But who are they, really? Are they gods, or are they men? Where did they came from? What do they want? Where do they live? Fruitless questions, some might say.

"But sometimes that is the best kind of question."

She paused, giving her words a moment to sink in. Storytelling was an art—pacing was important. The children remained silent, listening to her vigilantly. She smiled at them.

"Some say the Twins are gods who created the seven Prime Planets: Valar, Mar, Eryn, Sya, Y'abel, Ayel, and Ashi.

They made the planets and set them loose to drift in the universe, each a part of its own solar system. The Twins hid a part of their power on each planet, the legend says, waiting for elvenkind to find it and harness it.

"But some profess this tale to be a lie. They claim the Twins are simply elves, not gods—regular men who lived on ancient Valar before the Great Awakening. They were charismatic leaders, benevolent masters, loved by all. The Twins, in this story, were the greatest kings the world had ever known. Many swear that this is true.

"Still others say the Twins are moons, not men. The twin moons that forever orbit Valaralda, gazing down at us at night, guiding us, watching our paths. But watch as they might, the moons are powerless: just heaps of rock, swinging in great arcs through the sky. Silent, passive beacons in the dark.

"But many reject that story, too. So what truth remains? What *are* the Twins? Why do we worship them, curse them, use their signs? Why have we built great churches to them, written books about them, studied their origins? Surely there must be a nugget of *something* true, underneath it all.

"Which brings us to our final legend.

"In this story, the Twins are Trees: Tevelarel and Laravon. The Trees grew from seeds at the moment of the Awakening, bringing forth light and power and magic to the worlds. No one knows where the seeds came from—they just arrived.

"Now the Trees stretch forth their branches, embracing elves and men, sending forth waves of power from the high mountain where they stand. People and beasts and the very plants themselves embrace the Twins, feeding in the luxury of their magical wellspring.

"One Tree is black, and one is gold. The legend says they keep each other forever in balance, forever in check. For if one Tree were to destroy the other, it would throw the worlds into darkness such as none can imagine. And so the Trees are paired, a yin and yang, forever frustrating each other, forever keeping each other at bay.

"And their great power, such as it is, pulses in magnificent strands, flooding the planets with magic. Magic that the intrepid can harness, using for purposes good or ill. It is the very source of Prime magic: light and dark to rule all. This magic Awakened the minds of men, bringing about the Second Age.

"But the Trees, magnificent as they are, cannot be found. No one knows where they are. And if something cannot be found, can it be said to exist?

"These are all good stories. Powerful stories."

Kythaela stopped, letting her last words ring into the silence that followed. The fire crackled happily, smoke rising to the Valaraldan heavens. The children were silent, awed.

"Unfortunately," Kythaela said into the night, "none of these stories are true."

To be continued in THE ABSENT MEMORY...

To purchase, head to **jtf.link/metal6** or scan the QR code below.

ENJOY THE BOOK? HELP SPREAD THE WORD

Reviews are the most powerful tools in my arsenal when it comes to getting attention for my books. Much as I'd like to, I don't have the financial muscle of a New York publisher. I can't take out full page ads in the newspaper or put posters on the subway.

But I do have something much more powerful and effective than that, and it's something that those publishers would kill to get their hands on.

A committed and loyal bunch of readers.

Honest reviews of my books help bring them to the attention of other readers. If you've enjoyed this book, **I'd love it if you could leave a quick review.**

Head to **jtf.link/metalreview5** or scan the QR code.

ABOUT THE AUTHOR

Jeremy is a fantasy and science fiction author, living and writing in the San Francisco Bay Area. Fantasy is his first love —there's something about magic and mayhem that has interested him since he first cracked opened Lord Foul's Bane in the seventh grade. Also archery.

There always seems to be a lot of archery involved.

When not writing, Jeremy is a graphic designer, software developer, game designer, and music composer. He makes a really great Old Fashioned.

Check out his other work and sign up for his newsletter at **www.jeremythomasfuller.com**.

facebook.com/JeremyThomasFuller
instagram.com/jeremythomasfuller
amazon.com/author/jeremythomasfuller
bsky.app/profile/jeremythomasfuller.com

* 9 7 8 1 9 6 5 9 9 0 1 5 5 *